FOR CHEDDAR OR WORSE

A CHEESE SHOP MYSTERY

FOR CHEDDAR OR WORSE

AVERY AAMES

WHEELER PUBLISHING
A part of Gale, Cengage Learning

GALE
CENGAGE Learning·

Farmington Hills, Mich • San Francisco • New York • Waterville, Maine
Meriden, Conn • Mason, Ohio • Chicago

LIBRARY OF CONGRESS CATALOGING-IN-PUBLICATION DATA

Names: Aames, Avery, author.
Title: For cheddar or worse / Avery Aames.
Description: Large print edition. | Waterville, Maine : Wheeler Publishing Large
    Print, 2016. | Series: A cheese shop mystery | Series: Wheeler Publishing Large
    Print cozy mystery
Identifiers: LCCN 2016028173 | ISBN 9781410494207 (paperback) | ISBN
    1410494209 (softcover)
Subjects: LCSH: Large type books. | BISAC: FICTION / Mystery & Detective / Women
    Sleuths. | GSAFD: Mystery fiction.
Classification: LCC PS3601.A215 F67 2016 | DDC 813/.6—dc23
LC record available at https://lccn.loc.gov/2016028173

Published in 2016 by arrangement with The Berkley Publishing Group,
an imprint of Penguin Publishing Group, a division of Penguin Random
House LLC

Printed in the United States of America
1 2 3 4 5 6 7 20 19 18 17 16

To Kate Seaver, thank you for guiding me through the wonderful world of publishing! I treasure your input, expertise, and friendship.

ACKNOWLEDGMENTS

"Passion is one great force that unleashes creativity, because if you're passionate about something, then you're more willing to take risks."

— Yo-Yo Ma

I am blessed to have so many people in my life who love me and encourage me to follow my dreams and my passions. Thank you to my husband and my family for your love. Thank you to my talented author friends, Krista Davis, Janet Bolin, Kate Carlisle, and Hannah Dennison for your words of wisdom and calm. Thank you to my good friends who check in on me, especially when times have been rough. You know who you are!!

Thanks to all the author pals I've met over the past ten years, mainly via the Internet, who are in my life daily. I feel like we've been good friends our entire lives: my brainstormers at Plothatchers and my blog mates on Mystery Lovers Kitchen. Love you all!

Thanks to those who have helped make the Cheese Shop Mysteries a success: my fabulous editor Kate Seaver, as well as Katherine Pelz and Danielle Dill. Thanks to a terrific copy editor, Courtney Wilhelm, who has offered a critical eye to make this the best book possible. Thanks to my agent, John Talbot, for believing in every aspect of my work. Thank you, Sheridan Stancliff, for keeping me calm as I navigate the tricky world of social networking. Thank you, Kimberley Greene, for your support and your humor as I press onward. And thank you to a new member of my team, Madeira James.

Thank you to my cheese consultant, Marcella Wright. You have helped me more than you will ever know. This series is tastier because of you!

Thank you librarians, teachers, and readers for sharing the delicious world of a cheese shop owner in a quaint, fictional town in Ohio with your friends. Thank you to all who have posted such tasty, positive reviews!

And thank you Charlotte, Grandmère, Pépère, Delilah, Rebecca, Jordan, Urso, Meredith, Matthew, the twins, and the myriad other personalities who have populated A Cheese Shop Mystery series for coming alive in my mind and becoming a part of my life. You have enriched me with your personalities, your insights, and your love.

Savor the Mystery!

CHAPTER 1

I stopped dead in my tracks and listened, on full alert: a leaf fluttering in the early morning breeze, a creature skittering across the pavement; footsteps. I whirled to my right, but I couldn't see a thing. Dang. It was inky black out. The crescent moon had disappeared over an hour ago. *It's always darkest before the dawn,* my grandfather would say.

"Anybody there?" I whispered.

As if, I thought. As if someone wishing me harm would cry out, *Yes!*

Breathe, Charlotte. Doing my shallow best, I glanced at Rags, my adorable Ragdoll cat. I could make out the white of his dappled fur. He wasn't acting antsy, which meant I shouldn't, either, but sometimes the dark scared the bejeebers out of me. Why was I so jumpy? I couldn't put my finger on it. The month of May was a lovely time of year. The temperatures were growing

11

warmer. Birds were building nests and feeding newborns. Tourists were flocking to our fair town, which meant sales at Fromagerie Bessette — what many in town call The Cheese Shop — were good. No, not just good . . . booming.

"Let's go," I said to Rags and tugged on his leash. He was one of the few cats I knew that had taken to one. I think a leash made him feel safer.

If only some big, strong person had hold of my leash.

A breeze kicked up behind me. A chill shimmied down my spine. I spun again but didn't see any sign of danger.

"Think lovely thoughts," I muttered. "Raindrops on roses." We were on our way to the shop, walking instead of driving, as we often did. What could go wrong? Maybe I should have put on something warmer than a lacy sweater and trousers. Ah, who was I kidding? A jacket, mittens, and an ear-flapped snowcap wouldn't have been enough to warm me right now. Something was getting to me. What?

Then it dawned on me. It was the date my parents died. My shoulders tensed, my body flushed. Every year it happened. The memory of their deaths slammed into me like a thunderbolt. More than thirty years had passed, and yet that fleeting moment when the car went out of control and we crashed had changed my entire world.

A sudden death or two will do that, I thought wryly and mentally kicked myself. *Buck up!*

I forced the sound of screeching brakes and my parents' shouts from my mind and hurried ahead. I unlocked the front door of the shop and allowed Rags to cross the threshold first. "Let's switch on all these lights," I said to him. "We'll drum up good vibes. No wallowing."

I roamed the shop, drinking in the luscious aroma of cheese, drawing strength from what I, thanks to my grandparents, was able to call my own. Though the two darling people who raised me were both alive and in fine health, when my grandfather decided to retire, he turned over Fromagerie Bessette — Bessette being the family name — to my cousin and me. Ever since I moved in with my grandparents, under my grandfather's tutelage, I had learned to relish all things cheese. Prior to joining me in this venture, my cousin was a well-respected sommelier. He manages the wine annex portion of our shop.

"Not much to do, is there?" I said to Rags. Before leaving last night, I had straightened the boxes of crackers and jars of jam on the shelves, and I'd rearranged the displays on each of the slatted wine barrels. Decorative cheese knives and colorful plates nestled among the crystal wineglasses. Funky and traditional cheese graters stood beside chalkboard-style cheese markers, all set atop a huge wheel of Grafton Clothbound Cheddar, one of my favorite cheeses when paired with a dark chocolate, like Olive and Sinclair Southern Artisan Chocolate.

Rags meowed. I was pretty sure he thought his plea was packed with meaning that I, his human, could interpret. I couldn't, of course. I wasn't even good at sign language.

"Hungry?" I asked. I took him to the office — his home away from home — and freshened his water and treats.

Rags circled on his plush pillow in the corner and settled into a ball. Not hungry.

"What should I make for today's special quiche?" I asked as I nestled into the desk chair and wakened the computer. Rags offered no inspiration. "Maybe I'll add some secret item or spice that no one can figure out. Ooh, I know! I'll make it with peanut butter and apples and a dash of nutmeg. I'll use a simple Havarti." Havarti is a semi-soft Danish cow's-milk cheese, good for melting. "That combo will throw Pépère for a loop." My grandfather loves trying to guess

14

ingredients. "Don't you think?"

Rags couldn't be bothered. He was already snoring.

Every day at The Cheese Shop, in addition to the vast array of cheeses we peddled, we offered slices of quiche or specialty sandwiches. When the items sold out, we didn't make more. We weren't trying to compete with The Country Kitchen diner across the street. We just wanted our customers to feel they had plenty of time to browse the shop. If they cared to, they could slip into the wine annex and eat their items at one of the mosaic-inlaid café tables.

I clicked on the email icon and reviewed all the entries. A couple of orders topped the list. There was also an email from Jordan, my husband of three months. Subject: *I adore you.* He sent the note a half hour after I left home. *Our* home. Or rather, we were in the process of making it *ours.* We were revamping some of the bedrooms by repainting and switching out the window coverings. We were also upgrading the kitchen. We had ordered new appliances. Jordan loves to cook. So do I.

I typed a quick response: Love you, too, and I headed to the kitchen at the back of the shop.

An hour later, as I was removing the

quiches from the oven, the aroma of baked apples, peanut butter, and cheese filling my senses, Rebecca, my twenty-something assistant, entered the shop.

"Charlotte," she called. "You'll never guess what I did!" Rebecca, who was relentlessly perky, bopped into the kitchen while tying the strings of her gold apron around her bright pink dress. "Mmm. Smells fantastic. Nutty." She had a great sense of smell. "See?" She did a twirl.

"You cut your hair."

Usually Rebecca wore her long blonde hair in a ponytail. Not anymore. A swath of bangs swooped across her forehead. She swiveled a second time to reveal the back of her head, fringed in an A-line at the nape of the neck, not all that different from the style I wore.

"It's darling," I said. "Who made you so bold?" I remember her saying that she would never cut her hair. Ever. "The deputy?"

"No." Rebecca and Deputy O'Shea had been dating for a few months. They had performed in a play a few months ago and had been inseparable ever since, other than for work. I don't think they had gone past first base, to coin a phrase, which was so sweet and refreshing. "I won't let a man dictate how I wear my hair."

"My, my. Aren't you sassy today?"

Rebecca grinned. "I cut it because I saw this blog online —"

"You said you weren't going online anymore."

"To *shop*. I'm not going online *to shop*. And I haven't. But I like to read. Blogs especially." She flapped a hand. "Anyway, this blogger wrote that a woman should make a change to her look every few years, to keep life fresh and fun. I even added highlights. Can you tell? My hair is now officially multicolored."

I couldn't tell — the hairstylist had done a nice, subtle job — but I wouldn't burst Rebecca's bubble. When I hired her, she was an innocent right off an Amish farm, ready to spread her wings and taste all life had to offer. Within a month, she fell in love with the vastness of the Internet. She discovered clothing websites, home decorating sites, and more. Then she found TV reruns and became a mystery junkie. After that, she discovered books — everything from thrillers to classics — and movies. She was like an empty vessel ready to be filled. She had seen all the films starring Barbara Stanwyck, Meryl Streep, and Reese Witherspoon. Now she was lapping up movies featuring foreign-born actresses. I think Kate Winslet was her latest favorite, which might explain the inspiration for her haircut. Kate had cut off her curly tresses a month ago. Pictures of her with her new highlighted hairdo were popping up on covers of all the current magazines.

While I wrapped slices of quiche, Rebecca selected a wedge of Bleu Mont Dairy Bandaged Cheddar, an absolutely divine aged cheddar with caramel sweetness and a hint of mossy-grass flavor near the rind. She set it on the cutting board and carved off small morsels, which she placed on a pretty china platter. She set the platter on the Madura gold granite counter next to the display case. We offered a tasting of cheese to our customers daily. It was one of the best ways to sell our wares. Most people couldn't resist buying a wedge of cheese if they sampled it and liked it.

"Are you excited about the big event?" Rebecca asked.

"The brain trust? Absolutely."

"All packed?"

"Yep."

"Rags, too?"

I nodded. He was going to stay with my cousin Matthew and his family. Rags's canine buddy Rocket, a French Briard that

Matthew's ex-wife had given their twin daughters, would welcome Rags with open paws.

"Is Erin ready?" Rebecca asked.

"I'm sure she is."

Erin Emerald owned a spread at the north end of town called Emerald Pastures Farm, a local farmstead that had won awards for its goat cheese and now its Cheddar cheese. Erin and I had attended school together. I remembered the two of us, in fourth grade, spending a lot of time creating a historical diorama of Ohio; it involved glue and sugar cubes and giggles. Starting tomorrow, Friday, with the help of an event coordinator, Erin was putting on what was called a *brain trust* for cheese makers. About twenty people, including a few cheese makers, distributors, journalists, Jordan, and I, had been invited to participate. Jordan was invited because he knows the art of *affinage,* which is the careful practice of ripening cheese, and I was tagging along because I understood the marketing side of cheese. The inn on the property could house half of us. In a few hours, we were going to check in. The other attendees would stay at Lavender and Lace, the bed-and-breakfast next door to my . . . *our* . . . Victorian. During the two-day affair, Erin wanted us to

19

immerse ourselves in the world of cheese. We would talk shop and compare techniques while we stirred, cut, drained, and milled curd.

"The better question is," I said, "are you ready?" I was turning the shop over to Rebecca to manage through Sunday. "It will get busy in here."

Rebecca toyed with her hair. "Of course."

The brain trust idea had come to fruition because my grandmother, the town's mayor, had declared that, starting this year, our *annual* Cheese Festival Week would occur during the first days in May. The festival would start tonight and run until next Friday. Never one to shy away from setting up too many activities, Grandmère had enticed a number of local restaurants to offer cooking classes or specialty dinners. She had encouraged the farmers to hold creamery tours and wine tastings. Erin came to her with the brain trust idea, and Grandmère pounced on it. She had also dreamed up what she was calling the Street Scene.

For the event, a lane on each of the four main streets of Providence that girded the Village Green would be closed to traffic, allowing pedestrians to roam freely. A volunteer construction crew was putting the finishing touches on portable stages, upon which would appear singers, fiddlers, actors, and more. To cap it off, my grandmother had chosen Fromagerie Bessette to be the sponsor for the artisan cheese competition. There would be two rounds of tastings, ten artisanal cheese farmers in each round. At the end of each round, we would pick a winner. The two winners would compete a week from tomorrow for the grand prize. Grandmère hadn't told me what the grand prize was yet. I was eager to find out.

"Let's get hustling," I said to Rebecca. "Lots to do."

We worked side by side throughout the morning. Customers came and went.

Close to eleven A.M., the front door flew open. Grandmère, looking colorful in a yellow sweater and red slacks, hurried to the tasting counter and perched on a ladderback stool. Her face, though weathered, glowed with energy. "Charlotte, *chérie*! You will be so excited to hear."

"Hear what?"

My grandfather followed her inside. "Our Charlotte has heard it all."

"Heard what?" I glanced from one to the other.

Though Pépère was flushed and harrumphing like a disgruntled elephant, there was a twinkle in his eye. And why shouldn't there be? He loved coming to the shop and sneaking pieces of cheese — *sneaking,* because Grandmère continually put him on a diet. Perhaps the latest regimen was working. His stomach did appear less paunchy beneath his plaid shirt, and his typically chubby cheeks looked almost lean.

"Heard what?" I repeated.

Pépère rounded the cheese counter, clutched me by the shoulders, and kissed me, *la bise,* on each cheek. Then he plucked a piece of cheese from the tasting platter.

My grandmother *tsk*ed. "Etienne."

"What is wrong?" He took another and plopped it into his mouth while daring her to chastise him.

Grandmère frowned. What could she do? Pépère was going to help out Rebecca for the next two days. She couldn't eagle-eye him every minute. He would either have self-control or not. Most likely *not.* Grandmère turned her attention to me. "She has come."

"She, who?" I asked, intrigued.

"That woman." Grandmère waved a hand. "The cheese author. The one who writes about all the farms and cheese shops in America."

"Lara Berry?"

"Oui."

A thrill of excitement rushed through me. In my world, Lara Berry was a star. Years ago, she had started out as a simple cheese monger, like me, but now, in addition to being an author, she was a consultant who advised cheese makers on how to market their product, and she reviewed up-and-coming farmsteads. "Where is she?"

Grandmère said, "I saw her in La Chic Boutique buying a dress." The boutique was one of two women's dress shops in town. It offered classic styles at sky-high prices. "She is lean and tall, just like on the book cover."

"Why has she come?" I asked.

Grandmère squinted. "Is she not here to attend the brain trust?"

"She's not on the list of attendees. I've got to meet her."

"You have read all her works, *non*?" Grandmère mimed opening a book. *"Sont-ils de bons livres?"*

"Yes, they are very good books. *C'est fantastique.*" Occasionally my grandparents resorted to their native tongue. They migrated from France after World War II. "She is very knowledgeable." Lara Berry was the go-to cheese maven for American cheeses. "I've seen her on talk shows, too. She has quite a sharp sense of humor."

"Do you like her?"

"Yes. Of course."

"*Bon.* Then it will not matter that she is bossy."

"Bossy?"

"*Oui.* Bossy. This is the correct word. She barks orders." This coming from my grandmother, who could bark with the best of them. Some called her the little general.

"Was Prudence being rude to her?" I asked. Prudence Hart was the owner of La Chic Boutique. A woman with very strong opinions, she could rub people the wrong way.

"Perhaps." Grandmère chuckled. "Lara would not back down."

"Good for her." I appreciated a woman who could stand her ground.

The door to the shop flew open again. The chimes jangled. Matthew, my cousin, who reminded me of a Great Dane puppy mixed with a Sheepdog, all arms and legs with a hank of hair invariably dangling down his forehead into his eyes, raced in. "Have you heard?"

I nodded. "That Lara Berry is in town? Yes." Lara not only knew her cheeses; she also knew wine. Her latest book, *Educate Your Palate: a Connoisseur's Guide to American Cheese and Wine,* was a must-read for

24

people like Matthew and me. Thanks to Lara's research, I had discovered a wealth of new farms and creameries that put out excellent artisanal cheeses. Matthew had learned about a number of independent wineries, citing from Lara's book that at the turn of the century there had been about two thousand wineries in America; now there were over eight thousand. "Grand-mère saw her —"

"No," Matthew cut me off. "That's not what I'm talking about. Have you heard about Meredith?" His wife and my best friend. "She's pregnant!"

"What? You're kidding." I did a happy jig. "How far along is she?"

"Three months."

I stopped dancing. "Three months and neither of you said a word to me?"

"She thought if she said something, she might jinx it. We've been trying. She lost one last year."

"She what?" I yelped. She lost a baby and hadn't confided in me? What kind of friend was she? What kind of friend was I not to have sensed her pain?

Matthew shrugged. "What can I say? Everyone's got a secret."

CHAPTER 2

I sped to Meredith's house and found her decorating the baby suite. Seeing her in her splattered smock, glowing with hope, made my peeve vanish. I congratulated her, and we shared a bite of lunch and talked for an hour. When she said she needed rest, I left and dashed home. Jordan arrived minutes after me, looking delicious as all get out — his hair windblown, his white shirt opened a couple of buttons to cool him off. After a luscious kiss, he grabbed our weekender suitcases, and we headed to Emerald Pastures Farm.

The drive to the farm took Jordan and me a mere fifteen minutes. The inn, a white shingled traditional with a wraparound portico and modest columns, was located at the top of a bluff, far from any roads. It was so solitary that a visitor could easily hear the lowing of cows and the music of crickets in the fields.

Erin Emerald, a teensy woman easily five inches shorter than I — and I was barely pushing five-feet-four — welcomed us in the foyer. "I think you'll love your room. It's on the second floor." She skirted behind the check-in desk and nudged a register toward me. After I signed in, she told us to follow her. Her silky red hair swung to and fro as she moved ahead and flourished a hand toward the living room on our left. "This is where we'll have the cocktail reception tonight."

"It's beautiful," I said, taking in the space.

Two stately antique sofas faced each other in the middle of the room. There were clusters of comfortable reading chairs as well. An upright piano was tucked against the far wall. By the window stood a chess table with two darling hand-painted chairs. An antique grandfather clock with an astronomical moon phase dial also caught my eye. What I wouldn't do to own something like that. It was more than just a timepiece. With its intricate woodworking, it was a work of art. My grandmother had given me a great appreciation for furniture and the handiwork and love that went into making antiques. I had recently refinished an old desk in my office. Although I wouldn't be putting in those kinds of man-hours again anytime soon, I wouldn't mind investing in more items at a future date.

"Over to your right is the evening dining room. Beyond that, the breakfast room."

I said, "I love what you've done with the place, Erin."

She sighed. "It's a work in progress. You're seeing the first stages of a facelift. We need to do a lot of updates that we can't afford . . . yet. Although Emerald Finish, the farm's latest output, won first place in the state cheese competition, a ribbon alone can't pay for all the upkeep."

I had tasted the cheese. It was a creamy cow-sheep Cheddar with a tangy quality. Perfect with a glass of sauvignon blanc.

"Soon," Erin continued, "I'll complete my parents' vision for the inn, but the farm — the operation — comes first."

Jordan said, "The grounds look good. Well-tended."

"The structures have weathered well." Erin knocked on the wooden frame of a doorway. "Can't skimp on that." Her family had owned the farm for generations. "And the livestock are healthy, so I must be doing something right." Erin's parents passed away eight years ago. Her father, only in his fifties, died of a stroke; her mother died a month later of a heart attack. The next day,

Erin found herself swimming at the deep end of the farming pool. She hadn't been groomed to run the operation. She was just now grasping how to do the job.

"I'm certain the entire place will be up to snuff in no time," Jordan said. He had relocated to Providence a number of years ago and, until recently, had owned and operated a thriving spread called Pace Hill Farm.

"Thank you, Jordan. That means a lot coming from you. How is the restaurant business?"

"Swell." A few months ago, after one of our dear friends who owned an Irish pub was killed, Jordan purchased the place and handed over Pace Hill Farm to his sister. It wasn't a rash decision. Prior to moving to town, Jordan had owned a restaurant in upstate New York. A deadly encounter with a couple of thugs ended that. He was placed in the WITSEC program, settled in Providence, and kept a low profile as a cheese maker until the case went to trial.

"Jordan, I hear you've started offering cooking classes," Erin said.

"On Sunday evenings." Once the trial was settled and the people who had it in for Jordan were locked away forever, Jordan was free to pursue the career he loved: being a chef.

"The classes are a bunch of fun," I said. "For each meal, the amateur chefs don chef coats and prepare a four-course meal. In between courses, they taste their wares, each paired with an appropriate wine selection. You should take a class."

Erin smiled. "I just might."

Jordan and I had met at a cooking class at a local Italian restaurant. I would never forget the first look we exchanged. His eyes had sparkled with danger as well as humor. I was toast after that.

"Let's head upstairs," Erin suggested.

I trailed behind her, noting the fray of the dark green staircase runner. The railing could use a good polish as well.

Jordan must have noticed the wear and tear, too. He said, "Mind your step," and placed his hand at the arch of my back. Warmth radiated through his touch.

"The bags," I murmured.

"Got 'em." Jordan returned to the foyer, hoisted both pieces of luggage, and climbed the stairs behind me.

We passed a nook adorned with a vase of fresh spring flowers. I said, "The irises are gorgeous, Erin."

She peeked over her shoulder. "We have

flowers in abundance on the farm. The rain has been good this season. I hope you like your room. It was my parents' and has a beautiful view of the farm. It's one of the few I've recently renovated." Erin stopped in front of the room marked ~2~. "Here we are. You'll be right next door to me. I'm in four. Kandice is in the room a few doors down; number eight."

Kandice Witt was the genius who had come up with the idea of the brain trust. I had met her a couple of times. She used to run the dairy department at a college in the southeast, but according to her, the shift in the economy a few years back had made her eager to seek a new challenge. She wanted to be her own boss, roam the world, and meet new people. She currently helps regions throughout the United States put together cheese conferences.

"Kandice hasn't arrived yet," Erin added. "You'll see her at the cocktail reception."

I said, "I heard Lara Berry is in town."

"Lara?" Erin's eyes widened.

"Is she coming to the brain trust?"

"I suppose so." Erin didn't sound certain.

Apparently Jordan and I weren't the only ones in the dark. "Didn't Kandice mention anything?" I asked.

Erin shook her head.

31

Odd that Kandice would keep something that *big* a secret. "Have you met Lara?"

"Once. She —" Erin hesitated as if she wanted to say more.

"What?"

"Nothing."

"Do you have enough space to house Lara if Kandice hasn't arranged for her to stay elsewhere?"

"I've got one room left, on the third floor. Years ago, my parents changed the attic into three rooms. I haven't renovated them yet, but they're nice. All have pretty views. I'll text Kandice at once. Lara," Erin muttered under her breath. "Hmm."

"Is everything okay?" I asked.

"Oh, sure." Erin waved a hand as if to brush aside negative thoughts. "Everyone will be delighted to meet her. Everyone except Shayna, that is."

I turned to Jordan. "She's talking about Shayna Underhill, the cheese maker who owns Underhill Farm and Creamery in Wisconsin. Lara and she used to be partners."

"How do you know that?" he asked.

"I met Shayna at a cheese festival a few years ago."

"Prior to marrying Steven Underhill," Erin said, "Shayna was a big wheel in the corporate world, but a year after she said *I do,* her husband urged her to move to a farm and start making cheese. Unfortunately, he died a year later, leaving her to raise their girls and manage the farm all alone."

"That's when she took on Lara as a partner," I said. "Underhill won lots of blue ribbons for its Cheddar cheeses."

"However, in the mid-1990s, the winning streak stopped."

"When Lara and she parted ways." I eyed Erin. "I don't know why Lara left. Do you?"

"Not really. I —"

Something pounded the floor down the hall.

Erin gazed in that direction; her mouth turned down. "Sorry about that. My brother."

She was talking about Andrew. He was a good ten years younger than Erin and I. "He's autistic," Erin explained to Jordan.

Erin had been engaged once, but the guy backed out of the wedding when he realized Erin was never going to abandon her brother to someone else's care. Andrew lived in his own world, showing little interest in others. From kindergarten through high school, a special ed teacher had helped him cope with daily activities.

"He likes to count," Erin said. "Sometimes he counts minutes. By the second. Using a drumstick that was our father's. Daddy had a great sense of rhythm." She removed an old-fashioned key from her pocket. "Don't worry. Andrew only counts during the day. He won't be any problem at night. That's when he writes."

"What does he write?" I asked.

"Music. For the piano. It's quite good." She inserted the key into the lock for room two, twisted the handle, and pushed back the door.

A fluffy white cat darted toward us along the hallway. Before it could sneak into the room, Erin scooped it up. "Uh-uh, Snowball, bad boy. You know you're not allowed in any of the rooms by yourself." The cat squirmed but she wouldn't release him. "Isn't this room wonderful?"

We stepped inside. The window was ajar, its shutters folded open. Pretty green-themed floral drapes flapped in the breeze. The aroma of fresh-mown grass wafted inside. Two bottles of filtered water and a tray of sliced cheese covered in plastic wrap sat on a small dinette table. The duvet and pillows on the four-poster bed looked spanking new and comfy. A bookcase filled with books, magazines, and porcelain statues stood against the far wall. A forest green reading chair with floor lamp was situated near the bookcase. A hand-painted armoire with a beautiful rendering of the countryside abutted the far wall.

"Erin, it's charming," I said. "I love the variety of antique pieces you have in the inn."

"My mother and father purchased them from around the world. They loved old stuff." Erin handed me the key. "I'll leave you two to get settled. There's a bolt on the inside, too, for privacy." She aimed a finger and winked. "The cocktail reception starts at six thirty. When it concludes, we'll head to town to enjoy the Street Scene."

Erin closed the door, and Jordan set our suitcases at the foot of the bed.

I sidled up to him. "Lucky us. We get a second honeymoon."

"Who said we ever ended the first?" He wrapped me in a hug and planted kisses along my neck.

After Jordan and I unpacked, we took a walk around the grounds, talking the entire time about our lives, our concerns. Business — good. Our families — healthy. Meredith — pregnant. Jordan said his sister, Jacky, who moved to town a year after he relocated, was thriving on the farm. He was pleased that he had entrusted it to her.

On the way back to the room, Jordan stopped me and took me by the shoulders. "During the walk we skated around a certain topic," he said.

"Which was?"

"You."

Coquettishly, I raised an eyebrow. "What about me?"

He released me. "You talked so glowingly about Meredith."

Sure I did, when I wasn't carping about the fact that she had kept her secret from me.

"Do you want to have children?" he asked.

I gulped. In recent months, Jordan and I had skirted the notion but had never fully discussed the fine points. I was in my mid-thirties. *Ticktock* on the old fertility clock. Could I even bear a child? Jordan was older than I was by five years, not that men had to worry about that sort of thing. But did he want children now? We both had careers. His work at the restaurant often went well into the night. And we wanted to travel. Everywhere. Could we manage having children? Would it be wrong of us to have them if we couldn't devote quality time to them?

"Charlotte?" Jordan cupped my chin.

CHAPTER 3

"Oh, look," I said. "Guests have arrived."

An array of cars was parked in front of the inn: a Mercedes SL, a Mustang, and a Lincoln Town Car. A gentleman carrying two pieces of luggage was climbing the stairs to the porch.

Jordan didn't let go of my chin. "Charlotte, talk to me."

I rose on my tiptoes and kissed him on the lips. "We'll discuss plans after the weekend, okay? I'm desperately in need of snacks and a glass of wine."

We returned to our room, changed in a jiffy, and hurried downstairs to the party.

While we were taking our walk, Erin had set up the cocktail reception in the living room. She had brought in beautiful vases filled with spring flowers. Trays of appetizers plus platters holding a vast array of cheeses and fruits sat on a buffet table. A bartender, casually dressed in black trousers and a white shirt, stood behind a makeshift bar. He was pouring glasses of wine and other assorted beverages. A dozen people, including a couple of regional cheese makers and distributors whom I recognized, crowded his station.

"There's Shayna Underhill," I whispered to Jordan. "I want you to meet her."

Even from the back, I would recognize Shayna. She was a fifty-something earthmother type. At times I wondered if she had honed her fashion sense during the flowerchild era. Her long curly mass of auburn hair was tied back with a blue velvet ribbon that matched her blue Bohemian-style silk purse and the wide, faux-sapphire-studded belt that cinched her white gauze dress.

As if knowing my gaze was on her, Shayna swiveled. The hem of her dress billowed, revealing her bare calves and sandal-clad feet. I smiled. So did she.

"Charlotte, darling."

Shayna sashayed toward us while sipping a clear bubbly beverage in a wineglass. We kissed each other on the cheek, then Shayna nudged me to do a pirouette and appraised me. I had donned a pastel knee-length dress and a pair of strappy heels. She smiled. "Marriage suits you."

"Thanks."

Shayna turned to Jordan and assessed him openly from head to toe. "So you're Mr. Right."

"I am."

Shayna winked at me. "Good choice. He has kind eyes."

Jordan grinned and thumbed toward the bartender. "Charlotte, red or white?"

"Chardonnay if they have it."

"This could take a while."

"Don't hurry, Jordan." Shayna touched my arm. "Charlotte and I will catch up."

Jordan sauntered off.

"So, how did you meet your hunky man?" Shayna asked. "And does he have a younger or older brother? I'm not picky."

"Sorry, no." He'd had a younger brother who died years ago.

"Poor me. I love a man with an easy smile. I can see how much he adores you." She took another sip of her drink. "Tell me all about him."

I quickly brought her up to date on Jordan's life, how he had handed over his farm and bought the restaurant.

"And he cooks?" she whispered. "How charming."

"Is there a man in your life?"

"Sweetie, there hasn't been for years. Oh, sure, a few since Steven, but no one . . .

40

special. I don't mind being single," Shayna went on. "If I needed to pay attention to a man, I wouldn't have time to manage my empire."

"How are your daughters?"

Shayna laughed. "Between you and me, don't have girls. Both have put me through the wringer these past few years. They battled me coming out of the womb, and now they're fighting me tooth and nail, even though both have long since graduated college and have thriving careers."

"Are either married?"

"Ha! Never. Don't even talk to me about grandchildren."

"Neither of your daughters went into the cheese business?"

"And get their hands dirty? Heaven forbid." Shayna took another sip of her sparkling water. "How about you? Do you plan to have kids?"

I felt my cheeks redden.

Shayna tapped my forearm. "Don't tell me. You're pregnant!"

"No, but Jordan and I —"

"Are thinking about it?"

"We just opened the discussion a few minutes ago."

"Marvelous! However, do you want my two cents? Talk and talk about it. Find out how both of you feel. Make plans. Agree. My husband and I didn't, and it was rough. He wasn't there for me. I'm not saying this because he died. From day one, he wasn't . . . there. He loved the farm. That was his baby. All of us" — Shayna gestured to include everyone in the room — "rarely make vows in our lives. I had taken Steven's and mine seriously. He . . ." She rolled her eyes. "You need a partner during the whole process." She squeezed my arm. "Promise me you'll talk."

I nodded. "Speaking of partners, you and Lara Berry were in business at one time."

Shayna winced. "*Were* is the operative word."

"Erin and I were talking earlier, and neither of us knew why the partnership ended. Care to reveal why?"

Shayna's mouth quirked up in a tense way. "Let's just say Lara can be domineering. She has a lot of rules."

Based on the few times I had seen Lara Berry on television, I didn't consider her heavy-handed. She shared openly with interviewers. She smiled easily. I often thought I'd like to have her as a friend.

Shayna added under her breath, "A *lot* of rules. She is a perfectionist. I'm not. I couldn't measure up. I always disappointed her. She —" Shayna drew in a deep breath. "What does it matter? What's past is past. She took half of everything and went on her merry way. Water under the bridge."

"Half?"

"That was our agreement."

"She did well after she left."

"Yes, she has made quite a name for herself. From humble cheese monger to successful cheese maker to superstar." Shayna laughed, but it didn't sound genuine. "Truth be known, she was consulting and writing long before she broke off from me. She became bored with our little operation. It was inevitable."

"Hey, babe!" a man speaking into a cell phone said loudly. He didn't seem to notice that everyone around him went silent. "Yeah, it's me!" he continued. In his forties with a thick head of dark hair, bushy eyebrows that weaved together above his dark eyes, and a store-bought tan, he swaggered past Shayna and me. "Yeah, heh-heh." The guy reminded me of my ex-fiancé, not in coloring but with his bluster. *All hat but no cattle,* Jordan would say. "Yeah, I thought you'd want to hear from me." The guy moseyed toward the window, pulled a toothpick from his pocket, and proceeded to clean his teeth. A real charmer.

I turned to Shayna. "I gather he's another person you're not a fan of."

"Am I that transparent?"

I giggled. "Yep. Your nostrils flared. Your eyes grew flinty. Who is he?"

"Mr. Self-Important Victor Wolfman."

"I know that name. He owns Gourmet for the Masses, right?"

"That's the one."

GFM, as it was known in the trade, was an Internet-based group that imported cheese, meats, chocolate, specialty foods, and more.

"Keep your distance," Shayna advised. "Slime oozes off of him. He hits on anything in a skirt, although you're probably safe since you're married. There's nothing he likes less than a married woman. Unless, of course, you care to talk to him about French things."

"I'm not following."

"He's a true blue Francophile."

"Aha! I wondered why so many items offered on the GMF site are French."

Shayna nodded. "Anything French, according to Victor, is better than anything American, except taxes and health care. So if you agree with him, he'll talk your ear off and try to steal you from your man."

"He'd better not run into my grand-

44

parents," I said. "They're one hundred percent in favor of all things American." To show their unflagging support of their adopted homeland, they use quaint Americanisms with fervor.

Jordan slipped up beside me, carrying two glasses of white wine as well as a plate of sliced cheeses and skewered cheese-and-zucchini appetizers. He handed me a glass of wine and said, "Ladies, taste these Cheddars. The first is from The Farm House Natural Cheeses, in Canada."

"From one of the only Canadian cheese makers that binds its Cheddars in cloth," I said.

"Don't mind if I do." Shayna plucked a piece of cheese and hummed her appreciation. "Almost as good as mine." She winked. "It's certainly flavorful."

"The second," Jordan said, "is Yarg Cornish Cheddar."

"From Cornwall, England," Shayna said. "I've tasted it. Made from the milk of Friesian cows. Any American choices?"

"Actually, these morsels with the zucchini are made with Emerald Pastures' latest Cheddar. The flavors of the herbs and lime really give it a kick."

Shayna nabbed one and grinned. "I love a man who knows food."

"There are more over there to taste." Jordan gestured with his elbow. "I thought we'd pace ourselves."

"Good idea." Shayna popped the appetizer into her mouth and nodded as she finished it. "Mm. Good. So, Jordan, I hear you do *affinage* for the local farms."

"Not any longer. My sister —"

"Kandice!" Lara Berry, a leggy redhead about Shayna's age, although she appeared years younger, stormed into the room. Perhaps her youthful look was due to the trendy leather jacket and short skirt that she was wearing. Maybe it was her perfectly toned body or chiseled bone structure. "Kandice!" Lara's face was pinched with tension; her green eyes blazed with something that was a far cry from eager enthusiasm. She dropped her weekender suitcase on the floor with a *thud* and tugged her Prada tote higher on her shoulder while surveying the room. "Kandice Witt, show yourself!"

Uh-oh.

People exchanged glances and chattered in a whisper. I hadn't seen Kandice yet, and she was hard to miss, as tall as she was with her pink-white hair. When I'd first met her, clad in a pink mid-calf sheath, pink stockings, and a white feather boa, she had reminded me of a plump, thick-winged cockatoo. She had been dressed for an evening on the town; the woman liked to party.

"Kandice!" Lara yelled. "Are you hiding from me?"

Snowball, Erin's cat, scampered into the house and across Lara's feet.

"Back off, Furball!" Lara butted him with the toe of her shoe.

Snowball didn't need a second reminder; he tore off.

So much for Miss Nice, I thought, taking on Shayna's habit of labeling. Not my style, but what the heck? Lara's sense of humor, which was evident when she was in the public eye, was definitely *in absentia.*

"There wasn't a car to pick me up at the airport, Kandice." Lara's voice was as brittle as crackling ice. "Not a taxi to be had, either." She snaked through the crowd, assessing people as though one might be Kandice in disguise. "I had to rent a car. Without a reservation. Needless to say, standing in a line with minions was pleasant," she said, her sarcasm hard to miss. "*And* I got lost along the road, to boot. There are no signs whatsoever, and GPS is nonexistent. Big-city girls appreciate those things, or did you forget, Kandice?"

"Heavens," Shayna muttered. "Must she always make a despicable entrance?"

I had to agree. Lara had arrived in town hours ago, and Erin had contacted Kandice about the available room. Why wait until now, during the party, to arrive at the inn? Was this nasty display how Lara always acted? Was her cheery television persona fake?

"I had to talk to the locals, Kandice," Lara shouted. "The *locals.*"

Erin, looking darling in a green knit dress that crisscrossed her abdomen, popped over to Lara and offered her right hand. In her other hand, she carried a copy of Lara's latest book. "Miss Berry. Welcome."

Lara towered over her. She didn't take Erin's hand.

Erin kept her arm extended. "I'm Erin Emerald, owner of Emerald Pastures Farm." She offered a winning smile. I had to admire her pluck.

Lara relented and mumbled something unintelligible.

"What a pleasure to meet you." Erin waggled Lara's book, which featured a full-length, confident picture of Lara on the cover. "You're even prettier in person."

Lara softened at the compliment. Aha. There was a nice side to her. I was certain I hadn't imagined it. Phew.

"Maybe you'll autograph my book after I show you to your room," Erin said. "Let me help you with your bag." She didn't wait for Lara to agree. She gripped the handle of the overnighter.

Victor dashed to them. "Don't bother, Erin. I'll help." He took the suitcase from Erin. "Hey, babe," he said to Lara. *"Bon soir."*

"Victor." Lara threw him a contemptuous look but didn't say something rude. At least she had a tad of self-control. Good to know.

"I've got the perfect room for you, Miss Berry." Erin walked toward the staircase. "On the third floor. Number twelve. It's got the best view at the inn. Is your boyfriend coming?"

Lara sniggered. "Honey, he's been gone at least five years."

Erin blushed. "My apologies. I read an article —"

"In *Esquire?* Where he said he wanted me back? He doesn't."

I had read the *Esquire* article, too. Lara's ex-boyfriend was an advertising guy in New York. She had met him when she was working at a little hole-in-the-wall cheese shop on the Upper East Side. On a talk show, she had described their relationship as: *Love at first sight, followed by hate with one bite.*

"Again, my apologies," Erin said. "After you've unpacked and freshened up, we'll get you some wine and cheese, and we'll erase any memories of your travel woes." Erin guided Lara toward the stairs. "I'm sorry you had to ask for directions, but you're from the Midwest, aren't you?"

Lara said, "Rural does not mean you have to be a rube."

"Agreed." Erin couldn't have been more solicitous. "I've gotten lost once or twice around here. It seems I'm always directed toward the house with the white picket fence. Did you get that suggestion?"

"That or the big oak, like there's only *one.*"

"Everyone means well."

Lara's icy demeanor finally melted. She smiled and waved a hand. "*C'est la vie,* right, Shayna?" She swung around and leveled her gaze at her former partner. Shayna flinched but that didn't stop Lara. "*Une personne ne peut s'attendre à beaucoup de ceux qui sont sans education.*"

I blanched.

Shayna muttered, "How dare she! Me? Without education? I'm the one who graduated magna cum laude, not her. I'm the one who learned everything there was to know

50

about managing a creamery."

"Why did you partner up with her?" I whispered.

"Because, as it turned out, she had connections in the cheese world. She knew *everyone* who was anyone. She partied with the best of them. And she could market our wares like nobody's business."

"Is that why —" I stopped myself.

"Why the creamery floundered when she left? Why we didn't win any more awards?"

I felt my cheeks warm.

"Yes, that's why, but we're back on our feet again, so good riddance to bad —" Shayna blew out a frustrated breath. "I need air." She set down her glass and charged out of the inn.

Jordan whistled. "What just happened? What did Lara say in French?"

I translated for him. "Something like a person shouldn't expect much from those without education. I'm not sure what the dig meant, but it was definitely an insult."

"Wow." He clasped my hand. "I can hardly wait for the rest of the fireworks."

"Let's cut Lara some slack. She probably needs rest." I admired her work. I wanted her to be as genuine as she was on TV. "Traveling can be a strain."

My cell phone jangled in my purse, which,

thanks to Lara's outburst, made my insides whip into a frenzy. No one was supposed to call me during the brain trust unless it was an absolute emergency. I rummaged for my phone and exited to the porch to take the call.

"Charlotte," Matthew said before I could utter *hello.* "It's Meredith. Come quick!"

CHAPTER 4

Jordan drove like a bat out of you-know-where to get me to Meredith and Matthew's house. When we arrived, I flew upstairs. Jordan stayed in the living room with Matthew.

In a matter of minutes, I figured out the problem and realized why Matthew hadn't joined me in the master bedroom. My pal wasn't dying. She was livid. Her pretty, freckly face was hot pink with frustration.

"Twenty-plus weeks of bed rest!" she complained for the tenth time. "Are you kidding me?" She was propped up in bed by two pillows, a sheet tucked under her arms. The floral comforter, which was tri-folded back, only reached to her knees.

I sat beside her on the bed and petted her hand. "You can do it."

"Argh." She wrinkled her button nose. "This is going to send me to the loony bin."

"Nonsense." I grinned. "You've been wanting to complete a boatload of projects."

"Oh yeah?" She flipped her tawny hair off her shoulders. "Like what?"

"Updating your photo albums and organizing recipes, to name two."

"What will I do about the last couple weeks of school?" She moaned. "And what about heading up Providence Liberal Arts College?"

For the past ten years, Meredith had worked as an elementary teacher. Children loved her, and she adored them. Over a year ago, however, she took on a bigger project and spearheaded the creation of our local junior college. After construction was completed, the board of trustees clamored for Meredith to replace the temporary administrator and serve as the dean. Her duties were to begin in a month.

"You can do a lot of your prep from bed," I said soothingly. "Also, didn't the board plan to hire a temporary dean once they learned you were pregnant? They love you. They need you. They campaigned for you. No one is going to oust you because of this setback."

Meredith brightened. "You're right."

"Hey, you've been promising yourself you'd learn to knit. Now's the time! I'll go to the knitting store and pick up some supplies. What color?"

She made a face. "Not pink or baby blue."

"Yellow, then. To match the room. Perfect. I'll get a pattern for a baby blanket. That's easy to make."

Meredith threw an arm around my shoulders. "Charlotte, thank you. You always perk me up."

"What are pals for?"

Relieved that Meredith hadn't lost the baby and that she would survive as long as she didn't go nuts lying in bed, I asked Jordan to take me to Sew Inspired Quilt Shoppe so I could pick up supplies. We faced one setback of our own. Parking. Because of the Street Scene, finding a spot was impossible. In my haste to tend to Meredith, I had forgotten all about the event. It wouldn't be a fun trek in my strappy sandals, but I could manage.

Jordan parked on a side street and rounded the car to open my door. He offered a warm hand.

"Such a gentleman," I quipped. "How long will that last?"

"Forever. My mother raised me right."

Dusk had come and gone while we had tended to Meredith. Stars glimmered in the sky. Streetlamps offered a warm glow. At the corner of Hope and Honeysuckle, we drew to a stop to admire the view. In every direction stood portable stages, each stage assigned with a two-foot-high number from one to twenty, the latter being the premier stage. Each stage was fitted with front- and side-valances as well as pull curtains. People were milling about the streets, peering into shop windows. Many carried programs with showtimes. No performances had started yet. Discreetly, a cleanup crew in black jumpsuits picked up wayward trash that didn't make it into bins.

In addition to the upcoming entertainment, city-authorized pushcart vendors — permits only granted to people who owned a shop in town — were selling ice cream, pretzels, and more. Having missed most of the goodies at the reception, I begged Jordan for a treat. He bought me a scoop of Cheddar-chocolate stracciatella ice cream from the pushcart representing the Igloo Ice Cream Shoppe. Divine. The cheese offered a nice tang; the chocolate added a tasty crunch.

Jordan and I headed toward Sew Inspired, but I put a hand on his arm when I spied my grandmother, in a mid-calf-length dress and boots, marching in front of the premier stage, which stood in front of The Cheese Shop.

"Look," I said.

Delilah, my best friend next to Meredith, trailed my grandmother, her tangle of curls knotted at the nape of her neck. Dressed in black leggings and clinging black sweater, she looked like part of the stage crew, not the assistant director.

"*Oui.* That is correct," Grandmère said. Even from where we stood we could hear her. After all these years managing and directing shows at the Providence Playhouse in addition to addressing meetings as mayor of our fair city, she had trained herself to be heard without a megaphone. "Delilah, do you agree?"

"*Oui!* You" — Delilah called to a ropy woman who was holding a bolt of shiny gold material — "drape that fabric over the rack at the rear." Delilah, formerly a Broadway dancer-slash-actress, usually ran The Country Kitchen diner, but occasionally she wrote plays and assisted my grandmother with direction. "Allow for gathering on each side," Delilah suggested. Each stage sponsor could decorate according to its whim. "And let the material billow on the floor."

"Gotcha," the woman shouted.

Twang. Directly to our left on stage seventeen, a gray-haired man started warming up on an electric violin. The stage was decorated with ten-foot ficus trees in way-too-small ceramic pots. A number of performers crowded the space as well. A female singer started vocalizing, sounding like a lost cat crying *me-ow-me-ow* up and down the scale. I hoped for her sake that her songs would be more melodic. A guy with pewter-colored hair that was shaved along the sides of his head and thicker at top climbed onto the stage. Although his back was to me, I realized I had seen him for a brief moment at the reception at Emerald Pastures Inn. I had lost track of him when Lara made her boisterous entrance. I wondered what his name was and what he did in the cheese world. He picked up a preset electric guitar from a stand onstage and checked the amplifier. Performances weren't supposed to begin until eight P.M. or after.

Tap, tap, tap. On stage eighteen, which had been artfully draped with red fabric and set with a row of folding chairs, a lanky poet dressed in black and wearing a black chapeau, tested the microphone equipment. "Ahem! For the love of cheese, for the love of you, find your inner cheese." He stopped deliberately. "Tart, poignant, gritty, textured." He made another pause that you could drive a truck through. "To love cheese is to love yourself."

Folks watching the rehearsal offered polite

applause.

The poet bowed then turned to fellow artists occupying a few of the seats. "We're good to go."

I prodded Jordan forward, in the direction of the premier stage. "Grandmère," I yelled and waved.

She hurried to us and we exchanged kisses. *"Chérie,"* she said. "Jordan. Isn't it wonderful?" She swung an arm to include the entire town of Providence. "Everyone is so alive, so excited. We will have music. Poetry. We will even have a skit called *The History of Cheese* at nine P.M., right here."

Delilah joined us and buffed her nails on her chest. "I'm directing."

I faked a yawn.

Delilah thwacked me. "It'll be fun. We have dozens of ancient tools that your grandmother acquired for the show. Old churns and buckets. A butter and cheese cutter. A fabulous cheese slicer that looks like a horseshoe."

"A wooden wine/cheese press and sausage stuffer, too," Grandmère said. "It's quite unusual."

"Don't forget the French cheese scale that looks like a pendulum," Delilah added. "Very cool. Most are stowed behind the stage."

"Which reminds me, I have to fetch the last few." Grandmère patted my arm. "If you and Jordan come by later, you'll see."

I threw a goofy look at Jordan. He made a similarly silly face. We adored my grandmother, but at times she came up with the most oddball events. On the other hand, she was the main reason why Providence was a thriving community. She was convinced — and therefore had persuaded the city council — that locals as well as visitors would get involved, week after week, if they could experience something new and unique in town.

"What's going to appear on stage number one?" I asked. I indicated the stage past the premier stage.

Grandmère beamed. "I have scheduled a reading of *Who Moved My Cheese?*"

I knew the book. It wasn't about cheese. Written around the turn of the twenty-first century, its aim was to teach people how to eliminate anxiety about the future, not only in their lives but also in their work environment. Both Matthew and I had read it when we decided to take on Fromagerie Bessette. Maybe I should give a copy to Meredith. Thinking of her sent a frisson of fear through me. I hoped she and the baby would be okay.

60

Grandmère eyed me with concern. "*Chérie,* what is wrong? Your eyes . . ." She gently tapped my temples. "You are in pain."

"Not me. Meredith. She needs full bed rest until the baby comes."

"*Mon dieu.* That is terrible."

"I'm heading to the knitting shop to pick up some supplies for her," I said. "She's a novice."

"Perfect," Delilah said. "I can teach her."

"You knit?"

"My mother taught me as a girl. I used to make clothes for my dolls."

"Knock me over with a feather," I teased. "Should I tell your intended you're more domestic than you seem? Better watch out. He'll taunt you mercilessly."

"Oh, no, he won't."

"Yes, he will."

Delilah and our chief of police had reignited their on-again-off-again relationship a few months ago and were still wonderfully in the throes of love. I couldn't be happier for them. They laughed more than any couple I knew, except for Jordan and me and possibly my grandparents.

"No, he won't," Delilah repeated and poked me. "Not if he wants to live. Besides, he knows I knit, and he's told me he adores that domestic side of me."

"He's lying."

"I made him a winter scarf."

I twirled a finger near my neck. "The one with the orange popcorn stitches?"

"He wore it until the weather warmed."

"He was being kind."

Delilah swatted me again. I howled, in fun.

On stage seventeen, an emcee spoke into a microphone. "Folks, gather around. The show is about to begin. And a one and a —"

A fiddler kicked into a rousing rendition of "Pretty Little Girl." I squinted, surprised to see the fiddler was a redheaded female — Erin. The guitarist with the pewter-colored hair joined in, foot tapping, his oversized triceps bulging, his fingers pluck-ing the strings at a furious pace.

Nearby stood Kandice Witt, who was looking up at the performers and clapping in time. Once again, she reminded me of a plump exotic bird, dressed this time in a crimson, mid-calf-length dress, red stock-ings, and flats. Her hair was no longer pink-and-white but red-and-white to match her outfit. She had combed it into a dramatic peak at the top of her head.

Victor Wolfman stood beside her. I didn't see Lara Berry in the mix. Had she caught up with Kandice back at the inn? Kandice didn't look upset in the least. In fact, she seemed blissful.

Grasping Jordan's hand, I said, "Grand-mère, Delilah. We'll see you later." I tugged my husband toward Kandice and Victor. "They're good, aren't they?" I murmured to Kandice.

She swiveled and smiled. "Charlotte. What a delightful surprise." She was attractive, but not pretty, her nose a tad too long and her forehead a tad too high. She had aged since I had last seen her. What was she, forty-five or forty-six? Lines bracketed her alert eyes, probably from smiling too much. She had a wicked sense of humor. "I'm sorry I missed you at the inn earlier. My luggage didn't make my plane. Then my rental car went on the fritz and —" She hooted. "Like I always say, if I didn't have bad luck, I'd have no luck at all." She thrust a hand at Jordan. "You must be Charlotte's better half."

"Older maybe," he joshed. "Not better."

Kandice winked at me. "I love a modest man."

"Like me?" Victor asked.

"Victor, darling, no one would ever accuse you of being modest." Kandice regarded all of us. "Have you met? Charlotte and Jordan . . . Victor Wolfman."

"Gourmet for the Masses." Victor pulled a couple of business cards from the inside pocket of his jacket and dealt them to Jordan and me. They were glossy with frilly embossed letters. "At your service."

Kandice hooted out a laugh. "You are never at anyone's service, Victor."

"Except a beautiful woman's," he countered.

"Like Lara?"

"All beautiful women."

"Including me?"

"You, my dear —"

Kandice put two fingers to Victor's lips. "Don't be mean."

Victor shifted feet. "I was going to say you're too wonderful a catch for any man."

Kandice cackled. "Good recovery."

Without saying good-bye, Victor headed off toward a gathering of young women.

Semi-rude, I thought, but I kept my opinion to myself. I addressed Kandice. "How did it go when you and Lara met up?"

"Were you there when she made her grand entrance?"

I nodded.

"She chewed me out." Kandice shrugged. "No big deal. She also called me incompetent and threatened to ruin all my future conferences, but she didn't kill me, so I'll

live to breathe another day." Kandice too-
tled out another laugh. "How could I not
invite her to the brain trust with her credentials?"

"About that. Why wasn't she on the list
you sent to everyone? Erin was quite surprised."

"It was last minute. Lara . . . Let's just
say, she loves to be spontaneous. She rang
me up. I said *yes.* Give the woman an inch,
and she thinks she's a ruler." Kandice
chuckled. "Speaking of which, have you
seen Lara around? She said she was coming
to join in the fun."

I shook my head. The crowd had swelled.
Victor and the gaggle of young women had
already been swallowed up in the throng.

Erin and the guitarist finished their set.
The audience applauded with enthusiasm.

"More!" one eager fan yelled.

Erin saluted. "Thanks for the vote of
confidence, folks, but we're done." She
passed off her instrument to another musician and scrambled down the stairs at the
side of the stage. The guitarist followed her.
Erin saw our group and skipped to us. The
skirt of her dress bounced with merry
abandon. "Hi, everyone! So glad you could
make it. Charlotte, is Meredith all right?"

"She's fine." I explained that she needed

bed rest.

"Phew," Erin said. "What a scare. I can't imagine. I've never —" She balked. "Well, you know."

Been married, had children. I nodded in understanding.

"You play a mean fiddle, Erin," I said.

"Thanks. We're all sharing instruments tonight so we don't have to switch out the amplifiers." She shot a thumb toward the guitarist. "By the way, this is Ryan Harris. Have you met?"

"Not yet." I'd read his bio in the brochure that Kandice had sent out. He was a consultant who educated farmers on how to run their operations more efficiently. Seeing him up close was a lot different than from a distance. He was quite unique in the looks department. About the same age as Erin and me, maybe a year or two younger, he had thick arms and his torso was huge in comparison to his short legs. He wasn't height-challenged, just oddly proportioned. He also had a farmer's tan. An inch of pale skin showed beyond the short sleeves of his Mötley Crüe T-shirt.

"Ryan," Erin said, "meet Jordan Pace and Charlotte Bessette."

"Actually, I'm Charlotte Bessette *Pace,*" I said, enjoying saying my married name

66

aloud. I still used Bessette for business purposes, but I loved being Mrs. Jordan Pace. "Nice to meet you, Ryan."

"You, too." He grinned, revealing big teeth with a wide gap in the upper row, appealing in a good-natured way.

"Ryan used to be a cheese maker in Wisconsin," Erin said then blushed. "Of course, you know that already. You must have read his bio."

Kandice had asked each of us to deliver mini biographies for the brochure. All of us, that is, except Lara.

"Did you know Ryan lives in Texas?" Erin went on.

"He moved from Wisconsin," Kandice said. "That's where three of his sisters live." She smiled at Ryan coquettishly.

"He has six of them," Erin added.

Her focus, like Kandice's, was zeroed in on Ryan. Were the two of them vying for his attention? Sheesh, I was glad to be off the market . . . for good.

Ryan grinned. "I'm the only boy and the oldest."

"What a responsibility," I said. I had always wanted siblings, but I couldn't imagine having that many. Extended family and friends filled the void. "Is it nice to be near family?"

"Family is what it's about."

Kandice said, "What Ryan didn't include in his bio is he has also been featured in *Culture* magazine." *Culture* is a must-read magazine about cheese. "It's a wonderful article."

"I saw that one," I said. "I wouldn't have recognized you from the photo."

Ryan grinned. "It's the hair. I used to wear it shoulder-length. I cut it like this on a whim. A guy's got to change his look now and then, right?"

I thought of Rebecca and how she had reshaped her hair. Women and men. We weren't that different.

"Aren't you married to your high school sweetheart?" Jordan asked.

"I was. We're divorced now. My fault. I'm on the road too much."

I said, "How are your kids handling that?" According to the article, Ryan had three.

"They've rebounded well. They're easygoing, like their mom, and wicked smart."

"He moved them and his ex to Texas," Erin said.

Ryan jammed one hand in his pocket. "Tessie and I might have split up, but I wanted her and the kids to be near. She agreed. She didn't like Wisconsin winters much. She has already met a great guy.

They're engaged."

Kandice shifted feet. "Did you know Ryan has written a book called *Mastering the Art of Cheese Making: Cheddar is Better*? And currently, he's acting as a consultant to a struggling farm that is turning itself around by raising goats."

"Hey, Ryan," Erin said. "That's what I'm doing, too. They help out by eating what the other animals won't eat."

"Exactly." Ryan bobbed his head. "They keep weeds in check, and they —"

"Enough shop talk." Kandice patted Ryan on the arm. "We're here for fun, right? By the way, terrific job onstage. You should —"

"Watch out!" Ryan yelled.

CHAPTER 5

Ryan reached for Kandice. Not in time. A ficus tree in a ceramic pot hurtled offstage toward her. Luckily only the tree branches struck her. The pot smacked the cement with a loud *crack,* just short of her feet. Kandice stumbled sideways and careened to the ground; her right arm took the brunt of the fall.

The musicians stopped playing. Audience members gasped.

"Kandice!" I shrieked. Heart pounding, I crouched to help. "Are you okay?"

Erin kicked pieces of the ceramic and dirt away. Jordan dragged the ficus off of Kandice then knelt beside her.

"I . . . Ugh," she murmured.

Jordan said, "Can you wiggle your toes?"

"Half of them. I won't be doing a two-step anytime soon," she joked. "Am I bleeding?"

"Only your arm," I said and stroked her

shoulder. "Don't move."

But Kandice didn't obey. She struggled to sit while tugging down the hem of her skirt and smoothing her stockings.

Erin moaned as if the effort were hurting her. "Kandice, didn't you hear Charlotte? Don't budge."

"I'm okay," Kandice assured her, though her wincing face told me otherwise. "Mind over matter. If you don't mind, it won't matter." She forced out a laugh. "Get it?"

Erin said, "Got it. Ha-ha. Sit still."

Gently Jordan manipulated Kandice's arm. "I don't think anything is broken."

I yelled to the crowd, "Is there a doctor around?"

A woman emerged from the pack. "I've called my husband. He's nearby."

Another woman said, "My son went to alert your grandmother." Grandmère, as the Street Scene coordinator, needed to know of any incidents.

I turned back to Kandice, who was running her fingers through her short hair. "Did you hit your head, too?"

"No, but I must look a mess."

"You look fine."

Kandice swiveled her head and took in the stage. "What happened?"

I shook my head and gazed at Erin.

71

"I'm not sure," Erin replied.

Jordan didn't seem to have any idea, either.

Ryan. He had yelled for Kandice to duck. Maybe he could tell us what happened. I spied him standing close to the apron. Lara Berry was with him. She had changed into pinstriped trousers and a cashmere sweater that hugged every curve. Where had she come from? Why was she jabbing a finger into his chest? Her mouth was moving; her gaze, filled with fury.

A cluster of people inched toward them. Others craned an ear.

For goodness sake, what was wrong with the woman? Was she determined to alienate everyone? Hadn't she noticed the commotion and seen Kandice fall to the ground?

I bounded to my feet. "Erin, Jordan. I'll be right back." I approached Lara and Ryan. The crowd was whispering her name.

Ryan's voice rose above the din. "Ma'am, I told you twice already, I have no clue who you are."

"Oh, yes, you do. Yes. You. Do." Lara spit out the words.

"Only by bad reputation."

"Why you . . . hack," Lara hissed. "Just wait. The press will have a field day. I'm going to out you."

"Excuse me. You're going to *out* me? For what?"

"For borrowing some of my phrases."

Ryan scowled. "I *borrowed*? Are you implying I stole from you?" He exhaled forcefully.

"You did. I know it." Lara raised a hand to slap him.

He blocked the blow and seized her wrist. "Don't," he said through tight teeth.

Lara winced and pulled free. "You have no credentials, no right to —"

"Hey, Ryan." I beckoned him. "Can you help with Kandice?"

"What's wrong with Kandice?" Lara blurted. She glanced from me to where I was pointing. "Oh no." She dashed through the crowd to Kandice and knelt down. "Honey, what happened?"

Honestly? Hadn't Lara noticed the hullabaloo? Her warm-and-fuzzy triage-nurse act pleased me, although it surprised me, given how upset she had been with Kandice earlier. She ran a hand along Kandice's arm and whispered something to her. I thought I heard the words: *Got it.* Was she warning Kandice?

Kandice shivered. Did she think Lara had something to do with the accident? *Was* it an accident? I whirled around and studied the stage. What if someone had pushed that ficus onto Kandice? Someone like Lara, who had come out of nowhere.

"Kandice." Lara continued to stroke Kandice's arm. "You poor darling."

"I'm so *poor,*" Kandice said, "I can't afford not to *pay* attention." She thumbed toward the tree and yukked loudly. "Get it? Poor . . . pay."

Lara didn't crack a smile.

Get real, Charlotte. Lara did not shove the ficus at Kandice. It was an accident, pure and simple. No one wanted to hurt her. She was the weekend's event coordinator. Without her, the brain trust would fold.

And yet . . .

I studied the stage again. It looked wobbly; even more so with the musicians stomping their feet. The tree must have fallen of its own accord. Whichever numbskull had put those top-heavy ficus trees on the stage ought to be fired, except he couldn't be; everyone working at the Street Scene was a volunteer.

"Let me through," a man yelled. The local livestock specialist. He was tall and slender and carrying a black medical kit. He introduced himself and asked Erin, Jordan, and Lara to move aside — Erin and Jordan did; Lara didn't budge. After quickly assessing the situation, he started to apply goo and bandages to Kandice's bruised arm.

Knowing she was in competent hands, I focused on Ryan, who was shifting from foot to foot. Of course he should be acting edgy. Out of the blue, Lara had assailed him. She had called him a hack; I think she'd used the word improperly. In writer speak, a hack meant someone who was hired to write low-quality material on a short deadline. She had accused him of *stealing* her words. Were words or phrases copyrightable? I was of the belief that in order for material to be considered plagiaristic entire passages had to be copied or go uncredited to the author. Ryan had seemed astonished that Lara had accused him of such a thing.

I drew near. "Ryan, is everything okay between you and Lara?"

He shrugged. "I'd heard about her temper, but seeing as I've never met her, I hadn't encountered it one-on-one. My opinion? I think she needs meds. My mother, rest her soul, would say, 'Take it in stride.' "

"And your father? What would he say?"

"Dad . . ." He hesitated. "I don't remember anything he said. He passed away years before Mom did. I was fourteen." A muscle in Ryan's jaw twitched. He dropped his chin and studied his fingernails.

"I'm sorry," I murmured. "I totally understand. My parents died when I was three."

Ryan slowly met my gaze. "Then you know. You might not recall word for word what they said, but you know what they stood for."

I hitched my head at Lara Berry. "You and she haven't crossed paths before?"

"Nope. Isn't that astounding, seeing as we've been on parallel tracks? Even if we had, she and I are worlds apart. I like to bolster folks instead of insult them."

Clearly he held a bad opinion of her. I said, "It sounded like she was accusing you of plagiarism."

"I know, right? Where does she get off?" He shook his head. "Not a chance. Not me. Besides, we write with completely different styles. She's highbrow; I'm not. And in my book" — he winked — "I tell positive stories about people who succeed. She only talks about the folks she buried."

"Buried?"

"You know, ruined. With her reviews. She has given a lot of farms a bad rap." He scrubbed the top of his hair with vigor. "Jeez, I'll bet she's never read a word I've written. Provocative, that's what she is. Look at her and Kandice." Lara was hovering close and cooing over Kandice, petting her as if she were a delicate, injured bird. "They look like best buds now, don't they? Bullpuckey. It's a façade. You heard Lara back at the inn. She was ready to rip Kandice to shreds."

Lara's concern for Kandice should have set my fears to rest, so why didn't it? The accident wasn't anything more than that, right?

Ryan batted the air. "It's in the past. For Kandice. For me. History. *Let bygones be,* my mom would say."

"She sounds like a wonderful woman."

"She was kind to a fault, with the patience of Job when it came to us kids." He ground his teeth back and forth while staring at Lara.

"Do you see your sisters much?" I asked, trying to put him at ease. Being verbally accosted in front of a crowd could make anyone tense.

"I see the girls in Texas a bunch. They run a sheep farm called Udderly Delicious. They make a fabulous American-style Manchego; it's a really smooth cheese. The sheep they use are like family." He chuckled. "The three in Wisconsin own a delicatessen and work pretty much twenty-four-seven. Each, if you can believe it, has three kids. Count 'em. That makes eighteen. All boys. Enough for two baseball teams." He chortled. "Serves my sisters right, the way they ganged up on me." He pivoted. "I'd better join the lovefest."

He left me and knelt near Kandice. He offered his condolences. She murmured a response. Lara eyed Ryan warily, but she didn't lash out again.

Soon Kandice asked if she could rise to her feet. The doctor consented. Kandice offered to pay him for his services, but he wouldn't hear of it.

"Take care of yourself, young lady," he advised.

"Young? Ha!" she said. "I'm so old, they only put one candle on my cake."

The doctor offered a wry smile and disappeared into the crowd. Lara offered to escort Kandice back to the inn. Erin wanted to tag along, too. She encouraged Ryan to join them. Safety in numbers, she said. Ryan agreed and wrapped an arm around Kandice to support her. I noted that she was leaning on him a tad more than necessary. After all, she had injured her arm, not her leg.

They trooped away, and I joined Jordan. I wanted his input on what had just gone down. But we didn't get a chance to chat, because at the same time, my grandmother showed up. She was carrying a trio of cheese tools: a wood and metal hoop cheese cutter, a green-handled cheese slicer, and a box-shaped antique cheese grater that reminded me of a sledgehammer.

"*Chérie*, I am so sorry. I just heard," Grandmère said. "The brain trust lady. Kandice. She is all right?"

"*Oui.*"

"You look rattled. Come. Take your mind off the moment. Help me with *The History of Cheese.*"

"I can't." In all the commotion, I'd nearly forgotten our reason for coming into town. "Jordan and I have to get Meredith some knitting things and head back to the inn."

"All of that will wait, *chérie.* Meredith is not going to knit this evening, and there are no more functions tonight for your party, are there?"

I shook my head. "We have an early wake-up call."

Grandmère clucked her tongue. "Like you will fall asleep after all that has occurred. Come." She wouldn't accept *no* for an answer. She ushered me forward.

Jordan offered a consoling grin. "I'll go to Sew Inspired."

"But —"

"Freckles will be able to put together what Meredith needs," he assured me. Freckles, an adorable pixie of a woman, owned Sew Inspired Quilt Shoppe. "She'll offer to deliver it in person, too. You know her. Go." He shooed me away.

Oh, how I loved him.

My grandmother escorted me behind the premier stage. "Delilah, she is here!" She passed me the tools she was carrying. "As players step offstage, hand them the tools, one at a time."

"Is there any order?"

"*Non.* We are improvising. There are more props over there." She indicated a black-draped table.

"Didn't Delilah write a skit?"

"Are you kidding? She thought it would be more fun to keep the actors on their toes." Grandmère winked.

I laughed out loud. "Admit it. Delilah couldn't figure out what to write."

"*Oui,* you are correct." Grandmère tapped her temple. "Delilah is clever, but this time, she had too many ideas."

"I heard that!" Delilah scurried toward us. "Look, the history of cheese is not easy to pin down. It predates recorded history. I wrote an outline. As you are aware, cheese was first made while transporting milk in

80

bladders made out of ruminants' stomachs. No one truly knows whether the trend started in Europe or Asia or the Middle East, so I versed all my actors in the history, and I want them to wing it."

"Do you think your audience cares about the details?" I asked.

"The devil is in the details. Isn't that what Sherlock Holmes says?"

"Actually, it's 'God is in the details,' and Ludwig Mies van der Rohe, the architect, said it." I didn't mean to sound like a know-it-all, but some of my college education, particularly art history, had actually stuck in my brain.

"No matter," Delilah said. "I want it to be as factual as possible."

"Fast and funny would be better."

"I don't need a critic. Hand the tools to the actors," Delilah ordered, "but be careful not to get them caught up in your cute dress. Now, each actor has his or her mission. One will be writing in Egyptian tombs. Another will be reading from Homer's *Odyssey*."

"Is anyone actually going to use these tools?"

"*Oui,*" Grandmère said. "In the background we have actors miming the action. For example, with this tool —" She wielded the antique cheese grater with clamp and wooden handle and, *snap,* the wrought iron handle broke off in her hand. The grater head dangled. "*Sacre bleu!* I must fix this at once."

"Grandmère, don't overreact," I said. "It's just a cheese grater. Heavy and rusted, to boot."

"You do not understand. It was donated by Prudence Hart."

"Honestly?" I gawped, the notion beyond my ken. "Why would Prudence own such a thing?"

"She does not *own.* She collects and donates all of her findings to the Historical Society."

I'd forgotten that Prudence had taken on the responsibility of the museum after the former curator, a flaky woman, fled town.

"Prudence will be furious," my grandmother went on. "I must . . . I must . . ." She clutched the pieces. "What should I do?"

"Tape it together," I said.

"No, no." Her face was flushed, her eyes filled with angst. "I must have this fixed before Prudence finds out. Charlotte, please help Delilah with the rest." She pressed past the curtain and disappeared.

As the drapes settled down, a shiver

swizzled up my back.

Delilah gripped my shoulder. "What's wrong?"

"Is it almost a full moon?"

"Why?"

"Something . . ." Another quiver skittered up my neck.

Delilah scoffed. "Don't tell me you're superstitious."

"I'm trying not to be, but something is off. Really off. Things are breaking. Trees are falling off stages. People are snapping at each other. And with Meredith needing bed rest . . ."

A third tremor ripped through me, and this time rattled me to my core. What the heck?

CHAPTER 6

The History of Cheese was a huge success. The actors didn't play it as seriously as Delilah had expected, thank heaven. Laughter abounded. When the skit ended, I helped Delilah reorganize her props — a reprisal of the play was scheduled for tomorrow night — and then I located Jordan. As predicted, Freckles had insisted on taking Meredith the knitting goodies. She even said she would teach her to knit a stitch or two, if Meredith was up to it.

Later that night, when Jordan and I entered Emerald Pastures Inn, a number of people were sitting in the living room. Victor and Quigley Pressman, a shaggy-haired local reporter who had a penchant for wearing jaunty clothes, were playing chess at the table by the window. Quigley wasn't staying at the inn, but he had been invited to cover the brain trust event and intended to spend all the time he could with the participants.

He could be quite a gossipmonger. Shayna was nestled into a chair reading *Ten Little Indians,* one of my all-time favorite Agatha Christie mysteries. A lively Mozart violin concerto that I knew by the nickname of "Turkish" was playing through a speaker. Erin was stoking the fire in the brick fireplace. It crackled and spit at first, then the flame grew.

Erin caught sight of us and smiled. "Charlotte. Jordan. It's so good to see you. Want anything to drink?"

A few guests were sipping from mugs; others, from snifters.

"We'll pass. We're beat." I drew near and whispered, "How's Kandice?"

"Resting."

"How about Ryan?"

Erin's forehead creased. "Ryan?"

I told her about the mini-altercation between Lara and him.

"Ah." She grinned. "They seem to be hitting it off just fine." She jutted a finger. "They shared a glass or two of port over there. No harsh words were exchanged. Then Lara went up to bed. Ryan's in the study, reading. He said the ticking of our old clock was driving him crazy." She tapped her ears. "He's very sensitive."

"But cute," I said. "You two performed

well together onstage. Maybe when the brain trust is over, you two could date."

"He lives in Texas, remember?"

"A hop, skip, and a jump from Ohio."

"Oh, Charlotte."

"Don't 'Oh, Charlotte' me," I said. "He travels all the time, which means he could live anywhere, and he's dedicated to family."

"Stop!" She swatted my arm, but her eyes glistened with hope.

I bid her good night and followed Jordan upstairs to our room.

Soon after, I slipped beneath the bedcovers and snuggled into his arms.

He kissed my temple, his favorite spot — or so he said. "Have your willies subsided?"

"Yes. Sort of." I worked my teeth over my upper lip. "Where do you think the word *willies* comes from?"

He thought about it. "There's an Eastern European word *willi,* meaning wood nymph or fairy, which can be sort of eerie."

"How do you know that?"

"Crosswords, my love. You got me into them. Now sleep tight. I love you." He kissed me again.

I dreamed of nymphs, satyrs, and all sorts of odd creatures cavorting through the woods. In the dream just before waking, I was clothed in a flowing white gown and dubbed the forest priestess. Some animals were bowing to me; others were making weird gestures. Needless to say, it was all very unsettling.

Early Friday morning, a rooster crowed.

I bolted to a sitting position and muttered, "Can't fool him. Sun's up."

"It is not. He's early." Jordan ran a hand along my shoulders. "Lie down."

"Can't sleep. I'm awake." And the willies, for no good reason, were back. In spades. Drat. "I think I'll take a walk."

"I'll go with you."

The two of us washed and dressed for the day ahead — I put on a pair of chinos, a linen button-down shirt, and flats — and minutes later, we headed downstairs. The inn was as quiet as a tomb. No one, other than us, had taken the rooster's advice to rise and shine.

Quietly we opened the door and jogged down the steps. The sun was barely making its way over the hills to the east but offered enough light for a hike. A gentle low emanated from the small herd of cows; chickens skittered in the henhouse. A lone baby goat made its way to the fence that corralled the young ones and *maa* ed. Then it climbed up the fence and put its hooves on the top rung.

"Jordan, look." I strolled to the fence and scratched the goat's neck. "Hi, fella." Like a dog, he nudged my hand with his ear for more . . . *more.* I obliged then said, "See you around."

Jordan and I took off at a brisk pace. The trails were winding with slow-rising slopes and gentle downhill terrain. The sound of pressed gravel crackled beneath our feet. The scent of dew-kissed grass wafted up. Delightful.

Neither of us said a word for a half hour, not until Jordan's stomach grumbled.

"Hungry?" I asked. My tummy complained as well. The willies had vanished.

"Famished," he said and growled like a cartoon monster.

"Race you back." I tore ahead, my shoes smacking the trail.

Jordan won, of course. His legs were longer, his stamina fierce. But I wasn't far behind.

We jogged up the steps of the inn. The aroma of sizzling bacon and fresh-brewed coffee made my mouth water.

"Just in time," I said.

Many bed-and-breakfast inns in Providence served family-style meals. Everyone ate at the same time, or they didn't eat.

Erin had decorated the cheery breakfast room in blue and yellow gingham and furnished it with six picnic-style tables fitted with benches. On each table, Erin had set a pitcher of fresh-squeezed orange juice and a bowl of fruit. On a few of the tables stood stacks of Lara Berry's newest book. On other tables sat selections of Ryan Harris's book. Hmm. Had Erin or Kandice placed the books there, or had the authors? I didn't see Ryan in attendance. Maybe he didn't eat breakfast. I knew plenty of people who wouldn't, or couldn't. I nabbed a copy of both books and thumbed through Ryan's first. A family's name headed each chapter, the name representing one of the families he had consulted. Pictures were included throughout. Nice.

Eighteen guests were nestled at the tables; some had come from Lavender and Lace, the B&B next to my house. It wasn't that Lois, the owner, didn't make a superb breakfast, but the brain trust was set to start in less than an hour. The guests were wise to be present.

Kandice spotted me and patted her table. "Charlotte, Jordan. Join us." She looked rested. She had feathered a few strands of hair — once again highlighted with pink —

around her face. How she'd accomplished re-dying her hair with an injured arm amazed me. The peppermint-pink blouse with puffy short sleeves that she was wearing brought out the color in her cheeks. She had donned dangling pink earrings to match.

Lara, who was also seated at the table, reminded me of a haughty princess with her hair wound in a topknot and circled with an amber-and-black beaded headband. She was going over a schedule Kandice had given us and jotting remarks in the columns. Beside Lara sat Victor, who was texting someone on his cell phone. His face glistened, as if he had swathed it with lotion.

Shayna, who nearly matched the room in a blue sack-style dress, had taken a seat at another table. She wasn't conversing with anyone at her table. She seemed captivated by Ryan's book. Her tablemates didn't seem to mind. She glimpsed me as I passed, but she didn't set aside the book. Her eyes appeared puffy, the way mine would be if I'd cried myself to sleep.

I mouthed: *Are you okay?*

She nodded: *Fine.*

"Come on, you two," Kandice said. "Sit."

I started to slide in beside Victor, but when I caught a whiff of his overpoweringly musky scent, I opted to settle onto the bench beside Kandice instead. Jordan cozied up to me.

"I can't thank you two enough for helping me last night," Kandice said.

"How is your arm?" I asked.

"Sore, but I slept like a baby thanks to the pill the doctor gave me. Let's hear it for meds!" She leaned forward, fingering the bandage on her arm. "Between you and me, I don't like taking pills, except the pain was unbearable."

"How'd you manage to change your hair color?" I asked.

"Spray it on, brush it out. Easy-peasy." She mimed the action. "Hey, did you hear the rooster this morning?"

"Cock-a-doodle-doo," Victor crowed and continued texting.

"Good imitation, Vic." Kandice grinned. "Right afterward, something started tap-tapping next door to my room." She knuckled the table to illustrate. "I think there might be a resident squirrel living in the walls."

Or a resident autistic brother, I mused. Hadn't Erin mentioned Andrew to Kandice and the others?

Erin, wearing a darling yellow frock with a blue gingham apron, approached the table and offered us menus. Prior to the brain trust, she had sent out a questionnaire asking everyone about dietary issues. Apparently there were a few because the menu offered a choice of eggs cooked any way, ham or bacon, and regular cheeses as well as vegan cheeses like Miyoko's Kitchen Aged English Sharp Farmhouse, a delectable alternative to dairy cheese made with cashews and organic chickpea miso. Erin also offered a selection of muffins — either regular or gluten-free.

After we ordered, Erin pointed out Ryan's and Lara's books, thus settling the mystery of how they had wound up on the tables. She had put them there. Each of us could take one. She added that they were wonderful. She had read both.

Victor rapped his cell phone on the stack of Lara's newest book. "I'm telling you, it's great, Lara. Your best book yet. Very detailed. How did you do all the winery research?"

Lara grinned. "One glass at a time."

"I mean, alone or with a companion?"

"Why, Victor." Lara offered a wry look. "Are you hitting on me again? Are you hoping you can be the companion with whom I do my next taste test? Or did someone stand you up?" She wiggled a pinky at his cell phone. "Hand me your cell phone, and let me input my contact information."

"No."

"Yes." She grabbed his cell phone and stared at the screen. "Hmm. Who are you texting, darling?"

Victor snatched back the phone.

"Aw, Victor," Lara cooed. "Where has your sense of humor gone? You used to be *plein de vie.*"

Victor bridled. "I'm still full of life."

"You're full of something, all right."

"Lara, I'm warning you —"

"Say, Victor," Kandice interrupted. "I hear you're quite a collector."

"Of . . ." Lara asked leadingly. "Women? Phone numbers? French-made shoes and clothes?"

"Cut it out," Victor warned.

"French antiques," Kandice said, perfectly serious. "Tell us about some of them, Victor."

"Don't." Lara yawned. "It's so boring."

Victor shot her a murderous look and through clenched teeth said, "Sure, Kandice, I'd love to." His cruel gaze revealed he intended to stick it to Lara. He pocketed his cell phone and folded his arms in front of him on the table. "To begin with, I have entire rooms filled with exemplary examples of Louis XIII, XIV, and XV furniture. By the way, identifying the differences between the three can be taxing."

"Isn't some of the furniture in the inn's living room Louis XIV?" I asked.

Lara rolled her eyes at me as if willing me not to encourage him.

Victor, who seemed to be on surer footing thanks to an audience, ignored her. "Indeed, the stately sofas are. You have a good eye, Charlotte."

No, I didn't. My grandmother owned a Louis XIV table with cabriole legs. It was a cumbersome piece but so detailed.

"You see," Victor went on, "Louis XIII is a product of a more conservative time. It was massive and monumental. During Louis XIV's reign, furniture grew more elaborate yet more feminine." He continued enlightening us until breakfast arrived, then conversation turned toward what the day's activities would be.

I savored every bite of my gluten-free blueberry muffin and asked Erin if she would share the recipe because my niece Clair — actually, Matthew's girls, Clair and her twin sister, Amy, weren't really my nieces, more like my first cousins once removed, but *niece* was so much easier to say — had to eat gluten-free. Erin was quick to comply. She hurried to the kitchen and in a matter of seconds reappeared with a recipe card.

A quarter of an hour later, Erin announced that it was time to head to the facility. The brain trust was about to begin.

Emerald Pastures Farm had two cheesemaking facilities. The one where the farm made goat milk cheeses was a holdout from the earlier days of the farm. The other, where Cheddars were made, was state-of-the-art. The *make room* for Cheddar was much like the one at Pace Hill Farm. It measured about thirty-by-twenty feet and was windowless. A stainless steel vat, which was about half the size of the room, stood in the middle of the brick-tiled floor. Long whisk-like prongs were attached to a metal arm above the vat. Behind the vat was a conveyor belt loaded with metal boxes. Paddles, ladles, and other tools hung on the far wall. Unlike the facility at Pace Hill Farm, the far end of the *make room* consisted of a wall of clear glass. Beyond the glass, there was a visitors' room where, usually, the public could view the cheesemaking process. Not today.

Twenty of us, each wearing a white coat, latex gloves, and a hairnet — real attractive — clustered between the vat and the conveyer belt. Quigley Pressman, who was standing at the front of the pack, held up a tape recorder as Kandice drew in front of the crowd.

"Listen up, everyone," Kandice began.

A chill cut through me. My whole body started to shake.

Jordan wrapped his arm around me. "Are you okay?" he whispered.

"Yes."

"Liar. You're thinking about Tim."

A few months back, we had found our friend Timothy O'Shea drowned in a cheese vat. I hadn't been inside a cheese-making facility since. I had shared my reservations about doing the brain trust with Jordan, but he had convinced me that I needed to do it. FYI: Riding a bike was definitely easier.

I nodded. "I'm fine."

"Hey, gorgeous." Victor, wearing a supercilious grin, pressed in beside Lara.

She swiveled away and bumped into Ryan, who was slipping in at the last moment. His eyes were red-rimmed and tight, as if he had stayed up all night.

"Sorry," Ryan mumbled, even though he hadn't caused the collision. He skirted behind all of us and squished in between Erin and Shayna.

"Where've you been?" Erin asked.

"Talking to my kids." Ryan offered a what-can-you-do look.

She gazed at him with such desire. How I hoped he wouldn't break her heart.

"Thank you all for coming," Kandice said. "It is a pleasure to put on such a prestigious event. I'm excited to learn what each of you know. I hope you'll be open and forthcoming." She focused on Victor. "No room for smart-mouth remarks in here."

Victor held up his hands as if to say: *Don't look at me.*

"And now," Kandice said, "I'd like to turn the event over to Erin, our hostess."

The group applauded.

"Welcome!" Erin said in a booming voice.

I chuckled. Did she think she was in an auditorium and needed to project? Jordan elbowed me. I curbed my giggling.

Erin must have realized how loud she had sounded. She blushed and in a softer tone said, "Welcome. First of all, let me tell you what our process is, and then we'll dig in. We bring the milk from the holding tank at the dairy to here." She spread her arms. "By the way, the dairy is way across the property, if you didn't see it on your way in." She flapped a hand in that direction. "Next, we pour the milk into the vat, we pasteurize it, and then add starter culture to begin the

97

process. We allow the milk to ripen, which means the lactose, a form of sugar, begins turning to lactic acid. When the curds and whey are separated, most of the lactic acid is washed away, which is why most cheese, except fresh cheeses, have little or no lactose and are okay for those who are lactose intolerant. Pretty cool, right? Okay, moving on . . ."

I knew the next few steps. I imagined many of us did. They are similar among most cheese makers. Rennet is added to coagulate the milk. Once the cheese is of a tofu-like consistency, the cheese maker cuts the curd. Depending on how hard the cheese needs to be dictates how large or small the curd. For example, a soft cheese like Brie, packaged in a six- to eight-ounce box, may be one curd while the curds for a firm cheese like Parmesan will be the size of rice. Then the curds are stirred and left in the whey. Soon after, the whey is drained out, and the curds can be formed into rectangles on either side of the vat. At Emerald Pastures, the rectangles are then *cheddared,* a process that requires the rectangles to be cut into slabs, after which they are stacked, rotated, and stacked again. Next, the slabs are milled into long thin tubes, what some called *fingers,* to increase the surface area so the cheese can be salted. Salt impedes any further action by the starter culture.

"In general," Erin said, "three to four ounces of rennet are added to approximately one thousand pounds of milk. When diluting the rennet —"

"Excuse me," Lara cut in. "Where do you get your water? Is it pure?"

"Absolutely," Erin said. "We draw it from a spring on the property. Any impurities that cause the pH to be less than seven —"

"Has the spring been tested for impurities?" Lara asked.

"Yes. There's absolutely no chlorine, either."

"Which starter culture do you use?" Ryan said.

"O-culture," Erin replied. "The optimum growth temperature is typically twenty to thirty degrees centigrade."

Shayna said, "Do you ever add a yogurt culture?"

Lara threw her a scathing look. "Really, Shayna? How naïve are you? A yogurt culture when mixed with the O-culture is best for Camembert or Feta."

"Americans don't make Camembert," Victor said. "That's an AOC designation."

"Wrong." I held up a finger. "The name

Camembert is not protected. Americans do make Camembert, using pasteurized milk. So do the Italians."

Victor frowned. "Yes, but true Camembert —"

Kandice clapped her hands. "Let's keep on point, folks. The process that we're studying is cheddaring. Moving on."

We touched on the art of *affinage.* Kandice and Erin deferred to Jordan, since he was the expert. Victor, an obvious *anti* when it came to *affinage* — aging a cheese longer than the time the cheese maker had chosen to age it was a point of contention to him — took Jordan on.

"If Cheddar is ripened carelessly," Victor stated, "it can turn sulfuric and rotten-eggy."

"Nothing will spoil on my watch," Jordan said. "At Pace Hill Farm, we pay attention to what each cheese maker wants. We understand that our clients have a sweet spot." *Sweet spot* refers to the age where cheese makers think their cheese is perfect; they would prefer to have it consumed at that age. "*Affinage* is about more than letting a few wheels sit until some mystical timer goes off. It is about a series of repetitive procedures: washing, flipping, and brushing —"

100

"Except you aren't in charge any longer, are you?" Victor taunted. "Haven't you ceded the farm to your sister?"

"She will be as conscientious as I was."

"Maybe you should write a book about the art." Victor meant for the comment to sting.

Jordan's mouth twitched; he was doing his best to keep calm. "Maybe I will."

And so it went for the afternoon, each cheese maker, marketing expert, or connoisseur having an opinion as we stirred, cut, drained, and milled the cheese. Lara asked the most questions, posing hers to Kandice, as if trying to put her on the spot, no doubt as retribution for Kandice's bungling of the previous day's travel arrangements. Quigley surprised me and didn't ask one question. His mouth hung slightly open, as if he was in awe. Jordan, who understood the cheese-making process better than anyone, also kept quiet unless called upon. I loved that aspect of him. He knew when to observe and when to dive into a discussion.

If only I had the same self-control.

We wrapped up the session close to noon, tossed our hairnets into a garbage can on the way out — Kandice lost one of her pink dangling earrings in the process and scrounged to locate it; Shayna and Ryan helped her look; Ryan was the hero who found it — and we headed to lunch. No more bickering, the good humor of the group intact.

CHAPTER 7

Jordan and I followed the crowd to the cheery room where we had eaten breakfast. Guests were mingling as we entered. Two waitresses — Erin had employed twins who normally worked at The Country Kitchen; they were forty-something and identical in all aspects except for their hairstyles; one wore hers short and blunt, the other sported a long ponytail — roamed the room pouring glasses of water or iced tea. Usually when the inn entertained guests, Erin did all the waitressing duties. I was glad to see she had hired help.

Shayna stood in the far corner, worrying the seam of her sack-style dress while talking to Lara. No, not talking. She was poking a finger in Lara's direction, making a point. Lara batted Shayna's finger away and said something, her mouth curled up in a smirk.

The waitress with the ponytail did a

U-turn as she neared them. So did Erin.

After a moment, Lara grinned triumphantly. She patted Shayna on the arm. Shayna brushed Lara's hand away and mustered a smile. I wondered what they had discussed. The differences in styles of making Cheddar cheese? Men trouble? Their past? Whatever the debate had been about, they appeared to have put it behind them. They had *let bygones be,* as Ryan's mother would say.

Movement to my right made me turn. Kandice halted in the doorway. She was staring at Lara and Shayna longingly, almost in a teenager way, looking like an outcast, the quirky comedienne not good enough for the hot girls. Her head was tilted as if she were trying to listen in. After a moment, she shook off whatever was going through her mind, fluffed her feathery hair, and crossed the room to sit with Ryan. She tapped one of his books, which was still sitting in a short stack on the table, and said something.

Jordan nudged me with his elbow. "What are you doing?"

"Studying room dynamics."

Jordan and I often played a game when we went out to dinner. We watched people and made up their life stories. On our honeymoon, we must have dreamed up scenarios for at least twenty people. Most were running away from a dark and dastardly past.

"There are lots of egos in here," he said.

"You think?" I joked.

"Lara and Shayna seem to have made up, though."

"I'm not so sure."

Although Shayna had offered a smile at the end of the argument, she still looked teary. Was there something going on in her personal life?

Lara now stood near a window, a cell phone pressed to her ear. Her mouth was moving. Was she spilling some secret Shayna had imparted? To a tabloid magazine? To a supplier?

A prickle of irritation nicked my insides. I said to Jordan, "Why does Lara feel compelled to belittle others?"

"Some people get a tremendous sense of power from that kind of behavior. I think it's a coping mechanism."

"Wow, Dr. Pace," I teased. "Have you been boning up on psychology again?"

"Maybe." Jordan winked. "Hmm, let's see. Have you heard this one? 'The early bird may get the worm, but the second mouse gets the cheese.'"

"William Camden," I said. "1605." I wasn't super smart. I'd been studying up on cheese sayings, thinking I might use a few in my marketing strategy, and Jordan knew it. The Internet is a wonder when it comes to tracking down obscure things. Type in *cheese > quotes* and all sorts of witty sayings come up, like, "Age is something that doesn't matter, unless you are a cheese." Luis Buñuel Portolés, a Spanish filmmaker.

"Lara, over here," Erin called from the table by the window. She wasn't serving lunch. She intended to enjoy the meal with the rest of us.

Lara joined Erin, and the two immediately launched into a lively conversation about something. Erin laughed; so did Lara.

Victor entered after us, his cell phone in his left hand, his right hand furiously typing a message. He paused and observed Lara and Erin for a second. A cloud passed over his face. Was he, like Kandice, irked not to be included? Quickly he tagged Shayna and invited her to sit with him at a separate table. How could she refuse? Feeling she might need backup with Victor, I steered Jordan in that direction.

With deft speed, the twin waitresses delivered a meal that consisted of tasty grilled cheese sandwiches made with thin slices of Granny Smith apples, red onions, mustard, and Prairie Breeze Cheddar from Milton Creamery, an artisan cheese maker in Southeast Iowa. In addition, there was a daring fruit salad laced with wine and nutmeg. The staff offered a selection of white wines, but not everyone imbibed. Shayna didn't. Neither did I. A glass of wine at lunch could put me right to sleep.

Surprisingly, conversation during the meal didn't revolve around the cheese-making process. It gravitated toward regular life.

Victor speared a piece of mango. "My dear Shayna, have you ever visited France?"

She hadn't.

"You are missing something special. The flowers at this time of year" — Victor inserted the fruit into his mouth and chewed as he spoke — "are definitely the most beautiful in the world."

"Are there tulips?" Shayna asked. "I love tulips." She dragged the word out while pursing her lips. I got the feeling she was putting him on, tempting him to make a pass at her.

"Tulips? Of course there are tulips. Gorgeous tulips." Victor pitched toward Shayna, as if ready to steal a kiss. Was he calling her bluff? She recoiled; Victor smirked.

"I don't know, Victor," I said, rushing to Shayna's aid. "The irises and daffodils in *Ohio*" — I stressed the word — "are spectacular in May. And the grass?" Out a nearby window, I spied the beautiful rolling hills, blanketed with long grass speckled with white clover. The view made me whelm up. "How can you top this? Honestly, Ohio has France beat, hands down."

"You're wrong," Victor said. "America can't compare. The hillsides of France are greener and more expansive."

"I disagree."

Jordan nudged my foot under the table. He knew I was baiting Victor. "Sure you want to fight this battle?" he whispered.

I winked. "It's fun to rile him."

"You're on your own." Jordan pecked me on the cheek and excused himself to go to the restroom.

Victor didn't accept my bait. He swiveled to talk to Shayna exclusively. *Fine.* I tuned him out and bit into my sandwich. The grilled onions paired with apple and cheese was intoxicating. While doing my best not to swoon, I listened in on Ryan and Kandice's conversation at the next table.

"I'm made of rubber, I'm pretty sure." Kandice set down her wineglass and assessed her arm. "This is where I took the brunt of the fall, I think; honestly I don't know. It seems whenever I have an accident, I sort of —"

"Black out?"

"No, that's not it." She wagged a finger. "I go blank."

"You've had a few spills?"

"More than a few in my lifetime." She tittered.

"Do you think the ficus tree falling on you was an accident?" Ryan asked.

"Of course. What else . . . You don't mean . . ." Kandice's eyes grew wide with awareness. "No way. No one here wants to hurt me. Well, maybe Lara would like to take a swipe at me. She was certainly ticked off about the travel plans. But nah." Kandice sipped her wine. "I was voted the funniest and most popular girl in high school."

But was she popular now? Had the tree fallen accidentally?

Erin whooped out a laugh. I glimpsed her sitting beside Lara, and I was struck by the similarities between them: their hair color and vibrant green eyes, the tilt of their noses, their bone structure. After that, the similarities ended. Lara was a head taller than Erin, and Erin was animated, while Lara was stiff. Erin was talking about her brother, Andrew. She hummed a tune he had written; it reminded me of the quick-paced "Flight of the Bumblebee." I was pleased to hear she wasn't keeping his presence a secret any longer.

Lara nodded in sympathy. "My nephew suffers from attention-deficit disorder. Medication works for him. Is Andrew on any?"

Erin shook her head. "Unfortunately, there aren't a lot of options. Andrew really can't tolerate the two main ones. Besides, the meds don't treat the core characteristics, only the irritability."

"Some selective serotonin reuptake inhibitors are better than others, I hear." The medical term rolled off Lara's tongue like she was an expert.

"We've tried them all," Erin said. "Repetition works the best. Andrew is very bright. He appreciates schedules."

"I'll bet." Lara swirled the wine in her glass and polished off the remaining liquid.

"Andrew can do all sorts of math in his head," Erin went on. "Rapid calculations. He's what is known as a *calendrical* savant. He can calculate the day of the week with accuracy. Ask him when November 12th, 1979, was, and he'll tell you."

"Like I would know if he was wrong." Lara laughed. It was the first heartfelt sound

I had heard from her.

"He also has a brilliant ear. He knows what any note is. And he can repeat musical patterns, just like" — Erin snapped her fingers — "that."

"Sweet." Lara offered a supportive smile. "As for your farm, I gather you're struggling. Are you looking for a buyer?"

Whoa. Major conversation twist, I noted.

Erin stammered, "Why . . . No. We . . . I . . ."

"Hey, everyone!" Quigley shouted as he entered the room. His hair was mussed, his linen suit rumpled. "Am I late?"

Kandice barked out a laugh. "You'd be tardy for your own funeral, Pressman. Where have you been?"

"Posting notes about this illustrious event on all my social media sites. Keeping the world current." Quigley swaggered toward our table and slid onto the bench beside Shayna. "Do you all mind if I join you? Of course you don't. It's me. The storyteller."

Victor didn't look pleased. Shayna offered Quigley a smile of gratitude. Victor and his Francophile chatter had to be boring her to tears. Even cocky Quigley would make a better conversationalist.

Quigley set a napkin on his lap then waggled his tape recorder. "Never thought

I'd learn so much about cheese." He tossed the recorder onto the table. "I mean, sure, Charlotte, you've talked my ear off about cheese at the shop, and that's cool." Rebecca had done more of the ear talking. At one time she had been interested in Quigley until she found out that he enjoyed dating older, wealthy women. "But this," Quigley continued. "I'm learning about cultures and what to feed the cows and, well, everything. I thought you shook milk to make the cheese."

"That only makes a milkshake, silly." Shayna pinged Quigley's arm with her fingernail. Was she flirting with him to aggravate Victor? If so, her ploy seemed to be working.

Victor grunted and rose from the table. "Don't mind me." He jerked a thumb. "I've got a few business things to take care of."

Shayna wiggled her fingers. "Nice talking to you." She rolled her eyes at me as he strutted away.

I bit back a laugh.

Jordan returned and whispered, "What did I miss?"

"Dessert," I quipped.

When the group was once again reinstated in the cheese facility, the afternoon came and went in a blur. By five o'clock, I could only imagine how the others felt. I was accustomed to spending the day on my feet, and mine were aching with a vengeance.

Jordan and I retired to our room, freshened up, shared a kiss or two, and within an hour, headed downstairs for cocktails and dinner. We both looked sharp. Jordan wore a blazer and white shirt, open at the collar. I had donned a cream-colored sheath with a pair of gold sandals. My mother's pearl earrings finished off the ensemble.

The gathering once again consisted of the core group; the others were enjoying a special dinner that Lois had prepared at Lavender and Lace.

Ryan and Victor stood at the far end of the living room, bent over the chessboard by the window. Their match was heated. The group of war veterans who played chess on Sundays in the Village Green couldn't have repositioned their men faster. I heard Victor say, "Your sister!" as Ryan took a bishop.

Kandice lingered in the far corner by herself, speaking into her cell phone. Shayna hovered beside the bar. She was sniffing an opened bottle of cabernet and admiring its label.

Lara entered the room and marched to Shayna. She snatched the bottle from her hands. "Mine," she said. "It's not for you."

Shayna lasered Lara with a peeved look and threw both hands up in the air. "Fine." She pivoted and spotted Jordan and me. Her face relaxed. Joining us, she greeted me with a hug. "Have you had a good day?"

"Excellent," I said. "I'm learning so much." Nothing I could use in practicality, of course, but it was interesting information I could share with my customers.

When the ponytailed waitress announced dinner, we migrated to the formal dining room. Erin and the staff had elaborately draped the table with a white linen tablecloth and set it with Towle "King Richard" sterling silver flatware and Wedgwood white bone china. Light from a candle-style chandelier glittered on the gold walls and off the crystal goblets.

Lara positioned herself at one head of the table. Erin faced her, at the opposite end. Jordan, Shayna, and I sat on one side. Victor, Ryan, and Kandice on the other.

The dinner, which included a choice of two salads, each constructed from the farm's sustainable garden, as well as a beef dish served with a potato *galette* or an herb-baked spring chicken accompanied by chanterelle mushroom–Parmesan risotto, was a wonderful wealth of flavors.

Conversation about the day's event continued nonstop until Victor, who occupied the chair to Lara's right, stood and reached for the bottle of cabernet, which Lara had placed on a wine coaster near her.

Lara slapped his hand. "Uh-uh, Victor."

"I would like a taste."

"Stick to the white, like the others," she said. The remaining guests, excluding Shayna and Ryan, had opted for a local chenin blanc. "It's a much better match for the chicken."

I watched Victor and Lara intently, wondering what power play was under way between the two of them. Did she always need the upper hand? Victor glanced from the bottle to Lara. She didn't blink. Resigned, Victor slunk into his chair. He whipped out his cell phone and opened his text message app. As he typed, his gaze swung right and left, like a prairie dog alert for danger.

"Victor." Lara threw him a peeved look. "Care to put that away?"

"Not unless you care to share the red wine."

"Ha-ha. You are too funny." Lara poured herself more wine and slugged down a big gulp. "So, Shayna." She turned to her ex-partner. "How's business, darling?"

The ponytailed waitress appeared and asked if anyone would like a refill of wine. She lifted the bottle of cabernet.

Lara thrust her wineglass at the woman although she hadn't finished what was in it. "Yes, please."

The waitress poured a small amount. Lara waved for her to add more then indicated Shayna's glass. "Pour a little wine for my friend."

"I'll take some of that," Victor said.

"No, you won't." Lara eagle-eyed Shayna. "Darling, I asked you a question."

Shayna put her hand over the top of her glass. "No, thanks," she said to the waitress. Was she making a stand to support Victor, who was glaring at Lara? The waitress looked flummoxed. She set the wine back on its coaster.

"Aw, you're no fun." Lara's words were slightly slurred. How much had she had to drink? The bottle of cabernet looked about one-third full. She flitted her fingers at Shayna and took a long swallow of wine. "Business, Shayna."

Shayna answered, "Business is good."

"Is it thriving despite the blandness of your overrated cheese?"

Kandice warned, "Lara, don't."

Lara cut her a look. "Don't yourself. Keep

out of my affairs, and I'll keep out of yours."

"As if," Kandice said.

Lara tapped her chest with a thumb. "I know cheese."

"Not as well as you think," Ryan retorted. "I've been reading your latest book."

I had, too. Rereading. During our breaks. I'd forgotten how much I enjoyed the poetic words she chose to describe cheese: *chewy, pillowy, velvety.* They were words I used on a daily basis.

Lara arched an eyebrow and did a slow burn to Ryan. "Is that so? This from a —"

"Don't say it." Ryan brandished a finger.

"Hack!" Lara spit out the word.

I gulped. Jordan clasped my hand.

"I have credits," Ryan said.

"You know squat, Mr. Harris," Lara said. "Shayna's cheese is bland. Her farm is inadequately run."

Shayna's face tinged fuchsia. She fingered the knife on her table mat.

Lara tilted her head and threw Shayna a patronizing look. "Tell them, darling. I'm not lying."

"Lara, please," Shayna whispered.

But Lara didn't quit. "You have no finesse. You have nothing *new* to add to the market. Your cheese has always been bland. It didn't become popular until I showed up. I made people sit up and take notice. It's all about labeling. *Underhill* cheese. Really?" Her voice dripped with sarcasm. "How boring. But Underhill *Sizzling Summer* cheese. Now that's tantalizing. Tell them, Shayna."

"Stop it," Ryan hissed.

But Lara couldn't seem to help herself. She pressed on. "In our line of work, *new* is vital. Trite, banal, and dreary? *That* kills just about any —"

"Enough!" Victor stood. He snatched Lara's drink out of her hand, set it on the table, and clenched her wrist. "It's time for you to retire. Let's go."

CHAPTER 8

Lara wrenched free. "Why you!" Her arm flapped backward. She struck her hand on the top of the chair and yelped like a wounded animal. "I'll never retire, you fool, and you know it!"

Everyone in the dining room gasped, me included.

Under his breath, Victor said, "You know what I meant."

"Don't try to *handle* me," Lara went on. "A man like you will never *handle* me." She aimed a warning finger. "Besides, I'm not leaving until I've eaten dessert." She lifted her wineglass, took a defiant sip, and swung the glass toward Erin. "This isn't bad, young lady. Surprising, given the standards at this farm."

"I'm s-s-sorry?" Erin clutched the table with two hands to brace herself. "What's wrong with the standards?"

"You've let the place go." Lara waved her

free hand at the pair of mahogany hutches that held the crystal and china. "This place is a dump."

Bette Davis in *All About Eve* couldn't have uttered the line with more vehemence.

"Cut it out, Lara!" Shayna bolted to her feet. She banged the butt of the knife on the table. "You have no right to speak to people like this."

"Oh, but I do. It's America, darling. I have the right to speak my mind wherever I want, whenever I want."

I mouthed to Jordan: *Uh-oh.* What could we do to keep the evening from spiraling out of control?

Lara swung her gaze back to Erin. "What were you thinking, darling" — Lara hoisted her wineglass and motioned at the other guests — "inviting people here when your domain is in this kind of shape?"

"I think it's lovely," I said. "Quaint."

"The cheese facility is quaint, all right," Lara said. "As in small and understaffed. The grounds are a horror. Unplowed. Untended."

They were not; she was deliberately being malicious.

"Honestly," Lara continued, "have any of you really studied these relics Erin has on display?"

"Lara," Shayna warned.

"Lara," Victor echoed.

She ignored them and lasered Erin with a glance. "Don't you dust inside these cabinets? Oh, wait. Why should you? Nothing in them is valuable. That vase —"

Erin cut her off. "That vase is a Lismore Castle vase, I'll have you know, purchased in Ireland. It was my mother's favorite piece of Waterford."

Good for you, I thought. *Watch out, Lara.* Erin will defend hearth, home, and family. Back in school, I had seen her defend Andrew many times. Kids called him a nerd, a freak. On one occasion, a teacher sent Erin to the principal's office because she, a little bite-sized girl, slugged a bully.

"What about the ginger pots?" Like a knight unwilling to concede the duel, Lara jutted a finger as if it were an *épée.*

"My mother bought them in China." Erin's voice could have cut steel. "Those, as well as the jade carvings you see in the case."

Kandice tapped the table with a fingernail to get everyone's attention. "Hey, didn't a seller on that *Antiques Roadshow* find out her jade was worth something in the millions? Erin, have you had any of your things appraised?"

"No."

"You should."

"Kandice!" Lara swiveled and skewered Kandice with a lethal gaze. "Don't be ridiculous. I was looking at those items earlier. They're worthless."

"How would you know?" Erin asked.

Lara sniffed. "Because I am a collector of rare things."

Shayna scoffed. "You? A collector?"

"Indeed. I have a few Ming vases, some tooled silver from the Conquistadors, a Degas, a Miró."

"Here we go," Victor groaned.

"Here we go?" Lara's voice skated upward. "Victor, darling, you of all people *know* I speak the truth. You've seen my house."

Victor frowned. "All I saw were a few pieces of fine art and the cheese-related antiques like the *Liliput* cheese press by Carson and Toone. When did you get the rest?"

Lara offered a smug smile. "Time marches on, darling. I've enhanced my collection since you were there last."

Victor seemed less than convinced. "So now you need to brag about them?"

"I wouldn't push it, Victor."

"Why not?"

"I might reveal to everyone that you" — Lara wielded her finger — *"you know what."*

"Stop it!" Erin banged the table with her

fist. "That's enough, Miss Berry!" Her voice bounced off the walls. "This . . . this whole affair . . . this brain trust was supposed to be fun, but you —"

Overhead, someone started tapping. Loudly and furiously. Andrew. The tapping became pounding, then stomping. Something jangled, too.

Erin peered upward. So did everyone else.

Tears sprang to Erin's eyes. She zeroed in on Lara. "Look what you've done. You are so . . . I have a mind to . . ." She scrubbed her hair with her fingertips. "Ooh!" She raced from the room and charged up the stairs to the second floor. A door opened and slammed.

No one said a word for a long moment.

Ryan's voice pierced the silence. "Ma'am . . . Miss Berry . . ." His nostrils flared; obviously it required all his resolve to be polite. "I've visited and consulted lots of farms like this one. Yes, they are in need of work, but that doesn't mean they are going to seed. People do the best with the funds they have."

Lara scoffed. "Why don't these people pick another profession? Why engage in a losing battle?"

"Because sometimes a farm is a family's lifeblood," Ryan said. "You . . . you have no regard for any of these fine folks. Why, you've nearly ruined some enterprises with your reviews."

"Not nearly ruined," Lara cut in. "I have ruined them. And they deserved it."

My pulse started to chug. I wanted to tell Lara off — I was no longer a fan — except I couldn't because Erin entered the dining room. With her brother.

Andrew was taller than Erin by a foot and thicker all over — broad shoulders, broad forehead — but his features were similar and he had the same red hair. He carried a drumstick in one hand and a tambourine in the other.

"Sweetheart," Erin said. "These are our guests. Everyone, this is my brother, Andrew. I've told some of you about him." She seared Lara with a meaningful look.

Andrew peered above the heads of everyone, unwilling to make eye contact. "Guests," he said.

"Yes, sweetheart, guests. We were having a lively conversation. No one meant any harm."

"*Some* people meant harm," Lara said.

Anger throbbed in my temples. I wanted a crack at her. Just one. A single pop to the nose to set her straight. My typically sweet-natured husband looked almost as furious as I was.

Andrew wheeled toward Lara, his mouth drawn into a tight line. He craned an ear. Was he trying to determine whether Lara's was the voice of the person he had heard badgering his sister?

"What're you gawking at, Andy?" Lara challenged.

My mouth fell open. Gack. What had happened to the woman who told Erin that she *understood* what a person with autism suffered? Did Lara lie about having a nephew to win Erin's trust? She asked Erin if she wanted to sell her property. Was that Lara's real purpose for attending the brain trust? Ryan hinted that Lara helped destroy a few properties. Maybe unsettling Erin and forcing her to divest of her family's farm was Lara's endgame.

"Lara," I said, not sure what else I might add but ready to intervene.

Andrew tapped the drumstick against his leg.

Lara didn't falter. "Do you have a beef with me, Andy?"

Andrew's mouth moved in time to the tapping but no words came out. The tambourine jangled because his movements were so jerky.

"Andrew, don't," Erin whispered. "Sweetheart. Please." She glowered at Lara. "You said you understood that he's challenged."

"I do understand, darling," Lara said, her tone haughty, "but that doesn't mean I have to abide you parading him around to make a fool of me."

"I'm not parading —"

"Yes, you are. You want to win the sympathy vote. You want everyone here to think I'm an ogre." She gazed at Andrew. "Look at him. Not an iota of eye contact." Lara rapped the side of her head. "No one's home."

Andrew lashed the table near Lara with the drumstick.

"Andrew, no!" Erin cried.

Lara reeled back. "Get him out of here, Erin. Right. Now."

"Lara," I said, rising from the table.

Jordan echoed me.

"You two, stay out of it," she ordered.

Erin corralled her brother. She placed a hand on the drumstick. "Andrew, keep calm."

"Calm," Andrew echoed.

"Count."

"Count," he repeated.

"By tens."

Andrew began to tap the drumstick on the tambourine. "Ten, twenty, thirty . . ."

"Let's go to your room, sweetheart." Erin gripped her brother's elbow and guided him toward the foyer.

When they disappeared, I couldn't hold back. Every fiber in me was quivering with rage. "Lara," I said. "You had no right."

"Please. Not you, too. Why do I bother?" Lara pushed back her chair. She faltered. "I'm going upstairs. I have a splitting headache." She grabbed her Prada purse off the floor, swooped up the platter of cheese and fruit that was set in the middle of the table as well as the bottle of cabernet and the near-empty wineglass, and staggered out of the dining room.

I gaped at Jordan. His mouth was hanging open, too. Shayna's teeth were clenched. Ryan's jaw ticked with tension.

Kandice plucked at her hairdo. Her lips were quivering. "What just happened?" she asked.

Victor said, "Hurricane Lara blew through and decimated the island."

"Does she . . ." I stammered. "Do you know this side of her?"

Victor shrugged.

Silence fell over the lot of us. I could hear the *ticktock* of the grandfather clock in the living room. The twin waitresses entered through the archway, each carrying a tray of dessert selections, but no one wanted any of them. The sprightly nature of the event was doused. Minutes later, everyone went their separate ways.

By ten, Jordan and I were tucked into bed. He fell asleep instantly. I tried to read more of Lara's book — I wanted to reread the section on Midwest cheeses — but I couldn't get past two pages. I wasn't sure I could ever read another word written by her.

I slept fitfully. Around two A.M. I stirred. Had I heard a door open and close? I curled into Jordan and whispered, "Are you awake?"

He mumbled, "Now I am."

"Can I ask you a question?"

"Can I stop you?" He faced me and cupped a hand behind my head. "Go on."

"Do you think Erin will cancel the event?"

"She's a businesswoman. This brain trust has brought all sorts of people to the farm. The revenue will be a boon to her. She'll rally. Promise. In the morning, she will have found her smile, we'll continue with day two of the brain trust, and all will be well with the world." He kissed my forehead and said, "Go to sleep."

At four A.M. Saturday morning, I roused a second time. I heard footsteps in the hallway, and again heard a door click open and closed. I drifted back to sleep.

At dawn, the rooster crowed, and Jordan and I stirred. We dressed in casual clothes and took a brisk walk. At half past seven, we convened with the others in the breakfast room. The aroma of coffee and something sweet — pear-cheese Danish, I was pretty sure — permeated the air. I drew in a deep whiff. My stomach growled: *Feed me.*

"Let's sit over there." Jordan pointed to an empty table.

"Not feeling friendly?"

He grinned. "I'm hungry and don't want to share those pastries. We'll get a full basket to ourselves."

"Smart man."

We nestled at the table and each nabbed a pastry. Heavenly.

Kandice sat at the table beyond us, all by herself, reviewing a schedule.

Shayna, looking fresh in a white lace–on-blue dress, was sitting with Ryan and Victor. Ryan was scarfing down a roll. Victor was typing furiously on his cell phone. Had he come downstairs without looking in the mirror? His hair was mussed, his polo-style shirt only partially tucked in. Erin bustled between tables. Her hair, which was braided with ribbon, swung to and fro.

Shayna yelped. "You performed the rings, really?" She squeezed Ryan's bicep.

"Iron cross and everything. No joke. There's a picture on the bio page of my website. Check it out."

"I love watching the Olympics. Way back when, I had a crush on Bart Conner. When he won the bronze for the rings —"

"That was Mitch Gaylord," Ryan said. "Conner won a gold for the parallel bars."

"Can you do those, too?"

"Yep."

Victor kidded that he would have guessed Ryan was the kind of guy who would jump through hoops.

Ryan shot him a nasty look. "You're the jerk who seems to vault from one romance to another."

Victor sat taller. "Did you just call me a jerk?" He muttered something rude in French.

Ryan's lip curled up.

Jordan gazed at me. "I'm sensing tension between those two guys."

Erin slipped past us and whispered, "Surprise! Ryan's youngest sister dated Victor for a nanosecond."

"Small world," I said.

"From what I hear," Erin went on, "he

made a play for her after making a deal to sell her Udderly Delicious Manchego."

"Hold on a sec," I said. "Why would he want to peddle that cheese? It's American."

Erin giggled. "Yep. Victor might not like to buy American, but he has customers who do. He only buys artisanal. Emerald Pasture Farm's cheeses are included in his selections. Nothing large-scale."

Kandice's cell phone rang. She pressed Send and mouthed to everyone: *Sorry.* "Hey, what's up? Are you kidding? Swell. When it rains it pours. Yes, all right, see you soon." She ended the call and rose from the table. "Everyone, listen up. The shuttle from Lavender and Lace broke down." Her voice quavered; her *joie de vivre* seemed to be missing in action. "That was Quigley Pressman. He said they'll be an hour late and to start without them."

How horrible for Kandice, I thought. It is difficult enough to run an event under the best of circumstances. After last night's fiasco with Lara and now this snafu, she had to feel miserable.

While the waitresses served a feast of scrambled eggs, sausage, and pancakes, I whispered to Jordan, "I don't see Lara. Do you think she's too ashamed of her boorish behavior to show her face?"

"I doubt it. She probably overslept."

"Should we check on her? Maybe she needs something for that headache."

"Who are you channeling today?" He winked. "Florence Nightingale?"

"C'mon."

We excused ourselves and climbed to the third floor. Rooms ten and fourteen flanked Lara's room, number twelve.

I rapped on the door. "Lara? Are you awake?" She didn't respond. "Miss Berry," I said, opting to go with the more formal address. "It's Charlotte. We've started breakfast. Are you hungry?"

Still no answer. I didn't hear anyone moving about. The bedsprings didn't squeak. No water was running in the adjoining bathroom. Jordan tried the doorknob. It didn't budge. Locked.

I rapped again. "Lara, we're all sorry about last night." I hoped to appeal to her egotistical side. *We* were sorry; *she* needn't be. "C'mon. Open up. Join the party."

Deadly quiet.

"Jordan," I whispered with more urgency. "We've got to get inside. What if she's hurt? What if she went to the restroom and fell, and she hit her head and . . ." I gulped, unable to utter any more *what if*s. I had *snafus* on the brain. And *willies* at the pit of my stomach. "Break down the door."

"What?"

"You heard me. Open it. Something's wrong."

CHAPTER 9

Jordan kicked the door next to the handle. Four powerful kicks later, the door gave way. He lunged into the room and whirled to prop the door, which was hanging on one hinge against the wall.

I rushed past him. "Lara?"

She lay on top of the bedspread, eyes closed, arms at her sides. She was dressed in a slip and the blouse she had worn last night. Her skirt and her robe, sans belt, lay on the duvet. Her shoes were positioned on the area rug at the foot of the bed. A pair of white sleeping pillows and half a dozen decorative pillows, similar to the ones in our room, were strewn on the floor.

"Lara?" I repeated and drew near. I halted when I noticed the blue tinge in her lips, the ashen color of her skin. There was no rise and fall in her chest. "Jordan, she's not breathing."

He darted to the bed and nudged me to

the side. He touched her neck with two fingers. His eyes widened. He took hold of her wrist for a second and released it. He shook his head. "She's dead."

A small moan escaped my lips. I pressed the back of my knuckles to my mouth.

A cavalry of footsteps pounded the stairs. I spun around. Ryan stood near the doorway. He jutted his arm to prevent Victor and Erin from entering.

"What happened?" Ryan yelled.

Erin wouldn't be deterred. She ducked beneath his arm and darted into the room. "Charlotte, you screamed." I guess my moan wasn't as small as I'd thought. "Is everything —" Erin glanced beyond me. "Lara!" She tried to get past me.

I clasped her by the shoulders. "No!"

"Is she . . . Did she —"

"Die? Yes," I said. A bitter sadness filled my mouth.

Erin moaned. "How horrible." She wriggled out of my grasp and dashed to the others who had clustered into the room.

Kandice was now in attendance as well, but not Shayna. Where was she? The others looked horrified. The words *She's dead* and *She must have died in her sleep* circulated among them. Snowball slinked past

Kandice's ankles, his eyes as wide as saucers.

Erin spun around. "Charlotte, do you know what happened?"

"No."

I scanned the room. The door to the bathroom was ajar. The doors of the hand-painted armoire were hanging open. My gaze landed on the bedside table, upon which sat a sliver of cheese on a napkin and an empty wineglass — the glass Lara must have taken from the dinner table. The tray of fruit and cheese she had whisked off the table rested on an ornate escritoire across the room, as did the bottle of cabernet — empty.

Jordan pulled his cell phone from his pocket and stabbed in a number. "Chief," he said. "It's me. Can you come to Emerald Pastures Farms?" He listened. "A woman is dead. Lara Berry. Yes, *that* Lara Berry. In the inn. Third floor." Jordan worked his tongue around his mouth. "No idea. I'll leave that up to you." He ended the call.

"What will you leave up to him?" I whispered.

"Evidence."

Kandice gasped. "Do you think she was murdered?"

"I didn't say that," Jordan said.

"Then why will he need to collect evidence?" she demanded.

"Because all deaths are suspicious until proven otherwise," Jordan said as if by rote. Sadly, from experience, we both knew the next few steps in an investigation.

Jordan asked everyone to back out of the room. I didn't obey. I couldn't bear to leave Lara alone. In death she looked so vulnerable and meek, nothing like the terror that had stormed out of the dining room last night.

Erin grasped my hand and stood with me just inside the door. "Poor Lara. Do you think she had a heart attack?"

"I can't hazard a guess," I said. Our charming chief of police had at least taught me to reserve judgment. On the other hand, I wondered whether Lara might have committed suicide. I didn't see anything remotely like a bottle of pills, and yet something felt wrong about the scene.

Erin wove her hands together. "Someone should alert Lara's family."

"She has family?" I said.

"Everyone does at one time or another." Erin was speaking out of the side of her mouth, her gaze riveted on Lara.

"On a talk show last year," I said, "Lara told the hostess that her parents had passed away, and she doesn't have kids. She never married."

"True," Erin said. "But she mentioned a sister in the acknowledgment of her book." Her cheeks flushed pink. "Yes, I read her book. Front to cover. It was good. Informed." Erin hesitated, as if she wanted to say something else.

"What?" I asked.

"Nothing."

"You mentioned that you'd met Lara before."

"Mm-hm. Once."

"Where?"

"At a conference. In Cleveland. She was sharing her views on how to age cheese, and I approached her afterward."

"Did you talk?"

"Sort of. She was brusque, like a rock star who doesn't have time for fans."

Apparently, that had been Lara's modus operandi.

"When she arrived here," I said, "did she remember meeting you?"

Erin blurted out a sharp laugh. She covered her mouth with the back of her hand. "Sorry, that was rude of me. No. My farm is way too small a concern for her."

"Don't say that."

"It is. It's puny." Erin grimaced. "Anyway,

that wasn't the only time she was dismissive. When I was showing her to her room, she carped the entire time. 'I have to walk up three floors? To a room in the attic?' " Erin did a good imitation of Lara's abrupt speaking style. "Next, when she saw the number twelve on the door to her room, she cried, 'Why not give me room thirteen and be done with it?' I told her not to be superstitious. All of the rooms at the inn are even numbers. She asked why. I told her Andrew likes even numbers. He —"

A siren wailed outside and grew louder. Doors slammed. The front door to the inn squeaked open.

Jordan yelled, "Up here!" He edged closer to me. "Are you okay?"

I nodded even though my insides were in knots.

Chief of Police Umberto Urso, a linebacker-sized man with penetrating eyes and an easy calm, tramped into the room. Deputy Devon O'Shea, a hunky guy with an unruly hank of hair that unfailingly found his forehead, even when his broad-brimmed hat was in place, followed him inside.

"You arrived fast, Chief," Jordan said.

"I was just up the road, visiting my folks." Urso's parents owned Two Plug Nickels

Farm, one of the local participants in the cheese competition. "The deputy was nearby as well."

"U-ey," I started and quickly revised. "Chief Urso." U-ey is the nickname that many call him, a result of the pair of *U*s in his name. I try not to use U-ey when he is serving in an official capacity.

"In a minute, Charlotte. Let me get my bearings."

Urso and I had grown up together. For as long as I'd known him, he had dedicated himself to service. Eagle Scout. High School class president. At one point, I believed he might leave Providence and enter national politics, but he stayed. He loved Providence as much as I did.

He donned latex gloves and strode to the bed. He checked Lara's pulse, not that he didn't believe us, but he had to determine for himself that she was dead. He slid his hand beneath her armpit. A few moments later, he said, "She's not in complete rigor mortis, but she's been dead a number of hours. She's cool."

"The room is cool," I mumbled.

"True." Urso pulled a paper and pen from the breast pocket of his brown uniform. "First impressions, please." He regarded Jordan and me.

I recounted why we had come to Lara's room, how we had found her dead, and how the others had followed to check on us after I screamed. When I concluded, Urso asked everyone to step outside. Jordan, Erin, and I shuffled toward the door, but we didn't exit the room. Not because we meant to be disobedient; I don't think any of us wanted to leave Lara.

My throat grew thick as Urso toured the room. I couldn't seem to swallow away the grief. His focus rotated from Lara lying on the bed, to her shoes, to the wine and the cheese platter. In three long strides, he crossed to the bathroom and entered. I heard cabinets opening and closing. He returned to the room and strode to the bed. He crouched down and inspected the pillows and shams on the floor. He glanced upward at the skylight and downward at the green-toned area rug. Then he rose and stood in the center of the room, hands fisted on his hips.

"Chief Urso. Sir." Deputy O'Shea had also donned latex gloves. "Look at this." He was standing by the exterior window. He ran his fingertip along the edges.

Urso joined him.

"It's painted shut," O'Shea said. "No cracking. It hasn't been opened."

Erin edged in front of me. "All the windows on this floor are that way. I've renovated and upgraded the windows on the first floor and am halfway through the second floor. I haven't been able to do everything yet because —"

Urso held up his hand. "Thank you, Miss Emerald, I'll talk to you in a moment."

I gulped. He had called her *Miss Emerald,* not *Erin.* He was reverting to his impersonal cop mode. Uh-oh.

Urso returned to Lara and assessed her from head to bare toes. He bent close to her face and inhaled. Using two fingers, he pried open one of Lara's eyes then released it. The abruptness of his action made me gasp.

"What is he doing?" I whispered to Jordan.

"I'm not sure."

I cleared my throat. "Chief, do you think Lara died of a heart attack?"

He pivoted to face me. "No."

"An overdose? Did you find pills in the bathroom?"

"Nope."

"A gas leak?" I suggested, although the carbon monoxide detectors hadn't sounded.

Urso shook his head. "She was smothered."

I whispered, "As in murdered?"

His mouth twitched. "She didn't do it to herself."

"Are you sure?"

"There's lipstick on the pillowcase."

"I get lipstick on my pillowcase if I don't wash my face before bed." I mimed the motion.

"A smudge, perhaps," he said. "But a perfect print? Two full lips? I don't think so. And if suffocation or smothering has taken place, the eyes of the deceased will be bloodshot, which Miss Berry's are. This is definitely murder."

I shivered. *Not again. Not another body.* A sob burst from deep within me. "How?" I asked. "If the door was locked and the windows were painted shut?"

The crowd outside the room started to murmur. I heard a handful of questions: "What?" "How?" "What did Charlotte say?" "What was the chief's answer?"

I swiveled to look at them — Kandice, Victor, Ryan — and I couldn't help wondering whether one of them had killed Lara. Yes, she had been imperious and frosty, and she had verbally abused each and every one of them last night. On the other hand, just because she was a miserable soul didn't mean she deserved an untimely death.

Shayna materialized on Kandice's right. Kandice said something to her, and Shayna's mouth dropped open. Tears sprang to her eyes. Was her reaction genuine? Why hadn't she arrived earlier? Surely she'd heard me scream and seen the police's arrival. What had taken her so long to make it to the third floor? Could she have killed Lara out of spite? The termination of their partnership not only hurt her income, it had to have hurt her feelings.

I surveyed the room again and wondered, for a second time, how the killer entered if the door was locked and the windows sealed shut? How did he . . . or she . . . escape? Even I knew that to carry out most second-story-type crimes, the perpetrator came in through the window and exited through a window or door. Was there a secret entry like a hidden staircase behind the armoire or beneath the area rug?

Urso was standing beside the bed, speaking to the coroner on his cell phone. Deputy O'Shea was taking photographs: of the wine, the cheese platter, the window, the bed, the pillows on the floor, Lara's shoes — their toes turned away from the bed. Was that significant? O'Shea inspected something on the bedspread more closely. With gloved hands, he picked up a hair: red. Lara

144

had red hair. Then he picked up another one: white. The cat's, I imagined. The deputy tucked them into evidence bags.

Erin tapped my arm. "Charlotte, this will ruin Emerald Pastures for sure. I know it's wrong of me to be thinking of something like that because . . ." She slurped back a sob. "What am I going to do?"

I wrapped an arm around her. I had felt the same way when our landlord was found murdered in front of the shop. Years had passed, but the memory was still fresh: his body; my grandmother holding on to the knife that was used to kill him; the murmurs in the crowd wondering whether Grand-mère was guilty and whether Fromagerie Bessette would survive the bad publicity.

"Don't worry, Erin," I said. It was a weak response, but what else could I say?

Erin started to blink rapidly. "Wait a sec. How did the killer get in? Charlotte, you told the chief the door was locked, and Jordan, you kicked it in, right?"

Jordan nodded.

Kandice elbowed through the knot of people and aimed a finger at Erin. "You! Erin! You have keys to the rooms. You could have entered and left easily."

Erin shook her head vehemently. "No!"

"Of course you could have." Gone was

145

any semblance of Kandice's boisterous, fun-girl personality. Her tone was hard; her gaze, resolute. "Did you kill her, Erin?"

"No!"

I believed her. In my heart of hearts, I knew she didn't have it in her to kill anyone. She was kind and loving. She labored to keep her farm thriving and her brother safe. Besides, she was so petite. There was no way she could have overwhelmed Lara with a pillow. Lara was a head taller and pounds heavier.

"C'mon, Erin, admit it," Kandice continued. "No one would blame you. You killed Lara."

"I couldn't have," Erin cried. "I don't have another set of keys."

"Baloney. All proprietors do. Don't lie." Kandice's eyes were pink-rimmed, nearly matching the streaks in her hair. At the moment, she reminded me more of a mouse than a bird. A cruel mouse. "You and Lara didn't finish on the best of notes last night."

"Nobody did," Erin protested. "She argued with everyone."

Kandice shook her head. "She attacked you, Erin. Your home. Your possessions. She made fun of your brother. Did you use a key to enter her room and —"

"I didn't come in." Erin's skin turned ash

gray; her lips trembled. "I couldn't have because the keys . . . They . . ." She splayed her hands. "My brother lost them."

"A likely story."

"Two days ago," Erin said. "He was stimming."

I understood the term. *Stimming* is the repetition of physical movements or sounds that help an autistic person block out other stimuli that might upset him. Some autistics might flap their hands; others might rock or snap their fingers. Erin told me once that when Andrew was young he liked clacking door knockers and drawer pulls.

"He was outside near the well," Erin continued. "He was bouncing the ring of keys in his hand. He likes the jangling sound. Charlotte, you know how he likes that sound. That's why he carries a tambourine."

I nodded.

"Andrew accidentally lost hold of the keys," Erin said, "and they fell into the well. With all the preparations for the brain trust, I haven't had time to get copies of the keys made."

Kandice grunted, not buying Erin's account.

"Other than the housekeeper," Erin went on, "you each have the only key to your room. She doesn't live on-site. She won't arrive until noon today. She makes up the rooms during the lunch hour."

I spied Urso running his hand along the walls, and the notion I'd considered a moment ago returned. "Erin," I said, "are there other ways into the room? Perhaps a concealed entry to an old staircase?"

She shook her head.

"I don't see a chimney," I went on. "Was there one at any time? Or a dumbwaiter?" Maybe the killer had crawled through some kind of patched-over space. Beneath the bed? Behind the easy chair?

"The only chimney is in the living room. The third floor units — all of these —" Erin twirled a finger. "I told you, this floor used to be the attic. My parents refurbished it years ago, hoping to make the bed-and-breakfast a real draw for the farm, but we never had enough guests to utilize the rooms until now, which was why I hadn't gotten around to freeing up the windows. Lara's arrival" — a tiny sob escaped Erin's lips — "surprised me, but how could I tell her to stay someplace else? It's all your fault, Kandice."

"My fault?"

Erin jutted a finger at her accuser. "You kept Lara's arrival a secret from me. From

148

all of us. Why?"

"It wasn't a secret. It slipped my mind."

I gawped at Kandice. It had *slipped her mind* to tell the owner of the farm that Lara Berry, the most influential person in cheese today, was coming to the brain trust? No, I didn't buy that. Kandice was well prepared. She sent out a flurry of group emails, including attachments with schedules and reminders about what to wear and where to check in. How could she have made such a faux pas? Had she hoped to cause Lara grief? Had she betted on Lara losing her cool upon arrival? Maybe she killed Lara, but why?

"You should have warned me," Erin persisted. "Why didn't you?"

"I —" Kandice huffed. "You called me and said you had a room available."

Erin glowered at her. "I wasn't going to tell Lara to leave, and I —" She wrapped her arms around her petite body and drew in an agitated breath. "I was hoping she'd give the farm and our cheeses a good review. A word from Lara Berry is . . . was . . ." Her chest heaved; her shoulders sagged with the effort. "A word from her *could have been* gold. After I learned the news from Charlotte, I made up the room especially for Lara. Once she was over her peeve, she told me she liked the décor and the view. She found it restful."

Urso had moved to the center of the room and was pivoting slowly.

Erin said, "What is he doing?"

"Starting over as if he just walked into the room." *Rinse and repeat,* I mused. U-ey was nothing if not thorough.

I followed his example and tried to view everything with fresh eyes. Sadly, it all looked the same. Lara dead. The windows painted shut. Erin, at Kandice's insistence, the most likely suspect.

CHAPTER 10

Urso ordered Deputy O'Shea to wait for the coroner in Lara's room and asked the rest of us to convene in the dining room. In daylight, the room seemed less dramatic than it had last night. The maple table had been cleared, the dishes removed, the wood polished to a fine sheen. A needlepointed linen runner extended the length of the table. A vase of daisies — my favorite flower — sat atop the runner. Seeing them usually made me smile. Not today.

Erin flipped a switch and illuminated the crystal chandelier over the center of the table.

"Everyone, please take a seat." Urso crossed to a window. He opened it, allowing in a fresh breeze. Birds twittered outside. They sounded so merry. We were anything *but*.

The waitress with the blunt haircut scuttled into the room. "Miss," she said to Erin, "what's going on?"

Erin told her, and the woman burst into a flurry of questions while acting out how tall Lara was, as if to make sure she understood who had been murdered. Erin asked Urso if the waitress could bring water and coffee for everyone. It dawned on me that neither Jordan nor I had eaten anything substantial other than a pastry. My stomach growled in protest. I willed it to hush.

The waitress fled the room, and Erin slinked to the far end of the table. She pulled out the chair. The feet dragged and groaned on the hardwood floor.

Victor sat in the chair at the opposite end of the table, the seat Lara had filled last night. Was that an admission of guilt on his part?

Honestly, Charlotte, rein it in! But who had motive to kill her? Who had the drive, the will, to press a pillow over her mouth until the life was strangled out of her?

Kandice, Ryan, and Shayna nestled into chairs on one side of the table; Jordan and I on the other.

Urso removed a notepad and pen from his pocket and circled the group. He requested and jotted down each person's name while peering into his or her eyes, as if one would blab the truth by the mere strength of his will.

"I'll tell you what happened," Kandice said, jumping in before Urso could ask. "Erin and Lara argued. Erin lost it and killed her."

Erin spanked the table. "I did not kill her. Stop saying that."

Why was Kandice dead set on Erin being the killer? Was she trying to steer the suspicion away from herself? What motive would she have had to kill Lara? She and Lara didn't compete for clients. Lara consulted farms and wrote books; Kandice set up conferences. And yet I couldn't help remembering how Lara had fawned over Kandice after the accident at the Street Scene. What was their history?

"Lara fought with everyone," Erin said.

"Not me." Kandice squared her shoulders defiantly.

Shayna coughed. "I beg to differ, Kandice. Lara wasn't happy with her travel arrangements. She stormed in that first night ready to lay in to you."

Kandice flitted a hand. "She cooled down. She —"

"Lara was drunk last night, Chief Urso," Erin cut in. "She was saying horrible things."

"Like she always did," Kandice said. "You

were the only one to take offense."

Urso leveled his gaze at Erin, who recoiled.

I jumped in. "Erin didn't take offense, Chief."

"Sure she did," Kandice said. "Lara was dismissive about the farm and the family heirlooms. That threw Erin into a tizzy."

Erin spanked the table. "I did not fly into a tizzy."

I eyed the vases and urns in the cabinets and replayed last night's encounter in my mind. Lara taunted Erin, who sparred valiantly. Kandice added fuel to that fire. On purpose? Then Andrew stirred, and Erin had to subdue him. Did she go to Lara's room later to exact revenge? No. I didn't buy it. The motive was weak.

Kandice said, "Erin yelled at Lara to cut it out. Things spiraled out of control when her brother started making a racket."

"Andrew?" Urso asked.

Erin nodded. "Lara's outburst upset him."

"What outburst?" Urso asked.

Ryan recounted the altercation word-for-word.

Kandice cut him off. "Then Erin ran out of the room, steaming mad, and returned with her brother. That's when Lara lit into her a second time."

Ryan glared at Kandice. "Lara didn't light into Erin. She said nasty things about Andrew. She mocked him."

"Miss Berry made fun of Andrew?" Urso asked.

"Yes, sir," Ryan said. "He became anxious."

Urso hummed as if he understood. He and Erin had participated in many of the same activities in high school: student counsel, volunteer work. He must have met Andrew a number of times.

"Andrew almost jabbed Lara with a drumstick." Kandice jutted her arm to demonstrate.

"He was just trying to startle her," Erin argued. "He would never harm anyone. Ever."

"Erin couldn't take it anymore," Kandice went on. "She hustled Andrew upstairs, and Lara, a little worse for wear —"

"Drunk," Shayna said.

"Whatever." Kandice shrugged. "Lara stormed out. Victor made a comment that Hurricane Lara had made an appearance." She eyed Victor. "Was that your pet name for her, Vic?"

Urso swung around and peered at Victor, who shrank back.

Kandice said, "You knew her pretty well,

Vic. Admit it." She addressed Urso. "They had a fling."

How would Kandice have known about Lara's love life? Again I wondered about the relationship between the two of them. Did it matter right now? At least she wasn't targeting Erin anymore. She had zeroed in on the resident lothario. I breathed a little easier.

Urso studied Victor, who, surprisingly, had remained mute until now. "Mr. Wolfman, do you have anything to add?"

Victor drummed his fingers on the tabletop.

Urso strode to him. "Did you have a relationship with Miss Berry?"

Victor tilted his head up. His cheek was ticking with tension. "We dated."

"For how long?"

"Not long." He cut a hard look at Kandice.

"Were you in love with her?" Urso asked.

"As much as anybody here." A snicker escaped his lips; he bit it back. "Sorry. That was thoughtless of me. Lara and I dated for a month, but we didn't sync." He wove his fingers together to illustrate. Though he was trying to act nonchalant, his skin was slick with perspiration. "We were like oil and water. I cut bait and ran."

At the cocktail party on Thursday, Victor had acted like a sycophant, doting on Lara's every word. Had he really ended their relationship or had she? What if he —

A clinking sound drew everyone's attention. The ponytailed waitress entered through the doorway carrying a tray of poured beverages. Mouth grim, she moved from guest to guest, responding to each request for either a glass of water or a cup of coffee. She set a creamer and a bowl of sugar on the table and said, "Anything else?"

When no one responded, Urso told the waitress to hang out in the kitchen. He intended to interrogate the kitchen staff.

"None of us were here last night after dinner, sir," she said. "We washed the dishes and left."

Urso replied that he simply wanted to ask a few questions. The waitress wrung her hands as she exited the room. The door swung shut with a painful creak.

The *ticktock* of the grandfather clock in the living room could be heard over the silence.

Urso slowly circled the group. Jordan reached beneath the table and patted my leg. Feeling the warmth of his touch calmed me. I still couldn't believe it. Yet again a person I knew — had *met* — had been murdered, and it was highly possible that someone at the table had done the deed. What was it Agatha Christie said? *Every murderer is probably somebody's old friend.*

"When was the last time anyone saw Miss Berry?" Urso asked.

Ryan and Victor shifted in their chairs. Shayna combed her curls with her fingers. Kandice studied her chipped nails.

"I'll start," Jordan said. "Charlotte and I went straight to bed. That was the last we saw her. We didn't leave our room until we went on our walk this morning."

"Anyone else care to answer?" Urso asked.

"I will," Ryan said. He claimed he was so uptight after the row during dinner that he went to town and walked around. He listened to music, admired the window displays, enjoyed a decaf espresso at Café au Lait, and returned to the inn after midnight.

Kandice confirmed hearing someone climb the stairs around twelve fifteen. She was in her room tweaking tomorrow's presentation. She joked that she was so tired, she fell asleep using her inch-thick schedule as a pillow.

Shayna said she talked to her youngest daughter about *man trouble* and then took to knitting for a few hours; she couldn't fall asleep. When Kandice asked what she was

158

knitting, Shayna cast a dirty look and muttered, "A blanket. Why do you care?"

"Because I wish I'd learned to knit."

"Oh," Shayna whispered, red-faced. "Sorry."

Urso said, "Mr. Wolfman, your turn."

Victor leaned back in his chair and folded his arms across his chest. "I, like Ryan, went into town. The conflict at dinner had me wound as tightly as a coil." He eyed Ryan. "A wonder we didn't run into each other."

"Busy place," Ryan mumbled.

I glanced between the two men. Was one of them lying?

"By the way, there are some extremely good vocalists," Victor went on. "A young woman sang *'La Vie en Rose'* to near perfection."

"I heard her," Ryan said. "She sounded just like Piaf."

Édith Piaf was a cabaret singer who was once France's national star. "La Vie en Rose" was one of her most famous songs. My grandmother owned all of her albums.

"I also listened to some cheese poetry," Victor said. "Get this: 'Gruyère, Camembert, Swiss, or blue, served with wine and in fondue. To thine own cheese-loving self be true.' " He chortled. "Kid you not. That was the best the guy had to offer."

"How bad could it have been?" Ryan said. "You memorized it."

"I do that. Memorize. It's a gift."

"Or a curse."

"It's Cheese Week, you two," Shayna said. "Don't make fun."

"Shayna," Kandice cut in, "don't you mean let's be serious because Lara died?" The words came out sharp and reproachful.

Ryan set a hand on her shoulder. "We're all upset, Kandice. Keep cool."

She mouthed: *Thank you* and plucked a napkin from the stack the waitress had left. She set her coffee cup onto it. The cup and saucer rattled. She peeked at Urso self-consciously. He wasn't watching her. He was focused on Victor.

"Mr. Wolfman, what did you do next?"

"I returned to the inn. Must have been around eleven thirty. The place was still. I went to my room and took an Ambien, which makes me dead to the world." He gulped. "Sorry about the lousy choice of words."

"Gallows humor," Shayna said supportively.

Urso slipped a hand into his pocket, his manner easy and approachable. "Did any of you leave your rooms after you settled in, say, to roam the grounds or sneak a bite from the kitchen?"

A chorus of *no* from everyone.

"Who has the rooms on either side of Miss Berry's room?" Urso asked.

Shayna raised a hand. "I'm in number fourteen."

Victor said, "Number ten."

"There's no number thirteen," I told Urso. "All the rooms have even numbers."

Erin shrugged. "My parents did it for my brother."

Kandice twisted her coffee cup on the saucer.

Urso directed his gaze to her. "Yes? Do you have something to add?"

"Around eleven thirty, sir, I heard Lara play a violin. My room is directly below hers."

"No, it isn't," Ryan said. "Erin's brother's room is below Lara's. Our rooms are sort of underneath Shayna's room."

"Did you hear a violin, Mr. Harris?" Urso asked.

"Nope. Didn't hear anything."

"You hadn't returned," Kandice reminded him. "It wasn't a lot of noise, Chief Urso. Just a few notes. I don't know if they were bowed or plucked. Did you hear it, Shayna?"

Shayna's forehead bunched together in a troubled V. "I don't recall."

161

"Either you did or didn't," Kandice snapped.

Urso swung around to face Victor. "Did you hear a violin, Mr. Wolfman?"

Victor had just told Urso that he returned to the inn and went directly to sleep. Was Urso testing him?

Victor unfolded his arms and slung one over the back of his chair. "No, sir."

Urso's gaze swung up to the ceiling and returned to the group. "I didn't notice a violin in Miss Berry's room. Did anyone else?"

"Maybe it's under the bed," I suggested. "Or in the closet."

"Maybe Kandice heard a recording," Jordan suggested.

"Or the radio," Ryan countered.

"No, it was live," Kandice said. "It sounded like Lara was testing out the instrument for the first time."

Urso pulled his cell phone from his pocket and stabbed in a number. He waited a moment, then said, "O'Shea." He questioned the deputy about the violin. After the deputy's response, Urso asked whether there was a radio in the room. He listened. "Uh-huh. Yep. Thanks." He pressed End. "No violin was found. The radio — a clock radio — was tuned to static. There wasn't a

DVD or —"

The grandfather clock *ticktock*ed, then began to *bong*. Nine times. A raw feeling gnawed at my gut. More than an hour had passed since we went in search of Lara. I placed a hand on my abdomen to quell the uneasiness. Jordan sensed my misgivings. He draped his arm around my shoulders.

When the clock stopped clanging, Victor addressed Erin. "You play the violin."

"That's right, Erin," Kandice said. "Everyone in town heard you the other night."

The color drained from Erin's face.

"That was a borrowed violin," Ryan cut in. He placed both hands on the table. "Various performers onstage were using it, just like the guitar I played."

"Ask her if she owns a violin, Chief," Kandice urged.

Urso swung to face Erin. "Do you?"

Erin's cheeks flushed; tears pooled in her eyes. "You know I do, U-ey, I mean, sir. I played in the school orchestra with you."

Of course. I had forgotten. That was another activity that she and Urso had shared. Urso had played the trumpet. All students had to have their own instrument. The district budget couldn't afford to provide for every student.

"I only play it occasionally now," Erin

continued, "to soothe my brother."

"Where is the violin, Erin?" Urso used his softest voice. He wasn't into bullying suspects, especially one as fragile as Erin. I appreciated his sensitivity.

"In my room the last time I checked. Locked in my closet."

"I want to see it."

"Why?"

Kandice huffed. "Isn't it obvious, Erin? Because if it was in Lara's room and now it's in your room . . ." She peered at each person, seeking agreement.

Erin pushed back her chair and leaped to her feet. "I didn't kill Lara!" Her braid swished up and over her shoulder.

I flashed on the red hair I'd seen Deputy O'Shea pluck off the bed. It could have been Erin's hair, not Lara's, but that would be understandable. She was the proprietor of the inn. She had been in all of the rooms, and she candidly admitted to having made up Lara's room.

"Easy, Erin," Urso said, breaking his habit of solely using formal names during investigations. "Let's keep a cool head."

Erin breathed sharply through her nose. "Yes, Chief, Lara embarrassed me, and yes, she upset my brother, but that's not enough reason to kill her. I didn't even know her. I respected her and her work. She —"

Bang, bang, bang. From overhead. Someone — Andrew? — was pounding something on the floor.

CHAPTER 11

Urso peered upward. So did everyone else in the dining room. Without asking permission, Erin tore out of the room.

"Miss Emerald!" Urso barked.

"U-ey, let her go," I pleaded. "She's upset."

Jordan added, "Andrew reacts if he hears Erin is stressed."

"Chief." Ryan twisted in his chair. His jaw muscles were working overtime. "Why would it matter whether Lara had a violin in her room?"

"Because I heard it," Kandice cut in, "and then I didn't."

"Why was she playing it?" Ryan pressed.

"Maybe she was having a Sherlock Holmes moment," Kandice wisecracked, referring to the famous detective's penchant for playing the violin to quiet his mind so he could think. "Don't you see? If the violin is back in Erin's room, that establishes that

Erin was in Lara's room last night."

"If it was Erin's violin that Lara was playing," Ryan said.

Kandice clucked her tongue. "It had to have been. Who else brought a violin along?" No one responded. "Don't you see? Erin must have realized Lara stole the violin —"

"Whoa! Stole?" Ryan held up a hand. "Don't you mean borrowed?"

"Whichever. Erin killed her and took it back."

"Why kill her over a violin?" Ryan threw Kandice a nasty look, his feelings for Erin apparent. He didn't like seeing her thrown under the bus.

Urso flipped his notepad closed and jammed it into his back pocket. "Where is Erin's room?"

"Second floor," I said. "Next to ours. We're in number two. She's in four. Her brother is in six, right overhead."

Urso hustled out of the dining room, his cell phone pressed to his ear. Not eager to be left out of the search, the group followed him like a gaggle of goslings trying to catch up to their mother. Jordan and I trailed them. On the way upstairs, Urso communicated with Deputy O'Shea. When Urso arrived at Erin's door, he rapped on the wood.

No answer.

"She must be in Andrew's room," I said and started toward the room marked ∼6∼.

Urso cut in front of me. "Charlotte," he warned.

"After you."

He knocked.

Erin opened the door a crack. She had thrown a shawl over her shoulders. "What?" She sounded waspish. Her cheeks were streaked with tears. Beyond her, I caught a glimpse of the room. Stark. Very little furniture. Andrew was huddled in a corner, the tambourine and drumstick in his hands. He shook the tambourine rhythmically and chanted, "Up, up, up." He stopped for a moment, then said, "Down, down, down." He paused again, then resumed chanting, "Up, up, up," and so forth.

Urso motioned toward the foyer. "Please show me your room, Erin."

Erin jutted her chin. Defiance didn't suit her. It made her look as vicious as a feral cat. "The door is open."

"I'd like you to join us." Urso couldn't have sounded more solicitous. "I wish to inspect your violin."

Erin grunted. "This way." She cooed to Andrew that she would be right back. She didn't touch him. She knew better. He continued to shake the tambourine and recite his mantra.

Erin slogged forward, keeping close to the hallway wall while eyeing the others. Ryan watched her with concern; Shayna, with pity. Kandice and Victor clearly thought Erin was guilty.

What a zoo. How I wished I could sling blinders on Erin and protect her from their prying eyes. What would happen to her farm? Would a murder investigation drum up bad publicity? Would the farm deteriorate as a result? Jordan's farm had undergone intense scrutiny three months ago, after Timothy O'Shea's death. Luckily Jordan had been strong enough to suffer reporters' slings and arrows and had built up enough financial cushion to weather the storm. Now under his sister's watchful guidance, the Pace Hill Farm Double-cream Gouda planned for release in October was selling out in preorders.

Erin pushed open the door to her room. "Only you can enter," she said to Urso.

He stepped inside, arms hanging loosely.

I remained in the doorway. Jordan pressed in behind me. Ryan mumbled something to Kandice. Victor had Shayna's ear. I tuned them out.

The single-hung window in Erin's room

was open. The drapes billowed in the breeze. The bed, similar to the one in our room, was neatly made. Its plush pillows and shams were in place. A scruffy, well-loved teddy bear nestled on the center pillow.

Erin strode to an antique armoire situated against the far wall. Unlike the ones in the guest rooms that had been hand-painted with images of the countryside, this armoire was made of rich mahogany and painted in an art nouveau style. The mirrors on the doors caught Erin's reflection as she moved. Her face was taut; her gaze, riveted on her mission. She reached behind the armoire to retrieve something: a key. She returned to the front of the armoire, inserted the key, and twisted. She opened the right-hand door. It squeaked with the effort. She reached inside the armoire and withdrew a black violin-shaped carrying case. She closed the door, crossed to a table, and set down the case. She popped the clamps, opened the case, and pulled out the violin by the neck.

She displayed it to Urso. "Will you be checking it for fingerprints? Mine are on it."

"I would expect as much." Urso donned a new pair of latex gloves and reached for the violin. "It's beautiful. I remember when you got this. Your parents gave it to you when you were —"

"Fourteen."

"Before that you had a —"

"Garage sale violin." Erin caressed the scroll at the top. "My parents said if a daughter of theirs possessed a gift, then she should be encouraged to shine with a new instrument." Her smile flickered and faded. "They wanted me to have a career in music, and I did. I taught. But when they died, I moved home to take care of Andrew."

What a sad choice she'd had to make. I had seen her playing at the Street Scene. Her face had been lit up with joy. She truly loved her music. The life of a farmer is a calling; not everyone is bred to it.

"My violin is always in this room, Chief," Erin added.

"Chief," I cut in. "Maybe Lara slipped into Erin's room, borrowed the violin, and put it back while Erin was with Andrew."

Erin shook her head. "I don't know how she could have known about the violin. Even if she did, I've never told anyone where I keep it." She faced Urso. "Maybe she wasn't playing the violin. If she had the radio on —"

"No," Urso said. "Don't you remember? My deputy checked out that angle. Where is your old violin?"

"Long gone. It ended up as tinder in the fireplace. Maybe Lara brought her own violin," Erin suggested.

"Didn't you hear me before? Deputy O'Shea —" Urso pressed his lips together. I could see he was trying to temper his response. "The deputy didn't find anything in her room. No violin. No DVD player. No cell phone with a music list."

That detail struck me as odd. I slipped inside the doorway. "Chief, is Lara's cell phone missing?"

"Seems to be. Are you sure she had one?"

"Yes. I saw her talking on it yesterday."

Urso eyed the crowd hovering in the doorway. "Many of you said Lara stormed out of the dining room. Is it possible she left her cell phone behind in her haste?"

"No," I said. "She left with her Prada tote in hand."

"Hmm." Urso scratched his chin. "The deputy didn't mention a purse."

Had the murderer stolen it? Why go to the effort of making it look like Lara had died of natural causes and then do something like take her belongings, not to mention return the violin to its proper spot? Something wasn't adding up.

Urso jotted a few words on his notepad,

slipped the pad into his pocket, and refocused on Erin. "Miss Emerald —"

"Hey, Erin!" Kandice called from the hallway. "Why is the violin locked up? Is it valuable?"

Erin's lip quivered. "I lock up all my personal belongings. I'm not saying people who stay at the inn are thieves, but —"

"Your room wasn't secured a second ago," Kandice said.

Erin threw her a dismissive look. "That's because I came in here for a shawl and went immediately to my brother's room. I was shivering."

"Poor girl," Shayna said under her breath. She was twirling a long curl at the nape of her neck. How did she feel now that her ex-partner was dead?

I recalled the two of them having an argument yesterday. Afterward, Shayna had been near tears; Lara had appeared triumphant. What had they discussed?

"Officer," Victor said above their murmurs.

"Chief," Urso corrected him.

"Yes, of course." Victor cleared his throat. "Sir, might I see the violin? Perhaps Lara's interest in it was for aesthetic reasons. After all, according to her, she was adding to her antique collection."

"She didn't mention that she owned fine instruments," I said.

"That doesn't mean she didn't have any," Victor replied. "I mostly have art and furniture pieces, but I also own a flute from ancient France and a pair of drums from the French Revolution."

"For Pete's sake." Ryan stepped past me. "Enough about the violin. Lara borrowed it, for whatever reason. She put it back like you said, Charlotte, while Erin was in her brother's room. End of story."

"Or is it?" Victor thrust a finger at Urso. "As I was saying, Chief, if I got a closer look, perhaps I could tell you why Lara might have wanted to hold it."

Urso approached the door, violin extended, but he didn't offer the instrument to Victor. "I can't let you touch it."

"Understood." Victor inspected the scroll and tuning pegs, the *F* holes, and the chin rest. "My, my, my." He wiggled a finger, signaling Urso to reveal the backside. He uttered another chorus of *my, my, my.* When he was finished with his assessment, he said, "Do you know what you have here, Erin?"

"A violin," she snapped.

"Au contraire." Victor's eyes were gleaming with something just short of awe. "A Nicolo Amati original."

"No way," Erin said.

"That's valuable!" I exclaimed.

"How valuable?" Urso asked.

"Really, really valuable." I'd seen a special on television about Amati instruments. Members of the Amati family were the premier violin designers during the seventeenth century. Nicolo was the last of the line. How could Erin possibly own one of them? Weren't they all in museums? "Are you sure it's an Amati, Victor?"

"I am never wrong." Victor's fingers were twitching with a desire to grasp the violin.

"Erin, can you explain?" Urso asked.

"My parents traveled everywhere. To Europe. To the Orient. They often purchased antiques, like vases and statues. It was their passion. Sometimes they bought other things, like the violin." Erin swiveled toward me, back to Urso, and then to me again, as if begging for confirmation. "They never said it was worth anything."

"Never?" Urso asked.

"They told me to keep it in a safe place, that's all."

Kandice inched through the doorway and skirted in front of me. "Cut to the chase, Victor. How much is it worth?"

Boy, I was starting to dislike the woman. Her snippy attitude was just shy of Victor's snooty one. She no longer reminded me of a sweet cockatoo. With her longish nose and high forehead, she resembled a hawk, ready to consume its prey.

Urso waved for Victor to proceed.

Using his pinky, Victor indicated sections of the violin. "Note the inlaid *fleur-de-lis* design on the back and table, and see the inset gemstones? I believe this is a Louis XIV Amati."

Urso tipped back his hat. "How much?"

Victor grinned. "At least a million. To an avid collector, priceless."

Jordan whistled.

Ryan whispered, "Wow!"

Wow, indeed. Lara claimed she collected a few things. Paintings. Statues. Some items from the Conquistadors, of all things. Of what interest would Erin's violin be to her? How could she have known about it? Had she come to the brain trust with the express intent to steal it? She certainly didn't attend to offer her expertise. Other than grilling Erin and chiding Shayna, she hardly contributed at yesterday's session. I recalled Lara asking Erin if she was interested in selling the farm. Had Lara hoped to dupe Erin, an innocent from Providence, into selling the farm and every item on the premises just so she could own the violin?

"Erin," I said, "did you tell anyone about this violin?"

Erin didn't answer; she was pressing her lips together so tightly they had turned gray.

"Erin, answer me. Did you play it for anyone other than Andrew?"

"Only h-him," she stuttered. "Like I said, I d-do so to calm him."

"How about the housekeeper? Would she have known about it?"

"M-m-maybe." Erin shuddered; her eyes grew teary. "I don't remember."

"The high school orchestra saw the instrument," Urso stated. "For four years."

Erin swallowed hard. "Nobody could have known its worth. I didn't."

Kandice flailed a hand. "Does it matter, Chief? Its value gives Erin motive to have killed Lara. Like I said in the dining room, Erin must have realized Lara stole the violin, so she killed her and took it back."

"No!" Erin shouted.

Kandice whirled to face Erin. "Your farm is struggling. You could sell that violin for enough cash to spruce it up and make it shine."

"U-ey," Erin said, her tone desolate. "I didn't know how much the violin was worth. Honest."

Even if she did, would she sell it? She had

kept all the urns, jade, and statues that her parents had collected. Even a clueless person could realize that the commemorative value of the treasures was what mattered most to her.

"Besides," Erin went on, "I have an alibi. I was with my brother last night."

"From when to when?" Urso asked.

"From the moment I took him upstairs until breakfast." Erin's eyes flickered. Was she holding something back? Could she have slipped into Lara's room before heading to the kitchen to prepare the morning meal? I heard a door open and close twice in the wee hours of the night.

"I'd like to speak to Andrew," Urso said.

"No, Chief."

"Now."

Erin worked her lower lip between her teeth. "He won't remember last night. He forgets major chunks of time."

"No, he doesn't." Victor buddied up to Kandice, his face as judgmental as hers. "You told Lara yesterday that your brother has calendrical autism."

"What the heck is that?" Urso asked.

"He remembers dates" — Victor snapped his fingers — "like that."

"But he doesn't remember huge blocks of

real time," Erin said. "It's possible he won't remember me being with him."

CHAPTER 12

"Everyone, please return to the dining room," Urso ordered. "I'll be with you shortly. Nobody leaves. Erin, let's go see Andrew."

Erin gripped my hand. "I want Charlotte to come with us."

"That's not necessary."

"Yes, it is, Chief," Erin said. "I need someone I trust with me." She stood as tall as she could, the top of her head inches below mine. "Or I could call our family lawyer. My brother has rights."

"Fine." Urso shrugged. "Charlotte, please join us."

Jordan whispered, "Go with her. She's shaky."

"Sure, Erin," I said. "If you'd like."

She walked ahead of me. A person climbing to the platform of a guillotine couldn't have looked gloomier. Her shoulders were hunched. She heaved with each step. When we arrived at the room, Erin rapped on the door. She didn't wait for a response. She pushed it open, whispered, "Andrew, sweetheart," and beckoned us to follow her inside.

Moments ago, at first glance, I had considered Andrew's room stark. Now, standing inside it, I realized it was worse than stark. It wasn't exactly a prison cell, but it was bleak. Bare beige walls, beige carpets, a twin bed covered in beige bedding, a stack of books on the bedside table. Beside the books sat a ream of paper, a pencil, and an empty glass tinged with white film, the remnants of milk, I imagined. A metronome stood on top of the paper. If not for the rocking chair, upon which sat a well-loved teddy bear like Erin's and a needlepoint pillow decorated with a red, yellow, and blue alphabet, I would have assumed that color distracted or upset Andrew.

He was sitting cross-legged on the bed. He dwarfed the size of it. Rocking to and fro, he counted by ten. Rapidly. The tambourine and drumstick lay on the floor.

"Andrew, sweetheart, stop counting, please."

Andrew was nearing a thousand.

Erin strode to the bed and sat beside him. She put her hands down to balance herself, but she didn't touch her brother. "Andrew, sweetheart, can you stop counting and sit still, please?"

Either he wouldn't or couldn't. The rocking continued a tad more feverishly. His voice rose in pitch.

"Andrew, sweetheart, when you get to one thousand, I want you to stop counting and sit still."

He sped up his count. When he reached the number, he did as told. *Wham! Quiet!* As if he had gone on automatic shutdown.

"Look at me," Erin said gently.

Again Andrew either wouldn't or couldn't. He stared straight ahead, not making eye contact with any of us.

"Last night, Andrew," Erin continued, "after that lady named Lara upset you, I brought you to your room. Do you remember?"

"Up, up, up."

"Yes, we came here, and I tucked you into bed."

"Down, down, down."

Urso cleared his throat. "Miss Emerald —"

"U-ey, call me Erin. Please. It will help Andrew."

Urso's forehead creased with tension. After a moment, he sucked in a deep breath and let it out. "Erin, I'm not disputing that you came upstairs or that you retreated to this bedroom. Everyone witnessed that." He addressed her brother. "Andrew, did your sister stay in the room all night? I need you to answer me."

Andrew shuddered and started to count again, by tens, starting at ten. Faster than before.

Erin put her hand on his arm. "Shh." Andrew quieted.

I elbowed Urso and whispered, "You shush, too. Let her ask him."

"I'm sorry, Erin," Urso said. "Continue."

"Andrew, sweetheart, do you remember me staying in your room?"

"My room."

"I stayed up all night."

"Up, up, up."

"I sat over there." She pointed at the rocking chair. "You wrote your music" — she indicated the ream of paper on the bedside table — "while I read you a story."

"The Hound of the Baskervilles."

"Yes, that's right."

A Sherlock Holmes anthology was the topmost book on the stack of books.

"Bad Stapleton," Andrew muttered.

Erin smiled. "Yes, that's right. Stapleton is the villain in the story. Before you went to sleep, sweetheart, I got you a glass of milk

183

and some cheese and crackers. Do you remember?"

"Cheese." A faint smile tugged at Andrew's mouth. "We make cheese."

"Yes, sweetheart, that's correct. We do make cheese." Erin petted his arm. He didn't recoil. "Andrew, you woke up last night a couple of times. Do you remember seeing me dozing in the rocking chair?"

Andrew swiveled his head. "Teddy." He reached with two arms.

Erin fetched the stuffed toy and handed it to her brother. Andrew clutched the bear to his chest and resumed rocking.

"Did you see me, Andrew? In the chair? You woke up every hour." Erin whispered over her shoulder to Urso, "He doesn't sleep through the night, ever. He wakes up often."

Urso twirled a finger, signifying she should continue.

"Andrew, sweetheart." Erin licked her lips. I loved how she anchored him by using the word *sweetheart* when she said his name. "Did you see me?"

"I saw you."

Erin looked exultantly at Urso, but then Andrew moaned and started to bounce on the bed. The springs creaked beneath him.

Erin said, "What's wrong, sweetheart?"

"One, two, three, not four."

Urso jumped on that. "Not four?"

"He's counting," Erin said.

"No, he specifically said: *Not four.*" Urso took a step toward Andrew.

The young man leaned back. Panic filled his eyes.

I gripped Urso's arm to keep him from progressing. "Don't. He's afraid."

Urso grunted. "Ask him what he meant, Erin."

"Andrew, sweetheart, what did you mean, 'One, two, three, not four'?"

"Not four." His lips drew tight.

"Didn't you see me at four A.M.?" She gestured to the rocking chair.

"Not four."

Erin's eyes widened. "Oh, I get it. You didn't see me because I went to the restroom at four." She hitched her thumb at the opened door leading to the bathroom. "Is that what you mean?"

"Not four. Not four. Not four."

"Andrew, sweetheart —"

"Not four."

Urso stepped toward Erin. "Where were you at four A.M., Erin? Clearly not here and not in there." He jutted a finger.

Erin sucked back a sob. "Charlotte, help me."

"Chief, I heard a noise around then. A door opening and closing." I turned to Erin. "Were you wandering the inn?" I stroked her arm. "Trust U-ey. Tell him. He wants you to be innocent."

"I took a walk. Is that acceptable?" She sounded so defensive. Why shouldn't she? She had been caught in a lie. "I couldn't sleep. After Lara's tirade, Andrew was a mess. He fell right to sleep, but he tossed and turned. When he woke up around one, he started to pace. I couldn't have him pounding the floor and disturbing the guests. I sang to him. I read to him. I counted to a million with him. Around four, he fell asleep again, so I went outside. I needed air." She flailed an arm. Her eyes glistened with anger mixed with exhaustion. "I was outside for fifteen minutes, U-ey. Fifteen! Count 'em."

"Did anyone see you?" he asked.

"Charlotte just said she heard me. Isn't that enough?" She caved in on herself. "I didn't do it."

"Chief, you can't accuse her of murder," I said. "Not yet. You need to find out when Lara died first. I also heard a door open and close around two."

"That wasn't me," Erin said.

"When will the coroner arrive, Chief?" I asked.

"Soon."

"How about if we go back to the group? You can ask general questions. Maybe someone will slip up. Please." I put a hand on his arm.

Urso stared at my hand.

A flush of embarrassment coursed through me. "Sorry. I didn't mean to overstep or infringe on our friendship."

A smile tugged at the corners of his mouth. "Sure you did." He adjusted his hat. "Okay, Erin. Let's retire to the dining room."

Erin raised her trembling chin and mustered a salute. "Yes, sir."

CHAPTER 13

Everyone reconvened at the dining room table, taking the same seats they had occupied previously, but before Urso could ask a question, the coroner raced into the inn. He was a new guy, buttoned-down with Marine-cut hair and pinched features, and eager to get to the scene of the crime. Urso gave him directions to the third floor.

"By the way," the coroner said as he headed upstairs. "A mini-bus just pulled up outside."

Kandice moaned. "The others."

"What others?" Urso asked.

"The others who are participating in the brain trust. Their shuttle from Lavender and Lace broke down this morning. Until now, I'd forgotten about them. They —"

"Turn them away," Urso ordered.

Jordan said, "I'll take care of it, Kandice." He waited for a nod from Urso then sprinted out of the inn.

"Chief," Erin said, her voice soft and plaintive, "could I stay with my brother while you meet with the coroner? He gets so . . . All of this . . ." She twirled a hand. "You understand."

Urso agreed. He ordered everyone else to stay put.

"Before you go, sir." Ryan raised a polite hand. "I think we're all hungry. Is it possible —"

"Yes." Urso pivoted. "Erin, please get some food brought in before you tend to Andrew."

She agreed and exited toward the kitchen.

Urso departed. In his absence, we all went silent. The grandfather clock *ticktock*ed with even more vengeance, which made me less enamored of the dratted thing. For what seemed like an eon, no one said a word.

Right as Jordan returned to the table, my stomach growled. He clasped my hand and whispered, "Are you okay?"

"I'm hungry."

"And worried for Erin."

I frowned. "Yes. It doesn't look good." Quietly, I shared all I had learned in Andrew's room.

Jordan squeezed my hand. "U-ey will do the right thing. You know he will."

I nodded. I trusted Urso. "Any problem

189

with the folks you ousted?"

"That reporter Quigley Pressman wanted to hang around. I told him Chief Urso would have my hide if I let him. I promised him an interview tomorrow. With you."

"Me?" I squawked.

"You're much better at it than I am."

I whacked him fondly on his upper arm. "Chicken."

The waitress with the blunt haircut whooshed through the swinging door from the kitchen. She was carrying a tray of tea sandwiches. Her ponytailed twin entered after her. She held a tray filled with highball glasses and two pitchers, one of water and another of iced tea. Both women looked tight-lipped and worried. As the ponytailed one neared me, I whispered, "What's wrong?"

"Are we under suspicion?" she asked. "We only just arrived at dawn. We couldn't have . . . We wouldn't have . . . We had no reason to —"

I rested my hand on her wrist to calm her. "Don't worry. Chief Urso knows you well." U-ey is a daily customer at The Country Kitchen; the twins often waited on him. Not to mention, one of them, I wasn't sure which, had been his babysitter when she was a teenager. "He'll ask you a few questions, but you shouldn't fret. Just try to remember whether you saw anything out of the ordinary when you pulled in."

If only they had arrived at four A.M. and had seen Erin roaming the grounds. I sighed. *If only* wasn't to be.

I opted for a cream cheese and strawberry jam tea sandwich, but surprisingly after one bite, my appetite vanished. Swell. The minutes ticked on. Kandice and Victor continually checked their cell phones for messages. Ryan drummed the table, beating out a rhythm that sounded like Beethoven's Fifth. Shayna was scrolling through a series of email messages. When she caught me staring, she mouthed: *My youngest.*

A quarter of an hour later, Urso returned with Erin. She took her position at the head of the table, and Urso asked everyone his or her alibi again. In detail. No one deviated.

"Did anyone see me walking outside at four A.M.?" Erin asked. "Charlotte says she heard something, but that doesn't seem to be enough proof for Chief Urso."

"I also heard something at two A.M." I gazed at Kandice, my premier suspect because she was dead set against Erin, not to mention she had invited Lara to the brain trust. On the sly. I didn't expect her to admit to being out and about — if she did, she would be establishing that she had lied about falling asleep with her schedule as a pillow — but I hoped she would show a flicker of guilt: rapid blinking, gritting teeth, something. She didn't.

Ryan cleared his throat, but he didn't offer up anything.

Erin sucked back a sob.

"Sir." Deputy O'Shea emerged in the archway leading to the foyer. He said after searching Miss Emerald's room and the rest of the premises for a second set of room keys, which he did *not* find, he went in search of Lara's purse, which he *did* find. "This is it, right?" He held up a caramel-colored Prada tote. "It was tucked into her suitcase along with a hoard of files and a carry case of jewelry. Her cell phone is in the purse. As is the key to her room."

"Good work."

Kandice raised a hand. "Isn't the placement of the purse suspicious? I mean, stowing her purse in a suitcase. C'mon. Isn't that odd?"

"I do that when I travel," I said. "Out of sight, out of mind. A thief would have to look to find it, and thieves hate spending time."

Kandice smirked. "Since when are you an expert?"

"Don't attack her, Kandice," Shayna said. "She's only trying to help."

"Fine." Kandice slumped in her chair and crossed her arms over her chest.

"Is there anything significant on Lara's cell phone?" Victor asked.

Urso swung around. "Why would you ask?"

A fresh outbreak of perspiration glazed Victor's taut skin. "All I'm saying is what if Lara invited someone to stay with her? Someone *not* in this room. What if she arranged an *affaire d'amour,* and her paramour showed up after everyone retired? He brought her a violin, killed her, and split."

Ryan guffawed. "The door was locked, you dolt, or didn't you hear? And her room key was in her purse."

"Not to mention" — Shayna bobbed her head, agreeing with Ryan — "Lara wouldn't do such a thing. Inviting a stranger to her room? Get real." I was surprised and pleased to hear Shayna defend her former partner. It spoke well to her innocence.

The conversation continued, many acting testy, others growing morose: *How long would this take? Did she need a lawyer? How dare he be held against his will!*

Around noon, when Urso declared the brain trust officially over, there were moans

193

from everyone — whether from despair or relief, I wasn't sure. Urso allowed all of us, including Erin, to remain free on his or her own recognizance. Once he received the coroner's report about time of death, he would revisit the matter of alibis. No one was to leave town. Period. He asked for cell phone numbers and returned upstairs.

Chairs screeched the floor. Victor first, then Shayna. Ryan reached for Erin's hand. The warmth in his eyes said it all; he was falling for her. Erin peeked over her shoulder toward the foyer, probably wondering whether she should tend to her brother or remain here, drinking in Ryan's support.

"Dang, dang, dang it!" Kandice struggled to free the sleeve of her dress, which had snagged on her chair. She tugged hard; something ripped. "Drat!" Tears brimmed in her eyes. "I can't believe it. The brain trust is canceled? It's going to ruin me." She scrambled from her seat, flapping her arms like she might take flight. "Who will hire me to put on a conference after this fiasco?"

"How about me?" Victor said.

"You'd hire me?"

"Don't be absurd. If my clients find out I was here, I'm ruined."

"Why?" Kandice asked. "Because you did it?"

"Did what? Murdered Lara? Don't be ridiculous." Victor glowered at her but something flickered in his eyes. Did he kill Lara? I wouldn't put it past him. He said they had dated a while ago. He claimed he *cut bait and ran,* but did he? What if he fell in love with her? What if he got jealous because he thought she was, as he said, having an *affaire d'amour*? I pictured the scenario. He went to her room. She rebuffed him. He became enraged.

Kandice scoffed. "How could being here affect you, Victor? Online buyers don't look at the whereabouts of the site owner. They want cheap prices. You provide plenty of those."

"Are you saying my product is cheap? Why you . . ." Victor raised a hand. "Take it back."

Kandice snarled at him.

"Victor! Kandice!" Shayna shouted. "Cut it out. Do you hear yourselves?"

Ryan said, "That's all they hear. They don't listen to anyone else. They —"

"Ryan." Erin gripped his arm. "Don't fan the fire."

But Ryan couldn't seem to help himself. He wriggled free. "Victor, I didn't see you

195

in town last night. Why? Maybe you weren't really there."

"I was." Victor raised his chin.

"Did anybody see you?" Ryan challenged. "Anyone at all?"

Victor smacked his tongue against teeth. "Don't take me on, young man. I'm warning you."

Ryan flexed his arms. "You want a piece of me?"

Jordan stepped forward, hands raised in conciliation. "C'mon, fellas. Cool it. This isn't going to get us anyplace."

"Lara is dead." Victor spat out the words. "One of us killed her."

"Glad to hear you've included yourself in that group, pal," Ryan said.

"You know, *pal*" — Victor peered down his nose at Ryan — "you're the one who had a set-to with Lara the first night. She accused you of plagiarizing her. And you're strong enough to have smothered her."

"So are you."

"Yeah, but I wouldn't have. I loved her."

Aha! I knew it.

Ryan's nostrils flared; his upper lip curled into a sneer. "Victor, my man. At dinner last night, when you were questioning Lara about her collectibles, she told you to stop or she would tell us something about you. A secret. What was it?"

Victor poised himself, as if ready for a fight. Good thing he wasn't holding a rapier in his hand.

"I'd bet it has something to do with your business," Ryan went on. "Are you —"

"She had nothing on me. Nothing!" Victor glanced at the others. "I had no reason to kill Lara Berry. You have to believe me."

"Methinks the lad doth protest too much," Ryan said in a British accent. He leveled Victor with a glare. "The truth will out. It always does."

Flash!

Light flared through the window and bounced off the mirror on the far wall. Someone outside had taken a photograph.

CHAPTER 14

Jordan rushed to the foyer and out the front door. I followed. A man in a yellow plaid jacket darted around the corner of the inn. Quigley Pressman. Of course. Who else would own such a garish piece of clothing? How long had he been hanging outside? What had he heard? An engine sputtered to life, and seconds later Quigley zipped down the driveway in his black smart car.

"Jordan, what should we do?" I asked.

He shrugged. "We can't fight the freedom of the press."

"Quigley sure as heck won't get an interview out of me now."

Jordan wrapped an arm around me. "I never thought he would."

Because we lived in town, Jordan and I packed our things to return home. The thought of staying at the inn another night made me edgy. I felt sorry for the out-of-towners, but what could they do? They had nowhere else to stay. The rest of the B&Bs and quaint hotels in town were booked due to the Cheese Festival and Street Scene.

Before leaving, I assured Erin I would touch base with her tomorrow. I could not accept that she was the killer. Call it gut instinct or a total commitment to a friend, but I simply didn't believe it. I wouldn't. Erin barely heard me. Andrew was anxiously clacking the tambourine on the floor above while chanting: *up, up, up* or *down, down, down* loudly enough for all to hear.

On the drive back to town, I kept cycling the events through my brain. Lara's was a closed-room murder. There was no way in or out, so how had the killer gotten into and out of Lara's room undetected? Why had he or she moved the violin back to Erin's room if, indeed, that was what happened? There was no proof that Lara had been playing Erin's violin. True, Kandice claimed she heard the strains of a violin, but she couldn't convince me it was Erin's instrument, yet no alternative instrument had been found. The other niggling point was why Lara had played the violin in the first place? Near midnight? Had she stolen it and accidentally plucked it while trying to find a place to hide it?

Jordan and I swung by Matthew's house to fetch Rags. Amy and Clair, Matthew's preteen twins, met us at the door. Both were blossoming into lovely young ladies. Amy had grown another inch in the past month, nearly catching up to her older-by-a-few-minutes twin. Her dark hair had grown, too. She was wearing it swept into a ponytail. Clair still had her blonde hair styled in a bob. A blue ribbon held back the bangs that she was growing out. Six months ago, the girls would have tugged us into the kitchen for cookies and milk; now they hugged us for a nanosecond and tore off to watch a television show about a teenage detective.

"Meredith's asleep," Amy yelled over her shoulder as she took the stairs two at a time. "The animals are with her. Dad is making tea."

I was surprised to find Matthew at home on a Saturday. He explained that he had wanted to check in on Meredith. Even though Urso instructed us not to discuss the details of the murder, both Jordan and I felt we should let Matthew in on the drama. He would keep the news to himself.

While he poured us each a cup of Darjeeling tea, I did most of the talking. *Poor Erin,* he said a number of times. Meredith would be upset to hear. She had performed in the high school orchestra alongside Erin. Meredith had played the cello.

An hour later, we headed home. The first thing I did was open windows and let in a fresh breeze, anything to remind me that I was alive and breathing and life was continuing with gusto. Then I retreated to the kitchen. I fed Rags and puttered around for a few hours by cleaning cupboards and counters. I wasn't expected at the shop.

Close to dusk, I poured a couple of glasses of Chianti and pulled a bag of homemade spaghetti sauce from the freezer; I always froze the sauce if I had an amount left over in the initial batch. I made a simple meal of pasta and Solo di Bruna Parmigiano Reggiano, a mouthwatering cheese made by one of four cheese makers who draw their milk solely from brown cows. Even though the dinner was one of our favorites, neither Jordan nor I had much of an appetite.

Rags, as if he sensed he was supposed to have boarded with Rocket for the entire weekend, acted quite concerned to be home a day early. He repeatedly circled our ankles, swatting us with his tail while meowing. I tried to tell him there was nothing wrong, but he knew better.

Before going to bed, I called Rebecca to inform her of the change of plans. I would be available for work tomorrow, Sunday. I would open the store; she could sleep in. I also called my grandfather and let him know he didn't need to come to work at all. I was glad to have reached both of their voice mail recordings. The two of them were curious sorts. They would have begged to know what was up. I did not tell either about the murder. I wanted to explain in person.

The next morning around dawn, after a restless sleep — if Jordan hadn't encouraged me to stay under the covers, I swear I would have paced all night — I fetched Rags and headed to Fromagerie Bessette. He, like I, seemed thankful for the routine.

Walking to the shop took work. There was no spring in my step. My shoulders hung low, burdened by the memory of the events from the day before: finding Lara; the arguments that ensued among the guests; everyone on edge. I did my best to shake off my unease but failed.

Only a few people were up as early as I was. Some were walking their dogs. Others were exercising. Many were carrying out ordinary chores like delivering newspapers or slipping flyers under shop doors. Rags had no trouble keeping up with my sluggish pace.

As I opened the front door to The Cheese Shop, church bells pealed out. I startled, but then for some reason the chimes centered me, perhaps because I knew I could count on them to ring every Sunday morning, a steady reminder that there was more to life than, well, *death*. We all had responsibilities. People relied on us. We showed up and did our jobs.

"Time's a-wasting, Charlotte," I whispered and hurried inside.

I settled Rags in the office and donned an apron. Afterward, I prepared the daily quiche, a combo of ham, bacon, olives, and Cheddar, using Golden Glen Creamery River Cheddar, the Washington creamery's double-cream signature cheese. It smelled so fragrant that I cut myself a slice. I set my breakfast on the tasting counter, grabbed a fork, settled onto a ladder-back stool, and dove in.

Hot but delightful! Just what the doctor ordered. I fetched a glass of milk, and as I devoured the remainder of my meal, I revisited yesterday's interrogation.

Everyone had an alibi of sorts, but none could be corroborated. Shayna: knitting; Kandice: reviewing her schedule; Ryan: in town; Victor: the same as Ryan. All were asleep soon after midnight. By now, Urso had to know what time Lara had died. Would he reveal his findings? Would the time convict Erin, who had been out and about at four A.M.?

While washing and drying my dishes, I mulled over the violin that Lara had played . . . plucked . . . *whatever.* Was it Erin's? Had Lara borrowed or stolen it? Why, why, why was she toying with it so late at night?

I wrung the towel free of water. I hung it on its hook and noticed the sign I'd posted a year ago: *Your mother isn't here, so clean up after yourself!*

Following my own lead, I put away supplies for the quiche. As I did, I thought more about Lara and the violin. How could she have known the instrument was an Amati when Erin didn't even know its value? Had Lara seen it somewhere? Impossible. Erin played it solely for her brother.

I paused. That wasn't entirely correct. Erin had played it in high school. What if a friend of Erin's from back then had recognized its value and had mentioned it to Lara or to an acquaintance of Lara's? Better yet, maybe an image of the high school orchestra made it into a newspaper, and from there, onto the Internet. The group had been outstanding. It had performed at numerous events around the state. I remembered going to Cleveland to watch the orchestra play. I stayed in a hotel room with Meredith. We engaged in a pillow fight the first night that lasted two hours. Erin, as lead violinist, would have been in the forefront of any orchestra photograph.

What about Victor? Was he lying about Lara coveting the violin? Using the same scenario as above, had he learned of the instrument before seeing it? Maybe he stole the violin and hid it in Lara's room with the intention of retrieving it before Lara realized what he'd done.

I headed to the office. Rags stirred, but I instructed him to lie down. At my desk, I opened my computer browser and typed in Amati violin > image.

Hundreds of photographs came up. I perused pages of them. Most were close-ups of the instruments; the artistry was incredible. A few photos included noted musicians playing a similar instrument. I didn't see any high school pictures or Erin's face among the pack.

Discouraged, I returned to the kitchen and started toting the quiches to the cheese counter while considering my first notion. Did Lara invite Erin to her room? Did she order Erin — she wouldn't have asked nicely — to sell the violin? Did Erin go nuts and shove Lara onto the bed?

Erin was small; Lara had been tall and well built. Even though Erin had slugged the bully years ago, I didn't believe she was strong enough to hold a pillow over Lara's mouth for the time it would have taken to cut off her air. If she had, there should have been evidence of a struggle. Lying prone on the bed, Lara had looked downright peaceful.

"Hello-o-o!" someone called from the main shop.

I raced out of the office while smoothing my apron.

A seriously cone-headed man, made more prominent because he had shaved his head, grinned at me. I recognized him as one of the cheese poets. He wasn't a local.

"That cheese!" He motioned to a display of sheep's cheese made by a group called Bleating Heart Cheese. "Is that really its name?"

Fat Bottom Girl was indeed the name of the cheese he was indicating. The cheese monger, a newbie when she'd first created the cheese, had not only been inspired by a Queen song when making the first batch, but in a serendipitous accident, she had forgotten to flip the cheeses after removing them from their forms, thus creating the irregular or *spread* bottoms. No two cheeses were shaped alike.

The poet placed a hand over his heart and intoned: "Fat Bottom Girl. Delight of my soul. You make me whole. If only to taste. But never in haste. I hope you will love me and not go to my waist."

I applauded.

He pretended to doff a hat and take a bow. "A half pound of cheese. Please."

I prepared his order and met him at the register.

"Thank you, fair maid. See, you are paid."

He offered cash, and I made change, after which he skipped out of the shop. Odd but sweet.

The rear door to the shop opened, and Rebecca trotted in. "I'm so glad you're here," she said. "Today's the day!"

I did a double take, having forgotten how short she had cut her hair. She looked adorable and so radiant that I couldn't possibly tell her about the murder, not until she shared her good news.

"Today's the day for what?" I arranged the quiches in the glass-enclosed case, prettiest side forward. "Jordan's cooking class?"

About a month ago, Matthew and I made a pact to take off every other Sunday. I chose the even days; he opted for the odd. *All work and no play* was no fun, especially now that both of us were married. Often on my free Sundays, I would spend the day with Amy and Clair. They would sleep over, and I would drive them to school the next morning. Today was supposed to be my day; however, their mother had begged to take them on an adventure. Knowing the brain trust would conclude by nightfall, I had signed up for a cooking class tonight at Jordan's new restaurant.

"No, silly," Rebecca said. "Today's the day I take control. Forever. I made a vow this morning that after I get my next paycheck, I'm depositing it directly into the bank, and from there, paying off my very last credit card. Whee!" She did a twirl. "No more hyped-up interest. No more worry. I'm paying cash for everything from now on. I'm getting all my finances in order."

"Good for you."

"Devon is helping me keep blinders on." Devon O'Shea. Her boyfriend. The deputy who had assisted Urso at the inn. "He's very savvy when it comes to money," Rebecca went on. "He saves twenty percent of whatever he earns. Isn't that amazing?"

"It sure is."

Rebecca hung up her purse and slipped

an apron over her frilly white blouse and skirt, an outfit I'd seen her wear numerous times. The first year she had worked at the shop, she must have worn a different getup every day. When you added in all the Victoria's Secret items she had purchased as well, it was no wonder she had gone into debt.

"Why did you stop doing the brain trust?" Rebecca asked. "Didn't you like it? I mean, sure, some of the personalities are a little gung ho —"

I held up a hand. "Sit."

She perched on a stool.

"There's no easy way to say this." My voice cracked. "Someone died."

Rebecca gasped. "Not Erin. Please tell me it wasn't her."

"Lara Berry died."

"Heavens to Betsy. She was young, wasn't she? In her forties?"

"Fifties."

"Did she die of a heart attack or something?"

The image of Lara lying lifeless on the bed flickered in my mind, and a shiver slithered down my spine. "She was . . . murdered."

Rebecca leaped off the stool and threw her arms around me. "Oh no! I'm so sorry."

"Me, too."

"Who? Why?"

"We don't know anything yet. Erin is a suspect."

"Uh-uh, no way. Not Erin. She's the nicest lady around. She takes care of her brother, and did you know she teaches Sunday school?"

Yes, I knew. Was she there today? I doubted it.

Rebecca released me. "Erin must be beside herself. How is Andrew handling it? I remember the last time he was in here. He became fascinated with the bell above the door. As big as he is, he could reach it. He kept batting it like a kitten would." She reached high and chanted: "*Clang, clang, clang.* He likes simple cheeses, you know? White only. He reminds me of my uncle. I'm sure he had autism, too, though I'd bet he didn't see a doctor about it. The Amish . . ." She fingered her hairdo and sighed. "Erin has been so good about being on the forefront in that regard. She keeps up with all the new therapies, all the new treatments. I promise you" — Rebecca chopped one hand into the other — "she did not do it."

"I agree."

"Who found Lara?"

"Jordan and I."

"Ugh. Not again." Rebecca grimaced. "What happened? Was she shot? Stabbed?"

"I can't say. U-ey made us promise."

"Ahem. It's *me*."

"Sorry."

"But —"

"No," I stated firmly. "The police are handling it. That's all I'm going to share." I steered her toward a trio of platters I had set out in the kitchen. "Bring those in here, please. Before noon, we have to put together three cheese platters for different functions. Providence Playhouse has started rehearsals for its June production. All Booked Up is offering a specialty cheese poetry reading." I would wager our early-morning, cone-headed customer would attend that. "And the pet store is having an adopt-a-pet day. They want treats to lure in the humans."

Rebecca lifted the platters and carried them to the main shop. "Each of them will have a challenge negotiating the crowds. The Street Scene is a huge success."

"Good for my grandmother." It pleased me to know her efforts had been met with enthusiasm. "Help me with these." I pointed to a large wheel of Jarlsberg and a wheel of Farmhouse Cheddar Borough Market, made by the fabulous Mary Quicke in southwest England.

I lifted the Cheddar; Rebecca took the Jarlsberg. I set my wheel on the counter, removed its rind, and started slicing. I nibbled a morsel. The flavor was divine with overtones of mint, rarely tasted in a Cheddar, and it had a nice crunch. I fetched a Vermont Creamery Bonne Bouche, which was a creamy ash-ripened goat cheese that reminded me of a hockey puck — a squishy white hockey puck — and added it to the platter, for variety.

"You should have seen how busy we were Friday night," Rebecca said. "We didn't close until nearly eleven P.M. The tasting of Bleu Mont Dairy Bandaged Cheddar was a smash hit!"

"Say, did you see either Victor Wolfman or Ryan Harris in town that night? They're two guys from the brain trust. Do you know who I mean?" I was curious whether one or both of them had lied about their whereabouts.

"Ryan is the muscular one with the —" Rebecca waved a hand over the top of her head, indicating his thicker-on-the-top hairdo. "I saw him passing by. You know, he visited Thursday, before the trust actually started, and he sized up what we had in the counter. He told me about some cheeses from Texas. Have you heard of Pure Luck

212

Dairy? They make goat cheeses that have won all sorts of awards. We should order some."

"Will do." I waved a hand. "Go on. You said Ryan walked by Friday night. About what time?"

"Close to closing. He was carrying a to-go cup of coffee and one of those cheese stick thingies." She wiggled her fingers. "You know what I mean, like a churro but dipped in a caramel cheese sauce. Café au Lait makes the best —"

"You didn't see Victor Wolfman?"

"He's the older guy with the fake tan?"

"That's him."

Rebecca shook her head. "Nope, didn't see hide nor hair of him, but that doesn't mean anything. Like I said, we were packed. Is it significant?"

"Is what significant?"

She stopped slicing and slammed down her knife. "I can't!"

I startled. "You can't *what*?"

"I can't *not* know what's going on. You're investigating."

"I am not."

"Yes, you are. Why else would you be asking about Ryan or Victor's whereabouts? You're keeping me out of the loop. Talk! Now!"

CHAPTER 15

"Uh-uh," I muttered. "I refuse to be bullied." I kept mute and remained busy. I lined a second platter with a large paper doily; I rearranged the cheese case; I wiped down the counter.

Unfortunately, Rebecca was more stubborn than I was. She stood stock-still, arms folded. Soon her foot started to tap. Then she narrowed her eyes, and I got the feeling she was trying to channel the force from *Star Wars* so she could manipulate my mind. Sadly, her performance worked. My brain was so overloaded with theories, I had to blab. Dang.

"You are incorrigible," I hissed. "You'll dun me for information until you are blue in the face."

"Maybe."

"Fine. I'll spare you, and *me,* the pain. But you can't tell a soul."

"Promise."

"Especially Urso."

"As if."

I revealed everything. About Lara being smothered; the locked door; the sealed-shut windows; Kandice hearing the violin; finding a valuable Amati in Erin's armoire. I said, "It's worth at least a million dollars."

"Erin didn't have a clue?"

"None. However, that's not always the reason someone wants to own something. Often collectors don't care about the value, only how rare it is."

Rebecca whistled. "My grandmother used to play a violin. Her grandfather made it for her. It was a family heirloom. I remembered the sound. So sweet. She passed it on to my brother, who is a mean fiddler." Rebecca chuckled at the memory. "Can you imagine Erin's parents giving her something so valuable and not telling her its worth?"

Her comment made me stop. Erin's parents had invested in all sorts of antiques: urns, jade, china. Was that, as Rebecca had asked a minute ago, *significant*? Erin knew the origin of the Waterford vase. How could she not know that her violin was an Amati? Why would her parents have kept that information a secret?

"Tell me who you suspect," Rebecca pressed. "You know I might ask or say something that spurs your imagination."

Worry churned inside me. If Urso overheard us . . .

"Uh-uh. We've got work to do."

"Charlotte. C'mon. Spill."

I glanced outside. Neither Urso nor his deputies were in sight. The Street Scene wasn't under way yet. Not one customer was heading our direction. And a desperate need to come up with a suspect other than Erin was plaguing me like crazy. Maybe Rebecca's insight would spur my gray cells.

"Fine," I said. "I think Kandice Witt has it in for Erin."

"The organizer of the event? Why? She chose Erin's farm for the brain trust."

"Exactly. A little voice at the back of my mind is wondering why she did that. Emerald Pastures is not the brightest star in Ohio farms. It is suffering and in need of a real facelift. Not just the inn but the operation as well. Kandice could have selected other establishments. Why this farm? And why didn't she tell Erin that Lara Berry was coming?"

"She didn't?"

"Erin was totally surprised. She only had one room left, a room in what used to be the attic."

"With the sealed-shut windows."

I nodded.

"Kandice must have known that Lara would be isolated."

"She wasn't totally isolated," I said. "There are three rooms on that level. Shayna and Victor occupy rooms on either side of Lara's, although neither had direct access to Lara's room." I used a sharp-edged knife and cut the Bonne Bouche in half and then in quarters and placed the pieces on the second platter.

Rebecca said, "What's Shayna Underhill like?"

"Down to earth. Real. I don't think she killed Lara, although Shayna and Lara were once partners. Underhill Farm and Creamery won a ton of blue ribbons for its Cheddars, but the glory days ended about twenty years ago."

"When Shayna and Lara parted ways?"

"Yes."

"Ouch. That had to hurt Shayna financially." Rebecca mouthed the word: *motive.* She continued tweaking her platter, making it a visual fantasy by splaying the cheese here and there; cheese shouldn't always be plated in straight rows.

In the silence, I reflected on Shayna and the way she had dealt with Lara over the past two days. Always staring at her, assessing her. Had she been trying to determine whether she could overpower Lara?

Stop it, Charlotte. Shayna is a good lady. Mother Earth. On the other hand, her room was next door to Lara's, and she had a messy, possibly volatile past with Lara. If there was a hidden access between the rooms, she could have easily slipped in and out. Would Urso tell me if he had discovered something?

Rebecca said, "What about Ryan? What did you say his last name is?"

"Harris. He's a bit of an enigma." I finished a fan of cheese and covered it with a layer of cheese paper to protect it from hardening in the air. "He didn't know Lara before coming to the brain trust, but he instantly suffered her wrath. I think she saw him as a competitor. They've both written books and he, like Lara, consulted farms."

"He seems like a good old boy."

"With a lot of charm."

"And a deep dark secret?"

I threw her a bemused look. "Not everyone has one. I think he's sweet on Erin."

"Aww. She could use a little loving. I never see her with anyone." Rebecca fetched a jar of homemade strawberry preserves and set it in the middle of the platter she was creating. "The other night, I saw Ryan and Erin playing onstage together at the Street Scene."

"I didn't spot you there."

"I was incognito." Rebecca ruffled her hair in a sassy way. "Actually, I was part of the volunteer cleanup crew. We were all wearing jumpsuits. Very chic. *Not.*" Her mouth quirked up on one side. "Does Erin like Ryan?"

"I think she might, but right now, I doubt she can focus on anything other than proving herself innocent and protecting her farm."

Rebecca placed cheese paper over her array and started in on arranging another platter. "Say, I just remembered. That Victor guy" — she cut down hard on a round of cheese; her knife clacked the counter — "came in here yesterday. It must have been after . . . you know."

"The brain trust disbanded."

"Yeah. He wanted something to snack on. He likes that smelly cheese. Époisses." She snapped her fingers. "What did you tell me *Époisses* means?"

"It's actually a commune in the Burgundy region of France and has no specific translation, but I've seen it cutely translated by one cheese pundit to mean 'completely worth the effort.' "Though I preferred hard, nutty cheeses like Cheddar, I occasionally liked the flavor of a strong cheese. "Not many can take the aroma," I added, "but it's such a rich paste. Perfect when spread on a baguette and served with a glass of white Burgundy wine."

My stomach rumbled. I shouldn't have been thinking about eating after the healthy portion of quiche I had ingested, but certain combinations, like those that made me think about my marvelous honeymoon with Jordan when we traipsed across Europe tasting the various wines and cheeses of each country, stirred my senses.

Rebecca arranged the slices of Jarlsberg at the narrow end of the platter. "FYI," she said, "Victor didn't mention word *one* about the murder."

"Like I said, Urso advised us to keep mum."

"But you're talking to me." She winked.

"If he finds out —"

"I won't blab. I already promised." She crossed her heart. "Anyway, Victor was going on about how knowledgeable he is about cheese. He is so pompous." She withdrew a hunk of Tillamook Vintage White Extra Sharp Cheddar from the counter — for the money, one of the best Cheddars around. She cut it into slices and arrayed them on her second platter. "He also said how our stock didn't measure up to what he could offer online. The nerve, right?"

"I'm sure ours can't. We're small and we offer a lot of local cheeses, but his business is gigantic. He ships worldwide."

"Does he gouge customers?"

Her words drew me up short. Was that the secret Lara had hinted she would reveal about him? Did she have physical proof that Victor was manipulating the market? I said, "I wouldn't have a clue. Why do you ask?"

"He just seems the type. While I was preparing his order, he bragged about how he collected this and that, and he asked why we didn't have any cheese-type antiques in the shop." Using her knife to make a point, she said, "I told him in no uncertain terms that we weren't that kind of store. He could hightail it over to Memory Lane Collectibles, if that was what he was in the mood to buy. That shut him up."

I could just picture her telling off Victor, her narrow chin jutted forward, hands fisted on her hips. At times she reminded me of a spunky alley cat, ready for a fight.

"After a while, he left and went across the street to The Country Kitchen." Rebecca swiped the air with her knife. "Good riddance."

"He's not my favorite person, either," I confided as I added some darling disposable knives to the platter I was creating. Next, I packaged up two boxes of gourmet crackers and napkins to go with each platter. "My first encounter with him was overhearing him talking to a woman on the phone. He called her *babe.*"

"Devon calls me *babe.*"

"Victor said it in a sleazy, full-of-himself way."

"Oh, you mean like: *Hey, babe,*" Rebecca crooned in a low, gravelly timber.

"Exactly." I moaned. "Ick."

"Forget him. Back to the crime scene," Rebecca said. She could be so single-minded it was scary. "Are you sure someone couldn't have come into and gone out of Lara's room through the window?"

I shook my head. "The paint would have shown cracking. The deputy said it didn't. Urso inspected it, too."

"Then Erin has to be guilty."

"Or the housekeeper," I said, "if she's the only other person with a set of keys." But why on earth the housekeeper would want Lara Berry dead was beyond me. Why Erin would want Lara dead didn't make sense, either, other than to regain possession of her precious violin.

No, Charlotte. Erin is not a suspect. N-o-t!

"Hey!" Rebecca clacked her knife on the cutting board, interrupting my musings. "Maybe someone made a copy of Lara's key when she wasn't looking."

"That's not a bad idea." Why hadn't I thought of it? "For a short while, we thought Lara's purse might have gone missing, except it was found in her room, the key inside it."

"That doesn't mean the killer didn't borrow the key earlier, make a copy of it, and return it to Lara's purse." She waved her knife at me. "Which of course would make the murder premeditated."

"The killer couldn't have made a copy. No one left the property."

"Maybe the killer brought a key-making machine to the inn."

"Ha! Funny."

Rebecca jutted a hip. "Got any better ideas?"

I didn't and twirled a hand for her to continue. "What other theories are pinballing around in that overactive brain of yours?"

"That night, the murderer goes to Lara's room and knocks. Lara invites the killer inside."

"Why would she do that?"

"Because she was feeling vulnerable. She needed a friend after the fracas downstairs. The killer offers solace. They have a drink. You said there was wine in the room."

"There was."

"The killer" — Rebecca resumed fixing up her platter — "who has planned ahead, if my theory about the key is right, doses Lara's drink with some kind of drug. Lara, already tipsy, gets sleepy and lies down on the bed."

"She may have been perched on the bed already," I said. "There was only the one chair."

"All right," Rebecca said. "Lara gets drowsy. She leans back. She falls asleep. Once the murderer is certain Lara is out for the count, he . . . or she . . . smothers her and then poses her to make it look like she chose to lie down. The killer exits and, using the previously copied key, locks the door."

I swallowed hard. "That sounds so reasonable, it's scary."

Rebecca grinned. "I saw that in a movie. Was it *Dial M for Murder*?" She pursed her lips. "No, not that one. I've watched so many television shows and movies lately, the storylines are blending together. It doesn't matter. I saw it. All Urso has to do

224

is find out who has a copy of Lara's key."

I dashed to the telephone and dialed the precinct. When Urso answered, I laid out the theory.

"Already thought of it," he said in a clipped, official tone.

"You did?"

"Well, not me. Jordan. And Quigley. It seems we have a number of amateur detectives on the case." I imagined Urso leaning forward, drumming his fingertips on the desk, wanting to say something but practicing restraint.

"U-ey —"

"Stop, Charlotte!" he barked. So much for restraint. "I've got this under control. I've interrogated all who were staying at the inn. I've sorted through their belongings. No key matching Miss Berry's room was found. No key-making machine, either. Nothing. Good-bye."

"Wait, U-ey! The killer could have disposed of the key, maybe even tossed it down the same well where Andrew dropped the ring of keys. Erin's innocent. You've got to believe that!"

"We'll see." He hung up on me.

"Ooh," I groused. I hated when he did that. It wasn't like I was a numbskull. I was a concerned citizen, for Pete's sake. Each of us should be allowed to have our say. "Ooh," I repeated and moved behind the cheese counter.

Rebecca snickered. "By the sound of it, that didn't go well."

"Jordan and Quigley posed the same theory."

"Bah! Quigley." Rebecca's face pinched with loathing. "Why would he know anything about anything?"

"Because he was attending the brain trust."

"Why, for heaven's sake? He doesn't know diddly about cheese. He thinks that little round of deliciousness" — Rebecca pointed at the grayish-covered Bonne Bouche — "is rotten and should be tossed. He doesn't understand the benefits of mold." Bonne Bouche translates to *good mouthful,* and it was. "He —"

I held up a hand. "Whoa. Calm down. Quigley wasn't attending the trust to judge cheese. He was there to report about the people, the discoveries. He wasn't staying at the inn, either. In fact, that morning Urso ordered the busload of other attendees to leave. Quigley, when he got wind of a scandal, sneaked back."

"I would expect nothing less," Rebecca

muttered. "So what did Urso say about the key?"

I filled her in.

"That doesn't mean we're wrong," she said.

"No, but if there isn't a duplicate key, there isn't one. We can't prove anything without evidence."

Rebecca sighed. "What are you going to do to help Erin?"

"I don't know."

But I had to do something. I couldn't let her get bulldozed into jail. If only her brother could remember the details of that night.

CHAPTER 16

At dusk, although I was exhausted and no closer to knowing who killed Lara or exonerating Erin — I had racked my brain all afternoon — I headed to the cooking class at Jordan's new restaurant. The place used to be called Timothy O'Shea's Irish Pub, but after Tim was murdered and Jordan took ownership, he thought a name change was in order. Jordan didn't want the locals to think he was using Tim's tragedy to bring in business. He settled on the name *The White Horse* because when he was a boy, he had owned a white stallion named Spirit that took him on tons of adventures. Over valleys, through dales. Spirit even saved his life, pulling him from beneath a fallen tree.

In addition to changing the restaurant's name, Jordan had revamped the place and made it more upscale. The rustic booths were now a rich brown oak. Tables sported tablecloths. The bar, dismantled in Ireland

and reconstructed here, remained the same. How could it not? It was magnificent. However, instead of Irish music, the pub featured jazz musicians. Jordan loved all kinds of music, but particularly jazz. Many of the musicians were local talent. The menu had changed slightly, too. A number of Tim's appetizers were still featured on the menu — like O'Shea's potato skins, which were rich with cheese and bacon, and O'Shea's mini mac and cheese, tasty morsels served in ceramic tart dishes — but Jordan had substituted the burgers with fine steaks, and he had added a number of his specialty pasta dishes.

My favorite was penne pasta made with a spicy tomato-vodka-cream sauce, which those attending class tonight — Urso, Delilah, Rebecca, Devon, and I — would learn to make. The class was supposed to have included Matthew and Meredith, but due to Meredith's bed-rest order, Matthew and she had withdrawn. Tyanne, the town's premier wedding planner who occasionally helped out at The Cheese Shop, had asked to take Meredith's place. She promised Meredith she would do her proud and eat enough for two. I doubted she would because Tyanne, an attractive blonde who had transplanted to Providence from Louisiana

229

after Hurricane Katrina, had been in love with Tim. She hadn't fully recovered from losing him; she was pale and thin. I hoped tonight would bring her warm memories.

The first course was a simple Caprese salad of hothouse tomatoes and buffalo mozzarella drizzled with a basil pesto–olive oil dressing. Jordon put the women in charge of making the dressing. I ground the pine nuts. Tyanne chopped garlic. He gave the men the task of slicing the tomatoes and the cheese. When we completed our tasks, we sat at a preset table in the kitchen.

"Yummy," I said to Jordan after my first bite. He had paired the dish with a white wine from Italy: *divine.*

"It's my mother's recipe."

"Your mother wasn't Italian."

"Does that matter? She had a deft hand with spices, and her homemade buffalo mozzarella was not to be believed."

"Where did you grow up again?" I teased.

"On a farm in Jersey." He had no accent. He had worked hard to get rid of it when he entered the WITSEC program. So had his sister. "With Jersey cows, of all things." Jersey cows are a smaller breed of dairy cows, originally bred in the Channel Islands, England.

"Malarkey."

"God's truth." He held up three fingers, like a good Boy Scout, then said, "Switching subjects. Chief —"

I cast a warning look at Jordan. Before we scrubbed up, U-ey — that was what we were supposed to call him tonight, not Chief — had made it quite clear that there would be no talk about the investigation. We all agreed, though questions were churning inside my mind. I would bet there were even more scurrying around inside Rebecca's head. I wondered if she had been able to pry anything out of her darling deputy without admitting I had told her a thing. She could be wily.

"Don't worry." Jordan squeezed my wrist then blew me a sly kiss. "I was just baiting you."

"Fink."

He chuckled. "U-ey, tell us about the wedding plans."

"Wedding plans?" I shrieked and swatted Delilah. "You're getting married? When? How could you not tell me?" I batted her a second time.

"Ow. Cut it out." Delilah flicked me back. "We just decided. An hour ago." She whisked her dark curls over her shoulders and eagle-eyed Urso. "Obviously my adorable man told Jordan before I could tell you."

Urso winked at me. "Guys like to share things when they're slicing and dicing."

"I'll have to remember that," Delilah joshed.

"Okay," I said. "From the beginning. Have you two set a date?"

"We're thinking the fall." Delilah speared a piece of her salad.

Urso said, "I'm up for July."

"It's too hot in July." Delilah fanned herself coyly. "A bride doesn't like to sweat."

"It seems I don't have a vote." Urso elbowed her; she giggled.

Joy soared through me to see them so happy.

"Tyanne's going to put the whole thing together," Delilah said then popped a morsel of salad into her mouth.

"So, you know before me, too?" I said to Tyanne and eyeballed Delilah.

Tyanne tucked a hair behind her ear. "I'm envisioning pale orange —"

"Ew." Delilah plunked her fork on her plate. "Uh-uh. No way. I'm not a pale *anything.*"

"No kidding," Urso said.

Everyone laughed.

"Big, bright, bold." Delilah threw her

arms wide. "Maybe red."

Urso knuckled her in the ribcage. "You scarlet woman."

"I adore red. Haven't you paid attention? The color scheme at The Country Kitchen — that's mine."

The conversation during the rest of the salad appetizer revolved around which flowers and what music they should have for the ceremony. Neither Urso nor Delilah got annoyed that everyone had an opinion. It was like naming babies. Family members could chime in with ideas like Fred, Ned, or Zed, but in the end, it was the couple's decision. Personally, I liked the name Han Solo.

Kids . . .

"Charlotte?" Jordan was hovering behind my chair ready to move it backward. "Hello? Would you like to stand? We're moving on to the next course." He kissed my neck. "What were you thinking about?"

"Nothing," I lied. "A blank."

He gave me a knowing look. I dodged him and entered the kitchen. The good thing about cooking is it takes all my concentration. It works like a mental breather. I don't dwell on life's big questions or the horror of death.

"All right, everyone, aprons back on," Jordan ordered.

Although he had given the main restaurant a facelift, he hadn't altered anything in the kitchen. It was a well-designed space with a number of Vulcan ranges and ovens and plenty of prep counters. A kitchen staff member was cleaning up after us.

With Jordan's guidance, we cooked another hot appetizer as a tribute to Tim, a mini–potato skin stuffed with melted blue cheese. Tasty! Plating appetizers was always a challenge to me. I could create cheese platters without any problem, but making little morsels look scrumptious with just a sprig of parsley or a squiggle of olive oil was an art. Jordan did his best to show me how to wield a squeeze bottle, but my artistic talent fell short. Squirts came out as blobs or driblets. Swell.

We devoured the stuffed potatoes and moved on to the entrée.

In teams, we were assigned first to a prep counter and then to a grilling station. I was chopping parsley for my tomato-vodka-cream sauce when I heard Rebecca, who was working alongside her beloved at one of the Vulcan ranges, hoot with laughter.

"What's so funny?" I asked.

"Devon was coming up with lines from movies" — she couldn't contain herself; snickers burbled out of her — "but he was tweaking them to sound cheesy."

"Cheesy?"

"As in using cheese in the references. *Duh.*" She giggled some more. "And he was making me guess the titles. Get this: 'I love the smell of Parmesan in the morning.' "

"Apocalypse Now," Jordan said.

"Correct!" Rebecca winked at Devon. "How about, 'Puree it again, Sam'?"

"Casablanca," Tyanne chimed.

"Right!" Rebecca clapped her hands.

"Except there's no cheese in that line," I said.

"Don't be a stickler," Rebecca chided. "How about this one? 'May the fondue be with you.' "

"Star Wars," Delilah shouted.

"Yes!" Rebecca nearly cheered. "Aren't these fun? How about this? 'I've never kissed a Jarlsberg thief before.' "

"That's a stretch," I said.

"You know it?"

"Yes. You swapped *Jarlsberg* for *jewel.* It's from *To Catch a Thief.* And the line is 'I've never caught a jewel thief before.' " The Hitchcock classic is one of my all-time favorite movies. "Grace Kelly says it to Cary Grant."

Rebecca smiled. "That man is so yummy."

"Sugar, you're not kidding." Tyanne

235

sighed with a swoon. "Has anyone ever seen a dreamier cat burglar than Cary Grant? And those fireworks that light up the sky when they lock lips? Magical."

"Your turn, Charlotte," Rebecca challenged. "Do you have a quote?"

I thought for a moment and nodded. "How about this?" In a low, masculine voice I said, " 'I don't have to show you no stinkin' Brie.' "

Rebecca looked perplexed. "I don't know that one."

"Really?" I was shocked. I repeated the line, using a Hispanic accent. Still no response. "Are you kidding? You call yourself a film buff, and you don't know it?"

Urso said, "I believe the line is, 'We don't need no stinkin' badges.' "

"Yeah," Jordan chimed. "That's the line."

"Nope," I said, "but it is one of the most misquoted lines of film history." I couldn't believe I was the only one in the room who knew the correct line. Let's hear it for the film class I took during college. "C'mon, Rebecca," I goaded, wiggling my fingers, begging for the answer. "I know you've seen the film. Shh. Don't anybody tell her the title. Two Americans in Mexico, mining for gold."

"Oh, I remember now." A grin spread

across her face. "*The Treasure of the Sierra Madre* with Humphrey Bogart."

"And who said the line?" I challenged.

"It wasn't Bogart?"

"Nope. It was said *to* Bogart."

"Wait, wait, I know this!" Rebecca snapped her fingers. "His name is Alfonso . . . Alfonso . . ."

A fire alarm rang out. *Blang!*

"Uh-oh," I shouted and pointed.

Rebecca spun around. Huge orange oily flames were rising from her pan. "Oh, no!" Neither she nor any of us had been paying attention. *Oops!*

"I'm on it!" Jordan fetched a fire extinguisher and raced back with it aimed. "Watch out!" He doused the fire with a muddle of white goo.

After that, the easy, breezy feeling of the evening vanished.

CHAPTER 17

Later that night, when I was getting ready for bed — Jordan was nestled in and reading a thriller; I was standing in the bathroom scrubbing my face — out of nowhere, the fire incident at the restaurant struck me as funny. I pictured the look of horror and embarrassment on Rebecca's face. Like me, she hated making mistakes, especially in a crowd of friends. I wondered if she was still pacing her bedroom, scolding herself for being careless. If it weren't so late, I would call her to put her at ease. A week from now, no one would remember.

"What're you chuckling about?" Jordan asked.

I poked my head out of the bathroom and told him. "Fortunately, she didn't burn down the building," I added.

"Luckily no one got hurt."

His comment threw me for a loop. A pang of remorse scudded through me. *Luckily no one got hurt.* Or *dead.* Like Lara. No matter what people thought of her, she hadn't deserved to die, and she deserved justice as much as Erin warranted a good defense.

I assessed myself via the mirror above the sink. Thanks to the tension of the past few days, my eyes were not the eyes of a thirty-something. I looked more like a seventy-something going on eighty. I applied a generous amount of skin cream, doused my eyes with a dry-eye solution, and switched off the light.

Slipping under the covers, sorrow swept over me again. I shuddered and snuggled into my husband. "Who do you think —" I couldn't finish the sentence.

He clapped his book closed. "Who do I think *what*?"

"You know."

"Killed Lara?"

I nodded. How easily he picked up on my anxiety. My ex-fiancé, long gone from my life, had been so dense in that regard. I gazed up at Jordan and said, "Thank you."

"For *getting* you?"

"Yes."

"If you had your life to live over again . . ."

"I wouldn't change a thing. I live a dream life with a man I adore." Other than wishing I could have spent more time with my parents, I truly did have a perfect life. I loved my job, my family, my cat, and the town of Providence.

But then I thought of Lara again, and another wave of regret flooded over me. What kind of life had she led? Who had she loved in her life? Had Urso contacted her sister? Did she really *have* a sister, or was Erin mistaken?

I swiveled on my side and propped myself on my elbow. "Who could have wanted Lara dead, Jordan?"

He sighed. "Can't this wait until morning?"

"I won't be able to sleep and neither will you if I'm tossing and turning."

He set his book aside, kissed my forehead, and said, "Proceed."

"Do you know anything about the guests at the brain trust?"

His mouth quirked up on one side. "Does that mean you've ruled out the staff at the inn?"

"I know the waitresses Erin brought in from The Country Kitchen. They've worked for Delilah and her father for years. Besides, you heard. They left after clearing the meal; none of them stayed overnight. What grudge would they have had against Lara Berry, anyway?"

"True." He nodded. "What about others in the brain trust who weren't staying there?"

"The attendees who were rooming at Lavender and Lace would have had to cross town and risk being seen driving late at night."

"There are a lot of tourists in town, too," he said. "Someone outside the brain trust might have sneaked into the inn."

"Let's just start with the ones who were there: Kandice, Ryan, Victor, and Shayna."

"Don't forget Erin."

I grumbled my dissension then remembered the theory about the murderer copying Lara's room key and wagged a finger at Jordan. "By the way, you called Urso about the possibility of a duplicate key to Lara's room, so don't go acting like you haven't been thinking about the murder."

"Our conversation was supposed to be confidential."

"I called Urso about the same thing. He looped me in."

Jordan shrugged. "It was the most logical way to enter or exit her room and have the door remain locked afterward."

"In the wee hours of the night."

"Right."

I kissed his neck. "Which is why whoever

241

killed her had to have been staying at the inn."

"Except Urso didn't find a second key," Jordan stated.

"That doesn't mean it doesn't exist." I wriggled to a sitting position and swung my legs over the side of the bed. "Hungry? I'm starved. I need sugar."

"Charlotte, not now."

"We missed making that tantalizing chocolate cheese bombe at your restaurant because of the fire." I hesitated then snickered while saying, "*Bomb . . . fire.* Rebecca will never live this one down." I padded across the floor and shrugged into my plush terry bathrobe. "I still have a few slices of caramel cheesecake that I made last weekend. It's calling to us."

Jordan groaned. He was a sucker for cheesecake. "While we eat, I assume you want to bat around theories."

I threw him a sassy look over my shoulder. "Yep."

Rags stirred then nestled back into a ball. He wasn't up for a refrigerator raid.

I trotted down the stairs, breezed into the kitchen, and switched on the lights. While Jordan set the Shaker table with two gold place mats, napkins, and forks, I put on a pot of hot water for tea and pulled the cheesecake from the refrigerator. I cut two hefty portions of the cake and set them on simple white plates. I handed them to Jordan.

"A sliver would have done the trick," he said.

"Eat what you like."

"You know I can't resist."

I did. Cheesecake was one of my weaknesses, too. I whacked his taut abdomen with the back of my hand. "You'll exercise double tomorrow." He never missed a day. "Now, sit."

Jordan set the plates on the table and returned to the counter to switch on the iPod in its docking station. A Pandora easy-listening channel came on featuring orchestral music. Jordan played music all the time. Though I used to be a silence-is-golden girl, I had come to love the constant sound. The song switched to an upbeat tango, which the musician was performing on a rich string instrument. A cello, I was pretty sure.

"Nice," I said.

"It's Yo-Yo Ma."

"Are you sure?"

"Positive."

"Huh. I would've thought he only played serious kinds of music."

"Don't judge a musician by his, um,

243

album cover." Jordan quirked a smile and slid onto the bench at the table.

The teakettle whistled. I fixed quick mugs of Earl Grey tea — *quick* because I could never wait the full five minutes for tea to steep; I liked my brews hot-hot — and brought them to the table. I settled onto the bench beside Jordan.

He took a bite of his cheesecake and murmured his appreciation. "Tell me about Shayna. You seem to know her well."

I took a sip of tea and reiterated what I had told him cursorily at the cocktail party that first night about Shayna's brief corporate life, her marriage and move to a farm, the early death of her husband, and the beginning of the creamery. "She has two girls, now in their twenties, and neither is interested in their mother or her career." I relayed how Shayna confided to me during the morning portion of the brain trust that her youngest daughter, a junior lawyer, was madly in love with her boss, one of the partners. Shayna disapproved, of course. I added, "Her daughters give her a lot of grief about her life choices, even about her appearance."

"Are you kidding?"

"Shayna is a Bohemian. She loves the loose-clothing look. Casual hair. No

244

makeup." I took a bite of my cheesecake and savored the rich caramel that was not only drizzled on top but incorporated into the crust. I'd gotten the recipe from my grandmother, who was a whiz at sweets. "Shayna wasn't always that way. When she worked at her corporate job, she was buttoned down and sleek, but now, she embraces all things natural, including the way she makes cheese. Everything is organic. Nothing processed."

"Is her cheese good? Lara called it bland and boring."

"She was wrong. The cheese was . . . *is* . . . good."

"Why did Lara leave the partnership?" Jordan asked.

"Conflict of personalities is all I can figure out. Shayna said that Lara was rules-oriented." Was there some other reason Lara had walked out? An image of her lying dead on the bed popped into my head. I swallowed hard and set down my fork.

"Do you think Shayna resented Lara?" Jordan removed his tea bag from the mug, placed it on his cake plate, and took a sip of tea. Steam rose in front of his face.

"How could she not? When Lara left, she took half the proceeds, and the creamery struggled without her promotional efforts, yet, I can't believe Shayna killed Lara."

"Just like you can't believe Erin did."

Using my fork, I nudged a piece of cake around on my plate.

"Shayna is staying in the room next to Lara's," Jordan said. "That gave her the easiest access."

"True."

Jordan took another sip of tea. "Let's look at this from a different angle. Lara was the go-to person when it came to American cheeses. If you wanted to know whether a cheese was quality cheese, you asked Lara. Who will take her place? Who will become that voice? Shayna?"

"No. Never. I would imagine a woman in Vancouver, Washington. She's well versed and travels nonstop."

"What about Kandice?"

"She has the know-how, but there are one or two others who would reach acclaim first, which rules out motive for Kandice, I suppose." I bit back a yawn.

Jordan ran a finger down my arm. "Let's talk about the others in the morning."

"No. Tonight, please. I won't be able to sleep." I sat taller as I worked through a theory. Victor kowtowed to Lara that first night. The next day, Shayna flirted with Victor at one of the meals. I believed she had done it teasingly, but what if she had been seducing him in earnest? Did she hate Lara for having her pick of men? Would she have killed Lara to eliminate the competition? I said, "Is it possible Lara and Shayna ended the partnership because they were vying for the same man?"

"You are a romantic, my love."

Jordan was right. The idea was too *romantic,* too *high school.* I leaned back in my seat and focused on a previous notion regarding Victor. What if he went to Lara's room that night to win her back, and she refused him, so he lashed out in anger?

The closed-room aspect of the murder gave me pause. Whoever had killed Lara had locked the door after exiting. Would Victor, who most likely expected easy access to Lara, have thought to copy her key?

"Victor," I muttered.

Jordan choked back a laugh. "Yes, he's a jerk."

"He said he and Lara dated briefly. He said he cut bait and ran."

"Ha! A likely story. I know why it ended," Jordan said. "Lara booted him out. She was way too classy for him."

Was. I choked back a sob.

Jordan stroked my back. I appreciated the comfort it brought. A new song started playing. A solo instrument. Jordan tapped out the rhythm on the tabletop.

"Nice violin," I said.

"That's not a violin, sweetheart. It's a guitar. 'Partita for Violin Solo No. 3 in E minor,' by Andrés Segovia."

"How would you know that?"

"During college, I used to sit in the library, sling on headphones, and study for exams listening to Segovia. I would've given my soul to play guitar like him."

"You play guitar?"

"I tried. My grandfather gave me a standard Gibson acoustic guitar. He traded his pickup for it. The thing had wonderful bass tones." Jordan's eyes misted over; he looked as gaga as a kid who had received the keys to his first car.

"Where's the guitar now?" It was not in our house.

"Jacky has it. I could barely pluck out a tune. She has deft hands." Before taking on the farm, his sister had made gorgeous pottery and run a pottery shop in town.

"Hey," I said. "What if Lara was playing a guitar? Maybe it sounded like a violin."

"Urso would have mentioned seeing one, don't you think?" Jordan yawned. "I need to go to bed."

"Wait." Another idea struck me. "Victor

was the first to point the finger at Erin because she played the violin. Kandice backed him up. What if Victor was trying to cover his own tracks? What if he lied about his alibi? He said he roamed town, came back before midnight, and took a sleeping pill. Can that be verified? How long does Ambien stay in the system?"

"I would imagine a few days. A urine test or even hair test would show its use. But if Victor takes the drug regularly, that won't prove that he took it that night. Most commonly, the police search for a drug in a person's system if they suspect the drug facilitated an assault."

"How do you know that?"

"Because I work nights, so during the days I watch TV reruns. I'm hooked on mystery and crime shows."

"Just like Rebecca. Swell." Drinking in the strains of the guitar, I said, "The violin . . . if it was a violin . . . What if Lara didn't play it? What if someone else did, like Victor?"

"Why?"

"To implicate Erin. He recognized the value of the violin. Maybe he'd heard about its existence. He plucked it and replaced it, thus linking Erin to the crime."

"Or the killer accidentally plucked it while

removing it from the room."

"Why remove it?"

Jordan clicked his tongue.

"Don't say it," I warned. "Erin did not kill Lara."

Jordan rose and took our plates and mugs to the sink. I followed.

"Kandice was the first person to mention the violin," Jordan suggested. "Maybe she knew about the instrument and made up the part about hearing it to incriminate Erin." He rinsed a plate and handed it to me to dry. "You know, another question we should ask is how anyone knew where Erin hid the violin."

"Kandice!" I blurted.

"I just said Kandice."

I set the plate I was drying aside and paced the kitchen. "Hear me out." A scenario like a movie trailer running at double speed cycled through my mind. "Let's say" — I held up one finger at a time to make my points — "Lara discovered the violin's existence. I'm not sure how. Maybe she saw an Internet image or a newspaper article about the Providence High School orchestra. But she knew about it, and she contacted Kandice to find out more."

"Were they friends?"

"Don't you remember how Lara fawned

over Kandice after the incident at the Street Scene? The interaction suggests there was more to their relationship. On the other hand, they might just have a business relationship. Let's say Lara heard about the Cheese Festival and thought: *Perfect timing.* She hired Kandice to create a brain trust event, and she suggested Kandice negotiate the deal with Erin."

"You know, I've been wondering why Kandice chose Erin's farm. Pace Hill Farm and many others would have been better choices," Jordan said, echoing what I had said to Rebecca. "The cheese-making facilities aren't top-notch."

"Maybe she chose it because Emerald Farms is one of the few that has an inn."

"Good point."

I resumed drying dishes. "What if Lara knew about the violin, and she sent Kandice on a mission to locate it? While Kandice stayed overnight at the inn —"

"Did she do that?"

"Erin mentioned that she did. Kandice could have heard Erin playing the violin for her brother. She could have followed Erin to her room. Like a sleuth, she listened while Erin opened the armoire, pulled out the case, et cetera."

Jordan washed the mugs and handed them

251

to me. "Back up a step. Why did Lara play the darned thing if she was stealing it?"

"You said it before. Maybe she plucked it accidentally."

Jordan dried his hands on a fresh towel and drew me close. "We're overthinking this." He caressed my jaw with his knuckles. "Let's sleep on it, and maybe we'll come up with something by morning."

"Uh-uh." I poked him in the ribs and twisted free. "I want to keep hashing around theories."

He chuckled. "You are so predictable. Hey, you know who we haven't mentioned? Ryan Harris."

"Rebecca and I discussed him."

"You talked to her about the murder? Charlotte!" Jordan couldn't hide his disapproval. "U-ey told us —"

"Don't bark at me. We told Matthew and Meredith."

"They —"

I put a finger to his lips. "Remember how your mother warned your father never to go to bed angry?" I pecked his cheek. "Be nice. Soft voice."

"Leave it to you to remember everything I've ever told you," he groused.

"You don't have a long history," I quipped. Being in the witness protection program has a tendency to make a person reluctant to reveal the whole truth and nothing but the truth. I knew bits and pieces of his past. In time, I would learn more.

Jordan muttered something under his breath. I couldn't catch the words; I was pretty sure his muttering was for effect. At least I hoped it was.

I grasped his hand. "C'mon. You know Rebecca. She won't tell a soul."

Jordan's anger melted away. "Go on."

"Like I said, she and I talked about Ryan. He's a good man, a family guy. He helps people get their farms back on their feet. I think he's sweet on Erin. I doubt he would have taken the violin from Lara's room and placed it in Erin's armoire, knowing it might incriminate her."

"You're probably right."

I rubbed Jordan's arm and whispered, "Kandice. She's the ticket."

CHAPTER 18

Monday morning arrived in a flurry. I awoke groggy, but my head was swimming with ideas: about Kandice; about Erin. I wondered if I approached Erin privately, whether she could tell me more about Kandice's first visit. If a memory clicked for her and she could single out Kandice having concocted the whole brain trust idea with malicious intent, we could approach Urso.

But first, I went to the shop and met with my distributor — we had a full week's supply of cheese to unload and store either in the cellar, the kitchen walk-in refrigerator, or the cheese case. Next, I made sure Rebecca had everything well in hand so I could take off for a few hours. And then I decided to check in on Meredith. I'd missed seeing her at the cooking class last night. Because I didn't want to admit that I was worried about her health, I came up with the idea to tell her about Rebecca's fiasco. Laughter always made me feel better; I hoped it would buoy my pal.

Minutes later I arrived at Matthew and Meredith's house. Matthew met me at the door. The skin around his eyes was dry and tight. He was carrying a breakfast tray set with dry toast, a cup of tea, a jar of honey fitted with a spoon, and a crystal vase filled with pansies. Sweet.

"Hey," he said. "She'll be thrilled to see you."

"How's she doing?"

"Feisty."

"Feisty is good." I patted his cheek. "Go to work. I'll stay with her for a while. Where are the girls?"

"At school. Their mother took them." Soon after Clair and Amy were born, their mother, Sylvie, abandoned them and Matthew and fled to England to be with Dear Old Dad and Mum. To everyone's surprise, she returned a few years later and reinserted herself into the girls' lives. Thanks to a financial windfall, Sylvie now owned a boutique and spa in town. Matthew added, "She said she had such a good time with the girls yesterday, she couldn't stay away."

"That's a good thing, isn't it?"

"Maybe, maybe not." Matthew repositioned items on the tray for a better balance. "With Sylvie, you always have to question her underlying motive. I think she's worried that I'm going to leave my entire inheritance — all ten cents of it — to our new little bugger and cut out her girlie-girls."

Girlie-girls was what Sylvie called her daughters. The twins — and Matthew, in particular — hated the term, but what could anyone do? Sylvie didn't take orders. From anyone.

"You won't overlook the girls," I said. "They mean everything to you."

"Yes, but do you think Sylvie will believe me?"

I grinned. "She'll want you to sign a vow in blood."

"Exactly." He handed me the tray and hitched his head toward the stairway. "Fair warning. Meredith has, per your suggestion, taken up knitting, and it's not going well."

"No worries. I can handle a grouchy patient."

"Feisty."

I nudged him. "Go. Put Pépère to work. He showed up this morning and wants something to do." Our grandfather had the hardest time being idle. Creating birdhouses or tending to a rose garden just didn't fill enough of his hours. Occasionally he helped out at the Providence Playhouse, but seeing as he wasn't required for the production at the Street Scene and backstage construction for the theater's June musical hadn't yet begun, he was in need of stimulation. Working at the shop for a few hours would help. He often confided how much he missed being there on a daily basis.

"Swell," Matthew said. "Hey, does he knit? Maybe he could teach Meredith —"

"Hah! Not happening."

He bussed me on the cheek and hurried off.

I tiptoed upstairs, balanced the tray on one hand, and knocked on the master bedroom door. "Breakfast," I announced as I twisted the knob and bumped the door open with my hip.

Rocket, all ninety pounds of him, charged me. I backed up before his big French Briard head could smash into the tray.

"Sit!" I ordered. Rocket did so immediately. Over the past three months, due to weekly visits, I had been able to retrain him. "Stay."

He obeyed, reluctantly, his tail wagging nonstop.

"Charlotte, what a pleasant surprise!" Meredith was sitting in bed, propped up by a few pillows. A basket of knitting supplies sat near the foot of the bed. On the table against the wall lay a smattering of recipes and a pile of photo albums. Post-it stickums jutted from the album pages.

I winced at the sight of her. Her fair, freckled skin was as pale as I had ever seen it. "You look good," I lied as I placed the breakfast tray over her legs.

"Bah!" Meredith plucked at her limp hair. "Can you spell bored to tears?"

"Is this a pop quiz, Teach?"

"Very funny."

Rocket whined. I gestured to a spot beside my feet. He jogged over. I nuzzled his head, and he slumped onto the floor.

Meredith took a piece of toast and nibbled on it.

"Want me to get some jam for that?" I asked.

"Uh-uh. This is hard enough to swallow. I wish someone would put a feeding tube in me and be done with it." She sipped some tea.

Matthew had recently painted the room a cheery yellow. He had added a floral border to match the comforter on the bed, and yet the room felt dreary. I crossed to the window and opened the drapes. Sunshine, according to my grandmother, always elevated a person's mood.

"I see you're getting some projects started." I gestured at the knitting. "What are you making?"

"A baby blanket, like you suggested. Freckles told me it would be easy, but do you know how hard it is to make a popcorn stitch? Knitting and purling and then knitting and purling again, all into the same stitch. Delilah stopped by and tutored me, but honestly, I can't get the knack. I've had to pull out dozens of stitches because I forgot to purl or knit. Argh."

"Breathe." I drew in a deep breath and let it out.

"What are you now, a yoga coach?" she sniped.

I held up two hands. "Don't shoot the messenger. If you do, who's going to bring you the local gossip?"

"Omigosh. I'm being so selfish. You" — she set her tea down on the tray and reached for my hand — "found another body. And Erin. How is she holding up? Sit!" She patted the bed. "Talk to me!"

I perched beside her and filled her in about finding Lara and how Urso suspected Erin of the murder because of the violin.

"Of course Erin isn't guilty," Meredith said. "She's the kindest person I know, next to you. She couldn't smother anyone. Remember back in grade school how she was always saving birds or lost kittens? She even saved worms! And who could forget that time in seventh grade when she put together a fund-raiser talent show for the Children's Disability Home? We didn't know about Andrew at the time. In our minds, he was merely a hyperactive two-year-old, clacking dresser drawer handles with fierce abandon. When I think about it, Erin must have been worried sick that he would be forced to move into that home."

I recalled the evening of the fund-raiser. I had been dabbling in magic at the time and decided to show my style onstage. None of my tricks went off well. The coin that I was supposed to pull from behind my assistant's ear got stuck in her hair. The rabbit in the hat jumped off the stage, and everyone had to search for it. Meredith twirled a baton with ease. Delilah did an interpretive dance with scarves.

I said, "Didn't Erin play her violin in the talent show?"

"Come to think of it, yes."

Funny how memories can surface when another person provides the cues.

"You played in the orchestra with her," I said. "Do you remember when her parents gave her the violin?"

Meredith smiled. "How could I not? It was her fourteenth birthday. She came into the orchestra room and begged Mrs. Decker to let her play a piece by Saint-Saëns. 'The Violin Concerto No. 3 in B minor.' Of course, Mrs. Decker obliged. Erin gently withdrew the violin from the case and off she went. It was amazing. Professional quality. All of our mouths dropped wide open."

"You said she *gently withdrew* the violin. Do you think she knew it was valuable?"

"Don't read anything into that. It was new. Special."

"Did she ever mention to you that it was an Amati?"

"No. It is? Wow. She told me her family purchased it in Italy. They went there a lot to buy antiques."

"How could they afford to?"

"Some people go skiing. Her folks traveled." Meredith added a dollop of honey to her tea and stirred. When she clanked the spoon on the rim of her cup, Rocket peeped up at us.

"Go back to sleep," I ordered. He obeyed.

I mentioned the antique furniture that was set around the inn as well as the items housed in the cabinets in the dining room. "Erin took great pride in talking about each

261

piece," I added. "Lara intimated that it was all phony or subpar."

"No way."

"She taunted Erin."

"How awful."

"Erin told Urso she would never sell any of it, no matter how downtrodden the farm might get. They were her family treasures."

Meredith nodded. "Yes, she's that way. Devoted to family. To a fault."

I reflected on Erin's frustration with Lara, cut short because Andrew got upset and she had to handle him. Did Erin approach Lara later in her room to chastise her? Did she discover Lara had stolen the violin and lose control? No, something wasn't adding up. Lara's murder was subtle. She was smothered. The killer tried to make it look like Lara had died from natural causes. Spur-of-the-moment fury would have been messy. Objects would have been thrown or broken. And others in the inn would have heard a fight, right?

Again I wondered whether Lara had been drugged. Victor had snatched Lara's wineglass at the dinner table. Did he slip a crushed Ambien pill into it? It would have been a deft move. I, as an amateur magician, couldn't have pulled it off. An image of Shayna in the dining room that night flitted into my mind. When I entered the room, she was examining the bottle of red wine. It was uncorked. Was it possible she put a sleep aid into the bottle? Lara yanked the bottle out of Shayna's hands. Shayna refused red wine that night. Did anyone else drink some? Possibly not. Lara had suggested everyone opt for white wine with chicken. Should I suggest to Urso that the coroner look for some kind of drug in Lara's system?

"Talk to Erin," Meredith said. "Get her to trust you. I'm sure she wants the truth to come to light."

"That's where I'm headed next. I wish you could come with me."

"I wish I could, too, but" — she reached over the breakfast tray and plucked the knitting needles from her basket — "a woman's work is never done." She started unraveling stitches. "Never!"

A half hour later, I arrived at Emerald Pastures Inn. Erin was overjoyed to see me. She hugged me like I was a long-lost relative. She guided me to the terrace at the back of the inn. We took our places at a table set with bright yellow mats and napkins. A balcony hung overhead. Trellises of flowers rose upward. A bed of irises bordered the staircase leading from the terrace to the cow pastures, which were dotted with beautiful oak trees. Snowball, the scamp, was tussling with a ball of yarn on a patch of grass.

"Heaven," I whispered. At times I was sorry Jordan had given up his farm. I loved sitting on his porch and taking in the view, but where we lived now was much more convenient for both of us — in town, near work, with an upkeep that didn't require a staff of fifty.

The ponytailed twin from The Country Kitchen entered. Erin was keeping the sisters on through Wednesday, per their contract. The waitress served honey-sweetened iced tea decorated with a stick of pineapple. She reappeared minutes later with two mammoth-sized bacon-lettuce-tomato chopped salads and a basket of pop-overs.

"Eat," Erin said.

Before we could dig into our salads, I noticed two men strolling toward us. One was Deputy O'Shea. The other fellow was sandy-haired with a weathered face; he looked as if he had spent all his years in the sun. He wore jeans, a work shirt, and brown leather boots. Neither glanced our direction. Both were studying large sheets of paper.

"Don't mind them," Erin said. "They're reviewing the inn's architectural plans, searching for other ways into Lara's room. I don't think they believe me about there being no hidden entrances. My family hasn't always owned the property, so I might be wrong, but when Andrew was younger, he was always seeking out weird hiding places. He was good at it. None of those he discovered were secret passageways. I know because I was always the one who had to track him down." She sighed as if the weight of the world rested on her shoulders. "At least Chief Urso found the ring of keys where I told them they would be. At the bottom of the well. Right where Andrew dumped them."

"Did he find any other keys, like a single copy to Lara's room?"

Erin shook her head.

The men disappeared around the corner. Snowball trotted after them.

Erin said, "Eat."

I took a bite. Delicious. The blue cheese dressing with a zing of Tabasco sauce was divine, too.

"How do you stay so teeny eating like this?" I plucked a popover from the basket.

It was drizzled with Cheddar cheese, also made fresh on the farm. To die for.

"I don't dine like this all the time. Usually I eat protein and vegetables and no carbs. Andrew can't do them. They ramp him up."

"How is he? Does he remember any more of that night?"

"Not really."

"Is he still chanting *up, up, up* and *down, down, down*?"

"Yes."

"Do you know what it means?"

"It doesn't have to mean anything. And he's taken to repeating eleven thirty, eleven forty, two, two, two."

"Do you think he's referring to the time of day?"

She sighed. "I don't have a clue."

I took a couple of bites of the salad, savoring the turkey and bacon paired with avocado, and then I ate another bite of the popover while I considered the possibilities for Andrew's odd behavior. "Maybe he heard something going up or down at those times."

"We don't have an elevator."

"Maybe he detected a person on the stairs."

"Hey." Erin set down her fork with a *clack*. "Maybe he heard the violin. You know, the bow goes up and down." She mimed the movement.

"Except Kandice said whoever was playing the violin didn't use a bow. It was plucked."

Erin moaned. "I'm sure Andrew is trying to impart a secret, but I can't make any sense of it. I've tried using his music to get him to express himself. I've switched on the metronome. I've handed him paper and pencil. Nothing works." Tears pressed at the corners of her eyes. She dabbed them with her napkin. "Sorry."

"Speaking of Kandice," I said, trying to steer the conversation in the direction I wanted.

"Please." Erin dumped her napkin in her lap. "Let's not talk about that night. How's Meredith?"

I assured her she was thriving; the baby was well.

"Ultrasounds are important at our age," Erin said. "My mother was older when she had Andrew. They didn't do much testing back then. I wonder if she'd had some indication that Andrew would be a challenge —" She paused. "I think that's why she and my dad traveled so much. Mom needed breathing room." Erin took another bite of salad and swallowed. "Are you and

Jordan thinking about children?"

A shiver coursed down my spine. What was it about the topic of children that made me edgy? Was I afraid of something going wrong? Terrified I'd be an inept mother?

"We're starting to talk about it," I murmured.

"Spring for the testing." Erin stirred her tea using the stick of pineapple. "At our age, we have to be vigilant."

"Do you want children?"

"First, I'd need a husband. I wouldn't raise a child on my own. I'm not saying that's not okay for other women. I'm a forward thinker. It just wouldn't be right for me."

A silence fell between us. Cattle lowed. Crickets clicked. A flurry of birds scudded across the sky, twittering like crazy. And then —

Rat-a-tat!

CHAPTER 19

Erin swiveled in her chair and gazed at the toolshed. I followed her gaze. The building was older but well maintained. The door to the shed was propped open. The grounds around the shed were nicely manicured. Pansies grew in thick bunches along the sides.

The racket of a hammer hitting metal rang out again. Steady. Repetitive.

"Andrew," Erin said, as if that explained it all.

"He's in the shed?"

"He likes it there. Dad did all sorts of projects when Andrew was young. Those were some of the few times Andrew could remain calm. He loved the sound of Dad hammering or sanding things. Andrew keeps the door open so he doesn't feel trapped; however, a chorus of birds can startle him." Erin sighed. "He had an incident with birds when he was five. Crows attacked him." She shouted to her brother, "It's okay, sweetheart; the birds are gone!"

The hammering ceased, but Andrew didn't emerge from the shed.

"Is he all right?" I asked.

"Sure. He's regrouping. Almost like a computer rebooting after a shutdown."

"Where are the other guests?" I asked. I spotted Shayna sitting on a bench beneath one of the oaks. She was writing in a notebook.

"Ryan and Victor went to the breakfast room for a light lunch."

Leaning forward, I caught a glimpse of the two men sitting at a table beside a window. Ryan was resting against the back of his chair, arms folded across his chest. Victor was either giving Ryan a piece of his mind or, at the very least, a lecture. He repeatedly stabbed his forefinger in Ryan's direction. Suddenly Victor stood up and threw his napkin down on the table. Ryan hopped to his feet, too. Both men disappeared from view. Nerves were definitely on edge, I decided.

"Where's Kandice?" I asked, eager to turn the conversation toward her.

"She had a headache and went to lie down. She says Lara's death has hit her hard."

"How well do you know her?"

"I met Kandice for the first time when she came to the farm to discuss the brain trust. It was her idea."

As I had suspected.

"She'd heard about the annual Cheese Festival, and a lightbulb went off: *Bling!*" Erin popped her fingers to indicate fireworks exploding. "Or so she said. She's funny. She makes me laugh. Some might consider her quirky. I think she's colorful. Did you know she used to manage a dairy department at a college?"

I nodded.

"She didn't exactly fit into the university crowd. Rules, regulations, the standard of dress. Not for her. She quit. Got divorced. No kids. She's done rather well for herself in a span of a few years."

"Did she meet with other farm owners around here as possible sites for the brain trust?"

"She met with ten in the region."

"Why did she choose Emerald Pastures? Because it has an inn on the property?"

"I think that was part of it. After I gave her the full tour —" Erin hesitated.

"What are you remembering?"

"Come to think of it, she seemed more interested in the inn than the facility. She gushed over the antiques. She appreciated that I was refurbishing. She was absolutely enthralled by the grandfather clock. I gather she has quite an interest in timepieces. And she adored the chess nook. Her father was an avid chess player. Anyway" — Erin licked her lips — "at the end of the tour, based on the way she was talking about the number of people she intended to invite, I felt the farm wasn't big enough. The next day, however, she surprised me when she said it was perfect. She preferred intimate environments for the lectures."

"Did she stay the night?"

"Yes. She had the same room she's in now. She asked me my opinion about dividing the group into two and housing them at separate bed-and-breakfasts. I told her it sounded more manageable to me."

I pushed my salad around with my fork but didn't eat. "Do you know why Kandice didn't tell you about Lara taking part?"

"She said it was an oversight. She had so many details to attend to. Lara must have asked to join at the last second."

As before, I didn't buy that excuse. I believed Kandice deliberately omitted Lara's name from the roster.

"Looking back, you know what's odd?" Erin went on. "Kandice mentioned how quaint the antique keys were. She told me about a nightmare stay she had at a hotel in St. Louis. Locked out of her room. The credit card–style key, useless. No one at the front desk. A stranger had to show her how to slide the plastic key down between the door and the jamb. Can you imagine?"

Interesting. Kandice knew how to get in and out of rooms like a pro.

I said, "Do you think Kandice could have broken into Lara's room the same way?"

Erin flapped her hand. "Uh-uh."

"Why not?"

"Because Lara locked the inside bolt."

"Says who?"

"U-ey. A bit ago. You just missed him. He came along with his deputy and the inspector." Erin wiggled her fingers in the direction Deputy O'Shea and the weathered-faced man went. "The three of them examined Lara's doorway and determined there was no way to have unlocked the bolt from the outside. U-ey left. Now the deputy and the inspector are searching for other options."

Neither Jordan nor I had noticed that the bolt had been thrown, but why should we have? Jordan had used all his efforts to kick in the door, not scope out the construction of the locks.

"Erin, hello!" Kandice exited the inn wearing a pretty floral midi and bright pink leggings. She limped slightly as she neared us.

"Headache better?" Erin asked.

"Yes, that green tea worked wonders."

"It's filled with antioxidants."

"Is your leg okay?" I asked.

Kandice gazed at her leg, as though assessing if it might give her an answer. "It's actually my hip. Whenever I sit in a chair for a spell, it knots up. I'm going to stretch it out. See you." She hobbled away, head swiveling right and left as if searching for someone.

"Who's she looking for?" I asked.

"Who do you think?" Erin grinned. "Ryan. She has a big crush."

"What about you?"

"What *about* me?" Erin asked then raised both eyebrows, catching my drift. "Oh." A smile tugged at her lips. "Uh-uh. I'm not interested in Ryan or anyone. I don't have time. I have Andrew to think of. No man would . . . Uh-uh," she repeated.

"I think Ryan likes you. He defended you when Chief Urso was questioning us."

"Yes, but that doesn't mean he —"

Ryan loped out of the inn. "Hey, Kandice," he yelled. "Wait up!"

Kandice whirled around and flashed a broad smile. In a flirtatious way, she caught the side seam of her dress and started swirling the skirt portion to and fro. "Hi! Come take a walk with me."

"Sure, I'll —" He caught sight of Erin and glanced between her and Kandice.

"Go ahead," Erin said. "The walking trails are free to all." Her voice quavered ever so slightly, giving herself away — to me, at least. She *was* interested in him. What a shame she didn't feel she could pursue him. Considering the graciousness of how Ryan had dealt with his former wife and how dedicated he seemed to his family, I would bet he was the kind of guy who could love a woman with a challenged brother.

As Ryan and Kandice disappeared, Victor emerged from the house. His face was tight. His shirt rumpled and hanging over his designer jeans. He held a cell phone to his ear and was barking orders into it. "Sell. Buy." Was he talking to an employee or making a stock trade? He plowed down the steps, his designer high-tops kicking up dust and gravel, and hurried out of sight.

Erin shook her head. "Victor. He's so ridiculous, isn't he? He can't seem to help himself."

"Has he hit on you?"

"Me? Heavens. I've got too much baggage. Besides, he likes them young."

Except for Lara, I mused. And possibly Shayna, who had moved from under the tree and was heading languidly toward the enclosure of goats, like she hadn't a care in the world.

"Not to mention, Victor is too hairy," Erin continued. "Have you seen that tuft of hair sticking out of the top of his shirt? It's salt and pepper. Do you think he dyes the hair on his head?" She rolled her eyes.

"How well do you know him?"

"We've had numerous business dealings with him. As I said the other day, he brokers some of our cheeses online."

"What do you know about Lara's nasty inference that she had dirt on Victor? Do you think it had something to do with the way he manages his business?"

"He is ethical as far as business is concerned with our farm. He pays on time. We see all the paperwork."

I sipped my iced tea. "He seemed to know a lot about your violin."

She clicked her tongue. "I still can't believe it's an Amati."

"Honestly, your parents never told you?"

"They must have worried that I, had I known, wouldn't have touched it. I'm scared

276

to death of breaking things. As a girl, I was accident-prone. At six, I skidded on gravel and tore up my shin. At eight, I fell out of a tree and broke my ankle. I can't tell you how many baking trays of cookies or stacks of dishes I've dropped. I don't have a condition. I'm just always in a hurry and easily distracted. That's why I've never touched the jade urns or the crystal. Ever. I leave those to the housekeeper."

"Erin . . ." I ran a finger along the edge of the table. How to pry without being insulting? I plowed ahead. "How could your folks afford so many expensive things?"

"It's where they invested their money and why the farm is suffering. They took out loans. Both of them were obsessed. I couldn't fault them. All their lives, they were farmers. Born of the earth. Yet they had a deep appreciation for art and music. I think that's where they really connected, you know? They felt trapped on the farm, but not many farmers can move on like Jordan did." She pushed her plate away, folded her napkin, and placed it on top of the uneaten food. "I would like to meet a man who appreciated music."

Like Ryan, I thought, but kept my opinion to myself.

"Did you notice the small painting over

277

the chess table in the living room?" Erin asked.

"Of the woman and the girl sketching?"

She nodded. "It's the only pricey painting we own. Mother said it reminded her of us. I stunk at painting, but she would take me out in the fields, and we would create together. It's one of Monet's lesser works." She swiped the air with a hand. "Now do you see why I can't part with anything? My parents still live and breathe in this house through their collections, modest as they might be."

We finished our meal in silence.

Over a cup of coffee, I said, "What do you know about Shayna?"

"Not much. She has two girls. She's a widow. Never remarried. She makes excellent cheese. I could learn a thing or two from her about the cheddaring process."

"Lara called Shayna's cheese bland."

"She was mistaken. It's got grit."

"I agree."

"I'd compare it to an original Beecher's Flagship cheese. The fifteen-month version, not the four-year Reserve." Beecher's Flagship has a complex yet robust flavor and a nice crumbly quality.

"Why do you think Lara ridiculed her?"

"I have no clue, except —" Erin chewed

on her lip.

"What?"

"I don't know if I should talk out of school, but I heard Shayna and Lara chatting heatedly in the breakfast room the day before . . . you know."

She was referring to the discussion — the *argument*. I recalled that both Erin and the ponytailed waitress made a U-turn to avoid getting caught in the middle.

"I didn't hear the whole conversation," Erin continued. "Lara said something was Shayna's fault. Shayna apologized. Neither of them looked happy. Say, what if Shayna . . ." She pressed her lips together and exhaled. "You should question her."

"Shayna? Why?"

"You've got" — Erin reddened, like she was embarrassed to say more.

"C'mon, Erin. I don't bite."

"You've got a reputation for delving into things. You ask the right questions. People confide in you."

Heat suffused my cheeks. I could only imagine how much Urso and my new husband would appreciate hearing about my reputation. *Not.* Except they had heard before, from numerous sources.

"Please," Erin pleaded. "If Shayna had anything to do with Lara's death . . ." She didn't finish.

I clutched her hands. "Did you mention their conversation to the police?"

"It would be hearsay."

"Erin, you're in trouble."

She withdrew her hands and tucked both under her armpits.

"The police think you might have killed Lara to retrieve your violin," I said. "You should tell U-ey everything you know."

"I didn't do it, Charlotte. You have to believe me. What if . . . What if Lara didn't take my violin?" Erin gazed at me, her eyes filled with pathetic hope. "What if it was another violin, one she brought with her? The police didn't find Lara's fingerprints on mine."

"U-ey told you —"

Wood creaked overhead, as if giving under a footstep.

And then: *cra-a-ack.*

I peeked up. Saw something falling. Fast. "Dive right!"

Erin lurched out of her chair. Just in time.

A six-foot piece of wood railing slammed into our table. Plates erupted into the air. Our tea glasses pitched off the table and crashed on the porch.

I darted to Erin, who was balanced on all fours, her back arching as she gulped in

280

breaths. "Are you okay?"

"Uh-huh. Are you?"

"Yes." I wrapped my arms around her and helped her to a stand. She was shivering like an aspen. I didn't see anyone overhead. No tips of shoes, no shadows. I didn't hear anyone moving about.

Heart chugging, I scanned the grounds. Shayna had vanished from under the tree. Ryan and Kandice were out of sight. Where the heck had Victor gone? No one was fleeing down the staircase inside the inn.

A silhouette in the window by the door caught my eye. I swung around. Andrew was emerging from the toolshed. No, not from *inside* it. From *behind* it. His white shirt was smudged and hanging over his torn jeans. He wasn't wearing shoes. One hand was blocking the sun from his eyes. In his other hand, he carried a handsaw.

A shudder cut through me. I glanced overhead and back at Andrew. Did he saw through the railing and push it over the side to hurt his sister? No, impossible. He couldn't have dashed from the toolshed to the inn and back in the matter of time it took for Erin and me to tend to each other.

"Erin, Erin, Erin," Andrew chanted as he shuffled toward us. His eyes were pinpoints of worry.

She sprinted to him and comforted him, and a second notion jolted me. Had someone sent the railing off the balcony to strike me and not Erin because I was asking her questions?

"Erin, I'll be right back," I said and raced through the inn and up the stairs.

When I arrived at the sitting area beside Jordan's and my old room, it was unoccupied. There were no telltale signs of anyone having been in the vicinity. No half-drunk beverage; no magazine tossed aside.

The area opened to the overhead porch. I went outside. No one was there. I inspected the wood railing. It was raw-edged and rotten, not evenly sawn. The piece must have plunged to the terrace by accident.

CHAPTER 20

When I returned to the shop, I found Pépère at the counter. He was buzzing with good energy. His cheeks were flushed; his eyes, sparkling with gusto. Six customers stood in line to order. Four more were perusing the shelves or filling their baskets with goodies. One woman was eyeing the display of crystal wineglasses with outright lust. Her basket held four bottles of a pinot noir with cherry overtones that, according to my wine-savvy cousin, paired well with Cheddar cheese.

"We have been overrun," Pépère said. "The Street Scene is drumming up all sorts of new customers. That is the correct phrase, *non? Drumming up?*"

I nodded. "Where's Rebecca?"

"In the office. Weeping. *La pauvre fillette triste.*"

"Why is she a poor little sad girl?"

He threw his hands out. *"Je ne sais pas."*

Why would I expect him to know? "I'll be right back," I said and rushed down the hall. I whipped open the door to the office and stepped inside.

Rebecca sat curled in the desk chair, her hair a finger-tousled mess. A wad of used tissues rested on the desk. Rags was nestled in her lap.

"Rebecca," I said cautiously.

She peeked at me. Tears clung to her eyelashes and streaked her cheeks. Her nose was red and puffy. She had been crying for a while.

I hurried to her and rested a hand on her shoulder. "What's wrong?"

"Devon."

My pulse snagged. "Did something happen to him?" Images of horrible accidents popped into my mind.

"He's fine. He . . ." She hiccupped. "He wants to get married."

I took a step backward and scowled at her. "Then why are you crying like the world is about to end?"

"Because . . . I'm not ready to get married."

"You're not?"

"Devon is wonderful, don't get me wrong, but after being engaged to Ipo and everything . . ." Ipo was the honeybee keeper who

284

broke her heart when he returned home to Hawaii at his parents' insistence. Rebecca stroked Rags so hard he wriggled free and galloped to his bed. "I'm not sure I'm ready. I want all my ducks in a row."

"What ducks?"

"My credit cards. I want to be debt free."

"And you're doing that. With Devon's guidance. He's a good influence on you. He adores you." I perched on the desk, hands cupping the edge. "What's the real reason you're upset?"

She lifted her chin. "I'm a horrible, awful person."

"Why?"

"Because my eye still wanders. I look at other guys."

"Okay," I said slowly. For a naïve Amish girl, I understood how that might freak her out.

"Marriage is sacred and for life!"

"Yes, but it's normal for your eye to wander."

"It is?"

"Mine does."

"Really? But you're married to Jordan."

I grinned. "That doesn't mean there aren't other attractive men out there. I'm alive and kicking. I can admire. I just wouldn't, um, *dabble* because I love Jordan with all my heart and soul."

"Heart and soul," she murmured.

"That's what you have to figure out about Devon. Do you love every aspect of him? I'm not just talking about his good looks. Do you love his mind, his humor, his principles, his dreams?"

"I think so."

"You've got to *know* so." I bounded to my feet. "That's your next step. Tell him you're not ready because you don't know him well enough. You're both young. You've only been dating a few months. You have plenty of time."

Rebecca scrambled out of the chair and threw her arms around me.

I wiggled free and gripped her hands. "When I was your age" — *Listen to you, Charlotte, talking like you're an ancient woman* — "I didn't know what I wanted, either. I thought Chip" — Chippendale Cooper, nicknamed Creep Chef after he ended our engagement and fled to Paris — "was the end-all and be-all. He wasn't."

"You're not kidding."

"Do your due diligence. Ask questions. Know the man. You'll have your answer." I released her and patted her arm. "Go freshen up, and come to the counter when you're ready. The shop is hopping!"

I returned to the cheese counter and told Pépère he was free to go. He was grateful. His lower back was aching. He needed to stretch before he could help Grandmère with the Street Scene.

Rebecca joined me minutes later looking refreshed. She had fluffed her hair and had applied blush and a dash of lip gloss. "What can I do?"

"Wrap up those." I indicated chunks of cheese sitting on the prep counter. Pépère had been so busy, he hadn't had time to rewrap the baby Swiss and Appenzeller.

"I'm on it."

After the last customer departed, the door opened and Ryan Harris walked in. His face was sunburned. He must have forgotten to apply sunblock. Cool days in the spring can be deceptive and make tourists falsely think they are immune to the sun's rays. I greeted him. He nodded *hello* and sauntered to the tasting counter. He paused beside the platter of cheese and peered at the sticker I'd fashioned out of triangular yellow paper.

Reading aloud, he said, "*God gave us cheese to ease our burdens and to provide sweet mirth.* Nice." He hooked a thumb toward the street. "Perhaps you should do a reading on the poetry stage."

"Not likely."

He grinned. The space between his upper teeth made him look endearing. So why did an unnerving feeling zigzag up the back of my neck? The other day Rebecca suggested that Ryan might have a deep dark secret. Did he? Was I not seeing him clearly? Could he have pushed the inn's railing over the edge at me, to scare me so I'd stop talking to Erin?

Stop it, Charlotte. That was an accident. Besides, he wouldn't have risked harming Erin, and he had strolled off with Kandice, hence the sunburn, unless the two of them were in league together, and they had circled back, and . . .

I laughed at the notion. *Yeah, right.* Had anyone written a song titled "Paranoia"? Perhaps I should do so. I was acting like the poster child for the diagnosis.

"What is Scharfe Maxx?" Ryan asked, cutting off my mental ramblings.

"You haven't tasted it? It's yummy. An ultra sharp deliciousness paired with extreme creaminess."

"Is it a Cheddar?"

"Nope. It's a Swiss cheese, crafted at Studer Dairy near the Swiss-German border, and one of my favorites. Great for fondue."

"I'll take a quarter pound." He peered

past me at Rebecca, who was standing with her back to us. She must have felt his scrutiny; she peeked over her shoulder. "Hey," he said when their gazes connected.

Her cheeks flushed. "It's you." She abandoned her task and moved to the counter.

Aha. I got it now. Ryan was the one who had drawn her eye.

Rebecca hurried to say, "Charlotte, I told you Ryan came into the shop the other day."

"The day I arrived," Ryan said.

"He bought a sandwich."

"Erin hadn't planned lunch for us," Ryan explained. "All she had was tuna fish." He scrunched up his nose. "I hate tuna."

"Remember how I said Ryan told me about a cheese maker from Texas?" Rebecca chirped. "Pure Luck Dairy."

"Good memory," Ryan said. "I'll write down a few other creamery names for you. They're small concerns, but they make terrific cheeses." He jotted the information on a pad next to the register.

"Do you know how many jobs Ryan has had?" Rebecca said. "Farmer, delivery man, dog walker. He even worked at a spy shop."

Ryan shrugged. "Sold a lot of nanny cams."

"And he was a waiter."

"Only lasted a month at that job," Ryan

quipped. "Guess I'm not the customer-is-always-right person."

"He had to make ends meet for the whole family," Rebecca continued. "His youngest sister was ill a lot. She has chronic anemia. Ryan has a vitamin B-12 deficiency. That's why his hair is so . . ." She fluttered her fingers then paused, her face flush with conflicting emotions. Was she wondering how she had learned so much about a man in a matter of minutes? Deputy O'Shea played it close to the chest; Ryan appeared to be more candid. So much for him being a man of secrets. "Ryan needed to pay for insurance," Rebecca said, picking up where she left off, "so they didn't go bankrupt again."

"Is your sister healthy now?" I asked.

"No one can keep her down," Ryan said. "She's a bit of a rebel. She paints outside the lines" — he swiped the air to demonstrate — "if you know what I mean."

"I do." I packaged up his cheese, wrapped it in our special paper, and sealed it with a gold label. "Need anything else?"

Ryan swung to his left, plucked a box of crackers from a display, and handed them to me. "Lunch."

"Didn't you eat with Victor at the inn?"

Ryan's eyes wavered. "Nah. He lit into

me. I lost my appetite."

"Why did he yell at you?" I asked, happy for an invitation to discuss the set-to I had witnessed.

"He saw me talking with Chief Urso earlier. He demanded to know what I'd told him. I said I couldn't reveal anything. It was privileged information. Victor accused me of lying to the police to finger him for Lara's murder."

"Did you?"

"No, but" — Ryan glanced over his shoulder and back at me — "I told the chief that I saw Victor and Lara on the steps leading to the third floor before dinner that night. They were going at it."

Rebecca leaned in, totally enthralled with the tale. "*At it,* as in they were hitting each other?"

"No fists flew, but they were arguing. I think she was warning him."

"What about?" Rebecca asked.

I threw her a cautionary glance. "Ryan just said it's privileged information."

Rebecca fluttered her eyelashes at Ryan and smiled. "Is it really confidential?"

"Nah." Ryan jammed a hand into a pocket. "I just wanted to jerk Victor's chain."

Rebecca shot me a look. The triumph in

her gaze was hysterical. Perhaps she should consider a career in law. Any witness on the stand would be putty in her hands. She swung back to face Ryan. "Why was Lara warning him?"

"I'm not entirely sure. She was whispering so I couldn't catch everything. She said, 'I saw you text her,' and Victor said, 'I did not.' "

"Sounds like she was jealous," Rebecca suggested.

Ryan nodded. "Lara pressed him. She said, 'Do you think that kind of stuff vanishes in the wind?' "

Rebecca twirled a finger. "By that 'kind of stuff,' I'll bet she meant digital messages. Hackers can find anything if it's been sent digitally."

I rolled my eyes. My assistant and my husband, amateur CSI experts, thanks to television and the Internet.

Ryan continued. "Later, I saw Victor texting someone at the dining table, almost flaunting it at Lara."

I'd seen Victor typing messages, too.

Rebecca smacked her hands together. "Back to the argument."

"Right." Ryan bobbed his head. "Then Victor said, 'It's my business,' and Lara said, 'Don't contact her again.' "

"Did they say anything else?"

"Victor said, and I quote" — Ryan bracketed his fingers — " 'You are not the boss of me.' And Lara said, 'Is that so?' "

"Wow!" Rebecca gushed. "I wonder who he was texting. We have to see those messages."

"Uh-uh." I put a hand on her wrist. "*We* don't have to do anything. Chief Urso does."

Rebecca lasered Ryan with a look. "You told the police all of this?"

"Yup." He pulled his cell phone from his pocket and scanned the readout. Talk about timing. Someone had messaged him. "Gotta run. Nice seeing you." He paid for his purchases, offered Rebecca a flirty wink, and headed out.

"Back to work," I said to my sweet assistant. "No more sleuthing." I asked her to go to the cellar to fetch a couple of wheels of Grafton Clothbound Cheddar, our most popular cheese. We had run low. She sulked but did as told.

Just as Ryan was exiting, Kandice entered. She had changed her hairstyle into one of those odd new creations, with little bits and pieces of hair knotted into multiple rubber bands — trendy but unattractive on most females over sixteen.

"Hey, Ryan," she said and, as she had at

293

the inn, clutched her floral midi dress and swirled the skirt to and fro.

"Hey," he responded and edged past her to the sidewalk.

I greeted Kandice. She spun around. Her face revealed it all. She cared about Ryan and was stunned that he had snubbed her. She walk-limped toward the barrel that held the wine goblets. She lifted one. "These are lovely."

"How's your hip doing?" I asked.

"Fine." She peeked over her shoulder at the retreating form of Ryan. "Man, he can be aloof."

"Didn't you two have a nice walk around the property?"

"Not really. He left me about thirty seconds after joining me. Supposedly, his cell phone buzzed — I think he was lying; I didn't hear it — but he said he had business to attend to."

I peered after Ryan, who had stopped on the sidewalk and was talking to someone on his cell phone. Not just talking. Making a point, stabbing the air. His features were hard, his mouth grim. Seeing him so intense — a complete reversal from the sweet guy who had chatted with us seconds ago in the shop — made me zing back to the incident on the porch at the inn. Did he pretend to be interested in taking a walk with Kandice so she could verify his alibi when the wood railing fell? Should I suspect him of foul play?

No, I was reaching for answers that didn't exist. The wood was rotten. I was sure of it. Ryan had most likely abandoned Kandice because he was truly interested in Erin, and he didn't want her to be jealous.

"It's because of the way I look," Kandice went on. "Most men can't handle all of" — she flourished a hand along her curvy torso — "*this*. I'm too much woman. My ex told me so. I think that's a cop-out response, of course. Some men find a big, klutzy woman hot."

"You're not klutzy," I said.

"I'm certainly not graceful. After the accident at the Street Scene, Lara said —" Kandice hesitated. "Mustn't speak ill of the dead." Quickly she reset the goblet on the display barrel.

The move made me flash on Friday night and the way Lara and Kandice had sparred after Kandice made a big deal about the value of some of Erin's parents' treasures. Later that night, did Lara summon Kandice to her room to read her the riot act for making Erin aware of the value of her collectibles? I could just hear her: *How dare*

295

you give Erin the idea to have her treasures appraised? Kandice, not in her cups as Lara was, retaliated: *How dare you put me down in front of the others?* Kandice lashed out. Though she resembled a cockatoo, she was rather large and could have easily overpowered Lara, even with an injured arm.

"Kandice," I said. "Tell me about your relationship with Lara."

"Why?"

"I'm curious."

"We were colleagues."

I plucked a morsel of Marieke Aged Gouda, a sweet, nutty cheese, from the daily tasting tray and extended it to Kandice. "Try this."

She drew near and received my offering. "Mmm. Nice. Who makes it?"

"The Penterman family, which transplanted from the Netherlands to Wisconsin where there was a ton of land so they could continue the family business of cheese making." As she took another piece, I said, "When did you and Lara meet?"

"About six years ago. You'd think our paths would have crossed before then, considering all we did within the same circles, but they didn't."

"Were you close?"

Kandice hooted out a laugh. "With Lara?

Ha! She didn't *do* close. She liked to keep a healthy distance between herself and others. When I opened up to her about my divorce, like girlfriends do, she cut me off. 'Let's keep this business,' she said."

"She hired you?"

"Occasionally."

"The night she died —"

"I was in my room," Kandice rushed to say.

"We all were."

"Not Erin. She stepped out."

Her brittle tone made my teeth ache. "Why are you so set against Erin?"

"I'm not, but she seems to have the best motive to kill Lara."

"And you don't?"

"Why would I kill Lara?" She blinked. Rapidly. She had a motive. I was sure of it. Maybe Lara promised to split the proceeds from selling the violin if Kandice helped her locate it. Maybe that night, Lara reneged on the promise. Or there was something else Lara had on Kandice, something worthy of blackmail.

I handed Kandice another tasting of the Gouda. While she ate it, I said, "You were working on your schedule that night and fell asleep."

"I sure did." Kandice chortled; it sounded

forced. "I woke up with binder lines on my face to prove it. A hot water soak and mini massage helped." She surveyed the cheese counter and read one of the tags out loud. *"Cheese so sassy you might feel you have to slap it.* How darling! Who came up with that? Give me a quarter pound of that, please." She pointed to the Pistol Point Cheddar from Rogue Creamery, a chipotle-infused, orange-marbled cheese that added variety to any platter.

"Good choice."

"And that, too." She indicated another cheese. Her arms flexed.

While I wrapped up her order, I said, "You have very strong arms, Kandice. Do you work out?"

"Yes, I —" She eyed me with suspicion. "You're prying. Why?"

"No —"

"Do you think I killed Lara? I didn't. I told you, she and I were colleagues. Friends."

"No, you distinctly said you weren't *close."*

"That doesn't mean we weren't friendly. We helped each other out. I recommended her; she recommended me. Besides, there's no way I could have smothered her."

"Because of your sore arm?"

"Because of this." She hiked up her floral dress to a few inches above her knee and then rapped on her knee. It *clack*ed. "Hear that? My knee and calf are artificial. Phony. Non-human." She released the dress; it fell back in place.

"I'm so sorry. What happened?"

"I was sixteen. Out riding a sweet mare. We took a jump. She missed and tumbled sideways right on top of me."

I grimaced. If not for her demonstration and the apparent bulge from the hinge, I never would've known, but that explained why she occasionally limped and was always wearing mid-calf-length dresses and color-ful nylons.

"I couldn't have gotten enough leverage to kill Lara," Kandice continued, "no matter how hard I tried. I have no lower body strength."

The cellar door slammed. Rebecca emerged from the kitchen carrying a large round of clothbound cheese. "I'm back."

"Hey," Kandice said, "have you ever heard this one?" She cracked a wicked smile. "What's the best type of story to tell a horse? A tale of *whoa*. Get it?" She snig-gered. "Just so you know, I don't mind that you know about my leg. It's history."

Rebecca kicked my foot and mouthed:

What about her leg?

I whispered that I would tell her later.

"But I do mind," Kandice continued, "that you asked me my alibi. That means you don't know me very well."

"I'm sorry."

She waved a hand. "Forget it. 'Let bygones be.' That's what Ryan says." She glanced toward the street. Ryan had moved on. She turned back to me and pulled a wallet from her purse. "If it makes you feel any better, I've told the police everything I can remember. Like you, I'm naturally curious. I love murder shows on television. I'm a *Murder, She Wrote* fanatic. I've seen every episode dozens of times."

"Me, too!" Rebecca cried.

"Did you ever see the one with the kid who stole the bike?" Kandice asked.

"Except he didn't steal the bike," Rebecca replied.

"Exactly, but that woman at the precinct sure laid into the kid's mother. What a witch!"

Rebecca agreed.

After Kandice paid for her purchase and exited, Rebecca said, "I like her."

"I do, too."

But that didn't guarantee she was innocent.

CHAPTER 21

Midafternoon, I spotted Urso heading into
The Country Kitchen diner across the
street. Eager to find out if he had made any
progress on the case, I asked Rebecca to
watch the shop. There was only one customer browsing the wares, a regular who
adored Rebecca.

The diner was hopping. Every booth was
filled. I didn't recognize half the faces and
secretly hoped all the newbies in town
would venture into Fromagerie Bessette. We
valued new business.

I found Urso at the counter, his hat
removed and placed on the stool to his left.
Delilah, clad in her red waitress outfit, her
dark curly hair swept into a fashionable red-
ribbon hairnet, was standing next to him.
He must have said something funny. She
was laughing so hard her eyes glistened with
tears. When she saw me, she gestured to the
stool to the right of Urso.

"Pop a squat," she said.

I did; Urso eyed me with distrust.

"What?" I winked. "A girl can't get a bite to eat?"

"I happen to know you eat lunch at noon."

"I'm in the mood for an afternoon snack. A lemon meringue muffin." The diner made terrific muffins, packed with lemon-tart flavor.

Delilah said, "I'll be right back." She pecked Urso on the cheek and bustled to the kitchen.

Urso rested his chin on his fist. "What do you want to ask me?"

"Don't look at me like that."

"Like what?"

I mimicked his smirk and squeezed my eyebrows together toward the center. "Being suspicious doesn't become you."

He folded his arms on the counter. "It's my job. I repeat: Got a question?"

I fiddled with my napkin and place setting. "I'm curious. Where are you in the investigation?"

"Nowhere."

"Ryan Harris said he spoke to you."

"He did."

"And you're following up?"

"On what?" Urso wiped moisture off the outside of the glass with his fingertip.

I recalled what Erin said to me at the inn about people telling me things and trusting me. Not the chief of police, apparently. It wasn't my place to tell him that Ryan had blabbed about Lara and Victor's argument, so instead, I decided to address the questions Jordan thought were most important. "Did you find Ambien in Lara's system?" I asked. "Or in the wine she was drinking?"

Urso drew in a deep breath and released it with a hefty sigh. "You are relentless."

"No, I'm not."

"Yes, you are." He took a sip of water.

"U-ey, c'mon. It's me."

He set his glass on the counter with a *clack* and leveled me with a stare. "Miss Berry had a lot to drink. She had over the legal limit of alcohol in her system."

"I know. I was there. Did you find anything else? If not Ambien, then some other opiate that might have made her pass out?"

"Do you want the coroner's official evaluation?"

"Yours will do."

"She didn't pass out. She was knocked out."

"As in the killer used ether?"

"Chloroform." Urso swiveled toward me. "Understand, it is nearly impossible to render a victim unconscious using chloro-

303

form alone, but with the amount of alcohol in her system . . ." He let the rest of his explanation hang.

"How did you figure it out?"

"I detected the odor right off the bat."

I recalled him bending over Lara's body, his nose close to her face.

"It's sweet smelling," he said, "but I discounted it, figuring the aroma I was picking up had come from something she ate."

"Lara didn't eat dessert. None of us did."

"The waitstaff told me the same. After determining the contents of Miss Berry's stomach, the coroner confirmed my suspicions. He also added that attendants at the brain trust might know how to make chloroform. Many are chemists by nature. It is also fairly easy to purchase."

I eyed Urso's water and craved a sip. "Using chloroform changes things."

"How so?"

"Whoever killed Lara could have overpowered her easily. It means the killer didn't have to be someone strong, like Victor or Ryan." I told him about Kandice and her artificial limb.

"You've been questioning Miss Witt?"

"No. Not on purpose. She came into the shop and we chatted. She offered information freely." Well, somewhat freely. "She said there was no way she could have killed Lara. With both feet on the floor, leverage would have been difficult for her to achieve, but if Lara was sedated, Kandice could have scrambled on top of her and —"

"Anyone could have," Urso said, "including Erin."

I glowered at him. He stared back, his gaze ruthless.

Delilah arrived and set down two plates. "Here we are." One plate held a tuna melt for Urso; the other a muffin for me. "Coffee?"

"Water, please," I said. Coffee sounded too harsh for my churning, overly curious insides. She hurried off, and I switched the subject. "I saw Deputy O'Shea consulting with an architect at Emerald Pastures. Did they find a hidden entrance into Lara's room?"

"No. Whoever killed Miss Berry must have found another way in."

"Erin told me the door was locked using the inside bolt. That exonerates her."

"No, it doesn't. It doesn't clear anyone."

"Are you sure it was murder?"

"Yes! Charlotte, stay out of it, please."

"I can't. Erin is my friend."

"And mine."

"She isn't guilty!"

"That's it." Urso pushed his plate away, rose to a stand, and snatched his hat off the nearby stool.

"Did you get in touch with Lara's sister?" I asked, intent on keeping him engaged.

"She's coming to town to claim the body as soon as she can. She's in Europe." Without a good-bye, he jammed his hat on his head and stomped out of the diner.

Delilah reappeared with a glass of water and threw me a sour look. "Did you scare off my intended?"

"I think he's suffering from indigestion."

"Were you butting into the investigation?"

"I don't butt."

She shot me a knowing look.

"I asked a few questions, to which he didn't have the answers. Moving on . . ." I took a bite of my muffin. Super moist. Perfect. "How are the wedding plans going?"

"Great. U-ey and I agree on everything. The flowers, the chapel, the music, the date. Charlotte" — she pressed a hand to her chest — "I'm so in love, I don't even recognize myself. If you'd told me a year ago that he and I would be an item, I'd have laughed in your face."

"If I recall, you did laugh."

She scowled. "So you were right. Happy?"

"Ecstatic," I said, and I was, for her and for Urso, but at the moment, I couldn't erase the last encounter with her beloved from my mind. Erin was innocent. Why couldn't he see that?

"I saw Meredith," Delilah said.

"She told me. It was sweet of you to help her out with the knitting, but I've got to tell you, she hates it and is as bored as all get-out."

"I'll stop by after my shift and rouse her in a game of gin."

"Be careful," I warned. "She might be bored, but she hasn't lost her edge. You could fork over a lot of quarters."

Chuckling, Delilah headed to the kitchen. At the same time, the door to the diner swooshed open, and Clair and Amy ran in. "Aunt Charlotte!" they yelled as they scurried past booths to reach me.

Their mother, Sylvie, followed them inside. Typically she was a vision — okay, a *nightmarish* vision whenever she was clad in one of her over-the-top outfits. Today, however, her hair was one color, ice white, and her outfit was tame, a red sheath with bolero jacket.

I sidled off my stool and opened my arms. The twins flew into my grasp. "School's out already?" I glimpsed the huge clock at the far end of the restaurant, which read half past three. Time was flying. "How was it?"

"I love May," Amy said. "It's the end of the year —"

"And the teacher gets tired," Clair cut in.

"So she plays guitar." Amy mimed strumming.

"We all sing songs," Clair said. The twins invariably finished each other's sentences.

Sylvie peeled the girls off of me. "Sweethearts, don't choke Charlotte."

Actually, I was enjoying the hug fest.

"By the by, Charlotte," Sylvie said in her clipped British accent. "I'm looking for your grandmother. I was informed she was here."

"I haven't seen her. You look nice, Sylvie." I meant it. "What's the occasion?" Oops. That didn't come out right.

"I'm meeting with my lawyer."

Uh-oh. Sylvie and lawyers could be a caustic mix. "Why?"

"This Street Scene nonsense will be the death of my business. I want it to stop."

"Sylvie, get real. The event is only continuing for a short while longer. You don't have to resort to legal action. Besides, your business must have prospered because of the extra foot traffic."

"That's just it. It hasn't! Sales are down."

There could be a reason for that, I mused.

Sylvie sold extravagant clothing in her shop, items that might appeal more to people who attended haute couture fashion shows in New York or Paris. If she would change up her selections to please a more typical Providence clientele . . .

I said, "Perhaps you need to offer a special."

"What I need to do is talk to your grandmother with my lawyer present. Girls, let's go."

"We want to stay." Amy clasped her hands in prayer.

Clair copied her sister. "Please?"

I grinned. "I'll bring them to your shop in fifteen minutes, Sylvie."

Sylvie muttered, "Fine, but no sugar."

"What?" the twins cried in unison. "Since when?"

"Since now." Sylvie was the most quixotic woman I had ever met. Regularly, she bought the girls sweet treats like chocolate or even cotton candy, which is pure, unadulterated sugar.

"Don't worry about that, ladies," a woman with a throaty voice said behind me.

I spun on my stool and saw Shayna approaching from the rear of the diner. She wore yet another sack-style dress, this one pale blue, and thick-strapped Birkenstock sandals.

"The diner has a delectable sugar-free item on special," Shayna continued. "Grilled cheese with peanut butter and bacon."

"Perfect." Sylvie wiggled her fingers. "You can have that, my girlie-girls. Delilah!" she shouted, oblivious that using her outside voice might be irritating other diners. "Two of those cheese and peanut butter thingies."

I frowned. As attentive as Sylvie could be, occasionally she forgot to specify that Clair needed her food prepared gluten-free. Luckily the diner kept gluten-free bread in the freezer for Clair, and Delilah was conscientious enough to remind the chef to prepare Clair's food away from flour-contaminated prep areas.

Sylvie snapped her fingers. "Amy. Clair. Let's set you up in that booth over there."

As the girls scurried off, Shayna perched on the stool that Urso had vacated. "I remember the wondrous times my girls and I used to have going to diners, back when they were still thrilled that I was their mother."

"How's your youngest doing?" I asked.

"She isn't answering my phone calls. She's not crazy about my advice." Shayna leaned closer and whispered, "I don't mean to take you from the twins, but I saw you talking to Chief Urso a minute ago. Is there anything new on Lara's murder?"

"Nothing that he'll tell me."

"How I wish this would all be over. Poor Lara. And poor Erin. Lara had no right to lash out at her like she did."

"Erin didn't kill her."

"If you say so. But who else had motive? Mr. France-y Pants Victor? Or Kandice? Ryan Harris barely knew her."

I pushed my muffin aside, wiped my hands on a napkin, and spun on the stool to face her. "Shayna, what Lara said that night about the quality of your cheese had to hurt."

"Not a bit. I'd grown accustomed to her slings and arrows."

"You didn't hold a grudge?"

Shayna cocked her head. "If you're asking whether I killed her because she walked out on our partnership, the answer is no. I wouldn't have. Not in a million years."

"You two argued in the breakfast room. What about?"

"We didn't argue. We chatted. It was nothing." Her cheeks reddened with unspoken emotion. "Look, my farm is thriving. The reviews of my cheeses are good. In spite of Lara's exit, I've succeeded. In time, she would have found her way back to our friendship. I'm sure of it. My money is on Erin, Victor, or Kandice being the killer."

"There's still the problem of how someone got into the room."

"That is a puzzle. There are no secret passages in my room. I checked. I wish the police luck figuring that out." Shayna slid off the stool and patted my arm. "See you."

She strode to the exit, regal yet somewhat broken, and I sat there miffed at myself, realizing I should have pressed harder and learned what Lara and she had argued about. I didn't believe *it was nothing.*

I started to go after her, but Amy called out, "Aunt Charlotte!" I gathered my food and joined the twins at the booth. Sylvie had split without saying good-bye to me. How typical.

Clair said, "Mom said that lady you were talking to is very nice."

I smiled. *Mom.* Just a few months ago, they had called Sylvie *Mommy.*

"Mom is helping her out with her wardrobe," Amy added.

"Helping her how?" I asked.

Clair unfolded a napkin and placed it on her lap. "Mom stopped her on the street and pulled her into the shop."

I cringed. "She didn't."

312

Amy giggled. "Mom said the lady had no style. She owed it to the woman to fix her."

"That's not what she said," Clair interrupted. "She said the lady was so large, she needed a makeover."

Delilah arrived with two grilled cheese sandwiches. "Here you go, ladies. Gluten-free for you, Clair." She bent low and whispered to me, "Charlotte, you've got that look." She twirled a finger in front of her eyes.

Quietly I confided what I had asked Urso, how I had included Victor, Ryan, and Kandice in my list of suspects and that I'd left out Shayna, but realized now she should have been included in the mix. She had heft.

"Except heft isn't a factor. Chloroform was used to sedate Lara."

I gawped. "Did U-ey tell you that?"

"You're not the only one he talks to." She glanced over her shoulder and back at me. "Which means Erin can be a suspect along with the rest of them."

CHAPTER 22

Throughout the afternoon at the shop, I could barely think because Delilah's comment about Erin had thrown me for a loop. Did Erin kill Lara? I didn't want to believe it, but I couldn't be blind to the truth, either. Rebecca badgered me for information, but I didn't dare say anything lest I blurt out my fears.

Trying to block the dire thoughts from my mind, I chatted up customers and sold a vast amount of cheese, particularly the Jasper Hill Farm's Harbison, a scrumptious, soft-ripened cheese with a spoonable texture that we had set out for tasting. In addition, customers bought over fifty jars of Flying Bee Ranch blueberry honey, an amber-colored honey with a sweet, bold flavor that we had paired with the cheese. They also purchased nearly all the Italian ceramic platters we had stocked.

When the customers dwindled to two, I

suggested to Rebecca that she take a break. She didn't need me to say it twice. Quickly she donned a jacket and hustled outside to drink in some fresh air. Soon after, the front door opened, and Matthew entered with Victor. The two were shooting the breeze as if they were old buddies. Both carried a cup of something from Café au Lait. Matthew's hair stuck out all over, like he had just walked in a windstorm. Outside the wind had, indeed, kicked up. The drapes on the Street Scene stages were flapping with force.

Matthew strode ahead of Victor and said, "Make yourself comfortable. Check out the French wines we have in stock."

Victor blew past Matthew toward the wine annex while pulling his cell phone from his pocket. With only his thumb, he started texting someone. That took talent. I could barely text with two thumbs, and within seconds, I was making errors. Who was so important that the message couldn't wait until he was sitting down, his coffee cup set aside, both hands free?

I whispered, *"Psst,"* to Matthew and beckoned him with a finger. He drew near the register. "What's with you two? Are you best buds?"

"Me and Victor?" Matthew glanced toward the annex. "Nah. He caught up with me on the way out of the café. He's quite a talker. He said he wanted to pick my brain over the right Bordeaux to win a woman's heart."

"Which woman?" I asked.

"Got me."

Someone who had attended the brain trust, I imagined, or perhaps he had met someone else in the short time he had been here. He mentioned having heard a woman singing a Piaf song on the night Lara died. Maybe he had hooked up with her.

Matthew eyed me cynically. "You don't like him, do you?"

"I'm that easy to read?"

"Like a large-print book." He sipped his coffee and, while heading toward the annex, said over his shoulder, "Don't worry, whomever Victor has his eye on is a dalliance. He's not staying in town much longer. The moment Urso clears him to leave, he's flying the coop. If he had his druthers, he would move out of Emerald Pastures Inn, but he can't find anything else. All the B&Bs are packed."

Victor passed Matthew and approached the register with a bottle of wine in hand. "I guess this will do," he said.

It *should.* Even I recognized the bottle. A Lafite Rothschild Pauillac, one of the finest

316

wines we carried at the shop, valued in excess of four hundred dollars. His date was one lucky girl.

Victor plucked five hundred-dollar bills from his billfold and handed them to me.

"Any cheese to go with that?" I asked.

He surveyed the counter and stopped when he laid eyes on the Chabichou de Poitou, a buttery, tart cheese from the Loire Valley, presented in a little cylinder called a *bonde*. Aloud, he read the cheese tag I'd affixed to the wrapper: "*Flinty but flirty.* Honestly?" He arched an eyebrow. "Don't get cutesy when it comes to cheese."

"Why not?" I said, taking the challenge. "My customers like the fun sayings."

"Then they aren't serious cheese lovers."

The comment stung. I smiled tightly. "Have you tasted this cheese?"

"Of course. I have a well-educated palate. I'll take one *bonde*."

"The cheese would go better with a sauvignon blanc than a big hearty red like the one you've chosen."

"What do you suggest I order?"

"Beecher's Flagship Reserve." It was one of Beecher's tastiest Cheddars, a rich, four-year-aged cheese with a nutty and tangy finish.

"From Oregon?" Victor made a face.

317

"Yes, it's American," I said, unable to keep the bite from my response. "If that's not good enough, how about the Boerenkaas Gouda, from the Netherlands? Is that close enough to France for you?" The Boerenkaas was one of my favorite cheeses, with deep notes of caramel — some would say butterscotch — and cashews.

Victor nodded. "The Gouda is fine. A pound. I'll need crackers and honey."

I put together a nice assortment for him. He offered me another hundred-dollar bill. While he waited for his change, he texted another message. I was dying to peek at his texting history. Could something he had written convict him of murder? I wondered whether Urso had interrogated him after hearing Ryan's account about the argument between Victor and Lara. If only he would have confided in me at the diner.

"Here you go." I offered Victor the change and a bag filled with his treats, and he left.

No thank you. No good-bye. Downright rude.

Lois Smith, my neighbor who owned Lavender and Lace, a charming bed-and-breakfast that served the best scones in town, skirted Victor on her way in. Her nose twitched, as if she had smelled something bad. She flapped a violet-colored fan in front of her face — everything Lois owned was some shade of purple — and she drew near to the counter. Tucked under her left arm was the antique wrought iron cheese grater with clamp that my grandmother had broken and taken to be fixed.

"Are you okay?" I asked. "You look distressed."

Lois studied the retreating figure of Victor. "That man," she muttered. Lois was in her sixties and quite pale — paler since she had booted out her husband.

"Victor Wolfman," I said.

"He irks me. He's so" — Lois checked the shop; the one customer who had entered right behind her was far away — "misogynistic, don't you know."

"Why would you say that?" A misogynist hated women and often denigrated or beat them. "Did you see Victor hurt someone?"

Lois flicked her fan closed. "Not exactly, but that woman who died? Lara Berry?"

If only Lois would speak up. I could barely hear her. "Go on."

"I saw her and that man —"

"Victor."

"They were at Café au Lait. I'd run out of coffee. A few of my boarders requested it. Herbal tea is better for you, of course, and I had plenty of that on hand, but I try to accommodate when I can."

"Victor and Lara," I prompted.

"Right. I heard the two of them arguing. Around four in the afternoon on Friday."

After the brain trust concluded for the day and before the evening's dinner.

"What were they arguing about?"

"A woman." Lois spat out the word. "Lara said he shouldn't contact the woman anymore."

"Did Victor respond?"

"He told her in *no uncertain terms*" — Lois pinched off each word — "to keep her nose out of his affairs. Stop bossing him around. It wasn't her business. She disagreed. She threatened to expose him."

"For what?"

"How should I know? I wasn't listening in, don't you know. I only heard snippets."

Um, okay, it sounded like Lois had been listening in, but I wouldn't argue.

"The way he glowered at her," Lois went on, "I could see evil was running roughshod in his mind. I promise you —" She eyed the antique cheese grater she was holding. "Oh, my, seeing him put me off my errand. I came in looking for your grandmother. I need to return this piece to her. I repaired it."

"You?" I didn't mean to sound skeptical,

but Lois didn't strike me as the handy type.

"I have plenty of time now that —" She hesitated but didn't add: *Now that I sent my heel of a husband packing.* "It turns out I'm good with tools. I have all sorts of things I'd like to mend at the inn, so I've been spending my spare time reading how-to books. There are plenty of those at the Historical Society, don't you know." Lois's sister was the former curator who had fled town. "That other lady, the one who organized the brain trust, with the pink hair . . ." Lois drew her fan upward over her head.

"Kandice Witt?"

She jutted her fan at me. "She visits the museum daily. She's so lovely. We've been chatting quite a bit. She's the person who showed me a how-to book on antiques. She collects all sorts of cheese-making antiques, don't you know." Lois held up the wheel. "She knew exactly when this was made and who designed it."

Interesting. According to Victor, Lara had collected a number of antique cheese-related items. Had Kandice and Lara vied for the same pieces in the past? Had their rivalry been friendly, or would Kandice have killed Lara to get her hands on a specific antique? Erin told me Kandice had eyed a few of the pieces at the inn when she visited

Providence to scope out sites for the brain trust.

Lois handed me the grater. "I've got to run. Can you give this to your grandmother?" She headed toward the exit.

"Lois, wait. How much is something like this worth?"

"Nine hundred or a thousand dollars."

"Not enough to kill over," I muttered.

"Heavens! Who said anything about killing?" Lois peered at me like I was nuts.

Maybe I was.

CHAPTER 23

On Monday nights, I always made a point of joining my girlfriends for an evening out. Sometimes as many as eight of us got together. We would take a yoga or art class or go to a musical event. Last week we attended a self-defense-skills class. I was getting rather good at getting out of a choke hold. I still had to work on a frontal attack. On other occasions, we went to Timothy O'Shea's Irish Pub. After Jordan bought the pub and transformed it into The White Horse, I asked my pals if they still felt comfortable going there. All had given me weird looks, pretty much the way Lois had, like I was nuts: *Of course they were comfortable. Duh!*

Tonight, we were gathering for a spa experience at Tip to Toe Salon. Only Delilah, Tyanne, Jacky, and I could make it.

I called Jordan and asked him to escort me. I wanted a few minutes alone with him.

True, we hadn't been apart more than twelve hours, but I missed him. We strolled along the sidewalk, passing happy revelers enjoying the Street Scene, and I filled him in on my day, starting with the incident at the inn during lunch.

Jordan was upset that I hadn't called him right away. "You checked out the railing?"

"Yes. It was rotten wood. Not sawed by hand."

He muttered that I wasn't an expert, then shrugged and said, "Go on. What next? There's more, I gather."

I replayed the conversation with Ryan about Victor and Lara's argument and added that Lois corroborated the thread of the conversation. "They were two different versions," I admitted, "but the basics were the same."

"Have you told U-ey any of this?"

"U-ey." I grunted. I filled Jordan in on the terse conversation at the diner. "Needless to say, he wasn't forthcoming."

Jordan screwed up his mouth. "Charlotte, sweetheart, did Lois talk to Urso or any of the deputies?"

"I'm not sure."

"You've got to follow up."

"Haven't you heard me? Whenever I open my mouth, U-ey snaps at me."

"He doesn't mean to. He's on tenterhooks. Another murder. An upcoming wedding. I'm sure he appreciates all you've done to help him on previous occasions; not to mention, he worries about you."

"Ha!" I barked out a laugh.

"Just like I do."

We walked ahead, silence falling between us. Outside Tip to Toe Salon, we stopped, and Jordan ran a hand down my back. "I've been doing some thinking."

"Really?" I said. "You put your brain to work?"

"You're funny."

"A laugh a minute."

Jordan pulled me into a hug, his arms anchored at the small of my back. I tilted my head back to look into his eyes. He said, "We aren't spending enough time together. We have completely different schedules."

"Amazing."

"Be serious. Don't tease."

"I'm not teasing. I said *amazing* because we have been thinking exactly the same thing. We don't spend enough time together. What are we going to do about it?"

"I'm taking on an assistant manager."

"What? Who?"

"I'm thinking of poaching someone from La Bella Ristorante. It has three night managers. There are one or two who will never get a bump in salary or position. The new hire will be fully in charge at The White Horse three nights a week and assist me on Fridays and Saturdays." He took my hand and rubbed his thumb along the hollow.

"Are you sure you can give up that kind of control?"

"It's a risk, but we need time."

"I could hire another person, too, and take off an extra day. If we're going to have kids —" I pressed my lips together. How did those words pop out of my mouth?

Jordan burst into a smile. "So you have been considering it."

"Deep down, I know I want at least one."

"Me, too." Jordan kissed my forehead. "I love you."

I whispered the words back to him.

"Hey, hey," a man said. "No public display of affection."

We broke apart. Urso and Delilah were heading for us.

Urso singled us out with his finger. "Yeah, you two."

Delilah pulled his arm down and said, "Can it, goofball," and then stood on tiptoe and kissed him smartly on the lips.

Urso returned the favor. Afterward, he cuffed Jordan on the arm. "Got time for a beer before you take charge?"

"Always."

I whispered to Jordan, "You tell him."

Urso lasered Jordan with a look. "Tell me what?"

"About Lois," I chirped, and like a chicken, gripped Delilah's elbow and steered her into the salon.

Tip to Toe was decorated in a hip way, with black granite, silver accents, and bright yellow chairs. It pulsated with good vibes. Even on a Monday night, the place was hopping. A couple of female tourists who had come into The Cheese Shop earlier were perched at the station where a young woman was doing makeovers.

Delilah thumped me on the back. "Out with it. What did Lois say? Does she know who killed Lara?"

"Hey!" Jacky sailed into the salon right after us. She shrugged off a cardigan sweater and hung it on a coatrack by the door.

Delilah flicked my arm with her finger, demanding an answer. "Talk," she rasped.

I whispered, "No, Lois doesn't know who killed Lara, but she overheard Lara and Victor arguing. I'll fill you in later."

Jacky drew near. "Didn't you two hear me calling you on the street?" She had a sensuous, willowy figure, and, like Jordan, she

327

had dark hair, riveting eyes, and an easy smile. I would never forget our first meeting when I had mistakenly assumed she was Jordan's lover, not his sister. The memory still embarrasses me. Jealousy can be so unbecoming. Jacky and I soon became friends. She is one of the most down-to-earth women I know. She is an adoring mother, a passionate artist, and now a farmer. I love her as much as if she were my own sister. She hugged me and said, "I'm so excited to be here. I need a night out."

"Over here, ladies." Lizzie, the owner of Tip to Toe, Tyanne's energetic sister who migrated to Providence from New Orleans after Tyanne's husband walked out on her, beckoned to us. "On the double. Chop-chop." Lizzie always made me smile. She wore her red hair an inch long, and she layered herself with funky jewelry that complemented her colorful clothes. "I've set aside an entire section for y'all's mani-pedis." She wriggled her long, bejeweled nails at me. "I'm also serving a bit of the bubbly plus some of that scrumptious sheep's cheese you recommended, Charlotte. Manchego. Mm-mm. My favorite. I've put it on a platter with some nuts and dried fruits."

"Perfect," I said. I wasn't starved, but I

could nibble.

"Where is that sister of mine?" Lizzie asked.

"Right here!" Tyanne darted into the salon, a thick white album tucked under her arm. "Hi, sugar." She kissed her sister on the cheek.

Lizzie held her at arm's length. "Look at you." She forced Tyanne into a spin. "Honey, you have to start eating. You are way too slim." She pinched her sister's chin with two fingers. "And your eyes?" She clucked her tongue. "Stress lines."

Tyanne pulled away. "I'm working on it."

"Your loved one is gone," Lizzie stated matter-of-factly. "I understand. But, darling, you must reclaim your verve. Tim would be bereft if he knew how you've faded. And what would Mama say?"

Tyanne pulled free of her sister. "Mama would say I'm a grown-up, and I don't need my big sister ordering me about." She brandished a finger. "In fact, I think I'll add that to the book of Mama's sayings I've been putting together." She winked over her shoulder at me, her sense of humor in place. "Mama was one bright cookie."

"Speaking of books" — Lizzie pointed at the album Tyanne was carrying — "what's that?"

"Delilah's choices for the wedding so far."

"Let me see!" Lizzie snatched the album and started flipping through pages as she guided us to the rear of the salon.

I slung an arm around Tyanne's back. "I've missed you at the shop." Occasionally she helped out as a part-timer, but she had begged off lately. "Ready to start up again?" Maybe I could entice Tyanne to take on a full day so I could spend more time with Jordan.

"Sugar, it's wedding season. I doubt I'll have time, but I'll try to fit in an hour or two here and there."

We each took a seat in a spa pedicure station, the kind with footbaths attached and built-in massage rollers in the chair. I tucked my feet into the hot water and let the jets of air knead my feet. Heaven.

Lizzie handed the album back to Tyanne. "Honey, you have outdone yourself. Delilah, I love every bit of it. The red is striking." She sauntered to Delilah and plucked at Delilah's curly locks. "Maybe we should put these unruly things in an updo with cascading tendrils, or leave them down and weave red ribbon through them." Lizzie did all of our hair. She was a wonder. "Are you wearing a veil?"

"I am. A short, flirty one."

"Then an updo is an absolute must. No ribbon. And we'll definitely do a vitamin-rich conditioner." She rubbed Delilah's hair between her fingers. "Your hair is as dry as sandpaper and coming out in hunks. Stress will do that. But we won't think about that tonight." She brushed her hands together. "Y'all have fun. I have other customers to attend to." She blew each of us a kiss and hurried off.

Jacky said, "Let me see the album."

"Uh-uh, me first." I was sitting closest to Tyanne. She passed it over, and I opened to the first page. "Nice." It was a picture of the chapel in the woods with the stained glass panel windows flanking the altar.

Tyanne said, "The red theme will go well with the stained glass, don't you think?"

"Umberto loves it," Delilah said.

"*Umberto?*" I teased.

She shrugged. "He doesn't like me to call him U-ey."

Hmm. Maybe I should use his proper name from this point forward. Would my theories hold more weight if I did?

"We'll have lots of red roses," Tyanne said.

"And don't forget about the red butterflies," Delilah added.

Tyanne wagged her head. "Sugar, I've told you those are really rare in Ohio. We might

331

drum up ten, but we could have tons of black butterflies."

"As if!" Delilah snorted. "Black butterflies at a wedding? A funeral, maybe. Charlotte had blue ones at her wedding."

"Fine." Tyanne grinned. "Red it is, even if I have to import them. Does anybody know if that upsets the ecological balance?"

An employee brought us each a glass of sparkling wine and told us our spa technicians would be with us real soon. Then she set a tray of cheese on a portable table. Just out of reach. Drat. I was hungrier than I realized.

"No Pace Hill Farm Double-cream Gouda?" Jacky said, eyeing the array. "Harrumph."

I said, "I sold out of your cheese today at the store, if that makes you feel better."

"Definitely."

I took a sip of the sparkling wine. Bubbles tickled my nose. "How's it going at the farm, by the way?"

"Exhausting, even with the splendid crew I inherited. The scope of the operation is mind-boggling, but it's all fascinating." Jacky clasped a hank of hair and draped it forward over one shoulder. "Do you know that woman Shayna who's in town for the brain trust? She gave me some tips."

"How did you meet?" I asked. "Did she take a tour of the farm?"

"No, I bumped into her outside Café au Lait. What a sweet gal. She's very knowledgeable. By the way, tell me about that guy, Victor Wolfman."

"Whoa," I said. "That's a big U-turn in the conversation. Why do you want to know about him?"

"I saw him at Café au Lait, too, and out of nowhere, he hit on me. 'Hey, *babe,'* " she said, doing a perfect imitation of Victor.

"Steer clear," I warned.

"Don't worry. I did. Besides, I have my eye on someone new. I don't want to spoil that."

"Who?" Tyanne, Delilah, and I asked in unison.

"Not saying yet." Jacky grinned. "But he's local."

"That handsome art teacher," Tyanne guessed.

"Uh-uh," Delilah chirped. "He's too short and twenty years her senior."

"The new owner of Café au Lait?" I asked. Jacky visited the shop daily. She was a coffee fiend.

Jacky smirked. "I told you, I'm not saying. All in due time. Back to that Victor guy. He can be quite gabby. You know how people talk when they're waiting in line. He must have seen me talking to Shayna minutes before, because out of the blue he launched into the history of Shayna and her partner, Lara, and how Lara's exit from the enterprise bankrupted Shayna."

"I don't think it bankrupted Shayna," I said. "Yes, Lara took half, but, even so, she told me a bit ago that she was doing fine; the farm is thriving."

"That's not what Victor said. He claimed Shayna wasn't out of the red yet."

Had Shayna lied to me? Going into severe debt could give her a strong motive to want Lara dead: *revenge.*

Jacky cocked her head. "Here's what I want to know. Why would Victor tell me, a total stranger, something so intimate?"

Because he wanted to stir the pot so tongues would wag and divert suspicion from himself. His ploy was working.

CHAPTER 24

Climbing into a chilly bed alone that night didn't feel good. Rags, sensing my unease, pounced onto the bed and snuggled into me, but even his sweet kisses didn't help. I wanted Jordan — *his* kisses. I hoped he would be able to fill the position of assistant manager soon. Though I never would have complained about our work schedule conflicts, I was thrilled he had brought it up, and I looked forward to having more time with him. When I finally fell asleep, it was after midnight.

Around two A.M., Jordan slipped under the sheet, and I stirred. I mumbled something.

"Did you say 'babies'?" he asked me.

"Did I?"

"Yes, my love, you did."

"I must have been dreaming about them."

"A good sign." He kissed me gently on the cheek. "We'll work on making one soon."

■ ■ ■ ■

As always, I woke before the sun rose. A feeling of contentment washed over me. I peeked over my shoulder at Jordan — we had slept spoon-style, me tucked into him, all night. "I love you so much," I whispered and quietly slipped from beneath his arm.

I fed Rags, wrote a love note for Jordan, left it on the table with a homemade cinnamon-ginger-cream-cheese breakfast bar, and hurried to work.

Rebecca arrived an hour after me, exactly as I was removing the pine nut–carrot quiches from the oven. She inhaled and said, "Smells divine. What cheese did you use?"

"Kerrygold Dubliner." The cheese was a sweet, nutty, aged cow's milk Cheddar. "I cut a taster slice." I motioned to a plate holding a sizeable portion. "You can have a bite."

"Don't mind if I do." She slung on an apron and helped herself. "Mmm. Yum." She ate another morsel. "Any news?"

"About?"

"The murder. Have you spoken to U-ey?"

"Umberto," I muttered.

"Do I detect a touch of hostility?"

"Delilah says he likes being called Umberto now."

Rebecca jutted her fork at me. "You're not peeved about his name. Tell me what happened."

I hitched a shoulder like a disgruntled teenager. "I never told you, but I saw him at the diner yesterday."

"I figured."

"And he walked out on me."

"Uh-oh."

"It was my fault." It was; I had bungled it. While I organized the quiches on the counter, removed my oven mitts, and strolled to the walk-in refrigerator to fetch some parsley, I filled her in: how I tried to get information about Urso's chat with Ryan; how I spilled the beans about grilling Kandice; how I questioned Urso about the possible use of opiates. "He did reveal that chloroform was used to knock out Lara."

"Which means —"

"Anyone, even Erin, could have overpowered Lara." I described my chat with Shayna and ended by revealing what Victor told Jacky about Shayna.

"Getting revenge for burying someone financially is a powerful motivator, and she told you her argument with Lara was *nothing*? Poppycock." Rebecca eyed the quiche.

"I'm going to polish this off if you don't help."

"Go ahead." My appetite was nonexistent.

She gobbled up the rest and bussed her plate to the sink. "Did you ask U-ey . . . I mean, Umberto . . . whether he figured out how the killer got in?"

"Yep. He still doesn't have a clue. No secret passages. No trapdoors. Shayna said she checked her room for something like that, too, and came up empty."

Rebecca rejoined me at the counter. "Why would she mention that? Was she messing with you?"

"What do you mean?"

"Was she testing you to see if you could figure out how the killer escaped because she, the killer, knew how? You said Andrew keeps chanting: *up, up, up* and *down, down, down.* Maybe he's trying to say there's a secret passageway that abuts his room. You told me his room is right below Lara's."

"But —"

"Who has the rooms on either side?"

"Erin and Kandice, but —"

"Let's say —" Rebecca jutted both index fingers at me. "Stay with me on this. Let's say someone built a phony wall in Kandice's room. I saw that in a TV show. You could figure it out if you measured the rooms. The room will be narrower than the original."

"But Rebec—"

"Let me finish." She used her hands to illustrate. "Shayna somehow discovered the secret passage. Maybe she visited Kandice one night and scoped out the room. Whatever. She sneaked into Kandice's room that particular night, slipped into the passage, and climbed to Lara's room. *Up, up, up.* Maybe the trapdoor in Lara's room is hidden under —"

"No, it's impossible." I held up a finger to quiet her. "I've been trying to tell you . . ." I explained how Deputy O'Shea and the architect had looked for a secret passage and had come up empty.

"Rats." Rebecca smacked her hands together. "At least our illustrious chief of police is on the case."

A flash of blue swept past the front windows. Blue dress, blue tote. "Shayna," I whispered.

"What about her?"

"She's on the sidewalk."

"You should talk to her." Rebecca glanced at the clock on the wall. "We don't open for a bit. Go." She fanned me with both hands. "Ask her about the argument with Lara and the bankruptcy."

"I've tried."

"Try again. Say, 'Hi, Shayna, I know you said the farm was thriving, but how is it doing without you managing it on a daily basis? I know I'd be concerned if I left The Cheese Shop for more than a week.' Yada yada. Wing it."

"Wing it," I echoed.

Rebecca grinned. "C'mon. Do it. Ask her."

I had to admit I wanted answers. Honest answers.

A crisp morning breeze hit me as I exited the shop. I wrapped my arms around me and sped outside. Shayna had disappeared. Where had she gone? I noticed the door to Sew Inspired Quilt Shoppe hung open. I raced to the shop. Shayna stood inside.

Sew Inspired was a great place to roam. I wasn't a dedicated knitter, and I hadn't sewn much since high school, back when I made all my clothing, but seeing and touching the colorful wealth of material, yarn, and thread always stirred my senses.

I slipped inside. My buddy Freckles, dressed in a bright orange frock — orange is her go-to color — waved. I smiled and thumbed that I had come in to chat with Shayna, who had settled into a nook, one of many areas in the store where customers could sit and work on a project. Freckles had fitted some with chairs, others with beanbags. Shayna's tote rested on a polka-dotted armchair. She was rummaging through it, her mass of curls draping her face.

"Cup of tea, Charlotte?" Freckles said, indicating a tea caddy set with pretty china cups and a glass pot of tea sitting on a warming tray. "I'm going to have some. *Brr.*"

"No, thanks." I made a beeline for Shayna. "Hi. Fancy seeing you here. Have you lost something?"

Shayna swept a tress of hair off her face. "My skein of yarn. It's not lost, just stuck. I need to match it. I'm hoping Freckles has something close. I purchased my supplies up north. Voilà!" She presented a mussed ball of blue mohair. A strand trailed into her tote. She struggled to get the rest of her project out. "C'mon," she muttered. "Budge. *Oof.*" The wad, which included knitting needles and the lengthy beginning of what I assumed would become a blanket, popped out.

At the same time, the front door opened and Meredith entered the shop. Slowly.

"What are you doing here?" I called. "You're supposed to be at home. In bed." I started toward her.

Meredith held up a hand to keep me at bay. "Relax. Matthew drove me and

341

dropped me off in front. I can walk fifty paces without collapsing. Promise." She grinned. "I need some inspiration. My knitting is, suffice it to say, a wreck. I want to roam the shop and imagine myself with nimbler fingers. Maybe get a tip or two from Freckles."

She moved to the tea caddy. Freckles hugged her. They chatted and chuckled about something.

Shayna said, "Why do people do that to pregnant women?"

"Do what?"

"Freckles just patted your friend's tummy. Most people wouldn't dare touch a woman's stomach otherwise."

"I imagine they do it to feel like they're in touch with new life." Automatically I petted my abdomen. Would I ever feel a teensy being growing within me? The possibility sent a quiver of excitement through me.

"You're blushing, Charlotte."

"Am I?" Yes, I was. I felt a flush of warmth blossom up my chest to my neck. "Jordan and I talked again about starting a family."

"How exciting, but as I said before, be emotionally prepared. Kids love you" — Shayna brushed her hand over her knitting project; three rows of uneven popcorn stitches — "and leave you."

I heard Rebecca's voice in my head: *Ask her. Wing it.* "Shayna, I know you said things were thriving for your business, but how is everything really? With you gone for an extended time because of . . ." I faltered.

"Lara's murder? The investigation?"

I nodded, thankful for her help. "Are your farm and staff doing okay in your absence?"

Shayna assessed me. Her chest rose and fell with a sigh. "What do you really want to know, Charlotte? I don't mind you grilling me. After all, Chief Urso has asked very incisive questions. None of us staying at the inn has any privacy at this point." She dropped her wad of knitting onto the top of her tote and threw me a tolerant look. "Fire away."

Though I was embarrassed at being caught out, I pressed ahead. "Victor intimated to a friend of mine that your business" — I cleared my throat — "went bankrupt when Lara dissolved the partnership. He suggested that it never recovered and you hold a grudge."

"Ah, Victor. He's wrong. Like I told you at the diner, I'm flush. I have investors. I'm in the black. That Victor —" She huffed and pushed her curly locks over her shoulders. "Yes, it's true, I took a hit after Lara left. I had to refinance. I struggled for a number of years, and yes, before you pursue this thread, I was jealous of her success. How dare she become one of the most renowned voices for cheese in the United States! Sure, she knew a lot of people in the biz when we first met, but she didn't know squat about how to make cheese. I mentored her. I educated her. We became friends. And then . . ." She sighed. "I didn't resent her decision to leave. People make choices. Those choices don't always make others happy. We move on. I did. I'm stronger because of it. Anything else?"

"The argument Lara and you had at lunch on Friday in the breakfast room . . ."

"I told you, it wasn't an argument. It was a conversation."

"Not according to some."

"Who? That waitress with the ponytail?"

I didn't respond; I had no intention of implicating Erin. "Lara said something was your fault. You apologized. Talk to me, Shayna."

She plucked at her unfinished project. "It was personal. Leave it at that. What she said . . . Why I apologized . . ." She blew out a long stream of air. "Lara could be frustrating."

"You were near tears when you walked away."

"Hey." Meredith joined us. "I apologize for interrupting, but look what Freckles gave me." She displayed a knitting how-to booklet. "I'll be an expert in no time."

"Don't count on it," Shayna joked.

Meredith took a gander at Shayna's work. "Are you a newbie, too?"

I appraised Shayna's knitting project and flashed on the alibi she had given Urso. "Shayna, you said on the night Lara was killed that after talking to your daughter you knitted for hours."

Shayna's mouth turned down in an unattractive frown.

"I'm not much of a knitter, mind you," I went on, "but you certainly didn't stitch a lot of rows."

Shayna worked her tongue around the inside of her cheek. "That's because I was also watching a movie."

"Which one?"

Shayna glowered. "*National Treasure: Book of Secrets.* With Nick Cage. Love that guy. Anyway, I got distracted while doing popcorn stitches —"

"I know what those are!" Meredith exclaimed. "They're so hard."

"Yes, they are. About ten rows in, I realized I'd done them all wrong, so I pulled out row after row. I'm such a perfectionist."

Except she wasn't. She told me so at the cocktail party. And the stitches that remained in her work were downright sloppy.

She was lying, but I couldn't challenge her because right then Meredith moaned and clutched her stomach.

CHAPTER 25

"Charlotte, I need Matthew!" Meredith barked. "And I need to lie down. Now! And not in that order."

"Yes, ma'am."

Gingerly I ushered her from Sew Inspired Quilt Shoppe to Fromagerie Bessette and settled her onto the sofa in the office. Rags, the sweet boy, sprang beside her to nurture her. Giggling, Meredith fought off wet kitty kisses while I fetched Matthew, who begged off the rest of the workday and escorted his wife home. She was fine. No worries. But no more overdoing it.

Throughout the afternoon, in between sales, which thanks to the Street Scene soared beyond our expectations, Rebecca asked me to replay my encounter with Shayna. She picked apart every word Shayna said and decided she was *guilty*. Fine and dandy, I told her, but I had nothing I could share with Urso. It was all conjecture.

At dusk, just as I was turning over the *Open* sign to *Closed,* Pépère and Grand-mère arrived. Grandmère bustled to me and opened her arms for a hug. "Ready?" She kissed me on each cheek.

"For . . ."

"Have you forgotten? It is Tuesday evening. The first round of tastings is tonight. You are one of the judges."

The cheese competition. Of course. Yipes! My grandparents and I were to taste this evening's first-round selections of Cheddar cheeses and jettison nine competitors. Tomorrow, my grandparents and a local restaurateur would determine the second-round winner. All of us would judge the two finalists on Friday. A pair of city councilwomen would tally the ballots.

"You have forgotten," Grandmère said. *"Mon dieu."*

"I didn't forget. My days are simply blending together because . . ." I didn't need to finish. My grandparents nodded in understanding: *Lara's murder.* I mustered up a smile. "I'm game."

Rebecca winked. "No rest for the weary. Go. I'll close up."

The cheese competition stage, three times the length of any other stage, was set up near The White Horse. Ten competitors, made up of four large dairy concerns and six artisanal farmsteads including Two Plug Nickels Farm, which was owned by Urso's folks, were vying for the first-round win. Each competitor was stationed at a table with two chairs. Placards describing the cheese tastings stood on each table.

I roamed from one competitor to the next and found myself smiling while reading the various signs:

For a white Cheddar: *Nutty, funky, multifaceted. This cow's milk cheese from Holmes County has a gentle sweetness that shores up the other elements, sort of like Muhammad Ali, anytime other than when he was inside the ropes.*

For a rustic-colored bandaged Cheddar: *The rough-and-tumble Tommy Lee Jones of the cheese world, this Cheddar has a tan, leathery exterior that surrounds a gentle yellow paste.*

For a marbled Cheddar from Wisconsin: *Piano-playing cats. Wrestling puppies. Toddlers dressed in white, yet covered in mud. Do you see where we're going? Too cute for words. Yes, indeedy. This cheese is so cute you'll just want to lap it up.*

As I was polishing off a morsel of the *cute* Cheddar, which had a fine grit that finished with delicious notes of caramel and pecans,

Clair and Amy dashed to the raised stage and yelled my name. I waved. Both waved back. Matthew materialized behind them.

"It's late," I said. "Don't you girls have school tomorrow?"

"Yes," Amy replied, "but Daddy told us we needed to get out of the house."

"Meredith needs some alone time," Clair added.

A pit formed in the hollow of my stomach. I eyed Matthew with concern.

"Don't worry." He smiled tightly. "She's fine. She overdid it earlier."

"You should see Rocket," Amy said. "He's like a nurse."

"You mean a sentry." Clair paced back and forth. "One bark" — she *arf*ed — "means 'I love you, and I'm here for you.' "

"Double-bark" — Amy *yipped* twice — "means 'Get back in bed. Don't move.' "

The girls giggled.

Matthew nudged the twins. "Let's let Aunt Charlotte do her work." He nodded toward the cheese I had just tasted. "Good stuff?"

"Heaven." I wouldn't need dinner after all I had consumed, although a glass of an Italian prosecco would taste great. The White Horse had a terrific selection.

As Matthew and the girls moved on,

Grandmère poked my elbow. "*Chérie,* it's time. This way." She nudged me toward the end of the platform where we would fill out our ballots, rating each cheese maker from one to ten. "Have you selected a winner?"

"I have, but I won't tell you who."

Immediately after I cast my ballot, my grandparents suggested we go to Café au Lait for a coffee. So much for a glass of wine.

The tables outside and inside Café au Lait were filled. At one table, Sylvie sat with her archenemy Prudence Hart. Both were dressed in silver sweaters, and shock of all shocks, they seemed to be enjoying themselves. Had the two dress shop competitors established a truce? Was Sylvie trying to enlist Prudence's help in shutting down the Street Scene? Had she and her lawyer met with my grandmother?

Sylvie wiggled her fingers at me. "Hello, Charlotte . . . Bernadette." The latter she said with a sneer.

"Sylvie," Grandmère muttered with affected sweetness, which I took to mean that she *had* met with Sylvie and the lawyer, and the meeting had gone *her* way.

"Bernadette, a word, please," Prudence said. "Where's my antique?"

I realized I had forgotten to inform my

351

grandmother that Lois had repaired the cheese grater. I whispered the news to my grandmother and said it was resting on the director's chair in my office. She promised to fetch it tomorrow and, ignoring Prudence, prodded my grandfather inside the shop. A bullet train couldn't have fled from view faster.

"Well, I never," Prudence mumbled.

Sylvie harrumphed then tapped my arm. "Charlotte, love, stay a moment. You've got to hear what Pru just told me."

Pru? Only Prudence's closest friends were allowed to call her that.

"She heard Victor and that murder victim" — Sylvie paused for effect — "arguing. Right here. On Friday afternoon."

Join the crowd, I thought. Victor and Lara must not have been very discreet.

"Is that true, Prudence?" I asked.

Even on the best of days, Prudence looked like she had swallowed a lemon. There was tart judgment in her glare. "Yes."

"Just between us girls," Sylvie said, her voice half as loud as normal, "Pru has been spending a lot of time here lately."

Prudence spanked Sylvie's hand playfully. "Shh."

Sylvie swatted her back and continued in a whisper. "She's interested in the new

352

owner. Have you seen him? Quite the looker."

I said, "I thought you had your heart set on Herbert, Prudence." Herbert Hemming, the widowed owner of The Silver Trader, was dapper and well traveled.

Prudence sniffed. "He's fallen for someone else."

Was it Jacky? I wondered. At Tip to Toe Salon, she had been so secretive about her new love interest.

"What does it matter?" Sylvie said. "You know Herbert isn't good enough for you. And William" — she pointed inside Café au Lait — "is."

Inside the café, the new owner, who sort of reminded me of Victor Wolfman with his fake tan and thick mane of dark hair, was strolling between tables, spiritedly greeting customers. I couldn't imagine anyone *less* suited to Prudence.

"He's the right age," Sylvie went on.

"Age isn't everything," I said.

"True, but he's interested in all the same things that Prudence is. Art. Antiques. Books." Sylvie ticked them off on her manicured fingertips.

"I had no idea," I said. "Oh, look, he's heading this way."

Prudence tilted her face to Sylvie for

inspection. "How's my makeup?"

"Perfect."

I had to admit I was astounded by the women's budding friendship. Who'd have *thunk*! "Oh, wait," I said. "He's turning around."

Prudence sank sulkily into her bony frame.

"I've suggested Prudence ask him out," Sylvie said. "What do you think, Charlotte?"

"Why not? It's a brave new world. Say, while you're working up the courage, Prudence, fill me in on what Sylvie mentioned a moment ago. You heard Lara and Victor arguing."

Prudence bobbed her head. "Lara said she wanted him to stop."

"Stop what?"

"I'm not sure. She tried to grab his cell phone."

"Was he texting someone?"

"I assume so, but oh no" — Prudence brandished a finger — "he was having none of her interference. No, siree."

My mind percolated with theories as I replayed Ryan's and Lois's similar accounts. Whoever Victor was texting had mattered to Lara. Why? Did Victor kill Lara to keep his secret hush-hush?

CHAPTER 26

Later that night when Jordan arrived home, I was sound asleep and in no shape to talk about my various theories. I think I mumbled: *Victor's cell phone,* and I was pretty sure Jordan asked what I meant, but I couldn't remember answering.

At six A.M. Wednesday morning, my beloved was in about the same state of deep sleep that I had been in at two. I wrote him a note telling him I would call later, and then I fed Rags and headed to work. A glass of milk and a wedge of yesterday's quiche — there was only one slice left — made for a delicious and filling breakfast.

During the first two hours, I baked the daily quiches and assembled a dozen sandwiches: six on steak rolls using sopressata, chopped olives, and Meadow Creek Dairy's Grayson cheese, a luscious cheese with a reddish-orange rind and a solid earthy nuance, and six on Kaiser rolls pairing the sopressata with a tangy goat cheese.

Close to opening, Rebecca dashed into the shop. She let the door slam shut. "I'm sorry I'm late. I meant to call, but I got all wrapped up, and . . ." She clapped her hands. "Oh, Charlotte, it's so wonderful. It's done!"

"What's done?"

"I'm free! My last bill is paid off. I'm so happy, I want to jump for joy."

"Jump away."

"I did. This morning. On my bed." She spun in a circle and teetered to regain her balance. "I think . . ." She chewed her lip. "I want to go home and tell my father."

"Your father? Why?" She hadn't seen him since he came to town the day after her grandmother passed away. He brought Rebecca her grandmother's shawl. They didn't speak more than a dozen words. He was still upset that she had left the Amish community.

Rebecca said, "I want to brag about how well I'm doing. I know, bragging isn't holy, but Papa thinks I got sucked into the material world, and for a while, I did. Now I'm free. I can rebuild my life, starting with me from the inside out." She mimed unlocking shackles from her wrists. "Nothing has its hold on me. Isn't it wonderful? I want him to be proud. What do you think?"

"Do what feels right."

"I won't be gone for more than a couple of days."

"Take as long as you need."

Another wave of joy bubbled through her. She skipped to the rack near the rear exit to shed her coat and fetch an apron.

The front door opened, and Jordan strolled into the shop looking as handsome as I had ever seen him, casually dressed in a white shirt and jeans, hair tousled, eyes glistening with impish delight. What secret was he hiding? He said, "Are you open?"

"For you, always."

He offered a cockeyed grin, and I went gooey in the middle. How I loved the long dimple that etched his right cheek. I scooted around the counter, enveloped him in my arms, and planted a warm kiss on his lips.

He held me at arm's length. "Good morning to you, too."

"Why are you here?"

"Of all things, I need cheese, and I heard this is the place. Can you help me?"

While I put together a group of three cheeses for his restaurant to use as a dessert selection, including a buttery, peppery stretched-curd cheese called Suffolk Punch from Parish Hill Creamery, Jordan said, "By the way, I told you last night, but you probably don't remember. You were sound asleep. I've got two interviews scheduled this afternoon to hire a second-in-command."

"That's great. Who?"

"Elizabeth Lattimore, for one." Elizabeth was a sizeable woman in her fifties who had lived in Providence her entire life. She knew the restaurant business well, having run her folks' place for the past few years. She sold it a month ago, right after she buried her father.

"Who's the other?"

"Heather Hemming."

A pang of jealousy jolted me. Heather? Sassy, sexy Heather, the silver trader's daughter? All curves and bedroom eyes. Working side by side with Jordan. Holy smoke!

"She's the one I mentioned who has been trying to get ahead at La Bella Ristorante, but —" Jordan halted, a flash of concern in his eyes. "What's wrong?"

"Nothing."

"Liar." Jordan took hold of my hand and said to Rebecca, "Can you manage the shop alone for a sec? Charlotte needs a quick break."

"You got it." She greeted a customer who

was entering.

Jordan led me through the rear door to the town's communal garden that was located in the alley behind the shop, but he didn't stop by the bench in the garden. He guided me to the hothouse at the far end. We entered and he locked the door. "Talk to me."

"About?"

"You're worried."

"What would I be worried about?"

"Heather."

"Heather?" My voice was thin and reedy; I was no actress.

"Charlotte . . ." Jordan tucked a finger under my chin. "Why are you jealous?"

"I'm not . . . Okay, yes, I am and I hate myself for it, but Heather . . ." I pulled away. "She's so . . . Every man in town lusts for her."

Jordan gathered me into his arms. "I'm not every man. No woman, except you, will ever win my heart." He kissed me fully and deeply, for more than a minute. "Now do you believe me?"

"Yes."

He caressed my cheek. "Soon, we'll be spending evenings together again. That's why I'm hiring someone. Remember? And then you and I will have lots of time to work on making a family."

Without another word, he exited the greenhouse, leaving me breathless and fully focused on my age and my health and, well, not much else.

Not until I had returned inside The Cheese Shop did I realize that, swept up in the heat of the moment, I had forgotten to tell Jordan about Shayna or Victor or *anything*. I yanked my cell phone from my trouser pocket and punched in his number; he didn't answer. Rats.

"Charlotte," Rebecca said as she finished up with the customer at the register. "Look who's here."

Urso and O'Shea stood by the counter peering at the contents within. Both had removed their hats. "What's the special today?" Urso asked.

I said, "Two. Both with sopressata." I described the goat cheese I'd used, a Cheddar made by Avalanche Cheese Company, a concern in Paonia, Colorado, run by a former restaurateur who traveled the British Isles to learn the art of cheese making. "It's been aged for about a year, and made like a traditional British Cheddar, only with goats' milk. I've added crushed olives and basil. It's on a Kaiser roll."

I didn't need to describe the other choice.

Urso said, "Two of the goat cheese sand-wiches, please."

Rebecca joined me and whispered, "How do I tell Devon?"

"Tell him what?"

"About wanting to go home to see Papa."

"Are you worried you'll want to move back?"

"Uh-uh. No way."

"Then simply tell him." I nudged her with my hip. "Go outside. Now. To the garden. Talk. Communication is important."

Her cheeks flushed with heat. "Deputy," she said, "got a moment? I'd like to discuss something."

O'Shea turned to his boss for the okay.

Urso nodded. "But be brief. We have interviews to conduct."

Rebecca and O'Shea scooted outside.

"Speaking of interviews, U-ey . . . Umberto," I corrected myself. If Delilah could change her ways, so could I. "Have you met with Victor Wolfman?"

"About?"

"The murder, of course." I wrapped up the pair of sandwiches. "I assume that's what your interviews are about."

He didn't dispute me.

"Did Prudence Hart contact you?" I asked. "She has information about Victor."

"Charlotte, cool it. I'm going to stop coming in here if you grill me every time I do."

"Are you going to avoid me around town, too?" I sassed.

He sighed. "Just once it would be nice if you asked me about my life or the wedding or something other than murder."

I plopped the sandwiches into a bag and added a fork-knife-napkin package with a *thunk*. "How are the wedding plans going?"

"Great."

"How's your health?"

"Excellent."

"Super! We got that out of the way. Look, U-ey . . ." I drew in a breath and let it out. "Umberto, I'm allowed to know what's going on, and —"

"Quigley Pressman thinks he has the scoop," Urso snapped. "Read his byline."

"And" — I stressed the word, ignoring his testy interruption — "I'm allowed to tell you what I know. I hope everyone in Providence would do the same. Good citizenship is vital to the strength of a community."

"Says who?"

"Says my grandmother, the mayor."

I lasered him with a look. He mimicked me. We held the staring contest a full half minute. I know because I counted off the seconds in my head.

"Go on," he said, breaking the stalemate, which meant I won.

"Lara and Victor were overheard arguing. He was texting someone. She warned him to stop."

"Why?"

"I don't know. Maybe she was jealous. It might have been about his business."

"Who heard them?"

"Ryan, Lois, and Prudence."

"I've spoken with Mr. Harris."

"Which means neither Lois or Prudence has touched base with you." So much for good citizenship, I noted. "If you'll permit me . . ."

I motioned for him to take a seat. He settled onto one of the ladder-back chairs at the tasting counter. I perched on the other and fleshed out the sketchy details of each account.

"Disagreeing about the way to handle something is not necessarily a reason for murder," Urso said. "If so, either you or I would be dead." He offered a bordering-on-nasty grin. "But just to set you straight, no matter what the accounts, Victor Wolfman is cleared because he has an alibi for the time of death, which the coroner has set between ten P.M. and midnight."

I gaped. "Are you sure about the time?

363

What about Kandice claiming to hear a violin at eleven thirty?"

Urso clicked his tongue to make a point. "That pretty much limits the murder to a half-hour window, don't you think?"

"Unless the murderer strummed the strings on purpose to set a later time, or plucked the violin accidentally, while escaping."

"Aye, there's the rub. *Escaping.*" He thumped the counter. "In order to escape, one needs to have entered."

"You still haven't figured out how the killer got in or out?"

"Nope." In his tone, I heard a world of weary. "We've been over every inch of wall and floor space."

"Either way, the coroner's finding rules out Erin as a suspect."

"Does it?"

"Yes, because Andrew remembers her being in his room at that time."

"Does he?"

I squirmed. Who knew what Andrew would remember? *Up, up, up; down, down, down. Eleven thirty, eleven forty, two, two, two.* What was he trying to say? That Erin left the room at one or all of those times?

Reluctant to voice what was cycling through my mind, I said, "It eliminates

Ryan as a suspect, I guess. Not only did Rebecca see him in town after eleven, but Kandice heard him returning to the inn after twelve. What is Victor's alibi?"

"Your grandfather saw him in town at eleven fifty-five."

"But Victor said he came back to the inn at eleven thirty."

"He was off by a few minutes. No big deal. What matters is your grandfather came forward with his statement." Urso stood and pulled out a billfold. He ambled to the register to pay for the sandwiches.

I followed and took his cash.

"He, like you" — Urso winked — "is a concerned citizen."

"Pépère's eyesight isn't that good," I argued. "Especially late at night. He could have mistaken Victor for the new owner of Café au Lait, William what's-his-name. They look similar. Their thick dark hair, the way they strut."

Urso pocketed his wallet and wedged his hat onto his head. "Why do you want Victor to be guilty?"

"Because he's a fool."

"Being a fool doesn't make a person a killer. Otherwise —"

I jabbed a finger at him. "Don't say it."

Urso laughed heartily. "Be safe, Charlotte.

And call me U-ey." He strode to the rear door, whipped it open, and bellowed, "Deputy, let's go!"

CHAPTER 27

Hours later while closing up shop, I had a deep aching need to see Jordan. I didn't care if he could chat; I simply wanted to glimpse his face. I took Rags home, donned a peacoat, and walked to The White Horse alone. A crisp breeze made me button my coat. Music pealed through the air. Loads of people were still roaming the Street Scene. I spied Rebecca with Devon lingering by the poetry stage. They waved; I returned the greeting. I caught sight of Delilah and Urso strolling through the north gate of the Village Green. Neither saw me; they were deep in conversation. My grandparents were wrapped up in the second round of the cheese competition. I didn't intrude. Seeing them in their element, surrounded by eager locals and tourists, made me swell with pride.

Near the Free-for-All Stage, where children under sixteen could share any talent

— play an instrument, do a dance, you name it — I bumped into Tyanne and her children.

"Stay with us," Tyanne urged.

Onstage, a bewitching girl about the twins' age was playing an electric violin while singing a hearty bluegrass-style song.

I begged off and headed into The White Horse. The place was packed, the bar area three-people-thick in some spots. The sound of laughter and chatter filled the air. At the far end of the restaurant, two women, one a pianist and the other playing the bass viol, were doing a jazzy rendition of "The Lusty Month of May." I spotted Jordan standing near the kitchen door with his sister. He noticed me and held up his hand, fingers spread. He mouthed: *Five minutes* then mimed to get myself a drink.

At one end of the bar, Victor crowded in beside Ryan, who was paying for drinks. Neither talked to the other. Victor was typing something into his cell phone. Was he texting the person whom Lara and he had argued about?

He's innocent, Charlotte, I reminded myself. Urso confirmed that Victor had an alibi. So why was I itching to find out his secret? I moved in that direction.

"Charlotte!" a woman yelled.

I whirled to my right. Shayna was sitting at one of the bar tables with Erin and Quigley Pressman. Shayna mouthed: *Help!* and singled out Erin.

Poor Erin, I thought. She had gone out on the town for a brief, well-deserved respite, only to get hornswoggled by the wily reporter. If Rebecca were here, she would nab Quigley by the collar and hustle him out of the bar.

I signaled I would join them soon but continued to approach Victor.

Ryan spun around. We collided. Some of the amber liquid in one of the tumblers he was carrying sloshed over the rim. "Sorry," he murmured, his mouth grim, his eyes cloudy with fatigue.

"No worries. None splashed me. Are you okay?"

"Sure. Why wouldn't I be? I'm being held hostage in a small Midwest town, unable to get home. I'm as happy as a clam." He choked out a laugh. "Truth is, Mama's sick. My littlest sister is whining that I'm not there to help. I've called Chief Urso to plead my case. Of course, he's out for the evening. A slug of this" — he hoisted one of the drinks — "will help." He pushed past me to a table where Kandice was sitting. She watched him expectantly.

I caught a flicker of something in Erin's eyes as Ryan settled onto his chair and handed Kandice her drink. Did Erin wish she could change seats with Kandice?

Victor, who reeked of cologne, said over his shoulder to me, "This is taking a while. The two bartenders are overextended."

On occasion, Jordan helped out when the bar was crowded. Whatever Jacky and he were discussing must be urgent.

"Get you something?" Victor set his cell phone on the bar. A text conversation was visible on its screen.

"Sure. Thanks." Yes, my husband generally comps my drinks, but I didn't want to turn down Victor's offer. A guy buying a woman a drink might chat up a storm. My curiosity was stronger than ever. "White wine," I said and inched closer while shrugging out of my coat. "Are you as upset as Ryan about the police demanding you stay in town?"

Victor hitched a shoulder. "What can a guy do? The law is the law."

The bartender — newly hired; I didn't know his name yet — said, "What'll it be?"

While Victor requested three glasses of white Bordeaux, I peeked at his cell phone. The text was innocent enough. From Victor: Where R U now? Response: Getting cotton candy. Victor: Call me. Response: Come outside. Victor: You come in. I couldn't read the respondent's name. The font was too small.

"Got a hot date?" I asked.

Victor glanced between the text readout and me.

I smiled. "You ordered three wines. There are only two of us here. I deduce things."

Victor tilted his head. "I hear you've been asking around about me. It seems you alerted the chief of police that a *source* told *you*" — he stressed the words — "that Lara and I argued."

Urso revealed that to him? Sheesh. On the other hand, it meant he was following up despite the fact that Victor had an alibi. That was something, I guess.

I nodded.

Victor picked up his phone and waggled it at me. "Don't believe everything you hear. Or see, for that matter. Even if it's on a cell phone." He pocketed the device. "Want to know the truth?"

Did I ever!

"Yes, Lara and I argued."

"You were texting someone. She grabbed the phone."

"And she saw: *When can we meet? If he finds out, he'll kill me. Us.*" Victor clicked his

371

tongue. "You can imagine what Lara read into that exchange."

"She thought you were having an affair."

"No, she didn't."

"You told her to butt out."

"To put it mildly."

"You said she wasn't the boss of you."

"Your *source* had pretty good ears."

"You were loud."

Victor snorted. His nostrils flared in an unattractive, piggish way. "You've got half of the conversation right. Here's what went down. See, I was trying to get this woman to help me resolve a dicey issue."

"With?"

"One of my suppliers. A French cheese maker. The woman's boss."

"What was the dicey issue?"

Victor smirked. "Just to be clear, this started out as a prank. All in fun. The supplier is an old friend. He can be a royal pain. He claims his Brie is the best. No one else's can compare. You know the kind of braggart I mean."

I cocked my head. Who was calling the kettle black?

"Now, I am the first to admit that what I did wasn't entirely legit," Victor continued.

"What did you do?"

Victor shifted feet. "I repackaged an

inferior American cheese, a pasteurized Brie, and put his label on it."

I gawped. I knew someone who had done that sort of thing with wine. "That's illegal," I said.

Victor didn't even have the decency to flinch, the slug. "It was just a couple of packages," he said. "And I only shipped to people he and I know. Like I said, I did it in fun, but Lara didn't see it that way. She saw the text exchange. She said putting the ruse in writing meant the executive assistant, if she was a bitter woman and decided to turn the tables —"

"Bitter, why?"

"Because she and I, you know . . ." He chortled. "Hit the hay, as they say. A one-night stand. Anyway, Lara said the woman could publish anything I had written and get me in major hot water. Jail time."

The bartender set out three empty wine-glasses. He poured a swallow into one. Victor took a sip and then indicated the bartender could fill all three glasses.

"I told Lara to back off," Victor went on, "but she pressed the point. A couple of times."

"Did she threaten to expose you?"

"No, she did not. It wasn't that big a deal."

"She said it could cost you 'jail time.' "

"Lara was blowing it way out of proportion. Once she learned I intended to admit everything to my pal, she let it go."

"Just like that?" I snapped my fingers. "Did she give you a deadline, or *else*?"

Something flickered in Victor's eyes. A memory? Lara's last words, pleading for mercy? He quashed whatever was going on inside his brain and held out his cell phone. "Have a look at the conversation. You'll see I'm telling the truth. I showed the police the text exchange, by the way. They copied it, tracked it. Whatever."

I didn't take the cell phone.

Victor hiccupped out a laugh; it sounded forced. "Funny thing about Lara. She could be boorish and in your face, but she had a moral ethic. There was right and there was wrong. You should be punished if you did something wrong. My prank? It didn't warrant her wrath." He paid for the beverages, handed me a glass, and smiled easily, like we were having a good old time. "Mmm," he murmured with his first sip. "This is French. Primarily Sémillon grapes." He took another sip and said, "As for Kandice" — he peered in the direction of Ryan and Kandice; Ryan was doing all the talking; Kandice was smiling — "she didn't get so lucky when it came to Lara's charity."

"What do you mean?"

"Some people think she got fired from her job at the university because she was incompetent."

"Kandice was fired?"

"Yep."

"I heard she quit to start a new career."

"Nope. She was canned. Why? Because Lara let slip to some college bigwig that Kandice was having an affair with a professor."

"Why would Lara do something like that?"

"Like I told you, she had this thing about right and wrong. As fast as you can say *sacked,* Kandice was gone, her career ruined. Can you imagine sticking your nose into someone's life like that?" Victor's nostrils flared. "Lara didn't care. She was righteous and overbearing. Everyone had to fight, even me, to keep on equal footing. If you ask me, the police should take a long hard look at Kandice as the killer."

The door to the restaurant opened. In walked a luscious brunette carrying a cone of pink cotton candy. She was half Victor's age.

Victor cleared his throat. "Forgive me, but my date has arrived."

He skulked toward her like he was on the prowl. She didn't seem to mind. My skin crawled. Truth be told, if Urso hadn't said the guy's alibi was valid, I still would've thought he was guilty.

I turned my attention to Kandice. Why would Lara have stuck her nose into Kandice's business? Did Kandice hold a grudge against Lara? Was I wrong about the two of them working together to steal Erin's violin? Was the violin even an issue in the murder? Maybe Kandice lured Lara to the brain trust with the hope of getting her hands on the violin when all along her goal was to get even with Lara for ending her career.

Jacky joined me at the bar while tucking her long hair behind her ears. "Are you okay? You look lost in thought. Am I interrupting?"

"Heavens no. What were you and Jordan discussing?"

"Cheese, what else? *Affinage,* to be specific. I'm going to hire someone to help me with it at Pace Hill. Jordan could do it all by himself, big strong guy that he is, but I can't. My biceps are killing me, and my knowledge of the process needs honing." She thumbed in the direction of Victor and his date. "You two were quite chatty."

I explained our exchange in brief detail. "He swears he didn't kill Lara."

"I wouldn't be so sure."

"Urso says he has a pat alibi."

"Hmm. Maybe he should reconsider." Jacky opened an application on her phone to reveal an old *New York Times* news article. "I was going to take this to Urso. Have a look. The other day at the salon, you got me thinking about Victor, so I checked him out. Apparently Lara and he were quite the item. Paparazzi followed them wherever they went. To restaurants. To the theater. When she dropped him, the public display made headlines."

"Victor said he ended the relationship."

"He was lying. Lara learned he was stepping out with other women and ditched him over dessert." Jacky scrolled to a picture where Victor threw wine in Lara's face. The caption below told the tale. In all capital letters:

FRANCOPHILE NOT HAPPY AT BEING DUMPED

Jacky grinned. "Guess he wasn't well loved by the press." She stared harder at her cell phone and her eyes widened. "Wow, is that really the time? I've got to go. The babysitter has a final tomorrow." Jacky had the most adorable little girl. She pocketed her cell phone. "Oh, hey, I forgot to tell you. Jordan is going to be another minute. A vendor showed up."

"At this hour?"

"My darling brother wants to add more light in here. I told him he should invest in one of those ceiling windows."

"Do you mean a skylight?"

"That's it." She kissed my cheek and hurried off.

I glanced at the ceiling and the wood-beamed rafters, and a notion struck me: the skylight in Lara's room. Erin claimed all the windows on the attic floor were painted shut, but what if the skylights weren't? Urso said he and his staff had inspected the floors and walls. He didn't mention checking out ceilings or overhead windows.

I flashed on Andrew's haunting chant: *Up, up, up; down, down, down.* Was his hearing so attuned that he figured out the killer had gone *up* over the roof and *down* through the skylight?

Shayna and Erin were still sitting at their table. Quigley Pressman had left. I hurried over. "Erin, I've got a question."

She moaned. "Sorry, Charlotte. I'm interviewed out."

"This won't take long. The windows in the inn. On the third floor. Are they all

378

painted shut?"

"Yes. I told you —"

"What about the skylight in Lara's room?"

Erin's mouth fell open. She swung her head right and left, as if realizing along with me. "The skylights — all the rooms on the attic floor have one — are new. They were the last upgrades my parents made before they died."

"Did you tell the police that?"

"I didn't think —"

"How do you open the skylights? With a pole or something?" I couldn't remember seeing one in Lara's room.

"They are remotely operated." Erin mimed using a hand controller.

Shayna said, "I know what you're thinking, Charlotte, that the killer came in through the door and exited through the skylight, and it's a good theory, but there's no way anyone could have climbed up to it without a ladder. The ceiling is pitched. The window is too high. I don't have a ladder in my room."

My mind whirled with possibilities. Maybe the killer climbed on a chair, scrambled to the top of the armoire, and reached the skylight. No, that couldn't be the case. No one had set a chair near the armoire in Lara's room. The only one I'd noticed had been tucked under the escritoire.

What if the killer scaled the armoire? Victor was fit enough, but his alibi cleared him. Kandice had strong arms. She could probably climb the furniture even with an artificial limb. And what about Shayna? Was she dismissing my theory out of hand to throw me off track?

If the killer exited via the skylight, he . . . or she . . . would have had to descend the side of the inn or across the roof to reenter his or her room. Erin told Urso that some of the windows had been refurbished. Which ones would open and make it easy to reenter a room? Had all the windows on the second floor been upgraded like ours? It might have been easier to drop to the ground and enter through the front or rear door. *Up, up, up,* Andrew had chanted.

A chair scraped a floor; Ryan was rising from the table. I summoned up the conversation I'd overheard between Shayna, Victor, and Ryan in the breakfast room. Ryan said he was a former gymnast. He had competed in the rings, an event that required extreme upper body strength. He could maneuver the climb up the armoire to the skylight without the use of a ladder, but what motive did he have to kill Lara? Prior to the brain trust, he and she had never met. Or had they? Lara had hated him from the get-go. Why?

And what about Erin? Yes, she was my friend, but I needed to remain objective. Did she keep the information about the skylight from the police on purpose? She was teeny, but using hinges on the armoire as footholds, she could have scrabbled to the top of it and gone out through the skylight.

CHAPTER 28

Jordan slipped up behind me and kissed me on the neck. A shiver, the good kind, ran down my spine. "What a nice surprise," he murmured. "I've got two minutes."

I spun around to face him. "I don't. I've got to contact Urso." I explained why and punched Urso's private number into my cell phone. Urso didn't answer my call. I texted him and alerted him to the skylight and remote control. If my theory was correct, the killer would have taken the remote control along. How else would he or she have been able to close the skylight after exiting?

By the time I pocketed my cell phone, Jordan was busy with another restaurant task. I whizzed by him and whispered I would see him at home.

Outside the restaurant, Victor was standing beside a truck, wrapped in a feverish embrace with his young date and kissing her roughly. She pushed him away and made a U-turn. He didn't go after her. He spied me and halted. His face didn't move a muscle. A bad case of the heebie-jeebies shimmied through me. I tamped them down. Victor may be a creep, but he wasn't a killer. He had an alibi, right?

Even so, I kept a brisk clip all the way home.

As I neared my driveway, I heard the rumbling of an engine. An indistinguishable dark-colored sedan was driving toward me without headlights. My breath caught in my chest. The car slowed. I couldn't make out the driver. It was too dark. Suddenly the car picked up speed . . . and the headlights switched on.

"It's official," I muttered. "I'm paranoid." The driver had probably slowed to look for an address. Refusing to act like a damsel in distress and call Jordan, I hustled inside. Once I was standing in the foyer, however, anxiety gripped me full force, and I started to tremble. To shake off the tension, I jogged through the house making sure all the doors and windows were locked, then I nabbed Rags and brought him to bed with me.

An hour later, while reading but not absorbing a mystery, it dawned on me that I hadn't asked Jordan whether he had picked someone to be his second-in-command. I made a mental note to do so when he came home and, yes, I would tell him about the darkened car. He would put my mind at ease. But after I drifted off, both mental notes must have vanished because when Jordan crawled into bed with me, I couldn't remember muttering anything more than *I love you.*

At dawn Thursday, I took a gander in the bathroom mirror. Tossing all night is not good for the complexion. My skin was sallow; the area beneath my eyes, gray and dry. No amount of eye moisturizer would help. Swell.

I kissed my sleeping husband good-bye, dressed in taupe trousers and a peach V-neck sweater, and ate a quickie meal of eggs scrambled with Parmesan cheese, and then I hooked Rags to his leash, and we hurried to work. Routines mattered.

Around eight thirty, Rebecca entered The Cheese Shop, a bounce in her step. While preparing cheese, we discussed her plans to see her father. Devon was excited about the prospect, she told me. He believed in family first. When I asked her about her desire to postpone wedding plans, she said Devon was fine with that, too. He would wait for six months, but then he expected an answer. I was pretty sure she wouldn't wait that long to say *yes.* Devon was a catch.

Close to noon, Rebecca displayed a fistful of circular slogan buttons that read: *Say Cheese!* "Put one on," she said. "Grandmère ordered them to promote the Street Scene."

I obeyed. "When did she stop by?"

"When you were in the office on the telephone with suppliers. She didn't want to disturb you."

Matthew shuffled into the store via the rear entrance, his shirt hanging out on one side of his trousers, his hair scruffy and uncombed. "Morning," he mumbled and let the door slam shut.

"Did you forget to look in a mirror?" I pointed to his shirttail.

He tucked it in. "Guess so."

Worry whooshed through me. "Is Meredith okay?"

"She's fine, but how can I get any rest when she's making sounds like" — Matthew uttered a teensy groan — "and she pets her stomach all the time."

"That's normal."

"Since when are you an expert?" He jabbed an index finger at my abdomen. "Until you have a bun in the oven, you

385

don't know what's *normal.*"

"Touché."

"By the way, if you don't know how to knit, don't take it up after you're pregnant. Meredith and knitting are like oil and water. Who knew she had a mouth like a truck driver?" He slogged into the wine annex.

"Coffee for my cranky cousin," I whispered to Rebecca. "With a dash of cream. Now."

"On it," she chirped and darted away.

The front door flew open and Delilah rushed in. The skirt of her red waitress outfit fluted up. She was carrying a tall to-go cup of a beverage that required a straw. "That man!" She cut around the barrels of wineglasses and platters and made a beeline for me.

"U-ey?" I said, wondering whether he had received my text.

"I adore him," Delilah went on, "but he can drive a girl to drink milkshakes." She jiggled her cup at me. "My second this morning."

"What did he do?"

"Changed up everything for the wedding."

"Without asking you?"

"No, silly, of course he asked me. He was all sugar and spice about it. Would I be comfortable with twice as many people? His mother wants to invite out-of-towners." She took a sip of her shake. "Could I settle for red birds instead of red butterflies? I think Tyanne put him up to that one. She can't get her hands on the darned things." Another sip that elicited a big *slurp.* "Will I be happy if we say *I do* at five P.M. instead of three? His mom, again. I guess she thinks a late-evening supper is more fashionable."

Mrs. Urso, a loveable, squeezable woman, was the last person who would worry about being in vogue. She probably thought a five o'clock dinner offered a wider choice of menu.

Delilah flipped off the top of her milkshake and stirred the contents of her cup with the straw. "What do you think?"

"About?"

"About U-ey sticking his nose into every aspect of the wedding."

"You're back to calling him U-ey, not Umberto?"

"When he's in my face. Yes."

"I think it shows he cares."

"He does, but he's driving me crazy."

"Not a far drive," I teased.

The telephone at the rear of the shop jangled. Rebecca answered and said, "Charlotte, for you! It's the chief."

Delilah whispered, "Do you think he

knows I'm here?"

"Doubtful."

"Take this." She thrust the rest of her milkshake at me. "Don't let me have another, or I won't fit into my wedding dress." She dashed toward the exit. "And don't tell U-ey I was carping about him," she yelled over her shoulder. "I adore him."

I mimed locking my lips — her secret was safe — and raced to the telephone. "What's up?"

Urso said, "Didn't you see my text message response?"

"My cell phone is in the office."

"Thank you."

"For?"

"The tip. I'm red-faced to say it, but my team and I were lax. We never checked out the skylights at the inn. When Erin said . . ." He hesitated. "It doesn't matter what she said. We assumed, and you know what that makes us." He let out a low, self-deprecating laugh. "As it turns out, the skylights open easily and silently. We found evidence of rope fibers on the inside of the skylight in Lara's room."

"Meaning the killer could have come and gone through the skylight. No need to be let in by Lara."

Urso hummed his agreement.

"Did you find the rope?" I asked.

"For all we know, the killer tossed it into a lake."

"Or down the well," I suggested. "Except you already dredged that."

"And get this," Urso continued. "We found minuscule rope fibers in Victor's room. We also found the skylight remote control tucked between his mattress and box springs. We've taken him into custody."

"You told me he had an alibi, verified by my grandfather."

"That's the other thing. Your grandfather rescinded his testimony this morning. He said his eyesight isn't so good at night. He could have been mistaken about seeing Victor." Urso cleared his throat. "Did you coach him?"

"No. I —"

"Well, Victor is behind bars. You can relax now." Urso ended the conversation.

I stared at the telephone.

Rebecca sidled up to me. "What was that about?"

I filled her in.

"I told you." She toyed with a tress at the nape of her neck. "I never liked that Victor guy. *Babe,*" she uttered in Victor's sleazy way. "He made me uncomfortable."

"Me, too." I considered Victor's motive,

stronger now in light of the evidence. What if his swapping-cheese prank wasn't as innocent as he made out? The memory of Victor staring at me outside The White Horse made me shudder. Had he heard me talking to Erin about the skylights? Was he the one who had driven past me in the dark-colored sedan? Had he thought about harming me and then reconsidered?

"Case solved," Rebecca chimed. "Finding the remote control was a coup."

"Yes," I murmured. Or was it too easy? If Victor had ditched the rope, why wouldn't he have gotten rid of the remote control? Simple. Because he had intended to put it back in Lara's room when the body was found. Wait. How did he get the remote control in the first place? Lara must have left her room unlocked.

An image of Erin ducking under Ryan's arm to get into Lara's room popped into my mind. Erin had known about the skylight access. If she was the killer — *if* — she could have intended to replace the remote control in Lara's room, but when she couldn't, she hid it in the next nearest place: Victor's room.

A cluster of customers entered the shop all at once. The first needed a platter of cheese for a Street Scene crew, *pronto*. The second ordered a basket for an aunt who broke her leg. The third was shopping for a wedding gift and begged for our recommendation. Rebecca and I kept busy, nonstop, for over an hour.

When the activity died down, I concentrated on Erin again. I hated to think she was guilty, but I couldn't let friendship impede my judgment.

CHAPTER 29

Desperate to get answers, I drove to Emerald Pastures Farm. A number of cars were parked in the lot by the inn. Quigley Pressman's black smart car was among them. The guy was relentless, but I had to admit I was glad he was around if, indeed, Erin was the killer.

A tiny voice in my head shouted: *It's not her; you know it's not!*

I found Quigley and Erin sitting in the living room. Quigley was nestled on the pillow-packed sofa. Erin sat stiffly in a chair, her face gray, eyes lackluster, hair lank. Snowball had positioned himself at her feet like a protective sphinx.

"Charlotte." Erin offered a weak smile. "I'll be right with you. I hope."

Quigley grinned. "Just a couple more questions."

"That's what you said thirty minutes ago," Erin sniped.

The sounds of uneven footsteps and a clatter of wheels made me turn. Kandice, dressed in atypical black, her bleached hair devoid of colorful streaks, was lugging a large suitcase down the stairs. Her face was splotchy and eyes puffy, as though she had been sobbing all night. She was favoring her artificial leg.

"Are you crying about Victor?" I asked.

"Heavens no. If he killed Lara, he deserves to go to prison."

"Then what's wrong?"

Kandice grumbled. "I'm furious at Ryan. I thought I was going to get lucky last night, but he ditched me. I tried to slough it off, but obviously I can't. I'm so stupid. To think . . ." She cursed softly.

"Let me help you with your luggage." I extended a hand.

"I've got this." She did. Her biceps bulged with power. "Only two more pieces to go." She grunted. "Why can't I learn to pack lightly?"

Bad me, but I was suddenly wondering whether she had tucked a coil of rope into one of her suitcases.

"Down, down, down," a man said from above. Andrew materialized at the top of the stairs. In the low light, he looked hulking and ominous. He started to descend while tapping a pair of drumsticks. "Up, up, up."

Kandice said, "Stop it, Andrew."

But he didn't. He continued his chant: *down . . . up.* Kandice huffed and departed through the front door.

Andrew stopped next to me in the foyer. "Cheese."

"Hi, Andrew," I said.

"Cheese," he repeated, while staring at the button pinned on my sweater.

I smiled and said, "Cheese."

We went on like that for a few seconds, exchanging pleasant *cheese*s. I knew he wouldn't stop until I removed the button. When I did, he resumed his *up* or *down* chanting and headed into the living room. I followed him.

"No, Andrew, sweetheart," Erin said. "Not in here. I'm answering questions."

Quigley slung an arm over the back of the couch. "Say, can I ask Andrew —"

"Uh-uh." Erin bounded from her chair. "We're done. You don't get to question my brother. Only the police may."

"And did they?"

Erin's eyes blinked rapidly. "C'mon, Andrew, sweetheart. Let's take a walk. Good-bye, Mr. Pressman."

"I told you, call me Quigley."

"Good-bye." Erin ushered Andrew, all six-feet-plus of him, out of the living room, into the foyer. Snowball padded behind them. Erin waited for the reporter to exit — Snowball, the self-appointed guardian, followed Quigley out while nipping at his heels — then Erin slammed the front door and started for the stairs.

"Erin." I stopped her by touching her shoulder.

Andrew clacked the drumsticks together. "Up, up, up."

"In a sec, sweetheart," Erin said. "Yes, Charlotte? Why have you dropped by? Did you forget something in your room? I can ask the housekeeper —"

"I wanted to chat for a few minutes."

"About?"

I couldn't launch into an accusation right off the bat, could I? She looked so defenseless. I said, "Um, you must be happy the police arrested Victor."

"Thrilled." Her voice was flat, emotionless.

"Up, up, up," Andrew intoned.

"Charlotte, I have to go. My brother wants to go to his room."

"Down, down, down."

Hmm. That didn't sound like Andrew wanted to go upstairs. I said, "Did you ever figure out why Andrew is chanting those words?"

"No."

"What about his references to the numbers eleven thirty or eleven forty or two?"

Erin shook her head.

"Did the police question him?"

"What does it matter? They have Victor in custody. Lara's murder is solved. When all the guests leave, everything around here will get back to normal." Erin shuddered, probably realizing that the word *normal* would never apply to her brother or her life. She rotated her head to loosen knots in her neck. "I don't mean to be rude, Charlotte, but I need to get Andrew fed and settled so I can rest."

"I —"

The front door opened and Kandice entered.

Andrew very animatedly said, "Up, up, up!" He clicked his sticks at Kandice.

I eyed her. "Do you know what he's talking about, Kandice?"

"As *if.*" She marched up the stairs and disappeared from sight.

"Hungry," Andrew murmured.

Erin said, "All right, sweetheart. Let's get some food before we head upstairs." She directed her brother toward the kitchen.

"You're welcome to join us, Charlotte."

I started to follow but stopped when Ryan called to me from inside the breakfast room.

"Hey, Charlotte, did you hear about Victor?" He was sitting at a table by the window. Sunlight poured through the window and lit up his face. A glass of iced tea sat untouched in front of him. He was reading a book. Not just any book. Lara's book. He slapped the book closed, rose to his feet, and gestured to the table.

I murmured to Erin that I would catch up with her and moved toward Ryan.

"Great news, isn't it? We can finally put this puppy to bed," Ryan said. "I never did trust that guy, though I have to admit it surprised me. I didn't think old Vic had it in him. From all I could tell, he was smitten with Lara. What are you doing here?"

"I came to talk to Erin, but she's busy with Andrew."

"Sit." Ryan placed a hand on my back to assist me onto the bench opposite him then retook his seat. "If you're hungry, the housekeeper's around."

"I'm not."

"I hear she's a good cook. Ah, there she is."

An elderly, compact woman with wispy hair entered the room whistling. "Hiya, hon.

How about some tea? Hot or cold." She had a subdued Minnesota accent bordering on Canadian. "And a sandwich."

"Nothing, thanks."

She *tsk*ed. "Do you good. You're a tad on the thin side."

I wasn't, but relative to her I was. "Really. I'm fine."

She muttered, "Girls these days," and shambled out of the room while resuming her tune.

I regarded Lara's book and glanced at Ryan.

"Yeah, you caught me." Ryan grinned and, using his index finger, twirled the book on the table. "Call me crazy, but I couldn't resist. She really was knowledgeable. However, if you ask me, she was also certifiable. Have you read her acknowledgments?"

I hadn't.

"Usually the author puts extensive acknowledgments in a book," Ryan explained, "to recognize the people who have helped with research or support. Not Lara. One paragraph." He flipped open to that page to show me. "After that, she made it sound like she did it all herself. No mention of Shayna or anybody."

"You didn't like her."

Ryan shrugged. "Not because she attacked

me, but because she was affected and phony, caring for no one but herself. She ended the partnership with Shayna and left the business floundering. How many others did she hurt along the way?" He slugged down some iced tea and smacked his lips. "Speaking of Shayna, I guess it's okay for me to say this now, seeing as Victor is in custody. You might already know. She lied about her alibi."

"How do you know?"

"Because I spotted her from my window, sneaking into the inn at two A.M."

Two, two, two gonged in my head.

"I nearly missed seeing her. She was wearing all black like a jewel thief."

I thought of the silly movie-title game we had played at the cooking class last Sunday when all of us girls had gone gaga over Cary Grant, master jewel thief, handsome in black. A few moments ago, Andrew had grown agitated seeing Kandice all in black. Had he also seen Shayna at two A.M. on the night Lara was killed? Was that what he had been trying to chant-tell Erin? Did he believe the woman in black had something to do with Lara's murder?

"I told Shayna I spotted her," Ryan continued. "She begged me not to tell anyone."

"Where did she go?"

"She wouldn't say."

"For a walk?"

"I don't have a clue."

"You never told the police?"

"Why would I? Lara was killed before midnight."

"We didn't know that right away."

"No, but it was Shayna. I mean, c'mon, *Shayna.*"

I got it. He, like I at first, didn't believe she was capable of murder.

My cell phone buzzed in my pocket. "Excuse me." I pulled it free. *Jordan.* I pressed ACCEPT. "Hey."

"Where are you?"

"At Emerald Pastures Inn. Why?"

"Victor Wolfman" — Jordan sounded in a hurry — "has been released. A witness has come forward. A female, a very *young* female, claimed she spent the night with Victor the night Lara was killed. She was with Victor in his room at the inn all night. They were, in her words, 'Quite active.' She left via the back stairs before dawn. She didn't come forward before now because if her family found out —"

I didn't hear anything else Jordan said because with Victor exonerated, other scenarios, all involving Shayna, were cycling rapid-fire through my brain. Did Andrew

400

see or hear her go to the rooftop after eleven P.M.? Did he hear her leave the inn a bit after that? And did he see her return after two A.M.?

Where had she gone, to bury the chloroform and any other evidence of the crime?

CHAPTER 30

A desire to revisit Lara's room zipped through me. Maybe, standing inside the room, I would remember seeing a victorious smile on Shayna's lips or recall her glancing at the skylight.

I left Ryan to his reading and stole past the living room. The housekeeper stood within, whistling while fluffing the couch pillows. Eluding the woman's notice, I hurried to the third floor. The door to Lara's room, although damaged from Jordan's powerful kicks, had been rehung on its hinges. The crime scene tape had been removed. I slipped in and shut the door.

Standing just inside the doorway, I took in the room. It had been tidied. The pillows, both regular and decorative, had been returned to their rightful places on the bed. The armoire doors were closed, the chair pushed under the escritoire. The food and wine had been removed. Lara's discarded clothing had been taken — confiscated, I would assume, to test for evidence. Her suitcase was gone as well.

The police had found rope fibers on the inside rim of the skylight, which meant Lara's assailant hadn't needed an invitation to enter the room. Perhaps the killer slipped in after Lara fell asleep. Why use chloroform? To ensure she was unconscious and couldn't put up a fight. Would Victor or Ryan have needed to dose her with a potion? Either man would have been strong enough to pin down a sleeping, drunk woman. I didn't consider myself sexist, but chloroform seemed like something a female — Shayna or Kandice or, yes, even Erin — might use to get the upper hand.

Returning my focus to the bed, I edged closer and imagined Lara lying there. I pictured when Deputy O'Shea lifted hair samples off the bed. Strands of red and white hair. The white most likely belonged to the cat. The red could have been Lara's, but then shouldn't it have been on or near the head of the bed? No, not necessarily. I often found my loose hair around my house in places with no rhyme or reason, possibly tracked there by my shoes or by Rags.

Another image flickered in my mind. What if the killer planted the red hair on Lara's bed to implicate Erin? During the cheese-making session at the brain trust, each of us had been required to wear a hairnet. We discarded them in the trash on the way out. Kandice, who lost an earring, went back to the trash and scrounged through the garbage. Did she deliberately lose the earring so she could pluck a red hair from Erin's hairnet to place at the murder scene?

I readjusted my thinking. What if Shayna or Ryan had wanted to link Erin to the crime? Each had helped Kandice search for her earring in the garbage bin. Ryan was the one who found it.

And what about the dratted violin? Did it matter in the big scheme of things?

The door to Lara's room flew open. I whipped around.

Ryan stood in the doorway, backlit by the light in the hallway. "What are you doing here?" he demanded.

Alarm cut through me. I was alone. At the murder scene. With what could only be described as a fierce-looking man blocking my exit. His hands were flexing and closing. His hair . . .

I hesitated. Was it Ryan's pewter-colored hair and not the cat's hair that the deputy had found on Lara's bed? No, his was more silver than white. Kandice's bleached hair would have been a better match.

"What are you doing here?" Ryan repeated, an edge to his voice.

I was trapped. The window was painted shut. There was no escape other than through the skylight, which was *up, up, up.* My adrenaline spiked. *The best defense is a good offense,* my grandfather often told me.

I squared my shoulders and said, "I should ask you the same thing, Ryan."

"I was in my room and heard footsteps overhead. I thought Shayna had come back. I'm heading out. I wanted to say good-bye."

"Oh. Of course." His explanation sounded reasonable. Shayna's room was next door. I felt my cheeks warm. Maybe the edge I'd picked up in Ryan's voice was his fear of *me.*

"Did you find something?" he asked.

"I was —"

Ryan waved a hand. "You don't have to answer. I think we all suffer from morbid curiosity. I often returned to the barn where my dad died."

"You were fourteen, is that right?"

"Good memory."

"How did he die?"

"Let's just say it wasn't pretty."

"Ryan —" I thought again of the encounter between Andrew and Kandice on the stairs. Why had Andrew been so upset at the sight of her? Was Kandice the killer and not Shayna? "Did you happen to see Kandice enter Victor's room after the murder?"

"Can't say as I did. Why?"

"I was thinking it was mighty convenient finding the skylight remote control hidden in his room. Kandice was hanging outside his room after we discovered Lara dead. On the other hand, why would she implicate Victor? Why not point the finger at Erin, as she had all along?"

"You know, you're right." Ryan shifted his weight. "However, Shayna would have had an easier shot at planting it than Kandice, if that's what you're intimating, her room being on this floor."

A door slammed. A woman whistled. The housekeeper. She made quite a clatter as she descended the stairs.

Ryan glimpsed his watch. "Whoa! I've got to get going. I promised to do a gig with a band at the Street Scene, then I'm hitting the road. Nice knowing you." He exited and took the stairs two at a time.

I followed. On the second-floor landing, I spied the housekeeper entering Andrew's room. She was carrying a small bucket. Cleaning supplies poked out the top. Out of

406

nowhere, Snowball hurtled down the hall-way. He came to a screeching halt outside Andrew's room. The housekeeper said, "Uh-uh, you snip. Don't even think about it. Private. Keep out! P-r-i-v-a-t-e," she spelled. "Do you hear me? Scat! Shoo!" The cat scampered off, and the housekeeper slipped inside the room.

As she disappeared, the door to Erin's room opened. Kandice backed out. She tried to close the door quietly.

"Hey," I said. "What were you doing in there?"

Kandice whipped around, hand to her chest. Her face flushed a splotchy scarlet. "I . . . I . . ." She was about as deft with a comeback as I was. "I wanted to touch the violin."

"I don't believe you."

"It's true. I have an eye for fine things. Lara —"

"Liar. You've had it in for Erin from the beginning. You heard Victor was released. You thought you could plant something in Erin's room to convince the police she's the killer."

"No!" Kandice swallowed hard. "I would never —"

"You held a grudge against Lara."

"No, I didn't."

407

"She got you fired from your job at the university. Lara revealed to your superior that you were having an affair. You hated her for doing that."

"You've got it all wrong." Kandice's shoulders sagged; she sank into herself. "I was thankful. Lara saved me. From myself." She spoke in choppy gasps; her face grew splotchy. "Lara helped me get out of a toxic relationship. The professor was married. But I was in *love.* I believed . . . what every woman believes . . . that he would leave his wife for me. Yes, Lara changed the course of my life, but I will be forever grateful to her. I love what I'm doing. I never would have found the courage to move on. She wouldn't let me have a pity party, either." Kandice rubbed her thumb and forefinger together, as if playing the world's tiniest violin.

The image caught me up short. "Kandice, wait." I held up a hand. "What were you going to say about Lara earlier, in regard to the violin?"

"Lara wanted it something fierce."

"Why?"

"During dinner, when she said she collected a few things, *that* was an understatement. She owns . . . *owned* . . . all sorts of antiques. She told you about the Degas and Miró. She didn't mention the Archipenko sculpture or the Picasso. And books. She had a ton of them, all exquisite first-editions."

"Did you see these treasures?"

"Yes."

"She collected cheese-related antiques, like you."

"Like me? Ha!" She barked out a laugh. "Not on my modest salary. I admire from afar."

"Did Lara collect instruments?"

"A few. A harp from India. A piccolo from the Civil War. When she saw the picture of Erin with the violin —"

"What picture? Where?"

"On the Internet. In an article about autism. Lara stumbled upon it because she was reading up on her nephew. She knew instantly what Erin possessed." Kandice fluttered her fingers. "Anyway, Lara begged me to find out if Erin still owned the violin. The timing couldn't have worked out better. I saw Providence was having its first annual Cheese Festival. I brought the idea of a brain trust to Erin. Under the guise of seeking out locales for the event, I stayed at Emerald Pastures Inn, and as luck would have it, I heard Erin playing the violin that night."

"You followed her back to her room," I

said, reiterating the scenario I had come up with while talking to Jordan. "You hung outside in the hallway and heard her opening the armoire."

"Wrong. I *saw* her. She left the door open a crack."

"You reported back to Lara, who encouraged you to seal the deal on the brain trust, setting it at Emerald Pastures even though it wasn't a top-tier farm."

"Now you understand why I couldn't admit I knew about the violin's existence. The police would have thought I killed Lara."

I squinted one eye. "So you accused Erin and brought up the bit about the violin to implicate her."

Kandice didn't deny it.

"Did you or Lara steal the violin?" I asked.

"Lara."

"Who returned it to Erin's room?"

"I haven't the foggiest. I never touched it."

"Never?"

"Didn't you hear me? That's why I came here —" Kandice hitched her head in the direction of Erin's room. "To touch it. Lara told me at the Street Scene, after the accident when that tree clobbered me, that she'd taken it." She screwed up her mouth.

"Hey, maybe Shayna put it back. Lara and she were arguing Friday. In the breakfast room. And Shayna said" — Kandice glanced both directions; the hallway was clear — " 'Thanks to social media, you can't hide it forever.' Don't you see? *It* meant the violin."

"You were standing clear across the room. How did you hear that?"

"Elephant ears." She tugged on her right ear. "What if Shayna was warning Lara someone would find out about the theft and post it on the Internet? Lara said something more."

"What?"

"I missed it."

"You heard everything else."

"Not that." She frowned. "But whatever she said must have been cruel. Shayna looked really upset." Kandice ducked past me and darted down the stairs.

CHAPTER 31

Shayna, I thought. Did she kill Lara out of revenge and then return the violin to Erin as a final *gotcha,* knowing Lara had stolen it? Or was Kandice lying?

No longer needing to see Erin or Andrew — I was certain she was innocent and positive I had figured out what his chanting signified — I headed back to town with the plan to pick up Rags and track down Urso.

Navigating the various Street Scene stages was a challenge. It was dusk, that time of day when it was harder to see. Streetlamps didn't quite do the trick, and visitors were everywhere. The sights and sounds were great.

At stage fifteen, one of the cooks from The Country Kitchen acted as barker, encouraging people to learn how to make the perfect grilled cheese.

On stage eleven, three characters dressed up to look like wedges of cheese were chanting cheese poetry while doing a soft-shoe routine. Audience members clapped in time.

On stage seventeen, Ryan, who had made it back to town before me, was perched on a chair, playing guitar with a four-man band. He looked wrapped up in the tune, his chin tucked, his fingers moving rapidly. Victor stood among the spectators typing a text message on his cell phone. He didn't seem overjoyed with his release from jail. Rather, he appeared menacing. His jaw was ticking with tension; his eyes were steely. Maybe he was concocting a new prank or contacting another date that was barely of age. *Whatever,* as Rebecca would say. He had been exonerated. I moved on.

Nearby at the History of Cheese venue, audience members were roaring with laughter. I watched one vignette, where men and women in funny hats and robes entered and exited, some uttering one or two lines while others mimed their responses. The experience reminded me of a spoof Grandmère had staged at Providence Playhouse a few years ago called *The Complete History of America (Abridged)* by the Reduced Shakespeare Company. Although there was truth in the telling, silly fun was had by all. Me, included.

Drawing nearer to Fromagerie Bessette,

my stomach made a horrid noise. I rerouted to The Country Kitchen diner. I craved a cheeseburger, one of the diner's specialties. I would order one to go.

I perched on a stool at the counter and ordered from the ponytailed twin waitress who had helped out at Emerald Pastures Inn. Delilah, who was bustling from booth to booth, waved *hello.*

Beyond her, I caught sight of Shayna, also nestled at the counter. Her tote bag and a wad of knitting rested on the stool beside her. She was scrolling through something on her cell phone.

Before contacting Urso and making a fool of myself, I felt the urgent need to ask Shayna where she had gone that night. Here. In public. Where it was safe. She had lied about her alibi. Why not admit to the police that she left the inn and returned at two A.M.? What was the big secret? I also wanted to hear from her lips what Lara and she had argued about. Kandice's and Erin's hearsay accounts weren't satisfying me.

The stool on the other side of Shayna was free. I sat down. She regarded me icily.

"Have you tried the burgers?" I asked. "They're incredible."

"I ordered chicken soup." Shayna pushed

her cell phone aside. "My stomach is a little raw."

"You haven't gotten much farther on your knitting project."

"I was in Sew Inspired a few minutes ago, asking Freckles for advice. She said to toss it and start over." Shayna offered a weak smile. *"C'est la vie."*

The waitress set a bowl of steaming soup in front of Shayna. "Super hot," she warned. "Want a glass of water, Charlotte?"

I signaled *no* and kept my focus on Shayna.

"Did you hear?" Shayna said. "They nabbed Victor. He killed Lara."

"Actually, he's been released already. He's not guilty. He has a solid alibi. A young lady came forward — a very young lady — who said she was with him the whole night."

"How like Victor." Shayna inserted her spoon into the soup and stirred. "Do the police have another suspect? Are they going to rescind our right to leave town?" She lifted a spoonful of soup. Steam rose in waves. She blew on it, dumped the bite back in the bowl, and resumed stirring. Each movement seemed deliberate and thoughtful. Was she trying to figure out what she would say to the police if questioned again?

"I'm not sure."

The waitress returned with my burger packed in a to-go box. I set a twenty-dollar bill on the counter and told her to keep the change.

Shayna eyed the to-go box. "Did you sit by me to ply me for more information, Charlotte? Don't answer. I know you did." She sighed. "I thought we were friends, but I can't figure out who my friends are anymore."

"You and Lara had a complicated relationship."

"Yes, we did."

"I asked you before about the argument the two of you had during the break on Friday. You said it was nothing, but a source overheard you discussing social media."

"So?" Shayna folded her arms and glared at me. "I'm always in the market to grow my business. Lara had the inside track."

"The source said you warned Lara that she couldn't hide something any longer. Were you referring to the violin?"

"What? The violin? No. And your *source* heard wrong. It was the other way around. Lara said those words to me. She —" Two deep-set lines formed between Shayna's eyebrows. She tried to erase them with her fingertips. "It doesn't matter what she said. 'Forgive and forget.' That's my motto. I've spent a lot of years in therapy to learn that. 'God, grant me the serenity to accept the things I cannot change.' "

An *aha* moment struck me. I pictured Shayna holding a glass of sparkling water; Shayna eyeing a wine bottle; Shayna not sipping any wine. "Are you a recovering alcoholic?"

Shayna flinched but didn't respond. She ate a big bite of her soup.

"The Serenity Prayer," I went on. "You know it."

"Lots of people do."

"Where did you go the night Lara died?" I blurted.

"Huh?"

"Ryan saw you entering the inn at two A.M. You were dressed in black, like you had gone someplace incognito. You asked him not to tell anyone that you went out."

"Ryan . . . He . . ." She heaved a sigh. "All right, yes, if you must know, I went to an AA meeting."

"After midnight?"

"Even in little old Providence they have those. They're really, really private. Satisfied?" Shayna plunked her spoon into the bowl. "Do you want the truth, the *whole* truth, Charlotte? Lara's outburst at dinner made me want a drink so badly I

417

couldn't . . . breathe. She was being miserable to everyone. To me. To Erin. But when she attacked Erin's brother, I thought I'd get sick. She has a nasty streak, and it was out of control. I sat in my room and knitted and watched TV until I was nauseous. I had to get out. Get some air. Get some support."

"Earlier, before dinner, it made you angry when she removed the wine bottle from your hands, didn't it?"

"Angry. No, she was doing me a favor. She took it and whispered for me to be brave."

"Brave?"

"I wasn't brave years ago. It was why she ended the partnership. She said she couldn't stand by and watch me make a mess of my life. She worried that I would run the business into the ground with all the mistakes I was making. She said I would destroy my family. She refused to stick around and watch. The day she left . . . I was angry. Red-hot angry. The next day, I was devastated, and I quit drinking. Cold turkey." Shayna took a big slug of her ice water and *clack*ed the glass down. "It took a long time to repair the damage I caused with my girls, but I did. I thank Lara for that. In the end, she really was a friend."

"Will someone come forward to say you were at the meeting?"

"What does it matter? It took place after the time frame for Lara's murder, and what do you not understand about AA being anonymous, Charlotte?"

I shifted on my chair. "Where did you attend the meeting?"

"I repeat, what does it matter?"

"Because if you're telling the truth about one thing, I'd like to think you're telling the truth about everything. There's only one gathering after midnight in Providence. I happen to know where it's held because a friend who works late hours is an alcoholic."

Shayna sighed. "It was at a red house on Hope Street, beyond the hardware store. Happy?"

I was. She was telling the truth.

"For the record, Lara didn't want me to hide my sickness any longer. 'Come clean after all these years,' she said. If it was out in the open, no one on social media could *out* me." She paid for her soup, gathered her knitting, said, "Take care," and left.

I remained on the stool mulling over the facts. If Shayna and Victor were in the clear, and Erin was innocent — I truly believed she was — then that left Kandice and Ryan as suspects. Kandice swore she was forever grateful to Lara for turning her life around; she never would have hurt her.

How about Ryan? The other day Rebecca asked me if he was too good to be true. Maybe he was. He was the one, after all, who had made me think Shayna was guilty.

CHAPTER 32

Thinking of Rebecca and how I'd suggested she do her due diligence on Devon made me realize it was time for me to do the same for Ryan Harris.

I raced back to Fromagerie Bessette. The lights in the main shop were off. Rebecca was gone. Rags stirred when I entered the office. I switched on the light, set my to-go cheeseburger to the side, and clicked ENTER on my computer keyboard. The screen came to life.

Rags climbed into my lap and tramped in a circle. The pressure of his paws activated my cell phone; it glowed in my pocket.

"Off, Ragsie," I cooed, but he wouldn't budge. "Fine, settle down." When he did, he peered up at me and made a *mrr* sound, asking me if everything was all right. I said, "No, it's not." Rags gave me a questioning look. "Ryan Harris. You don't know him." Did I? Only a day ago, I believed he was the kind of guy who could love Erin and help with her challenged brother. Was I wrong?

I typed Ryan's name into a Google search. A number of listings emerged, some with middle names, some with middle initials. Ryan Harris, no middle name or initial, had a website, a couple of social media sites, and plenty of images of him roaming farms, standing behind lecterns on daises, and shaking hands with well-known people. I clicked on his website, which not only provided information about his consulting services but featured his latest book. A visitor to the website could read the first chapter, review the table of contents, and order the book.

On the *About Ryan* page, the biography was five times longer than the one he had provided for the brain trust brochure. The first paragraph recapped what I already knew: Ryan was divorced with three children; he resided in Texas; prior to that, he had lived in Wisconsin; he taught farm owners how to manage their operations for maximum growth and income.

I read on. Sprinkled throughout the bio, he had included pictures of his mother, sisters, and him on their family farm, and of the grown-up clan, many with children, at a Christmas reunion. There were pictures of an incredibly serious high school–aged Ryan with his gymnastics team, as well as individual pictures of Ryan while performing on the rings. There was a younger picture of Ryan merrily climbing a rope hanging from a tree. Not proof positive that he was the killer who had entered Lara's room via the skylight, I told myself. Lots of people climbed ropes. I had loved doing so as a girl.

The subtitles beneath the family pictures named each of the members. The one beneath the team picture stated Ryan and his teammates went to regionals and then nationals. Two of the team members, including Ryan, had been Olympic hopefuls.

The caption beneath a picture of Ryan from the back doing an Iron Cross on the rings, a task that required him to support himself with both arms shooting straight out from his shoulders, legs hanging straight down, said he had excelled at the move. Something in the photo made me pause. The last name; it appeared to be shorter than Harris. I zoomed in. The name on Ryan's shirt read: *Yeats.*

When and why did he change his surname? I skimmed the biography and learned his mother's maiden name was Harris. Ryan must have changed his name after his father died. I read further in his biography, but I couldn't find the reason for the switch.

In the search engine line, I quickly typed in *Ryan Yeats* and added a caret symbol > and the word *father.*

Up popped an article about Samuel Yeats titled "What Would You Do?" Eighteen years ago, the Yeats Family Farm suffered a setback — it went bankrupt. Thrown into despair, Samuel Yeats drank . . . and drank. One night, he went into the family barn and hanged himself. Ryan, at the vulnerable age of fourteen, found his father's body the next morning.

My insides snagged. My throat grew tight. Ryan had told me that finding his father wasn't pretty.

According to the article, the day after his father's funeral, Ryan put aside his dreams of becoming an Olympic athlete. He performed odd jobs while learning the art of farming. He was, after all, the eldest child and only son.

Something niggled at the back of my brain. Ryan had mentioned that a number of Lara's reviews had ruined small farms. Did she destroy his family's farm? The night Lara antagonized everyone — the night she was killed — Ryan said to her, in defense of Shayna, that a farm is a family's lifeblood.

He accused her of having no regard for anyone. Had he really been referring to his own farm . . . his own family?

I searched Samuel Yeats's name in regard to Lara. Indeed, the Yeats Family Farm was one of many that went belly up after one of Lara's critical reviews. Samuel put the farm up for sale, but no one would touch it. I stopped scrolling. I could guess the rest.

Ryan had acted as though he had never met Lara, but he had met her, as a teen; it had been she who hadn't recognized him. I doubted Ryan came to the brain trust expecting to see her. Kandice hadn't included her on the roster. She was a surprise attendant. However, when he saw her that first night and she subsequently harassed him at the Street Scene, old memories must have surfaced.

Did Ryan return to his room that night and plot how he would kill her so no one would suspect? How had he known the skylights weren't sealed shut? Maybe Erin had taken him on a tour of the inn and described, in detail, her renovation plans. The first morning of the brain trust, Ryan had skipped breakfast and arrived late at the cheese facility. Had he been busy testing out his plan? Did he, like a jewel thief, climb to the roof and steal across to the skylight above Lara's room? Did he test opening it with the remote control he swiped? If it worked, then all he had to do was find some rope.

I had to tell Urso my findings. Unable to reach my cell phone with Rags nestled in my lap, I picked up the receiver to the landline telephone and dialed the precinct. The clerk answered. I asked for the chief. She said he was tending to a three-car pileup in the north part of town. Cow's fault, she added. She asked if my issue was urgent. I said it was. I was at The Cheese Shop. I needed him to call me ASAP; it was about Ryan Harris.

When I cradled the receiver, Rags wakened. His ears perked. He twisted his head toward the door.

"What is it, fella?" I whispered.

A floorboard squeaked. Someone was in the shop. Rebecca would have called out; my grandparents, too.

Rapid footsteps. The door to the office burst open. It slammed into the wall. Ryan stood beneath the arch, his face dripping with perspiration, his eyes merciless.

Butterflies — no, *hornets* — took flight in my gut. Stinging, zapping. There was no way for me to escape. No windows, no skylight. I wouldn't get past Ryan.

"Is your set over?" I asked, the tension in my voice even shriller than yesterday when I had pretended to my husband that I wasn't jealous about Heather. How petty that all seemed right now.

"Don't play stupid," Ryan said. "You know why I'm here."

"Let's talk." *Talk?* Honestly. Since when had I become a therapist? Since when did I know how to negotiate? I set Rags on the floor and said, "Go!" But he wasn't listening. His ears were laid back, his face jutting forward, his tail at attention. He snarled and charged Ryan.

In one swift move, Ryan nabbed Rags and tossed him out of the office. On all fours. Ryan closed the door and locked it. Rags yowled with anger.

The pitiful sound drove me to distraction. I needed to focus. I tamped down my fear and glared at Ryan. "How did you know I was here?"

"I planted a bug on you."

Embarrassment coursed through me. "In the breakfast room earlier today," I said. "When you helped me to the bench."

He nodded.

If only I had been more alert. Rebecca said Ryan had worked at a spy store. He'd sold mostly nanny cams. "You carry bugs around with you?"

"I like to be prepared."

"Why me?"

"At The White Horse, you were poking your nose where it didn't belong. At the inn, too, when you were having lunch with Erin."

Fear zinged through me. "You. You did it. You hurled the rotten wood railing at me."

"Yup. Missed."

"You could have hurt Erin."

"I'll admit I wasn't thinking straight. I thought a scare would frighten you off."

"Did you cause the ficus tree to fall on Kandice?"

"Now, why would I do that? That was a pure accident."

"You followed me home from The White Horse Inn in the dark sedan."

He grunted.

"When I showed up at the inn today —"

"I knew you were snooping again. I had to control the situation."

"You followed me to Lara's room."

"If that darned housekeeper hadn't shown up . . ." Ryan inched forward, his teeth bared.

Keep him talking rang out in my head. Urso would learn that I had reported in. When he returned my call and I didn't answer the phone, he would check up on me. Or would he? He was upset with me for prying into his investigation. If only I had touched base with Jordan.

Up, up, up chimed in my head.

"Andrew heard you," I said.

"Heard me what?"

"You came back to the inn before midnight the night Lara died. You went up to the roof at eleven thirty. You went down at eleven forty-five. He heard you."

"He heard something. He can't confirm it was me."

"Later, after you killed Lara, you sneaked out and entered through the front door so someone — Kandice — would hear you come in after midnight. Clever."

He grinned.

"Your father hanged himself," I said, trying a different approach. "I'm sorry for your loss."

"No loss. Dad was weak. He caved." Ryan grasped a pillow off one of the director's chairs positioned along the wall. Did he intend to smother me like he had Lara? Had he brought a dose of chloroform to facilitate the process?

I wouldn't succumb easily. I would fight. But I needed a weapon. The computer was too unwieldy to hurl. Same with the chair. The blotter and pen set were useless. So was the cheeseburger in its to-go box.

Think, Charlotte. You've taken defense classes. What's your move? I'm nimble. If Ryan came at me, I could duck past him. Open the door. Pick up Rags . . .

Not a chance. Ryan would nail me from behind.

I said, "You blamed your father for destroying your family, didn't you, Ryan?"

"Darned right I did. He left us. Mom and six girls."

"And you with no future, no Olympics."

Ryan sneered. "If only he had manned up. But he couldn't. Mom was all-forgiving."

"You took your mother's name."

"It was her family that started the farm. She let my dad rename it as her fifteenth wedding gift to him."

"And then Lara Berry came calling."

"Lara." He snarled her name.

"Did your father do something to incur her wrath?"

"Dad had a mouth. He spouted off sometimes. He talked to reporters. He —" Ryan rubbed his forehead hard, like he was suffering a severe migraine. "I. Don't. Know."

"What did Lara do?"

"She took a tour of the farm. Told Dad and Mom she loved the place, the lying phony. Then she wrote a bad review. She said our product was inferior. She sent out notices to cheese shops and suppliers. Dad fought her. He got the newspaper involved. He hired an attorney."

"That doesn't sound like he was weak."

"He waited six months to start the process. Too late. By then, our business had soured."

Rags scratched the door. Ryan swung around and hissed. During the distraction, I glanced left: notepads, pens, a digital calculator about three ounces in weight. Nothing hefty.

"Your mother advised you to 'take it in stride,' Ryan. Did she mean your father's death?"

"Everything: death, life, success, loss."

"She also said, 'Let bygones be.' She didn't want you dwelling on the past."

Ryan's face twisted with pain. "Good old Mom. All she ever dreamed about was making cheese. Our cheese. The family cheese. History, she said, mattered."

History. I looked to my right. The antique wrought iron cheese grater that Lois had repaired was still sitting in the director's chair where I'd left it. Grandmère hadn't picked it up yet. Would it work as a weapon? It was about sixteen inches long and as heavy as a mallet. If I swung with both hands and caught Ryan on the arm or shoulder, maybe that would give me time to run. Get Rags. Flee.

I inched from behind the desk. Toward the enemy. I had to risk it. "You hated Lara Berry for destroying your family. No matter how angry you were at your father, she —"

"Was the devil!" Spittle flew from Ryan's mouth.

"You followed her career. You patterned yours after hers. Except you tried to use your power for good."

"I wanted people to have faith. To grow their businesses. To thrive."

"What about your kids, Ryan? What will they do when they find out their father is a murderer?"

Ryan halted. His gaze flickered. Hadn't he considered the repercussion of his actions? "Cut it out! Don't mind-game me." He massaged his neck again.

"Tell me about the violin, Ryan," I asked. Anything to keep him from attacking me.

"The violin?"

"I figure Erin told you about it while you were jamming at the Street Scene. You didn't know it was valuable, of course, because she didn't have a clue, but when you saw it in Lara's room, you realized its worth."

"How could Erin not know?" he whispered.

"It enraged you when you realized Lara intended to hurt Erin, someone you loved."

"Liked."

Semantics, I noted. I flashed on the crime scene; the bed; Lara's robe. The belt had been missing. "You tied the violin to your body using the belt from Lara's robe. You accidentally plucked the instrument as you exited."

His eyelids blinked rapidly.

"You escaped through the skylight and scaled the building to Erin's room. You climbed in her window. It isn't sealed shut. Andrew heard you. Her room is right next to his." *Down, down, down.* "You replaced the violin in Erin's armoire. How did you know about the key?"

"Child's play. One of my kids tapes her diary key to the back of her dresser."

"You didn't consider that when the police found the violin in its rightful place, it would implicate Erin in Lara's murder."

Ryan moaned. "I didn't mean to."

"Of course you didn't. You're one of the good guys, Ryan." I inched toward the director's chair. "You know what confuses me, though? Why did you put the skylight remote control in Victor's room? Why not toss it?"

Ryan's mouth drew up on one side, forming into a malicious grin.

"Aha," I whispered. "You *meant* to finger him. You didn't like Victor because —" I pictured Ryan playing chess with Victor in the living room. It had been a heated game. Later, Erin revealed that Ryan's youngest sister had dated Victor for a nanosecond. "Because Victor jerked your sister around."

"He's a sleaze. But enough about that. We're done chatting." He charged me.

I lunged for the cheese grater. Wielding it like a mace, I swung upward. I missed his bicep. He swiped at me with a massive arm. I ducked.

"You have nothing!" he bellowed. "No evidence."

"Yes, I do." I recalled two conversations with Rebecca. The first, when she said her hair was multicolored, not just one shade; Ryan's silver could contain some white strands. "White hairs were found on Lara's bed," I rasped and swung the cheese grater again. Toward his torso. Missed.

"Big deal."

The second conversation involved Ryan specifically. "The hair will be hard to explain away if any matches your DNA. Yours will reveal the vitamin B-12 deficiency."

434

"Why would the police think to compare hair?"

"Because I'll tell them to do so."

I swung a third time. Ryan seized the head of the cheese grater. Twisted. In defense class, I'd been taught to give up my purse if an attacker came at me. *Release and run.*

I let go of the cheese grater. Ryan careened backward. He stumbled against the director's chair. I swooped at him and kicked the foot of the chair. The chair crashed to the ground. Ryan went with it.

Heaving with exertion, I dashed out of the office and scooped up Rags while pulling my cell phone from my pocket. I dialed 911 and hustled for the exit. "Pick up, pick up," I chanted.

At the same time, Urso rushed into the shop through the front door. Ryan must have left it open. He grabbed me by the shoulders. "Charlotte, what's going on?"

"Ryan Harris." I gulped in air. "In my office."

Urso drew his revolver and barreled headlong down the hall.

CHAPTER 33

On Saturday night, we convened at my grandparents' house.

"Charlotte," my grandmother said. "You and Jordan tend to the roast." She had called the family together to celebrate the end of the Cheese Festival. She jiggled a finger. "Matthew, uncork the wine. Etienne, Clair, and Amy, come with me." She clasped Pépère's arm and whisked him out of the kitchen into the dining room. The twins, each carrying a condiment, trotted behind them.

The entire family, other than Meredith, was at the house. Urso, Delilah, Rebecca, and Devon were joining us as well.

The cheese competition had gone off without a hitch. The finalists had included Two Plug Nickels Farm and the maker of the *cute* Cheddar from Wisconsin. As much as I had liked the cute one, I had to admit Urso's parents had done a bang-up job with their new clothbound Cheddar. It was nutty and savory with a hint of honey. Heavenly. The grand prize was a trip to England to see how original Cheddar cheese was made. The Ursos hadn't traveled anywhere, ever. They were over the moon.

Jordan fetched the carving knife and faced the roast that had been sitting on the cutting board for nearly fifteen minutes. He twisted the board until the roast was at the proper angle, and then he made his first cut. "How are you holding up?"

"Me? Great. Never better."

Okay, yes, all day yesterday and most of today, I got a case of the shivers whenever I replayed the encounter with Ryan Harris. Urso took him into custody, and before leaving Fromagerie Bessette, read me the riot act. I argued that I hadn't baited Ryan; I had no idea he was the killer until I researched him online. Urso, the big mean bear, grumbled and roared, but in the end, he forgave me. He, more than almost anyone other than Jordan, understands my dedication to friends and family. Within hours, Urso informed Kandice, Victor, and Shayna that they were free to go. The three of them couldn't get out of town fast enough.

"I feel badly for Ryan's family," I murmured.

Jordan nodded. "Like the families of all murderers, they will have to cope."

I shot him a wry look. "Pragmatism doesn't suit you."

"Sure it does. Always has." He pecked me on the cheek. "Any worries about my decision?"

"To hire Elizabeth Lattimore? I'm thrilled." Heather Hemming had decided to keep her job at La Bella Ristorante. At some point, she hoped Luigi would retire and she could buy the place. Her daddy was a rich man. Elizabeth had been so eager to get going that she had shadowed Jordan all day yesterday and today at The White Horse and offered to take on the place tonight so he could be with family.

While I tended to the salad and side dishes, Jordan set slices of the roast on a serving dish preset with parsley and orange wedges.

He said, "I heard Quigley Pressman got the exclusive with Ryan."

"Yep. He'll be hard to live with." I grinned. "By the way, did you hear about Erin?" Friday morning, she had left me a message. She was tearful — she had truly hoped Ryan was the man for her — but she was thankful that the nightmare had come to an end. "Some of the townspeople, folks who went

438

to high school with her, have come together to help her raise money to update the farm. They don't want her to sell the Amati violin."

"You're kidding."

"There are good people in this world, my love. As for other news, her brother stopped chanting *up* and *down* the moment Urso told Erin about Ryan. Erin thinks Andrew sensed Ryan was the killer, but he couldn't get the words out."

The door to the kitchen opened. Matthew poked his head in. "Almost ready?"

"Yes." I handed him a dish filled with Dauphinoise potatoes, one of my all-time favorite recipes, a luscious mixture of Gruyère cheese, crème fraîche, and onions. "Take this to the table. Send the girls in for the salad." I had shredded Emerald Pastures Cheddar on top of chopped fresh vegetables, which we had gathered from my grandmother's garden.

Grandmère said *Grace* before we started the meal, we all said *Amen,* and then she addressed Matthew. "How is Meredith holding up?"

His mouth quirked up one side. "She's still grumpy, but she's happier now that the baby is kicking."

"What?" Delilah and I said in unison.

"Isn't it too soon?"

"Nope, right on target," Matthew said. "The doctor set the conception date as the end of January when Meredith and I went on that two-day —"

"Too much information!" Amy and Clair chimed, both forming their hands in a capital T.

Everyone at the table laughed.

Grandmère held up a hand. "Umberto and Delilah, do you have an official date?"

Urso slung an arm over the top of Delilah's chair. "You tell them."

"I love a man who defers to me."

"Only on occasion." He winked.

"The first Saturday in September," she said. "And there will be no red butterflies." She batted her eyelashes at her intended. "Who says I'm not flexible?"

"Not I," Urso replied.

She elbowed him.

I glanced at Rebecca, who hadn't eaten a bite of food. "How are you holding up? How are the travel plans?"

"Good. My father wrote back and said it was okay to come home." She gulped. "I'm so nervous." She clutched her sweet deputy's hand. "Devon is driving me up. He said he would stay in his car until midnight, just in case I need a ride back. But I'm sure I'll be fine. I'm a big girl now. A grown-up."

"Says who?" Devon teased.

Rebecca thumped him on the arm. "I do, and when I get back to town, you and I are setting a date!" She eyed me and said, "Since we're all on the hot seat, how about you?"

"Huh?"

"You look sort of . . . colorful." She fluttered her fingertips next to her cheeks. "Got news to share?"

"News?"

"Are you and Jordan, you know . . ." She pointed at my belly.

I gawped and turned to Jordan. His face flushed with happiness.

"Are we?" he asked.

I grinned. "Yes." I had visited the doctor yesterday for a check-up. Just as we arrived at my grandparents' house, I noticed a voicemail from him. *Surprise!* I was going to tell Jordan the news later, in private. "We're having twins, which means now, more than ever, I have to find a few more people to help out at Fromagerie Bessette. I am going to take some time off!"

RECIPES

ZUCCHINI WITH CHEDDAR KEBAB APPETIZER
À la Emerald Pastures Inn
(SERVES 4)

1 pound medium or small zucchini
1 lime or lemon
Salt and pepper to taste, about 1/2 teaspoon each
3 tablespoons extra virgin olive oil
2 teaspoons dried bouquet garni or basil
4 ounces white Cheddar cheese

Slice the zucchini squash lengthwise, about 1/2-inch thick, and then slice into bite-sized pieces, about 3/4-inch wide.

Mix together the juice of one lime (or lemon), salt and pepper, olive oil, and seasonings. Toss with the zucchini bites. Cover and refrigerate for four to six hours.

Remove from the refrigerator.

On a cutting board, cube the Cheddar

cheese. Pin a cube of Cheddar onto a piece of zucchini using a toothpick.

Serve as an appetizer or put 5–6 on a plate to serve as a salad.

[Note from Erin: These morsels are so easy to make. When my brother, Andrew, was little, he liked to help my mother and me in the kitchen. He couldn't concentrate for long periods of time. A more complicated recipe would have stymied him, but he liked to chop things, and he liked to poke the toothpicks into the cheese. He prefers white cheeses, which is why we went with the white Cheddar.]

BLT SALAD
À la Emerald Pastures Inn
(SERVES 2)

1 head iceberg lettuce
2 tomatoes, diced
4 green onions, diced
2 stalks of celery, diced
4 strips of center-cut bacon, cooked and crumbled
1/2 pound turkey breast, cubed
1/4 cup blue cheese dressing, (page 446)
2 ounces of blue cheese, crumbled

To assemble the salad, set out two plates. Chop the lettuce into 1″–2″ pieces. Split the lettuce between two plates and arrange, mounding slightly in the center.

Dice the tomatoes; set aside. Dice the green onions; set aside. Dice the celery; set aside. *Note:* if your celery seems limp, you can refresh it in a bowl of ice water.

Cook the bacon until really crisp, let cool, then crumble and set aside. You can cook it either of two ways. Traditionally, you can sauté it in a pan on medium high for 8–10 minutes until crisp, then drain off the fat and place the bacon on paper towels to cool, OR you can place a large paper towel on a dinner-sized plate, set the slices of bacon on the paper towel, cover with another paper towel, and cook in the microwave on high for 3–4 minutes until crisp. Let cool, then remove the paper towels, crumble the bacon, and set aside.

Cube the turkey breast. I use fresh-cooked turkey, which has been cooled overnight in the refrigerator, but you can use a deli turkey that is low in sodium and gluten-free. Your choice. *Note:* To cook a small turkey breast, wrap the breast in foil and cook in the oven at 300 degrees Fahrenheit for 40 minutes. Remove from the oven, and remove the foil. Let the turkey breast cool on a cutting board. Wrap in fresh foil or in a resealable plastic bag and keep in the refrigerator until needed.

Now, to arrange all the items on top of the lettuce. Pick a pattern. I like to imagine wedges of a pizza. Set out a wedge of turkey, then tomatoes, then green onions, then turkey, celery, and bacon.

In the center, place 2 tablespoons of blue cheese dressing (recipe below), and top with a few pieces of crumbled blue cheese.

Serve cold.

BLUE CHEESE DRESSING

1/4 cup cider vinegar
1/4 cup olive oil
4 ounces sour cream
2–3 ounces blue cheese
1–2 shakes Tabasco
5 grinds of a peppermill

Put all the ingredients into a blender. Whir. Serve over a crisp salad of your choice.

[Note from Erin: This salad was one of my parents' favorite salads. We often use vegetables grown in the garden on the farm. My mother always said to use a cow's milk Roquefort for the best "kick." I like to use Cowgirl Creamery Point Reyes blue cheese. It's without a doubt one of the best around.]

GRILLED CHEESE, APPLES & ONIONS
(PER EACH SERVING)

2 slices of bread, your choice

2 tablespoons butter

1–2 tablespoons cream cheese

1 tablespoon spicy mustard

1/4 Granny Smith green apple, peeled (4–6 slices)

1–2 tablespoons chopped red onions

2 ounces (approximately 6–8 thin slices) white Cheddar cheese

Butter each slice of bread on one side. Spread the cream cheese on the other side of the bread.

Spread mustard on the cream cheese.

To assemble: Now comes the tricky part. In order to construct this without everything falling out, it is easier if you set one of the pieces of bread, butter side down, on the grill (whether stovetop or panini maker — see below). Then top with apples, onions, and cheese. Top with the other piece of bread. Okay, proceed . . .

If cooking on a stovetop: Heat a large skillet over medium heat for about 2 minutes. Set the sandwich on the skillet (as instructed above) and cook for 4 minutes, until golden brown. Flip the sandwich, using a spatula, and cook another 2–4 minutes. You can compress the sandwich with the spatula. Turn the sandwich one more time. Press down with the spatula, and remove from the pan. Let cool about 2–3 minutes, and serve.

If cooking on a panini or sandwich maker: Set the sandwich on the griddle (construct as mentioned above) and then slowly lower the top. Cook for a total of 4 minutes. Remove from the griddle and let cool 2–3 minutes, then serve. Beware, the inside ingredients might ooze out the sides. If the lid is too heavy, you might want to consider resorting to the stovetop method.

[Note from Charlotte: I was introduced to this grilled cheese sandwich while at the brain trust event. I mentioned it to Delilah, and now it is a regular offering on the Country Kitchen menu. The mustard and red onion makes the sandwich so savory. The apple pops with a delicious sweetness. Enjoy!]

PENNE WITH
TOMATO-VODKA-CREAM SAUCE
À la Jordan
(SERVES 6)
2 cloves garlic, minced
1/2 teaspoon paprika

2 tablespoons extra-virgin olive oil

1 28-ounce can mini-diced tomatoes

3 tablespoons vodka (*I use Grey Goose)

1/3 cup freshly grated Parmigiano Reggiano

1/3 cup chopped fresh parsley

1/3 cup heavy cream

2 teaspoons kosher salt

1 teaspoon freshly ground black pepper (10 grinds of peppermill)

12 ounces penne, raw (about 4 cups cooked)

Extra Parmigiano Reggiano for garnish

Extra parsley for garnish

Bring a large pot of water to boil.

Meanwhile, in a large saucepan over medium-high heat, sauté the garlic and paprika in the extra-virgin olive oil until the garlic sizzles, about 30 seconds. Add the tomatoes (including the juices) and the vodka. Bring to a boil.

Reduce the heat to a simmer, cover with a lid tilted slightly, or use a screen top so extra moisture escapes, and cook to reduce the sauce, about 10–15 minutes.

Remove from heat. Stir in the grated Parmigiano Reggiano, parsley, cream, salt, and pepper. Simmer to integrate the cream, and reduce the sauce a bit more, about 5 minutes. Reduce the heat to low and keep warm.

Meanwhile, make the pasta according to package directions. Rinse in a colander with warm water.

To serve, divide pasta among four to six bowls. Top with sauce and extra Parmigiano Reggiano, plus a sprig of parsley.

Serve warm.

[Note from Jordan: This is my mom's recipe. She wasn't Italian, but when she was a girl, she fell in love with Italian food. As a teenager, she apprenticed in an authentic Italian restaurant. Later, she taught everything she learned to me. At The White Horse, I want to share these flavors with my customers. I'll still give them what they expected from Timothy O'Shea and his terrific pub menu, but I hope to open their eyes and hearts to new food experiences.]

BACON OLIVE CHEDDAR QUICHE
(SERVES 6)

4–6 slices bacon, cooked and crumbled
1 1/2 cups whipping cream
1/2 cup milk
4 eggs, slightly beaten
1/4 teaspoon salt
1/4 teaspoon white or black pepper
1/4 pound Cheddar cheese, shredded (about 2 cups)

2 tablespoons chopped green onions

10–12 black or Greek olives, pitted and sliced in half

1 9-inch pie shell, baked (*see below) and cooled

Preheat oven to 375 degrees F.

Pre-cook bacon. I like to microwave for no mess. To do so, on a plate, set a large piece of paper towel. Place 4–6 strips of bacon on top. Cover with another paper towel. Microwave on high for 3–4 minutes until very crisp. Let cool, then crumble into small bits. Set aside.

In a saucepan, heat cream and milk on medium-high for about 1 minute. Remove from heat.

In a bowl, whisk the eggs and seasonings. Add the eggs slowly to the hot cream and milk, stirring constantly. Stir in the shredded Cheddar cheese, crumbled bacon, chopped green onions, and sliced olives.

Pour the mixture into an unbaked pastry shell. Bake for 30–35 minutes, until the custard is golden and set. It shouldn't "jiggle."

[Note from Charlotte: If you'd like this recipe to be gluten-free, all you have to do is switch out the pie shell. The ingredients are gluten-

free. I've found some great frozen gluten-free pie shells at the store. Here are two recipes, below: one for regular pastry dough; the other for gluten-free pastry dough.]

Pastry Dough for Quiche
(MAKES 1 PIE SHELL)
1 1/4 cups sifted flour
1 teaspoon salt
1/2 teaspoon white pepper
6 tablespoons butter or shortening
2–3 tablespoons water

Put flour, salt, and white pepper into food processor fitted with a blade. Cut in 3 tablespoons of butter or shortening and pulse for 30 seconds. Cut in another 3 tablespoons of butter or shortening. Pulse again for 30 seconds. Sprinkle with 2–3 tablespoons water and pulse a third time, for 30 seconds.

Remove the dough from the food processor and form into a ball using your hands. Wrap with wax paper or Saran wrap. Chill the dough for 30 minutes.

Heat your oven to 400 degrees F.

Remove the dough from the refrigerator and remove the covering. Place a large piece of parchment paper on a countertop. Place the dough on top of the parchment paper.

If desired, cover with another large piece o
parchment paper. This prevents the dough
from sticking to the rolling pin. Roll out
dough so it is 1/4-inch thick and large
enough to fit into an 8-inch pie pan, with at
least a 1/2-inch hang over the edge.

Remove the top parchment paper. Place
the pie tin upside down on the dough. Flip
the dough and pie tin. Remove the parchment paper. Press the dough into the pie
tin. Crimp the edges.

Bake the pastry shell for 5–10 minutes
until lightly brown. Remove from the oven
and let cool.

GLUTEN-FREE PASTRY DOUGH RECIPE
(MAKES 1 PIE SHELL)

1 1/4 cup sifted gluten-free flour (* I use a
combination sweet rice flour and tapioca
starch; you can use store-bought like
Bob's Red Mill or King Arthur gluten-
free flour)
1/2 teaspoon xanthan gum
1 teaspoon salt
1/2 teaspoon white pepper
6 tablespoons butter or shortening
2–3 tablespoons water

Put gluten-free flour, xanthan gum, salt, and

453

e pepper into food processor fitted with
blade. Cut in 3 tablespoons of butter or
shortening and pulse for 30 seconds. Cut in
another 3 tablespoons of butter or shortening. Pulse again for 30 seconds. Sprinkle
with 2–3 tablespoons water and pulse a
third time, for 30 seconds.

Remove the dough from the food processor and form into a ball using your hands.
Wrap with wax paper or Saran wrap. Chill
the dough for 30 minutes.

Heat your oven to 400 degrees F.

Remove the dough from the refrigerator
and remove the covering. Place a large piece
of parchment paper on a countertop. Place
the dough on top of the parchment paper.
If desired, cover with another large piece of
parchment paper. This prevents the dough
from sticking to the rolling pin. Roll out
dough so it is 1/4-inch thick and large
enough to fit into an 8-inch pie pan, with at
least a 1/2-inch hang over the edge.

Remove the top parchment paper. Place
the pie tin upside down on the dough. Flip
the dough and pie tin. Remove the parchment paper. Press the dough into the pie
tin. Crimp the edges. [Note: Gluten-free
dough, unlike regular dough, has a tendency
to break. Don't worry. Use a little water and
with your fingertips press back together.

Nobody will see the bottom of the quiche.]

Bake the pastry shell for 5–10 minutes until lightly brown. Remove from the oven and let cool.

PINE NUT CARROT QUICHE
(SERVES 6)

1 frozen 9-inch ready-made pie shell (regular or gluten-free)
2 cups shredded carrots
1 1/2 tablespoons olive oil
1 teaspoon garlic powder (if you prefer, you can use 2 cloves real garlic, chopped finely)
1 teaspoon salt
1/4 teaspoon white pepper
1 teaspoon dried sage or 1 tablespoon fresh sage, chopped
1/2 cup pine nuts, toasted
1 cup Cheddar cheese, grated
1/4 cup Parmesan cheese, grated
1 cup milk
2 large eggs

Preheat the oven to 350°F.

Remove pie shell from the freezer and thaw for ten minutes. Prick the bottom with a fork and bake for 7–10 minutes, until lightly browned.

Remove crust from the oven to cool.

Peel the carrots and chop finely, or if you have a Cuisinart or food processor, peel and chop the carrots, and then add to the Cuisinart and shred. So easy!

Heat olive oil in a sauté pan on medium-high. Reduce heat to medium. Add garlic powder (or garlic cloves, chopped), chopped carrots, salt, white pepper, and sage.

Cook, stirring constantly, for about 1 minute. Stir in pine nuts.

In a small bowl, mix Cheddar and Parmesan cheeses. In another bowl, whisk milk and eggs together.

Sprinkle 1/4 cup of the cheese mixture on the cooled piecrust. Top with half of the carrot–pine nut mixture. Add 1/2 cup cheese mixture and then remaining carrot mixture. Top with remaining 1/2 cup cheese mixture.

Don't worry — I didn't forget the milk mixture.

First, place the pie pan on a sheet pan. Carefully pour in the milk mixture.

Bake for 40 minutes. Check. If necessary, cook another 5–10 minutes, until a knife inserted into the center comes out clean.

Cool slightly before cutting.

[Note from Charlotte: If you prefer to make a homemade pie shell, see recipe choices on pages 452 and 453. No matter what, savor

the combination of the nuts with the carrots. This is a perfect quiche for the Thanksgiving holiday. Its autumn flavors are divine.]

PEANUT BUTTER QUICHE
Gluten-Free or Regular *
(SERVES 6)

4–6 slices bacon, cooked and crumbled
3 eggs
1 cup milk
1/8 teaspoon nutmeg
1/2 cup peanut butter
1 (9-inch) pie shell, baked (*see note on page 458) and cooled
2 green apples, peeled and sliced thin
1 cup shredded Havarti cheese

Pre-cook bacon. I like to microwave for no mess. To do so, on a plate, set a large piece of paper towel. Place 4–6 strips of bacon on top. Cover with another paper towel. Microwave on high for 3–4 minutes until very crisp. Let cool, then crumble into small bits. Set aside.

Preheat oven to 375 degrees F.

Combine eggs, milk, and nutmeg in a mixer bowl. Turn up speed to medium-high and whip 30 seconds more.

Add peanut butter. Mix on medium-high until well combined, about 1 minute.

Sprinkle bacon evenly in the bottom of a pie shell. Layer the sliced apples on top of the bacon. Pour egg–peanut butter mixture over both, and sprinkle with Havarti cheese.

Bake at 350°F for 25–35 minutes, or until knife inserted comes out clean.

Let stand 5 minutes before serving.

[Note from Charlotte: I know, you'd never have thought to add peanut butter to a quiche, and neither would I, except I was in a playful mood and hoping I could stump my sweet grandfather when he wanted to taste one of the quiches we prepare at the shop. And this one did. He picked up on the peanut butter and the bacon, but he missed the apples, which add such a nice flavor to this dish. This can be served as an entrée or dessert quiche.]

[Second note from Charlotte: If you'd like this recipe to be gluten-free, all you have to do is switch out the pie shell. I've found some great frozen gluten-free pie shells at the store. Or use the GF pastry dough recipe on page 453 and omit white pepper.]

CHEDDAR-CHOCOLATE
STRACCIATELLA ICE CREAM
À la the Igloo
(SERVES 6)

1 cup whipping cream

2 tablespoons espresso coffee (brewed, liquid)

3/4 cup sugar

1/8 teaspoon salt

1 (12-ounce) can evaporated low-fat milk

3 large egg yolks

1 tablespoon vanilla extract

1 cup Tillamook sharp Cheddar cheese, shredded

1 Ghirardelli dark chocolate bar, or your favorite dark chocolate

In a saucepan, over medium heat, cook whipping cream, espresso coffee, 1/4 cup of sugar, salt, and evaporated milk. Cook for 3–5 minutes, until tiny bubbles form around the edges. DO NOT BOIL.

Remove from heat and let stand 10 minutes.

In a medium bowl, combine the remaining 1/2 cup sugar and egg yolks. Stir well. Gradually add the hot milk mixture to the egg mixture, stirring constantly.

Return the mixture to the saucepan. Cook over medium heat for 3–5 minutes, until tiny bubbles form again. DO NOT BOIL.

Remove the pan from the heat. Cool at room temperature and then set in refrigerator for 2 hours.

Pour chilled mixture into ice cream maker

and churn for a half hour.

When the consistency of the ice cream is like soft-ice, melt the chocolate. Here's how: Chop the chocolate and put into a microwave-safe small bowl. Set the bowl in the microwave. On medium-low, zap the chocolate for about 30 seconds at a pop, stirring in between; this usually takes 1–2 minutes.

Pour the chocolate very slowly into the ice cream as it churns. When the hot chocolate hits the cold ice cream, it will solidify into small pieces.

Freeze the ice cream per your ice cream maker suggestions.

[Note from Charlotte: I adore ice cream. The salty-sweet combination of the Cheddar and chocolate is delicious. A scoop or two, and it's a perfect afternoon as far as I'm concerned.]

CARAMEL CHEESECAKE
(SERVES 8–12)
1 pound (16 ounces) ricotta cheese
1/4 cup rice flour or tapioca starch or corn starch
1/2 teaspoon xanthan gum
4 egg yolks
1/2 cup sugar
1 tablespoon lemon juice

1/2 teaspoon vanilla

1/2 teaspoon salt

1 pound (16 ounces) cream cheese

1/2 cup sour cream

4 egg whites (no yolks!)

1/2 cup MORE sugar

1/2 cup crushed graham crackers (*for gluten-free version of dessert, use gluten-free graham crackers)

2 tablespoons butter whipped cream, if desired

Caramel Sauce Ingredients:

1 can sweetened condensed milk

To make the caramel sauce:

Open the can of sweetened condensed milk and set the can in a saucepan. Fill the saucepan with water to halfway up the side of the can. Turn on the heat and bring the water to a boil. Turn the heat to low and let the condensed milk cook for about 2 hours, until it turns a warm brown color. [Make sure you don't run out of hot water around the can; replenish if it starts to get too low!] Using tongs or mitts, remove the can from the saucepan and let cool. [This can be made a day ahead. Keep at room temperature.]

To make the cake:

Preheat your oven to 300 degrees F.

In a large bowl, using a hand mixer, mix ricotta cheese, rice flour, xanthan gum, egg yolks, 1/2 cup sugar, lemon juice, vanilla, and salt until well blended.

Add cream cheese and sour cream and mix well.

In a small bowl, using a hand mixer, mix separately: egg whites (with no egg yolks in them) and the other 1/2 cup sugar until egg whites form a soft peak (about 6–8 minutes).

Fold the egg white mixture gently into the cheese mixture.

In a springform pan, set 1/2 cup crushed graham cracker cookies. [Note: if you want to ensure this is gluten-free, use gluten-free graham crackers.] Drizzle with 2 tablespoons butter and press with your fingertips to create a "crust." Now drizzle with 4 tablespoons of the caramel sauce in concentric circles.

Pour cheese mixture on top of the graham cracker crust.

Bake for 60–75 minutes. Turn OFF the oven. Let the cake STAND IN OVEN for 2 hours so the cheesecake will set and not droop.

When ready, remove cake from oven and

run a knife between the cake and the springform pan, then pop open the springform
spring and remove the cheesecake from the
pan.

Set the cake on a platter and cover with
plastic wrap. Cool the cake in the refrigerator 1–2 hours. When ready to serve, drizzle
with the remaining caramel sauce. Top each
slice with a dollop of whipped cream, if
desired.

*[**Note from Grandmère:** There is nothing
more satisfying to me than a rich cheesecake.
It reminds me of when we moved to the United
States. Etienne and I landed in New York, at
Ellis Island. We stayed the night in New York
and we tasted our first cheesecake. I will
never forget the rich flavors and the sweetness. It will forever be our reminder of the
sweet life we came to seek . . . and found.]*

Dear Reader,

You may not know this, but I write two culinary mystery series under two names — my pseudonym, Avery Aames and my real name, Daryl Wood Gerber. As Daryl, I write the Cookbook Nook Mysteries. Fans of the Cheese Shop series often enjoy the Cookbook Nook series.

If you haven't yet had a *taste* of any of the Cookbook Nook mysteries, let me introduce you to Jenna Hart, a former advertising executive who, two years after losing her husband in a tragic accident, moved home to the beautiful coastal town of Crystal Cove, California, to help her aunt open a culinary bookstore and to find her smile. Jenna is an avid reader, a marketing whiz, and a foodie, but she doesn't have a clue how to cook. As the series develops, Jenna is learning her way around the kitchen. She hopes to become an expert cook someday. The Cookbook Nook sells cookbooks, foodie fiction, and culinary goodies for the kitchen. In addition, there is The Nook Café, an adjunct of the shop, which serves up delicious meals throughout the week. During the year, the store and the town offer all sorts of specialty events. In the fifth installment in the series, *Grilling the Subject,* due out in 2016, Jenna celebrates along with the rest of the town as the Wild West Extravaganza comes to town. *Yee-haw!* But when a bonfire lights the morning sky of Crystal Cove, and hours later Jenna's father is suspected of roasting a land-poaching neighbor, the revelry fades. To add to Jenna's distress, an unexpected guest blazes into town like a tornado and throws her life into a tailspin. Can she keep calm while she grills suspects that include the victim's tepid husband, a saucy Realtor, and the extravaganza's sexy Casanova? Will Jenna clear her father before the killer turns up the heat and rakes Jenna over the coals? Can she survive the personal upheaval, too?

I hope you will join Jenna and her loyal friends and family as Jenna once again seeks to right a wrong. Perhaps you'll even find a new zesty recipe or cookbook title to share with friends!

For those of you who love the Cheese Shop Mysteries, sadly, the series has come to an end. Charlotte, now an expectant mother, will forge a new life with her family. Wish her well on her way! I will be writing more series and stand-alone novels! Please keep in touch with me via my website

and by joining my newsletter!
    Savor the mystery and say cheese!
                           Avery aka Daryl

ABOUT THE AUTHOR

Avery Aames is the Agatha Award–winning author of The Cheese Shop Mysteries and, as Daryl Wood Gerber, The Cookbook Nook Mysteries. She loves to cook and enjoys a good wine. And she adores cheese.